RED AS A ROSE IS SHE.
A Novel

RHOD.

CHAPTER I.

Have you ever been to Wales? I do not ask this question of any one in particular; I merely address it to the universal British public, or, rather, to such member or members of the same as shall be wise enough to sit down and read the ensuing true and moving love story—true as the loves of wicked Abelard and Heloise, moving as those of good Paul and Virginia. Probably those wise ones will be very few; numerable by tens, or even units: they will, I may very safely aver, not form the bulk of the nation. However high may be my estimate of my own powers of narration, however amply Providence may have gifted me with self-appreciation, I may be sure of that, seeing that the only books I know of which enjoy so wide a circulation are the Prayer-book and Bradshaw. I am not going to instruct any one in religion or trains, so I may as well make up my mind to a more limited audience, while I pipe my simple lay (rather squeakily and out of tune, perhaps), and may think myself very lucky if that same kind, limited audience do not hiss me down before I have got through half a dozen staves of the dull old ditty.

Have you ever been to Wales? If you have ever visited the pretty, dirty, green spot where Pat and his brogue, where potatoes and absenteeism and head-centres flourish, *alias* Ireland, you have no doubt passed through a part of it, rushing by, most likely, in the Irish mail; but in that case your eyes and nose and ears were all so very full of dust and cinders—you were so fully employed in blinking and coughing and enjoying the poetry of motion—as to be totally incapable of seeing, hearing, or smelling any of the beauties, agreeable noises, or good smells, which in happier circumstances might have offered themselves to your notice. Perhaps you are in the habit, every midsummer, of taking your half-dozen male and female olive shoots to have the roses restored to their twelve fat cheeks by blowy scrambles about the great frowning Orme's Head, or by excavations in the Rhyl Sands. Perhaps you have gone wedding-touring to Llanberis on the top of a heavy-laden coach, swinging unsafely round sharp corners, and nearly flinging your Angelina from your side on to the hard Welsh road below. Perhaps you have wept with Angelina at the spurious grave of the martyred Gelert, or eaten pink trout voraciously at Capel Curig, and found out what a startlingly good appetite Angelina had. But have you ever lived in the land of the Cymri? Have you ever seen how drunk the masculine Cymri can be on market days, or what grievous old hags the feminine Cymri become towards their thirtieth year? Have you ever, by bitter experience, discovered the truth of that couplet—

"Taffy was a Welshman, Taffy was a thief?"

I *have* lived in Wales, so I speak with authority; and for my part I don't think that Taffy is much more given to the breaking of the eighth commandment than the *canaille* of any other country. He is not a bright fellow, is not Taffy; happiest, I think, when rather tipsy, or when yelling psalms in his conventicle or schism-shop—for Taffy is addicted to schism; he will tell you plenty of lies, too, and will not season them with the salt of a racy, devil-me-care wit, as Pat would. But he is very civil-spoken, and rather harmless; seldomer, I think, than his cleverer neighbour over the border does he hanker feloniously after his neighbour's spoons, or hammer his wife's head with the domestic poker.

But why am I drivelling on, like a sort of Murray and water, on the manners and character of this, to my thinking, not very interesting nation? I will waste no more "prave 'ords" upon them, as the few men and women whom I am going to tell you about, and whom I shall want you to like a little, or dislike a little, as the case may be, are not Taffies, only they happen to have stuck up their tent-poles in Taffy-land when they first make their low bow to you. These men and women were nothing out of the way for goodness, or beauty, or talent; they did a hundred thousand naughty things, each one of them. Some of them did them with impunity, as far as this world goes; some of them, capricious Megæra and Tisyphone lashed with scorpions for their derelictions. This is going to be neither a "Life of Saints," nor a "History of Devils;" these are memoirs neither of a "Hedley Vicars," nor of a "Dame aux Camellias;" so, whoso expects and relishes either of those styles of composition may forthwith close this volume, and pitch it (if it be his own, and not the battered property of a circulating library) into the fire. Those who love a violent moral, or violent judgment for sins and follies—a man struck dead for saying "damn," or a woman for going to a ball, as the *Record* would charitably have us believe is the way of Providence—equally with those who enjoy the flavour of violent immorality, will be disappointed if they look this way for the gratification of their peculiar idiosyncracies. Of my friends presently to be made known to you, and criticised by you, "the more part remain unto this present, but some have fallen asleep."

Once upon a time—I like that old, time-honoured opening; it makes one so nobly free, gives one so much room to stretch one's wings in, ties one down to no king's reign, no hampering, clogging century—once upon a time there was a valley in Taffy-land; there is still, unless some very recent convulsion has upheaved it to the top of a mountain, or submerged it beneath the big Atlantic waves; a valley lovelier than that one in "Ida," where "beautiful Paris, evil-hearted Paris," pastured his sheep and his jet-black goats, and inaugurated his rakish course; a valley where there are no dangerous, good-looking Parises, only one or two red-headed Welsh squires, who have each married, or will in the fulness of time each marry, one lawful wife—red-headed, too, very likely; and have never made, will never make, love to any Enones or other ill-conducted young shepherdesses. In fact, in that Arcadia there are no such shepherdesses; the daughters of the Cymri do not "ply the homely shepherd's trade," nor would they shed much romance over it if they did; for with sorrow be it spoken, blowsy are they mostly, hard-featured, toothless; and, moreover, the little nimble, lean sheep that go scrambling and jumping and skurrying about the rough crags and steep hill-sides do not need any crook'd and melodious Dowsabellas or Neæras to look after them and guide them in the way they should go.

In that valley there are plenty of houses, squires' houses and peasants' houses, where the propagation of the Cambrian is conducted with much success; houses big and little, red-faced and white-faced and dirty-faced, old and new. But we have at present to do with only one of those houses, and it comes under the head of the littles and the olds. Halfway up a hill-side it stands, looking across the valley to other higher hills that swell out softly against the sky, and go sloping gently down to the sea twenty miles away. They always remind me—I don't know why—of the distant hills in Martin's picture of the "Plains of Heaven;" so mistily do they rise in their hazy blueness. It is a snug, unpretending little house enough, with its black and white cross-beamed front and unwalled kitchen-garden straggling steeply up the slope at the back. Many and many a day has it stood there, seeing generations and fashions come in and go out; has stood there since the far-away days when men wore curly wigs half-way down their backs, and sky-blue coats, and fought and died for prerogative and King Charles, or fought and lived for England and liberty: when most houses were black and white, like its little elderly self, before plate glass or stucco, or commodious villa residences, five minutes' walk from a station, were dreamed of. The name of the little house is Glan-yr-Afon.

CHAPTER II.

"Jack and I got in our last hayload to-day, without a drop of rain; the first bit of good luck that has come to us, I don't know when. If we had any land, I should imagine that we must have a bit of consecrated ground among it, to account for our ill-fortune; but as we have not of our own enough to pasture a goose upon, that cannot be it. Such an odd thing happened to-day—Robert Brandon proposed to me: it is the first offer I ever had, though I was seventeen last month. If it is never a more pleasant process than it was to-day, I hope sincerely it may be the last. I said 'Yes,' too; at least, a species of Yes after half-a-dozen Noes; I cannot imagine why, for I certainly did not feel Yes. I suppose I must have been pleased at any one wishing for my company during the term of his natural life."

The name on the fly-leaf of this journal-book is Esther Craven, Glan-yr-Afon, and the date July 10, 186-. July is very often a rather wet month—not so this year; all through its one-and-thirty days the sky was like brass, as it looked to Elijah (the Seer's) eyes on the top of Carmel, when, by his faith, he brought up the tarrying rain from the sea's chambers. London is pouring out her noble army of haberdashers and greengrocers into Ramsgate and Margate, and Scarborough and Llandudno. The John Gilpins of to-day are not satisfied with a modest outing to the "Bell" at Edmonton, "all in a chaise and pair."

Armies of schoolboys are devouring arid sandwiches and prime old buns in railway refreshment rooms—schoolboys emptied out of every school and seminary and college all over the country. Highly paid instructors of youth are stretching their cramped legs up the steep sides of Helvellyn and Mont Blanc, and surveying the "frozen hurricane" of the glaciers through their academic spectacles. And young Craven's (of Glan-yr-Afon) last hayload is safely stacked, as you heard from his sister's diary. This morning the highest lying of the upland fields was hilly with haycocks: to-night it is as flat as Salisbury Plain. All day long the waggons have gone grinding and crunching up and down the rocky mountain road between field and rick-yard. All day long Evan and Hugh and Roppert (sic) with their waistcoats open and their brown arms bared, aided and abetted by various Cambrian matrons, with bonnets standing upright on their heads, and pitchforks in their lily hands, have been tossing the scented bundles—sweeter in death than in life, like a good man's fame—into the carts; loading them till of the shaft horse nought but ears and nose and forelegs appeared, save to the eye of faith. All day long Esther has been sitting under a haycock, as one might fancy Solomon's wise woman doing, "looking well to the ways of her household." The hay moulds itself pliably into a soft arm-chair for her young, slight figure, and the big hay-spiders walk up her back at their leisure, and explore the virgin forests of her thick dusk hair. She has had her luncheon brought out to her there—bread and milk in a white bowl. It is unsocial, surly work, eating alone; one feels reduced to the level of a dog, cracking bones, and lapping up gravy out of his trencher, all by himself, with tail well down, like a pump handle, and a growl and a snap for any brother dog who may approach to share his feast.

The haymakers were much cheerier—"couched at ease" under the nutty hedgerow; bringing slices of unnaturally fat bacon out of blue and white spotted pocket-handkerchiefs, gabbling to one another in the Welsh tongue, which, to one who occupies the room of the unlearned, has always a querulous, quarrelsome, interrogative sound; and digging their clasp knives into the ground to clean them, when their services were no longer required. Jack is out for the day, and the place feels stupid without him. There is not much melody in "I paddle my own canoe," but one misses it when one is accustomed to hear it echoing gaily over the crofts and through the farm-yard and orchard. It would be impossible to talk more dog-Welsh than Jack does to his workmen; but even the mellifluous tongue of the Cymri, with its three or four consonants standing together, undissevered by any vowel, is made harmonious, enunciated by a young, clear voice, that sounds as if it had never been the vehicle for sorrowful words.

"The   village   seems   asleep   or   dead, Now Lubin is away,"

and Esther, though she has entered upon her eighteenth year (an age which a century ago would have been rather overripe—Chloe and Cynthia and Phyllis being considered in their prime at fifteen, and toasted accordingly), has as yet no Lubin but her brother. Now and again, Gwen the cook, and Sarah the housemaid, came panting up the hill in lilac cotton gowns and trim white aprons, bearing beer in every jug and mug and tin pipkin that Glan-yr-Afon affords, as Evangeline brought the nut-brown ale to the reapers of the village of Grand Pré. And the haymakers drink insatiably, and wipe the thirsty mouth upon the convenient sleeve as artless Nature bids. By-and-by artless Nature makes them rather unsteady on their legs. As they lead the heavy-laden cart to the last remaining haycock, the one on which their mistress sits enthroned, I am not at all sure that they do not see two haycocks, two wide-leaved white hats, two Esthers. Perceiving their condition, though too old an inhabitant of Wales to be in any degree surprised at what is, after all, the normal condition of the Welsh, Miss Craven rises precipitately. Driven from her fortress, she picks up her needles and threads, and Jack's shirt, from which, as usual, the frequent button is missing, and runs lightly down the mountain path in her strong country boots, which bid defiance to the sharp stones that crop out at every step through the limestone soil. At the hall door—a little arched door like a church's, with a trellised porch and benches, such as one sees Dutch boors sitting on with their beer and schnapps, in Teniers' pictures—-Sarah meets her. Sarah is an Englishwoman.

"Mr. Brandon is in the parlour, 'm."

"Parlour! My good Sarah, how many times shall I adjure you, by all you hold most sacred, to say drawing-room?"

"He has been there best part of half-an-hour, 'm."

"Poor man! how lively for him! why on earth didn't you come and call me?"

"He said as he wasn't in no partikler hurry, and he'd as lieve as not wait till you come in. Stop a bit, Miss Esther, you have got some hay on your frock behind."

"People of seventeen wear gowns, not frocks, Sarah. Oh! there, that will do. If I had a haystack disposed about my person, he would never be a bit the wiser."

Half-an-hour passes, and Mr. Brandon is still in the "parlour." It is seven o'clock, and dinner-time. Would you like to know what it is that Mr. Brandon takes so long in saying, and whether it is anything likely to reconcile Miss Craven to the loss of her dinner? A little room that looks towards the sun-setting; a little room full of evening sunshine and the smell of tea-roses; a light paper, with small, bright flower-bunches on the walls; white muslin curtains; a general air of crisp freshness, as of a room that there are no climbing, crawling, sticky-fingered children to crumple and rumple. A young woman, rather red in the face, standing in one corner. She has been driven thither apparently by a young man, who is standing before her, and who is still redder. At a rough calculation, you would say that the young man was seven feet high; but put him with his back against the wall, with his heels together, and his chin in, and you will find that he is exactly six feet four; that is, four inches taller than any man who wishes to do work in the world, and find horses to carry him, ought to be. His clothes are rather shabby, and he looks poor; but, from the crown of his close-clipped head to the sole of his big feet, a gentleman, every inch of him, though he has no "gude braid claith" to help to make him so. His features may be Apollo's or Apollyon's, for all you can see of them, so thickly are they planted out with a forest of yellow hair; but tears do not seem to be at any immense distance from eyes blue as the sky between storm clouds, fearless as a three-years'-child's.

"Don't you think that we do very well as we are?" says the young woman, suggestively.

"I don't know about you, I'm sure. I know I've lost a stone and a half within the last year," replies the young man, very ruefully.

Esther laughs. "There is some little of you left still," she says, with rather a mischievous glance up at the two yards and a half of enamoured manhood before her.

This is what has been over-roasting the mutton. He has been asking her to take his heart, his large hand, and the half of one hundred and twenty pounds a year (the exorbitant pay of a lieutenant in Her Majesty's infantry), of an old hunting watch, and a curly retriever dog; and she has been declining these tempting offers, one and all. The minute hand of the gilt clock, on which Minerva sits in a helmet and a very tight gown, with her legs dangling down, has travelled from 6.30 to 7.5, and within these five-and-thirty minutes Miss Craven has refused three proposals, all made by the same person: the first, very stoutly and mercilessly, from Jack's arm-chair, where she had originally taken up her position; the second, decisively still, but with less cruelty, from the music-stool, to which she had next retired; and the third, in a hasty and wavering manner, from the corner, in which she has taken final refuge, in a strong, fortified entrenchment behind the writing-table.

"But—but—" says Esther, her rebellious mouth giving little twitches every now and then as at some lurking thought of the ridiculous—"it's—it's such a very *odd* idea! I don't think I ever was more surprised in my life. When Sarah told me that you were here, I thought that, of course, you had come to say something about that bone-dust. Why, you never said anything at all tending this way before."

"Didn't I?" answers the young giant, with a crestfallen look. "I tried several times, but I don't think that you could have understood what I meant, for you always began to laugh."

"I always do laugh at civil speeches," answers the girl simply. "I don't know how else to take them: I suppose it is because I have had so few addressed to me; they always sound to me so *niais*."

"I'm not a bit surprised at your not liking me," he says, with humility. "I don't see how any one could at first. I know that I'm ugly and awkward, and don't understand things quick———"

"I don't *dis*-like you," interrupts Esther, with magnanimity, quite affected by her lover's description of his own undesirability. "Why should I? There is nothing in you to dislike; you are very good-natured, I'm sure," damning with faint praise, in the laudable effort not to be unqualifiedly uncomplimentary.

"I know what an unequal exchange it is that I am offering," says Brandon, too humble to resent, and yet with a dim sense of mortification at the quantity and quality of praise bestowed upon him. "I know of how much more value you are than I!"

She does not contradict him; her own heart echoes his words. "I am of more value than he; I shall find it out practically some day."

"That was why I was in such a hurry to speak," he says eagerly. "I felt sure that if I did not, you would be snapped up directly by some one else."

She laughs rather grimly. "You might have laid aside your alarms on that head, I think. I don't know who there is about here to snap me up."

Silence for a few minutes: Esther takes up a penwiper, fashioned into a remote resemblance to a chimney sweep, and studies its anatomy attentively. "Shall I upset the writing-table and make a rush past him? No, the ink would spoil the carpet, and he would only come again to-morrow, and hunt me into the other corner. Poor fellow! I hope he is not going to cry, or go down on his knees!"

Whether mindful or not of the fate of Gibbon the historian, who, having thrown himself on his knees before his lady-love, was unable, through extreme fat, to get up again, Brandon does not indulge in either of the demonstrations that Esther apprehended. He stands quiet, cramming half a yard of yellow beard into his mouth, and says presently:

"Well, I suppose I must not worry you any more; it is not good manners, is it? A man ought to be satisfied with one No; I have given you the trouble of saying three."

"It's very disagreeable, I'm sure," says Esther, wrinkling up her forehead in an embarrassed fashion, "and I hate saying No to any one: I don't mean in this way, because nobody ever asked me before, but about anything; but what can I do?"

"Try me!" he says very eagerly, stretching out his hand across the narrow table (all but upsetting the standish *en route*). "I don't want to threaten you, saying that I should go to the dogs if you threw me over, for I should not; that always seemed to me a cowardly sort of thing to do; and, besides, I should have my mother left to live for if the worst came to the worst; but you must see that it is everything in the world to a fellow to have one great hope in it to keep him straight."

4

Soft music in the distance; some one whistling "I paddle my own canoe" somewhere about the house; Esther, in an agony between the fear of subversing the table, and the hundredfold worse fear of being discovered by Jack in an unequivocally sentimental position, of which she would never hear the last. "Very well, very well, I'll—I'll *think* about it; could you be so very kind as to loose my hand?"

He complies reluctantly, and she, that there may be no further discussion about it, hides it discreetly away in her jacket pocket. "I paddle my own canoe" dies away in the distance; apparently it was on its way to dress for dinner. Esther draws a sigh of relief. "I thought that some one was coming."

"And if they had?"

"Why, I did not relish the idea of being found driven into a corner, like a child at a dame's school, and you, like the dame, standing over me," answers she, abandoning the struggle with the corners of her mouth, and bubbling over with the facile laughter of seventeen. Utterly unable to join in her merriment, he stands leaning in awkward misery against the wall; all other griefs are at least respectable; love-sorrows, alone, are only ludicrous.

"It really is so silly," says Esther, presently, compassionate but impatient. "Do try and get the better of it!"

"Easier said than done," he answers ruefully. "I might as well advise you to get the better of your affection for Jack."

"I don't see the parallel," rejoined she, coldly, feeling as if there was sacrilege in the comparison. "My love for Jack is a natural instinct, built too upon the foundation of lifelong obligations, endless benefits, countless kindnesses. What kindness have I ever shown you? I sewed a button on your glove once, and once I pinned a rose on your coat."

"I have the rose still."

She says "Pshaw!" pettishly, and turns away her head.

"Perhaps you are afraid of marrying on small means?" suggests Brandon, diffidently, after a while.

The gentle clatter and click of dishes carried into the dining-room enters faintly through the shut door. Esther's heart sinks within her. Is he going to begin all over again?—round and round, like a thunderstorm among hills?

"I am afraid of marrying on *any* means," she says, comprehensively. "I particularly dislike the idea; marriage seems to me the end of everything, and I am at the beginning."

"But I don't want you to marry me *now*," cries Robert, stammering.

"Don't you? You told me just now that you did."

"For pity's sake, Esther, don't laugh! it may be play to you, but it is death to me."

"I'm not laughing."

"Perhaps some day you will feel what I am feeling now."

"Perhaps" (doubtfully).

"And you will find then that it is no laughing matter."

"Perhaps" (still more doubtfully).

The clamour of a fresh cohort of plates shaking noisily upon a tray warns Brandon that his time is short.

"Esther!" with a sort of despair in his voice, clashing the ridiculous with the pathetic—they are always twin sisters—"I could live upon such a little hope."

"What would you have me say?" she cries, standing with fluttering colour, tapping feet, and irritated eyes. "I have told you the plain truth, and it does not please you; must I dress up some pretty falsehood, and tell you that I fell in love with you at first sight, or that after all I find that you are the only man in the world that can make me really happy?"

"Say nothing of the kind!" he answers, wincing under her irony. "I have not much to recommend me, we all know that, and I start with the disadvantage of your thinking me rather a bore than otherwise; but other men have overcome even greater obstacles; why should not I? Give me at least a trial!"

She is silent.

"Say that you will *try* to like me; there need be no untruth in that."

"But if I fail!" says Esther, wavering—partly in sheer weariness of the contest, partly in womanly pity for sufferings which owe their rise to the excess of her own charms.

"If you fail you will not have to tell me so; I shall find it out for myself, and—and I shall bear it, I suppose." He ends with a heavy sigh at that too probable possibility.

"And you will console yourself by telling all your friends what a flirt I am, and how ill I treated you." Apparently he does not think this suggestion worthy of refutation; at least he does not refute it. "Or, if you don't, your mother will."

"Not she" (indignantly).

5

"Or, if she does not, your sisters will."

"Not they" (less indignantly).

"And if—if—after a long while—a very long while—I succeed in liking you a little—mind, I don't say that I shall; on the contrary, I think it far more probable that I shall not—but if I do, you won't expect me to *marry* you?"

He smiles, despite himself. "I can hardly promise that."

"I mean not for many years, till Jack is married, and I am quite, *quite* old—five-and-twenty or so?"

"It shall be as you wish."

"And if, as is most likely, I continue not to care about you, and am obliged to tell you so, you will not think the worse of me."

"No."

"You are certain?"

"Certain. Whatever you do, I shall love you to-day, and to-morrow, and always," says the young fellow, very solemnly; and his eyes go away past her, through the window, and up to the blue sky overhead, as if calling on the great pale vault to be witness between him and her.

As for her, her prosaic soul has wandered back to the mutton; she takes the opportunity of his eyes being averted to steal a glance at the clock. Apparently, however, he has eyes in the back of his head, for he says hastily, with rather a pained smile: "You are longing for me to go."

"No—o."

"I ought not to have come at this time of night. I ought to have waited till to-morrow, I know."

"It is rather late."

"But to-morrow seemed such a long time off, that I thought I must know the worst or the best before the sun came up again. I don't quite know which it is now; which is it, Esther?"

"It's neither the one nor the other; it's the second best," she answers, all smiles again at seeing some prospect of her admirer's departure, and forgetting, with youthful heedlessness, the price at which that departure has been bought. "It is that I really am very much obliged, though, all the same I wish you would think better of it, and that I'll try; I will, really; don't look as if you did not believe me."

So with this half-loaf he goes, passes away through the little wooden porch, that is so low it looks as if it were going to knock his tall head, past the stables, and through the oak woods, home.

CHAPTER III.

"It   is   the   hour   when   from   the   boughs
The   nightingale's   high   note   is   heard;
It   is   the   hour   when   lovers'   vows
Seem sweet in every whispered word—"

As saith that most delicious of love poems that makes us all feel immoral as we read it. It is the hour when chanticleer retires to his perch in the henhouse, lowers his proud tail, sinks his neck into his breast, and goes to sleep between his two fattest wives. It is the hour when animal life and wild humanity retire to bed; the hour when tamed humanity sits down to dinner. The more we advance in civilisation the farther back we push the boundaries of sleep and forgetfulness. When we reach our highest point of culture, I suppose we shall hustle the blessed, the divine Nepenthe, off the face of the earth altogether.

The dining-room at Glan-yr-Afon is, like the rest of the house, rather small and rather pleasant. It will not dine more than twelve comfortably; it is seldom asked to dine more than two; and these two, being young and void of gluttony, do not spend much of their time in it. In youth the dining-room is not our temple, our sanctuary, our holy of holies, as it often is in riper years. In youth our souls are great, and our bodies slender; in old age our bodies are often great and our souls slender. The one wide open window looks on the gay little garden—the window, all around and about which the climbing convolvulus is blowing great white trumpets. There are two or three pictures on the walls; good ones, though dim and dusty. Thomas Wentworth, Lord Strafford, very dark and haughty and saturnine, in blue grey armour, scowling at whosoever looks at him, as he might have scowled at Pym and Hollis. Erasmus, astute and lean, in a black skull cap: and Mary, Queen of Scots, very pale and peaky and indistinct, for time has washed and scrubbed all the carmine out of the cheeks and lips that sent Europe mad three centuries ago. An old sheep-dog is lying on the hearth-rug, with his wise old eyes fixed on his master, licking his

6

chops every now and then when he sees some morsel more tempting than ordinary conveyed to another mouth than his.

This evening Lord Strafford is scowling, Mary Stuart simpering, down upon two people dining together, and on a third person whisking about in a clean cap and an aggressively well-starched print dress in attendance upon them. There is a great pot, full and brimming over with roses—a beanpot our forefathers would have called it—in the middle of the table. They were plucked but half an hour ago, and their faces were still wet with the dew-tears that they wept at being torn away from their brothers and sisters on the old gnarled rose trees up the kitchen-garden walk.

But the freshest, the sweetest, the largest of the roses is not in the beanpot with the others; it is on a chair by itself; there are no dew-tears on its cheeks, it has no prickles, and its name is Esther.

"Have some roast chips, Essie? I cannot offer you any roast mutton, because there isn't any; I dare say there was an hour ago, but there certainly isn't now."

This speech is made by Jack. Jack is a young person with not a single good feature in his face; with a baby moustache, which, like the daguerreotypes of fifteen or sixteen years ago, is only visible at rare intervals in one particular light; and with cheeks and nose and chin and throat all as brown as any berry that ever ripened under the mellow autumn sun.

"It's a fault on the right side, dear boy; it's better than quivering and being purple," says Esther, with a pout which a lover would have thought entrancing, but which a prosaic brother, if he perceived it at all, considered rather a distortion than otherwise.

"I wish that people would remember that there is a time to call and a time to dine, and that the two times are not the same," he grumbles, a little crossly.

A man may bear the untimely cutting off of his firstborn, the disposition evinced by the wife of his bosom to love his neighbour as himself, the sinking of his little all in the Agra Bank, with resignation and fortitude truly Christian; but what hero, what sage, what archbishop, can stand the over-roasting or under-boiling of his mutton, the burning of his soup, or the wateriness of his potatoes, and bear an *æquam mentem?*

Esther looks rather conscious, purses up her pink mouth into the shape of a noiseless "Hush!" and says "*Pas avant*," which idiomatic phrase is intended to convey to her brother the indiscreetness of making comments on Sarah's presence on Mr. Brandon's enormities.

From long familiarity with the sound, Sarah has become entirely acquainted with Esther's specimen of Parisian French, and always pricks up her ears when it appears on the scene.

Then they are silent for a little space. One is not apt to say very brilliant things in one's family circle; it requires the friction of mind with mind before bright sayings spring into being, as the flint and the steel must be married before the spark leaps into life.

"How long the days are now!" Jack says presently, as he looks out on the evening light lying like a great bright cloak all over the land.

The earth is so very fair, all pranked with "smalle flowres" and green leaves, that the sun is grievously loth to leave her. Fair-weather friend as he is, he cannot be in too great a hurry to desert her, when she lies poor and bare and faded in the dull November days.

"One always says that this time of year," Esther says, smiling. "It would be much more worthy remark if they didn't get longer; if one kept a journal of one's remarks for a year, what an awful tautology there would be in them! What a pity that one cannot say a thing once for all, and have done with it!"

"If you resolved never to say anything that anybody had said before, you would make mighty few observations, I take it," Jack answers, a little drily. "Most remarks have been pretty well aired in the course of the last six thousand years, I fancy."

So, with a little flagging talk, the dinner passes, and the modest dessert appears: scarlet pyramids of strawberries, great bag-shaped British Queens, and little racy, queer-tasted hautbois.

Sarah retires, and the embargo is taken off Esther's speech.

"Is she gone—finally gone?" she cries, very eagerly. "Heaven be praised for that! I thought she would never have done clattering those spoons. Oh, Jack, what a heavy weight a piece of news is to carry! How I sympathise with the woman who had to whisper to the rushes about Midas' ears! I have been dying all through dinner for some rushes to whisper to."

"To whisper *what* to?" asks the boy, his eyes opening very wide and round.

"Jack, do I look taller than usual to-night?"

"No."

"Broader?"

"Not that I perceive."

"More consequential?"

"Much as usual. You never are a woman with 'a presence.'"

7

"Is it possible that there's no difference at all in me?"

"None whatever; except that, now I look at you, your cheeks are, if possible, redder than usual. Why should there be any?"

"Because" (drawing herself up) "I have to-day passed a turning-point in my history. I have had—a proposal."

"Who from?—one of the haymakers?"

"No. That would not have surprised me much more, though. Let me get it out as quick as I can, now that the string of my tongue is loosed. Robert Brandon was here to-day."

"As I know to my cost," says Jack, with rather a rueful face at the recollection of his unpalatable dinner.

"And—and—how shall I word it prettiest?—asked me to be his."

"The devil he did!" exclaims Jack, surprised into strong, language.

"Yes, the devil he did! as you epigrammatically remark."

"And you, what answer did you give?" asks the boy, quickly, his mouth emulating the example of his eyes, and opening wide, too.

"I said I was much obliged, but that, for the present, I preferred being my own."

"You said 'No,' of course?"

"Yes, I did; ever so many 'Noes.' I did not count them, but I'm sure their name was Legion."

Jack gives a sigh of relief, and throws a biscuit to the ceaselessly attent sheep-dog. "Poor beggar!" he says. "Here, Luath, old man. You old muff! why did you not catch it? He is as good a fellow as ever I came across, and now, I suppose, it will be all different and disagreeable. Hang it! what a plague women are!"

"But, Jack——"

"Well, Essie, not done yet? Any more unlucky fellows sent off with their tails between their legs?"

"No, no; but, Jack" (looking down, and staining her fingers with the henna of the strawberries), "I—I'm not quite sure that, after all those 'Noes,' I did not say something that was not quite 'No.'"

"That was 'Yes?'"

"No, not 'Yes' either; not positive, actual 'Yes;' something betwixt and between; a sort of possible, hypothetical 'Yes.'"

"More fool you!" said Jack, briefly.

"Don't scold me, you bad boy!" she cries, running over to him and putting her gentle arms about his neck in the caressing way which sisters affect so much, and which brothers, in general, disrelish so highly, "or I vow I'll cry, and you know you hate that."

"I hate your making a fool of yourself worse," growls Jack, mollified, but struggling. "I say, you need not strangle a fellow."

"Wait till I do make a fool of myself," she says, very gaily. "I'm only talking about it as yet, and there's a good wide ditch between saying and doing."

"More shame for you to say what you don't mean."

"Jack, dear boy, don't you know that I hate saying things that vex a person? I never had a faculty for telling people home-truths; I'd far sooner tell them any amount of stories; and I got so tired of saying 'No,' and he seemed to take it so much to heart, that I said 'Yes,' just for a change—just for peace. In fact, 'anything for a quiet life' is my motto."

"And may I ask what you intend to live upon?" asks Jack (the romantic side of whose mind lies at present fallow and uncultivated, and whose thoughts, Briton-like, speedily turn from "love's young dream" to the pound, shilling, and pence aspect of the matter).

"On love, to be sure. On—what is it?—6s. 6d. a day; and perhaps I may take in soldiers' washing," Esther says, bursting out into a violent fit of laughing.

"Uncommonly funny, no doubt!" Jack says, laughing too, but sorely against his will. "And do you mean to tell me that you like Brandon all of a sudden enough to be such an abject pauper with him for the rest of your days? Why it was only yesterday that you were laughing at him, saying he danced like a pair of tongs."

Esther has slidden down to the floor, and sits there tailor-fashion.

"I don't mean to tell you anything of the kind," she answers, gravely. "Poor dear fellow!—it is very odious of me—but between you and me I think I should survive it if I were to know that I should never see him again; only, please don't tell him I said so."

"Love, who to none beloved to love again remits——"

she repeats softly, musing to herself; "that is a very lovely line, but it is horribly untrue."

"What do you mean to do then, if it is not an impertinent question?" asks Jack, throwing back his young head, and looking in an inquisitorial manner at the penitent at his feet from under his eyelids. "Marry a man that you don't like, and who has not a farthing to keep you on, merely because he is the first person that asked you?"

"Nothing is farther from my intentions," says Esther, getting rather red. "And how unkind of you to twit me with my dearth of admirers. I mean *you* to interpose your parental authority and forbid the banns; I intend to shift the odium of the transaction on to your shoulders," she says, relapsing into levity,—"poor, dear shoulders!" (patting them very fondly) "they are not very wide, but they are broader than mine, at all events; to them I transfer my difficulties."

"*That* you shan't!" cries Jack, with animation, shaking off her hand, and looking very indignant and honest. "You are to do shabby things, and I am to have the credit of them! Thanks, very much, but I don't admire that division of labour. I don't think I ever heard a meaner proposition."

Esther's little head, rich in a soft plenitude of dusky love-locks, sinks low down towards her lap; she is very easily snubbed, especially by Jack.

"A nice name you'll make for yourself, Miss Essie," pursues the young Solomon, severely, still brandishing the metaphorical birch-rod over his sister. "I expect you'll make the country too hot to hold us in a short time."

Esther lifts up two sudden, tearful eyes, that look like great jewels seen through running water, and says, piteously, "But, Jack, you know, as you said just now, it was the first time; one never does things well the first time one tries; one is always clumsy at them; I shall know better next time."

"I don't see what 'next time' you are likely to have," says Jack, inexorable in his young severity. "It will be rather late in the day for people to propose to you when you are Bob Brandon's half-starved or whole-starved wife."

"But I'm not, Jack," cries Esther, very eagerly.

She looks grave enough now; rather alarmed at the little gay sketch her brother has drawn of her future destiny.

"I'm not going to marry him or any one else, *ever*. Do you think I'd leave you to marry the Angel Gabriel, if he came down from heaven on purpose to ask me?"

"Why did you tell Brandon that you would then?" asks the young fellow, not a bit disarmed by her sweet flattery.

"I did not tell him so; I said I would try; but even if I do try, I need not succeed; and even if I do manage to get up a sort of liking for him, I need not *marry* him. You are in such a hurry to jump at conclusions; *there's* the beauty of his being so poor, don't you see? He cannot expect me to marry him, when he has no bread and butter to put into my mouth."

"Then why be engaged to him at all, my good girl?" asks honest Jack, rather bewildered by these new lights—these subtleties on the subject of betrothal.

"Why do people give babies gin?—it is not good for them, but it keeps them quiet; *that* is precisely my principle. Being engaged to me may not be good for Robert, but it is *gin* to him; it keeps him quiet," answers Esther, on the battle-field of whose small face smiles and tears are fighting.

Her brother does not seem to see the beauty of this ingenious mode of reasoning in a very strong light.

"I won't have you playing fast and loose with him," he says, very decisively, shaking a stern young head—stern, despite its curliness and its total dearth of those care-lines that are supposed to be Wisdom's harsh footprints. "He is much too good a fellow to be played tricks with; mind that, Miss Esther!"

"I have not the slightest desire in life to play tricks with him; if I ever do play tricks, I hope it will be with some one more amusing," answers Essie, very pettishly, looking excessively mutine and ill-humoured. "I don't care if I never hear his ugly name again; he has spoilt the dinner and made you as cross as two sticks; and—and—I wish he was *dead, that* I do!" concludes happy Mr. Brandon's *fiancée* weeping.

CHAPTER IV.

Morning is come again. The sun cannot bear to be long away from his young sweetheart, the earth, so he has come back hasting, with royal pomp, with his crown of gay gold beams on his head, with his flame-cloak about his strong shoulders, and with a great troop of light, flaky clouds—each with a reflex of his red smile on its courtier face—at his back. He has come back to see himself in the laughing blue eyes of her seas and streams, and to rest at noontide, like a sleepy giant, on her warm green lap.

9

The daily miracle—the miracle that none can contest, to which all are witness, has been worked—the resurrection of the world. And this resurrection is not partial, not limited to humanity, as that final one is towards which the eyes of the Christian church have been looking steadfastly for eighteen centuries and a half; but every beast and bird and flower has shaken off Death's sweet semblance, his gentle counterfeit, and is feeling, in bounding vein and rushing sap, the ecstatic bliss of the mystery of life. If we never slept, we should not know the joy of waking; if we never woke, we should not know the joy of sleep. How, I marvel, shall we *feel* the happiness of heaven, if we never lose, and consequently regain it?

The thrushes and blackbirds are already in the midst of their glees and madrigals and part songs. They sing the same songs every day, so that they are quite perfect in them; and they are all very joyful ones. In their sweet flute-language there are no words expressive of sorrow or pain; they know of no minor key. There were twenty roses born last night, and the flowers are all rejoicing greatly. They are smiling and whispering and gossiping together; the sweet peas, like pink and purple butterflies,

"......on   tiptoe   for   a   flight,
With wings of delicate flush o'er virgin white,"

each half-inclined to hover away with the young west wind that is sighing such a little gentle story all about himself into their ears. The lambs, grown so big and woolly that one might almost mistake them for their mothers, are leaping and racing and plunging about in the field below the house, in the giddiness of youth, unprescient of the butcher. Hated of Miss Craven's soul as much as ever were the blind and lame of King David's are those too, *too* agile sheep. Grievously prone are they to ignore the low stone wall of partition, and work havoc and devastation among the aster tops and cabbage shoots of her garden.

"The   king   was   in   his   counting-house,
Counting   out   his   money;
The   queen   was   in   the   parlour,
Eating bread and honey."

The King of Glan-yr-Afon is not counting out his money, because he has not any to count, poor young fellow. He is sitting on a garden-chair, reading the *Times*, and thinking how much better he would rule the Fatherland, how much less mean and shabby and selfish he would make her in other nations' eyes, if he might but have the whip and reins for six months or so. Old Luath lies at his feet, with dim eyes half closed, snapping lazily at the flies, and catching on an average about one every quarter of an hour. Esther is in the stack-yard, holding a levy of ravenous fowls. She has tied a large white kitchen-apron round her waist; with one hand she is holding it up, with the other she is scattering light wheat among a mixed multitude. Baby Cochins, in primrose velvet; hobbledehoy Cochins, *au naturel*, with not a stitch of clothes on their bare, indecent backs; adult Cochins, muffled and smothered up to the chin in a wealth of cinnamon feathers, and with cinnamon stockings down to their heels; Rouen ducks, and scraggy-necked turkeys. She is doing her very best to administer justice to her commonwealth, to protect the weak, to prevent aggression and violence; but like many another lawgiver she finds it rather up-hill work. Strive as she may, the ducks get far the best of it. They have no sense of shame, and can shovel up such a quantity at a time in their long yellow bills. The turkey-cock, on the other hand, gets much the worst, by reason of the long red pendant to his nose, that gets in his way and hinders him. They say that Nature never makes anything for ornament alone, divorced from use; but I confess to being ignorant as to what function that long flabby dangler has to fulfil. The stack-yard is all on the slant; it slopes down with its many stack-frames, to the old rough grey barn that is stained all over—walls and roof and door—with the stormy tears of a score of winters. There is no lack of voices all about the farm to-day: voice of Sarah chattering in the drying ground, where she is hanging Esther's cotton gowns and Jack's shirts on the lines; voice of Evan Evans, the carter, talking friendly to his heavy team in that deplorable tongue which, we trust, will soon be among the abuses of the past; voice of Seryn (Welsh for Star), from the pasture, lowing for her calf, which a day ago became veal, and a day hence (Oh blessed short memory! why cannot we take lessons from a cow?) she will have forgotten utterly. Presently comes another voice, clearer, stronger, nearer than the others—comes sailing up through the July air.

"Es—ther!"

"Ye—es!" responds Esther at the tip-top of her voice, and consequently not particularly harmonious. It is only the lark that can talk at the top of his voice and yet not be shrill.

"Where are you?" (*Forte.*)

"In the stack-yard." (*Fortissimo*).

Obedient to this direction, in about two minutes the owner of the voice, and of the excellent lungs which sent it out, makes his appearance in loose cool clothes and a smile—Jack, in fact, looking very ugly and pleasant and good-natured.

"Jack, dear boy, open the gate. Quick! Out of the way! Don't let him get under the stack-frame. Shoo!" cries Esther, in great excitement, rushing wildly about in her big apron, in pursuit of a large drake with a grasping soul, and a wonderful rainbow neck, who, with bill wide open and wings half extended, is waddling, flying, quacking away from Nemesis as hard as his splay feet and his full crop will let him.

Jack obeys. "There is a person in the drawing-room wanting to speak to you," he says, leaning his arms on the top of the gate, and looking rather malicious.

"What sort of a person?" Esther asks abstractedly, craning her long neck round the corner of the barn, to see whether the drake shows symptoms of returning. "There he is again! Shoo!"

"What was the name of Esther's husband? the man that bullied his first wife so. Oh! I know; his name, oh Queen Esther, is Ahasuerus, which, being interpreted, is Bob."

Esther's apron drops from her fingers and the wheat rolls down in a shower on to the broad backs of the Cochin householders. Fiercely the war of chickens—the pushing, the fluttering, the pecking—rages about her feet. "Already!" she says: and in her voice there is none of love's sweet quiver, nor on her cheeks is there any sign of love's pretty flag being hung out, neither the red nor the white one. She only looks a little blank—a little troubled.

"Yes, already," says Jack, mercilessly; "and not only has he come himself, but he has brought all his household gods with him. He has come with a great company of old women at his back. I fancy they have brought a notary or a scrivener, or what do you call it? with them, and that there is to be a grand betrothal in form."

"Nonsense!" says Esther, and she comes all over to the gate, and clasps two little petitioning hands on his shoulder. "You will come with me, won't you, Jack?"

"Not I!" says Jack, stoutly. "I would not trust myself with those old maids, in their present excited state, if you were to give me my next half-year's rent: they would be employing the notary in my case too before I knew where I was."

"Jack, is my hair pretty tidy?" stroking it down with the improvised brush and comb of her slim fingers.

"Extremely so: it looks as if the chickens had got into it, and been scratching there by mistake."

Meanwhile Master Brandon and his old women, to wit, his mother, Mrs. Brandon, and his sisters, the two Misses Brandon, are posed about the drawing-room, waiting. Waiting is always a painful process, from the modified form of suffering involved in the ten minutes before dinner, when every man's tongue is tied, and his wits congealed by the frost of expectant hunger; upward to the Gehenna of a dentist's antechamber. Robert is all on wires this morning: he cannot sit still; he keeps shuffling and twisting his long, awkward legs about, beating the devil's tattoo on the floor with his nailed boots, and hammering an ugly little tune with a paper knife on an old Book of Beauty on the table. "How you fidget, Bob!" cries his sister Bessy.

Miss Elizabeth Brandon is ten years older and about ten feet shorter than her brother; she is in process of souring, like cowslip wine that has been kept too long, or small beer in thunder. She is not so very sour, after all, poor little virgin! only ten years ago she was, and ten years hence she will be mellower than she is now.

"All right!" says Bob, "I won't;" and he stops, only to commence, two seconds later, a new noise, seven times worse than the first; a very disagreeable sort of scraping with the hind legs of his chair. Is not it one of Miss Yonge's goody heroes, who, when he feels disposed to be impatient, sits down and strums away at the "Harmonious Blacksmith?" Bob could not get through a bar of that soothing melody this morning. Mrs. Brandon is just beginning to say, "Do you think the servant could have told her?" when the door opens, and a little vision comes in with delicate hair ruffling about her sweet, shining eyes; a little vision that ought to be walking on rosy clouds, Bob thinks, with cherubim and seraphim holding up her train, instead of on shabby oil-cloth and faded carpet, dragging her train behind her.

"I—I'm very sorry; I'm afraid I have kept you waiting: I did not" (did not expect you so early is on the tip of her tongue, but she remembers just in time that it would be about the impolitest remark she could make. Never, until the millennium, will the marriage of Truth and Civility be solemnized)—"did not know you were here till Jack came and told me a moment ago," she substitutes so adroitly that none of her auditors perceive the rivet that joins the two halves of her sentence together.

"I don't know what your brother will say to us for taking his house by storm, but you must blame *him*, my dear, you must blame *him!*" says Mrs. Brandon, nodding her head towards

Bob, and looking as if there was something peculiarly humorous in the idea of Esther being in a condition to blame him for anything he could do or leave undone.

Mrs. Brandon is an old woman, with a smooth, holy face, and a villainous black poke bonnet: she kisses Esther, and the Misses Brandon likewise come forward and inflict a prim sisterly salute with their thin old-maid lips, on the velvet rose-leaf of her cheek. They had never kissed her before, and she felt as if the manacles were being fastened round her wrists, and the gyves about her ankles. She longs to cry out and say, "What are you all about? you are quite mistaken, every one of you; Mrs. Brandon, I am not your daughter; Miss Bessy, I am not your sister; I don't want to be: take back those kisses of yours, if you please, if they mean that!" Had she been alone with Robert, she would probably have said this; have said it without much difficulty, but now the words seemed infinitely, impossibly hard to frame. There is upon her the shyness of a young woman with an old one; the shyness of one against three. She feels, too, that it seems ungracious, churlish, when they are so glad to take her in to themselves, to adopt her as their own, not to be very glad too. When a person says to one, if not in words, yet with looks and gestures, "Our people shall be thy people, and our God thy God," it is not easy for a plastic, gracious nature to say "No, they shall not!" however little they may relish the arrangement. So, in her muteness, Esther accepts the Brandon God and people as hers.

Wordless and demure, she sits down on a little low seat as far removed as may be from Robert. Esther will, no doubt, be an ugly old woman; she makes rather an ugly photograph; but who can deny that she is a delicious bit of colour as she sits there right in the eye of the morning sun, and not at all afraid of his strict scrutiny? So many women, now-a-days, are neutral-tinted, drabbish, greyish, as if the colours that God painted with were not fast, but faded, like Reynolds'. Esther's colouring is as distinct, as decided, as clean and clear as that on a flower's petal or a butterfly's wing. Nobody speaks, except the clock with the short-waisted Minerva on it, and it does not say anything particularly original. Then the old woman bends towards the young one, and says in a kind, low voice, "You see Robert has told us his news, my dear." There is flowing in through the French window a broad river of yellow light from the great fountain in the sky; it is deluging Mrs. Brandon's bonnet and Esther's hair. The bonnet is black, and the hair is black; but there are blacks and blacks. The May grass is green, and a beer bottle is green; but the resemblance between the two is not striking. Esther has not the remotest idea what answer to make; so she chooses one of the shortest words she knows of, and says "Yes!" half-assentingly, half-interrogatively.

"And we could not rest till we came and told you what good news we thought it," pursues the old lady, encouragingly.

Esther says nothing. Her eyelids feel glued down to her cheeks; she is conscious, with inward rage and vexation, of looking blushing, bashful, everything that a young betrothed should look.

"I'm an old woman," concludes Mrs. Brandon, rather moved by her own eloquence, "and I cannot expect a great many more years of life. You know what the Psalmist sweetly says, love; but I trust I may be spared to see God bless both my children, and make them His happy servants for this world and the next."

As she speaks she lays one hand on Esther's head. Bob is happily too far off, or she would lay the other on his, while the two little virgin clerks from the sofa cry "Amen!" in a breath. Esther is half-frightened. What with the serious words, with the three women's solemn faces, she half feels as if she were being married on the spot; her thoughts fly to Jack and the notary; after that "Amen!" she is not quite sure that her name is not Esther Brandon. She shrinks away a little, but not at all rudely.

"You are very kind," she says, in her gentle voice, "and it was so good of you coming all through the wood—such a long walk for you, too; but I think—I'm afraid that there is some mistake about—this—about me; there is nothing settled—nothing at all, I assure you. I told your son so yesterday quite plainly, only I'm afraid he did not understand me," she concludes, looking rather reproachfully over at him.

"I did understand you," protests poor Bob, eagerly, jumping up, upsetting his chair, and never thinking of picking it up again, "I did, indeed. I told mother your very words, only she would have it that they meant—what we all wished they should mean," he ends, looking very downcast and snubbed and disconsolate.

There is another pause, then Mrs. Brandon rises and puts out her hand to Esther—in farewell this time.

"I'm afraid I've been in too great a hurry, my dear," she says, trying not to speak stiffly, and not succeeding quite so well as she deserved. "But you'll forgive me, I'm sure; you see, mothers are apt to be partial people, and I could not imagine any one trying to love my boy, and not succeeding."

But Miss Craven can never let well alone. She would marry Old Nick himself sooner than that his mother or sister should look askance at her, or seem hurt and grieved with her for expressing any want of relish for him, hoofs and tail and horns and all.

"Oh no, you must not go!" she cries, in her quick, eager way, putting up two anxious hands in deprecation; "you must not be vexed with me; I did not mean to be disagreeable. I shall like very much to belong to you, I'm sure. I was only afraid of your expecting more from me than I had to give *yet*," she ends, with head drooped a little, and cheeks reddened like a peach's that the sun has been kissing all the afternoon.

The stiffness goes away: nobody can be stiff for long with Esther Craven, any more than a snow-ball can remain a snow-ball under the fire's warm gaze.

"We don't want you to belong to us if you don't wish it yourself," the old woman says, very gravely, yet not ill-naturedly.

"I hardly know what I wish," answers the girl, naïvely, in a sort of bewilderment.

Then they go, and Robert walks off with his old mother on his arm. He would walk down Pall Mall with her in that identical poke bonnet, and the two little dowdy vestals pottering behind in the most perfect unconsciousness and simplicity, even if he were to know that his brother officers, to a man, were looking out at him from the "Rag" windows.

"Oh, my cheeks! my cheeks! will they ever get cool again!" cries Esther, flinging herself down on the oak bench in the porch, and laying her face against the cold ivy leaves.

"You look rather as if you had been poking your countenance between the bars of the kitchen grate," responds Jack, with all a brother's candour. Jack has been dodging behind the laurel bushes, after the fashion in which the English gentleman is fond of receiving his friends when they come to call on him.

"Why did not you come to my rescue, you unnatural brother? What chance had I, single-handed, against those three Gorgons? Pah! it makes my head ache to think of mamma's coiffure."

"When a person gets into a scrape themselves, I make it a rule to let them get out of it themselves, as it makes them more careful for the future," replies Jack, with philosophy.

"But I'm not getting out of it; I'm floundering deeper and deeper and deeper in, like a man in an Irish bog," says Esther, ruefully. "Oh, Jack!" she concludes, laughing, yet vexed (laughter is as often the exponent of annoyance as of enjoyment, I think), "if you could have heard the stories I was forced to tell, I'm sure I deserve to be wound up, carried out, and buried, as much as ever Ananias did."

CHAPTER V.

This world is divided into poor and rich; into those who do things for themselves, and those who get other people to do them for them. The Cravens belong to the former class. On the afternoon of the day mentioned in my last chapter, Miss Craven is doing for herself what she had much rather that some one else should do for her. She is sitting at her sewing-machine, with a pile of huckaback cut up into towel-lengths beside her. As long as civilization remains at its present ridiculous pitch of elevation, people must have towels, and there is a prejudice in favour of hemmed versus ravelled edges. In the kitchen garden the maid-servants are all busy, picking currants and raspberries for preserving. Owen, the gardening man, is helping them; they are combining business with pleasure; fruit-picking with persiflage. How loudly and shrilly they laugh! and yet loud, shrill laughter expresses mirth and cause for mirth, as well as low and silvery. Esther, grave and alone, catches herself wondering what the joke was that caused such general merriment two minutes ago. Probably, did she know it, she would not laugh at it, would see no point in it, perhaps, but she would be glad to hear it. The huckaback is thick and heavy; bending down one's head over one's work sends all the blood in one's body into it. Phew! How hot! How much pleasanter to be out of doors, tweaking off dead rose heads, watching the great red poppies straightening out their folded creases, pulling the green nightcaps off the escholtzia buds! A shadow darkens the French window, causing Miss Craven to give one of those starts that make one feel as if one literally jumped out of one's skin, and fill one with ungodly wrath against the occasion of them.

"I rang several times," says Robert Brandon, apologetically, "but nobody came."

"Oh! it's you, is it?" she says, with a tone not exactly of rapture in her voice; "our servants always manage to be out of the way on the rare occasions when any one calls. They are all in the garden, picking currants; one would have been plenty, but they prefer working, like convicts or navvies, in gangs."

"I came to see whether you were inclined to take a walk?" he says, hesitatingly, for her manner is not encouraging.

"Too hot!" she answers, lazily, leaning her head on the back of her chair, and closing her eyes, as if his presence disposed her to sleep.

"Not in the wood?" he rejoins, eagerly. "Under our oaks it is as cool and almost as dark as night, and there is always a breeze from the brook."

"I am busy!" she says, pettishly, annoyed at his persistence, and taking in with a dissatisfied eye his *tout ensemble*—yellow beard, frayed coat-sleeves, vigorous rustic comeliness.

He does not pursue the subject further, but stands leaning wistfully and uncertain against the window.

"Jack is not at home, I'm afraid," she says, stiffly, by-and-by.

"I did not come to see Jack," he answers, bluntly. She does not invite him to come in, but he, crossing the threshold diffidently, takes a seat near, but not aggressively near, her. "Don't let me interrupt you!" he says, deprecatingly.

She takes him at his word, and continues her homely occupation. Up and down, up and down her foot goes, keeping the wheel in motion; prick, prick, prick, the needle travels with its quick, regular stabs. If, as I have said, the process of bending over work on a July afternoon is heating, the consciousness that another person is watching every quiver of your eyelids, counting every breath you draw, and every displaced hair that straggles about brow or cheek, does not conduce to make it less so. The magnetic influence that sooner or later compels the eyes of the looked at to seek those of the looker, obliges Esther, after awhile, to raise hers—reluctant and protesting—to Robert's.

"I wish my mother could see you!" he says, with a smile of placid happiness. Mr. Brandon carries his mother metaphorically upon his back, almost as much as pious Æneas did the old Anchises literally. Esther suspends her employment for a moment.

"I beg your pardon; this machine makes such a noise that I did not catch what you said."

"I was only wishing that mother could see you now."

"It is a pleasure she enjoys pretty frequently. Why *now* particularly?"

"She would see how thrifty and housewifely you can be."

"I am glad she does not, then," answers the girl, drily, beginning to work again faster than ever, and flushing with annoyance; "she would form a most erroneous estimate of me. I dislike particularly to be found by people in one of my rare paroxysms of virtue; they take it for my normal state, and judge and expect of me accordingly."

"I shall tell her that, at all events, my judgment of you was nearer the truth than hers," says Robert, triumphantly.

Esther laughs awkwardly.

"I don't know whether you are aware of it, but you are conveying to my mind the idea that your mother has been pronouncing a very unfavourable verdict upon me and my character."

"She thinks you are too pretty and lively, and—and—" (frivolous had been the word employed by Mrs. Brandon, but Robert cannot find it in his heart to apply it to his idol)—"too fond of society to care about being useful in tame, humdrum, everyday ways."

Esther gives her head a little impatient shake.

"Mrs. Brandon adheres to the golden axiom, so evidently composed by some one to whom beauty was sour grapes, that it is better to be good than pretty; an axiom that assumes that the one is incompatible with the other."

So speaking she relapses into a chafed silence, and he into his vigilant dumb observation of her. At the end of a quarter of an hour, as he still shows no signs of moving, finding the present position of affairs no longer tolerable, Miss Craven jumps up, flings down her heap of huckaback on the floor, and says abruptly, with a sort of forced resignation:

"I will come to the wood, if you wish; it will be all the same a hundred years hence."

"I am perfectly happy as I am," he answers with provoking good humour, looking up in blissful unconsciousness at her charming cross face, and the plain yet dainty fit of her trim cheap gown.

"But I am not," she rejoins brusquely; "indoors it is stifling to-day; please introduce me as quickly as possible to that breeze you spoke of; I have not been able to find a trace of one all day."

She fetches her hat and puts it on; too indifferent as to her appearance in his eyes to take the trouble of casting even a passing glance at herself in the glass, to see whether it is put on straight or crooked.

The Glan-yr-Afon wood is a fickle, changeable place; like a vain woman, it is always taking off one garment and putting on another. Three months ago, when the April woods were piping to it, it had on a mist-blue cloak of hyacinths—what could be prettier?—but now it has laid it aside, and is all tricked out in gay grass, green, flecked here and there with rosy families of

14

catch-fly and groups of purple orchis spires. Do you remember those words of the sweetest, wildest, fancifullest of all our singers?

"And the sinuous paths of lawn and of moss,
That led through this garden along and across,—
Some open at once to the sun and the breeze,
Some lost among bowers of blossoming trees,—

"Were all paved with daisies and delicate bells
As fair as the fabulous asphodels,
And flow'rets that, drooping as day drooped too,
Fell into pavilions white, purple, and blue,
To roof the glowworm from the evening dew."

They describe Glan-yr-Afon wood much better than I can. It is a great green cathedral, where choral service goes on all day long, and where the rook preaches impressive sermons from the swinging tree-tops.

"Had we not better walk arm in arm?" asks Esther, sardonically, as they march along in silence. "I believe it is the correct thing on these occasions; at least Gwen and her sweetheart always do on Sunday evenings."

He turns towards her; an expression of surprised delight upspringing into his eyes.

"Do you mean *really*?"

She is mollified, despite herself, by the simple joy beaming in his poor, good-looking face—face that would be more than good-looking if only some great grief would give it fuller expression; if only a few months of late hours and mundane dissipations would wear off its look of exuberant bucolic healthiness.

"No, no; I was only joking."

"Shall we sit here?" asks Brandon, presently, pointing to a rustic seat that stands under a great girthed oak, taller and thicker-foliaged than its neighbours. "See! did not I tell you true? Hardly a sunbeam pierces through these leaves, and the brawling of the brook comes up so pleasantly from below."

Esther looks, but the situation does not please her; it is too secluded, too sentimental; it looks like a seat on which Colin and Dowsabel might sit fluting and weaving

".... belts of straw and ivy buds,"

and simpering at one another over the tops of their crooks.

"I don't fancy it," she says, beginning to walk on; "it looks *earwiggy*."

"Only the other day you said it was quite a lovers' seat!" he exclaims, in surprise.

"Exactly; and for that very reason I prefer waiting till I am more qualified to sit upon it."

By-and-by Miss Craven finds a position that suits her better; one nearer the edge of the wood, in full view of the Naullan road, along which market women, coal carts, stray limping tramps, go passing, and where loverly blandishments are out of the question.

The sun slides down between two birch stems that stand amid rock fragments, and riots at his will about her head, as she sits at the birch foot on a great grey stone, all flourished over with green mosses and little clinging plants. Below, the baby river runs tinkling; it is such a baby river that it has not strength to grapple with the boulders that lie in its bed; it comes stealing round their hoary sides with a coaxing noise, in gentlest swirls and bubbled eddies. The squirrels brought their nuts last autumn to Esther's stone to crack; the shells are lying there still; she is picking them up and dropping them again in idle play. Little dancing lights are flashing down through the birch's feathery-green locks, and playing Hide and Seek over Esther's gown and Robert's recumbent figure, as he lies in the repose of warmth, absolute idleness, absolute content at her feet. An hour and a half, two hours to be spent in trying to like Robert! Faugh! She yawns.

"That is the seventh time you have yawned since we have been here," remarks her lover, a little reproachfully.

"I dare say; and if you wait five minutes longer, you will probably be able to tell me that it is the seventy-seventh time."

"You did not yawn while we were indoors."

"I had my work; what is a woman without her work? A dismounted dragoon—a pump without water!" She stretches out her arms lazily, to embrace the dry, warm air. "Does every one find being courted as tedious a process as I do?" (Aside.) Aloud: "Some one said to me the other day, that no woman could be happy who was not fond of work. It is putting one's felicity on rather a low level, but I believe it is true."

"In the same way as no man can be good-tempered who is not fond of smoking," says Bob, starting a rival masculine proposition.

"I don't know anything at all about men," replies Esther, exhaustively. "No woman in the world can have a more limited acquaintance with the masculine gender than I have."

"You are young yet," says Brandon, consolingly.

"I was seventeen last May, if you call that young," she answers, her thoughts recurring to "Heartsease," the heroine of which is

"Wooed and married and a'"

before her sixteenth birthday.

"You are eight years younger than I am."

"Am I?" carelessly, as if such comparative statistics were profoundly uninteresting to her.

"Yes; I am glad there is so much difference in age between us."

"Why?"

"Because you are the more likely to outlive me."

She passes by the little sentimentalism with silent contempt. "I shall *certainly* outlive you," she says confidently. "Women mostly outlive men, even when they are of the same age. We lead slower, safer lives. If I spend all my life here, I shall probably creep on, like a tortoise, to a hundred."

"But you will not spend all your life here?" he cries, eagerly.

She shrugs her shoulders. "*Cela dépend.* I shall live here as long as Jack remains unmarried."

"That will not be very long, I prophesy," cries Brandon, cheerfully. "A farmer requires a wife more than most men."

"More than a soldier, certainly," retorts she, with a malicious smile.

He laughs; too warm and lazy and content to be offended, and makes ineffectual passes at a gnat that has settled upon his nose. "Has he never yet shown even a *preference* for any one?" he asks, feeling a more personal interest than he had ever before experienced in Jack's amours and amourettes.

"Not that I am aware of; Jack and I never show preferences for any one, nor does any one ever show a preference for us; we are a good deal too poor to be in any demand."

"I am glad of it."

"You may have the doubtful satisfaction of knowing that no one ever showed the slightest inclination to be your rival."

"So much the better; I don't want you any the less because nobody else wants you."

"Don't you? 'A poor thing, but mine own,' that is your motto, I suppose?"

A pause. An old woman, with a myriad-wrinkled Welsh face rides by along the road on a drooping-headed donkey; a large blue and orange handkerchief tied over her bonnet and a basket on each arm.

Esther watches her as she jogs along with a feeling of envy. Fortunate, fortunate old woman! she has no lover!

"I wish you would not look so happy," Miss Craven says suddenly, flashing round an uneasy look out of her great black eyes at her companion.

"Why should not I? I *am* happy."

"But you have no right to be, no reason for being so," she cries, emphatically.

"I have, at all events, as much reason as the birds have and they seem pretty jolly; I am alive, and the sun is shining."

"You were alive, and the sun was shining, this time yesterday," she says drily; "but you were not so happy then as you are now."

At the decided damper to his hilarity so evidently intended in this speech, a slight cloud passes over the young man's face; he looks down with a snubbed expression.

"I suppose I am over-sanguine about everything," he says, humbly, "because I have always been such a lucky fellow; my profession suits me down to the ground; I have never had an ache or a pain in all my life, and I have the best woman in England for my mother."

A body free from disease, a commission in a marching regiment, a methodistical, *exigeante* old mother. These would seem but a poor *chétif* list of subjects of thankfulness to Fortune's curled and perfumed darlings.

"Your acquaintance amongst old ladies must be extensive to justify you in that last statement," says Esther, with a smile.

"The best woman I know, then."

"It is a pity that when you went, like Coelebs, in search of a wife, you did not try to find some one more like her," rejoins Esther, piqued and surprised, despite her utter indifference to his opinion of her, at finding that, notwithstanding the imbecile pitch of love for herself at which she believes him to have arrived, he can still set a dowdy, havering, brown old woman on a pedestal, above even that which she, with all the radiant red and white beauty of which she is so calmly aware, all the triumph of her seventeen sweet summers, occupies in his heart.

"You are young and she is old," says Robert, encouragingly; "I don't see why you should not be like her when you are her age."

"I think not; I hope not," says Miss Craven, coolly, strangling her twenty-fifth yawn. "Without meaning any insult to Mrs. Brandon, I should be sorry to think that, at any period of my life, I should be a mere reproduction of some one else."

Another long pause. (Have we been here an hour yet?) The brown bees go humming, droning, lumbering about, velvet-coated: a high-shouldered grasshopper chirps shrilly: the dim air vibrates.

"Just listen to that cricket!" says Esther, presently, for the sake of saying something. "How noisy he is! I read in a book the other day that if a man's voice were as strong in proportion to his size as a locust's, he could be heard from here to St. Petersburg."

"Could he?" says Bob, absently, not much interested in his betrothed's curious little piece of entomological information; "how unpleasant!" Then dragging himself along the grass and the flowers still closer to her feet, he says, "Esther, mother hopes to see a great deal more of you now than she has done hitherto."

"Does she? she is very good, I am sure," answers Esther, formally, with a feeling of compunction at her utter inability to echo the wish.

"She bid me tell you that she hopes you will come in as often as you can of an evening. We are all sure to be at home then; the girls read aloud by turns, and mother thought that——"

"That it might improve my mind, and that it needs improving," interrupts Esther, smiling drily; "so it does. I quite agree with her; but not even for that object could I leave Jack of an evening; he is out all day long, and the evening is the only time when I have him to myself."

"You find plenty to say to *him* always, I suppose?" says Robert, with an involuntary sigh and slight stress upon the word *him*.

"Not a word, sometimes. We sit opposite or beside each other in sociable silence."

"*How* fond you are of that fellow!" says Robert, sighing again, and thinking, ruefully, what a long time it would be before any one would say to her, "*How* fond you are of Bob Brandon!"

"He is the one thing upon earth that I could not do without!" she answers shortly, turning away her head.

There are some people that we love so intensely that we can hardly speak even of our own love for them without tears.

"I should be afraid to say that of any one," says Bob, bluntly, "for fear of being shown that I *must* do without them."

"What have I in all the world but him?" she cries, a passionate earnestness chasing the slow languor from her voice, all her soft face afire with eager tenderness; "neither kith nor kin; neither friends nor money. I am as destitute, in fact, though not in seeming, as that girl that passed just now, shuffling her bare feet along in the dust, and with three boxes of matches—her whole stock-in-trade—in her dirty hand. But for Jack," she continues, in a lighter strain, "you might at the present moment be carrying half a pound of tea or four penn'orth of snuff as a present to me in the Naullan almshouses."

Robert looks attentive, and says "Hem," which is a sort of "Selah" or "Higgaion," and does not express much beyond inarticulate interest.

"I often think that he is too good for this world," says the young girl, mournfully, picking an orchis leaf, and looking down absently on the capricious black splashes that freak its green surface.

Bob is a little embarrassed between his love of truth and his desire to coincide in opinion with his beloved.

Jack is not in the least like the little morbid boys and girls in his sister Bessy's books, who retire into corners in play-hours to read about hell-fire, to whom marbles and toffee and bull's-eyes are as dung, and who are inextricably entangled in his mind with the idea of "too good for this world." He evades the discussion of the alarming nature of young Craven's goodness by a judicious silence.

"I am such an expense to him," continues Esther, lugubriously, the corners of her mouth drooping like a child's about to cry—"what with clothes, and food, and altogether. Even though one does not eat very much every day, it comes to a great deal at the end of the year, does it not?"

"If you come to me, you would be no expense at all to him," Robert answers, stroking his great, broad, yellow beard (beard that will have to disappear before he rejoins his gallant corps in Bermuda), and looking very sentimental; yet not that either, for sentimental implies the existence of a little feeling, and the affectation of a great deal more.

17

"He would have to provide me with a trousseau and a wedding-cake, even in that case."

"I would excuse him both."

"Would you?" she says, jestingly; "I wouldn't; it has always seemed to me that the best part of holy matrimony is the avalanche of new clothes that attends being wed."

"You shall have any amount of new clothes."

"I should be an expense to you, then," she says, giving him a smile that is grateful and bright and cold, all in one, like a January morning. Cold as her smile is, it is a smile, and he is encouraged by it to refer to a subject nearer his heart than Jack Craven's excellences.

"If you cannot spare time to come to us of an evening, would you let me—might I—would you mind my joining you and Jack—now and then—for half an hour or so—if I should not be in the way?"

Her countenance falls, more visibly than she is herself perhaps aware of.

"Of course," she answers, in a constrained voice, "if you wish; we shall always be glad to see you, of course."

"I would not come often," says the poor young man wistfully; "once a week perhaps—so that we might get to know one another better; mother says——"

"Don't tell me any more of your mother's speeches to-day, or we shall have none left for to-morrow," interrupts Esther, with a sort of ironical playfulness, flapping about with her pocket-handkerchief at a squadron of young midges, and looking mild exasperation at the unlucky six-foot slave at her feet. Then she stretches out her hand, plucks a dandelion, or what was a dandelion a week ago, but is now a sphere of delicatest, fragilest, downspikes, and blows it like a child to see what o'clock it is. "One, two, three, four, five, six. Time to go home!" she says, flinging away the hollow stalk and springing up.

"It seems only five minutes since we came," says Robert, with a great sigh of good-bye, looking down at the long stretch of bruised grass that indicates his late resting-place.

"Do you think so?" exclaims Esther, opening her eyes very wide, and the most violent negative could not have expressed dissent more clearly.

So they pass home through the loudly vocal wood, and he parts from her under the porch. He had meant to squeeze her hand at parting; perhaps still bolder forms of adieu flitted before his mind's eye, but a certain expression in her face makes all such plans take to their heels. He looks as if he would come in if he were asked; but he is not asked, therefore, courage failing him, he departs. She stands in the shadow watching him, and thinks, "What bad boots! and is not one shoulder rather higher than the other?" It is not the least bit higher; no young fir is straighter than he; but when a thing belongs, or may possibly belong, to oneself, one waxes marvellous critical.

CHAPTER VI.

"Something new! something new!" cried the Athenians; and across two thousand years we catch up and echo their greedy cry. But why do we? We all know well enough that there is nothing new; there was not even in King Solomon's time—not even in all his treasure-house, nor among his seven hundred wives. What an advantage those ancients who saw the world's infancy had over us—over us, who have to content ourselves with the lees of the wine, which the few dropped ears scattered about the great reaped wheat field! Who would not fain have lived in the days when nothing had yet been said—when everything, consequently, remained to be said? Who could be trite then, in that blest epoch when platitudes were unborn, when *Tupper* was an impossibility, and even the statement that two and two make four had something startlingly novel about it? *Then* a man's thoughts were his own, his *very* own, his own by the best of all rights—creation; *now* they are the bastard product of ten thousand buried men's dead ideas.

Original is a pleasant word, is it not?—fair and well-sounding; but it is like the sample figs at the top of the box: it represents nothing, or something infinitely smaller than itself behind and underneath it. Is it too much to say that it is impossible to find an original idea in any writer we wot of? You meet, perhaps, some day in a book a thought, an image that strikes you. You say, "This is this thinker's own; there is the stamp of this one individual mind upon it;" when lo! mayhap but a few hours later you are reading the thoughts of some elder scribe, one that has been dust nigh ten or twenty centuries back, and you find the same thought, half fledged or quarter fledged, only in the egg, perhaps—but still it is there. There is nothing new under the sun.

And if this is true of other subjects, how much truer of that most outworn, threadbare old theme, Love! The world has been spinning round six thousand years at the lowest, most exploded computation; in any thousand years there have been thirty or forty generations, and each unit in every one of those generations, if he has lived to man's estate, has surely loved after one fashion or another. Whosoever has done any worthy thing, whosoever has sent out his thoughts in writing or speech or action to the world, has felt the stirrings of this strange instinct; unconsciously it has moulded and permeated his deeds and his words: and yet, old as it is, we are not tired of it, any more than we are of the back-coming green of the spring, or the never-extinguished lamps of the stars.

"The harvest is past, the summer is ended;" at least well nigh ended. Jack and Esther are at breakfast: outside the scarlet geraniums are blazing away in the morning sun, trying their best to shine as brightly as he is doing, and the gnats are dancing round and round on the buoyant floor of their ball-room—the air. I wonder that that incessant valsing does not make them giddy. I am not sure that human beings, like the lions and tigers and uneasy black bears in the Zoological, look their best at feeding-time; but such as they are, here they are.

Esther in a chintz gown, sown all over with little red carnations as thickly as the firmament with heavenly bodies. She looks as fresh as a daisy—as an Englishwoman, to whom morning *déshabille*, wrapper, slippers, undressed hair, are unknown Gallic abominations—and is eating porridge with a spoon. Jack reading his letters, which look all bills and circulars, after the fashion of men's correspondence; for what man made after the fashion of a man, would sit down to indite an epistle to another man, were it his *alter ego* unless he had something to say about a horse or a dog or a gun? Presently he finishes this cursory survey, crumples up the last blue envelope in his hand, flings it with manly untidiness into the summer-dressed grate, and says, resuming a conversation which had been interrupted a quarter of an hour ago by the entrance of prayers and the urn, "I cannot imagine what you have done to the fellow! he used not to be half a bad fellow to talk to. Never a genius, you know, but still I used to like to have him to walk over the farm with me—not that he knows a swede from a mangold: don't see much sign of his old mother's farming mantle falling upon him. But now he has not a word to throw to a dog; he is as stupid as a stuck pig."

"I have not cut out his tongue or tied it up in a bag, if that is what you are hinting at," says Esther, with a smile as confused as a dog's, when, not quite sure of his reception, he sneaks up to you sideways, lifting his upper lip, and from tail to muzzle one nervous wriggle. "Perhaps he is like the birds, and gets silent towards the end of the summer."

"Why you keep him dangling after you, like the tail of a kite, I cannot conceive," Mr. Craven cries, crumbling his bread with a little irritation. "It must be such a nuisance having a great long thing like him knocking about under your feet morning, noon, and night."

Esther is silent; only her head droops lower, lower, till her little nose almost immerses itself in her stirabout.

"Whereas," pursues Jack, helping himself to a great deal of cold beef, "if you were to give him his *congé* now (Jack is by no means neglectful of the *g* in the French word), he would be all right again in a fortnight, ready for the shooting."

"He would, would he?" says Esther, lifting up her nose and reddening with vexation.

No woman likes to think of her empire as anything short of eternal.

"If you don't like to do it yourself, I'll do it for you," pursues her brother, making a magnanimously handsome offer. "I would say to him, 'My dear fellow, it is no good, she does not seem to care about you,' as soon as look at him."

"What a delicate way of breaking the news!" cries Esther, ironically. "Commend me to a man for gentle *finesse*."

"I don't believe in *breaking* news," replies Jack, sturdily. "If you were to go off in a fit, or the bay colt was to break his leg, or anything to go wrong, I'd far sooner people would tell me so without any humming and hawing and keeping me on the tenter hooks. Breaking news is like half cutting your throat before you are hanged, making you die two deaths instead of one."

"But suppose I do seem to care a little about him?" suggests Esther, blushing furiously, but holding up her head bravely, and looking straight at her brother.

"Suppose the cow jumped over the moon," replies Jack with incredulity.

"I don't know whether the cow has accomplished her feat, but I have accomplished mine," says Esther, trying to make her face as brass, and failing signally.

Jack puts up his hand, and strokes the future birthplace of his moustache, to hide an unavoidable smile.

"I don't wish to be rude," he says; "but may I ask, since when? Was it a week ago, or less, that you requested me to accompany you on one of your joint excursions to that everlasting wood, and told me you thought your watch wanted cleaning, the time seemed to go so slow?"

"A week!" cries his sister, indignantly. "Three weeks, or a month, at least."

"Wrong, Essie, wrong; it was this day fortnight, Ryvel Horse Fair, which was the reason why I had to decline your invitation."

"What does a week one way or another signify?" she cries, becoming irrational, as a worsted woman mostly does.

"Nothing to a woman or a—weathercock."

This last insult is too much for Miss Craven.

"I see you are determined to turn me into ridicule; I see you don't believe me!" she cries, preparing to rush from the room like a tornado.

"My good Essie," says Jack, jumping up, taking her two hands, and manfully repressing his inclination to laugh—"here I am; tell me *anything*, and I'll swear by the tomb of my grandmother to believe it."

"Why should not I like him? What is there in him so hateful as to make my being fond of him incredible?" asks Essie, unreasonable and sobbing.

"Nothing that I know of—except his *boots*, and you told me *they* were—"

"So they are," she says, smiling through her tears—"more than hateful; they haunt one like a bad dream."

"He is not the least penitent about them, I can tell you: only yesterday he showed them me with ungodly glee, told me he had got them at Hugh Hughes's, at Naullan, and advised me to go and do likewise."

"But—but—his boots are not he; he is not his boots, I mean," remarks Miss Craven, with meek suggestion; "mercifully, they are separable."

"He was not born in them, you mean? I did not suppose he was; he would have been worse than Richard the Third, who made his appearance with all his teeth in his head—didn't he?—if he had."

"It is quite true—perfectly true," continues Esther, leaning her two hands on the back of a chair, and tilting it up and down, "what you say about his being so stupid; he *is* extremely stupid: often I feel inclined to box his ears, for the thing he says, and for not understanding things, and having to have them explained to him; but after all, do you know, I am not sure that it is the people who say clever things, and snap one up all in a minute, that are the best to live with."

"You contemplate living with him then, eh? Last time I was favoured with your plans, you were to be a vestal to the end of the chapter."

"A provision for old age: I cannot expect you to be satisfied with me always," she answers, with rather a sad smile. "And when I am superseded, a good worthy simpleton, with obsolete chivalrous ideas of *Woman* in the abstract—*Woman* with a big *W*—who will laugh at my worst jokes whether he sees them or not, and make none himself, is better than nothing."

"All right," says Jack, calmly, walking towards the door, and unfolding the *Times* with a crackling that nearly drowns his voice: "please yourself and you'll please me: only be so good as to tell me when the wedding day is fixed, as I must get a new coat. I suppose that the one I had for Uncle John's funeral will not do, will it?"

Who is it says in the "Tempest," if neither Ferdinand nor any other beautiful young Prince had come on the scene, yet if Miranda had remained alone with her father, and the storms and winds and water-spirits, she would have ended by loving Caliban? I do not know about Miranda, but I am sure that if Esther had been in Miranda's place she would have so ended; would have carried faggots in her slender arms for the shaggy monster—have called him caressing diminutives, and asked him little interested questions about his dam Sycorax.

The desire to be loved is strong enough in us all; in this girl it amounted to madness: it is the key to all the foolish, wicked, senseless things you will find her doing through this history's short course. If she could have had her will, every man, woman, and child, every cow and calf and dog and cat that met her, would have watched her coming with joy and her going with grief. Add to which, in the summer time most women like to have a lover; it is almost as necessary to them as warm clothes at Christmas. In winter the fire is lover enough for any one. The frosty splendour of the stars and the chill flashing of the northern lights provoke no yearning in any one human soul towards any other; we peep at them through our icy casements, then drop the curtain shivering, and leave them alone to their high cold play in the sky. But who can look at a July moon alone?

You will say that Esther was not alone, that she had her brother to look at it with her; but who will deny that a brother who makes agricultural remarks about the Queen of Night, and observes that the haze round her royal head looks well for the turnips, is worse, immeasurably worse than nobody? To me it seems that there is nothing absolute, positive in all this shifting, kaleidoscope world; everything is comparative. There is nothing either good, bad, pretty, ugly, large, small, except as compared with something better, worse, prettier, uglier, larger, smaller. Measure two men together, and you find one tall and the other short; put the short one by himself or among a world of pigmies, and straightway he grows tall. Lacking a standard to go by, we make egregious errors. I have known many a woman to pass through life with a pigmy beside her, taking him for a giant all the while, nor undeceived to the end. Esther has no man to measure her Robert by; none at all, save the cowman, the carter, and the groom. Intellectually, morally, physically, he outtops them in stature, and that is all she can as yet know about him. Moonlight, propinquity, total absence of objects of comparison—these three must be Esther's excuses.

Robert is not much like her ideal, certainly—the ideal whose picture she has been painting life-size on the canvas of her mind during the vacant moments of the last two transitional years; but if we all waited to be wed till our ideal came knocking at our doors, the world would be shortly dispeopled of legitimate inhabitants. Miss Craven's ideal is dark; at seventeen, most ideals are dark: he has long, fierce, sleepy, unfathomable eyes. Robert is straw-coloured: his eyes are blue; very wide awake: they say exactly what his tongue does, neither more nor less, and there is absolutely no harm in them—a doubtful recommendation to a woman. The ideal's nose is fine cut, delicately chiselled; his cheeks are a little haggard, slightly hollowed and paled by five and thirty years or so of the reckless life of one that has lived, not existed. Robert's nose is broad and blunt; his cheeks have the roundness and bloom of a countryman's five and twenty. The ideal breaks most of the commandments with easy grace; is inclined to be sceptical and a little sarcastic over the old world beliefs, and facts hoary with time and reverence. Robert nightly prays on bent knees to be "not led into temptation but delivered from evil;" he believes firmly every thing that he ever was taught, from the Peep of Day upwards, and he could no more shape his honest lips into a sneer than he could square the circle. Before the fell shafts of the ideal's eyes women lie slain as thick as Greeks lay beneath the arrows of Apollo in the Iliad's opening clash; the number of Robert's female victims is represented by a duck's egg.

"Je ne comprends pas l'amour sans effroi," says one of the characters in the best French novel I have read this many a day. The ideal inspires fear equally with love; you can imagine his being harsh, fierce, cruel, to the woman he loves. In none of the most hard-hearted of created beings could Robert provoke alarm. Children who see him for the first time come and thrust their little dimpled hands into his, and laugh up with confident impudence in his face. Dogs to whom he has never been introduced come and rub their shaggy heads against his knees, and curl and wriggle about his friendly feet.

Esther can indulge no faintest hope that he will bully her. The ideal rides straight as a die, and is as much a part of his horse as a centaur. Robert is very fond of getting a day's hunting when he can afford the two guineas requisite for the hiring of a horse, which is not very often; and he likes to get his money's worth by blundering blindly over everything that comes in his way, but he has about as much idea of *riding* as a tailor or a cow. The ideal is an idol to be set up and worshipped—a Baal to be adored with tears and blood and knife-gashings. Robert is a worshipper to be encouraged by a cold look and smile flung to him every now and then, like a bone to a dog, or spurned away with disapproving foot, as Cain was from his unaccepted altar. To worship is to a woman always sweeter than to be worshipped. To worship one must look up; to be worshipped one must look down....

Come with me this August Sunday through the wood from Glan-yr-Afon to Plas Berwyn—from Esther's home to Robert's. It is but a few hundred yards of shade and shine, a small, scarce trodden wood-path whose narrow, faint track the ripe grasses and the seeded ferns have wellnigh obliterated, flinging themselves across it in all the *abandon* of their unspeakable grace. The apples' round faces are reddening in the little Plas Berwyn orchard; the shorn fields slope barely, slantwise along the hill-side in their yellow stubble. For weeks and weeks the corn has been whitening under the sun's hard, veilless stare, and now at last it has fallen; the barley has bowed its bearded head beneath the sickle's stroke, and the oats their tremulous ringlets. They are all gathered in, and garnered in Mrs. Brandon's stout, well-thatched stacks; to thatch a stack is the one thing a Welshman can do.

It is an hour past noon, and the Reverend Evan Evans has released the bodies of his congregation from that white-washed, tumble-down old barn that he is pleased to call his church, and their minds from the tension necessary to take in the ill-strung-together, misapplied texts that he is pleased to call his sermon.

Plas Berwyn is a house of about the same size as Glan-yr-Afon, but the rooms do not look so large, they are so full of large things and large people. The dining-room is crowded up with a great mahogany table, a great mahogany sideboard, great mahogany chairs—inconvenient relics, fondly clung to by people who from a larger house have subsided into a smaller one—a sort of warranty of past respectability like the cottager's japanned tea-tray and brass candlesticks. There is an atmosphere of lumbersome age and gravity about the whole place; none of the fragrance and light and melody that youth, sheer youth, even divorced from any other attractive qualities, brings with it.

Of all the gods of the Greek mythology I will bring my votive crowns and my salt cakes to Bacchus. Not the bloated old gentleman striding drunk over a barrel, as we figure him, but

Bacchus eternally young. What is there so worthy of adoration in this aging, wrinkling world as never ending youth?

Most people are cross and most people are unusually hungry on Sunday. I do not know why it is, but if you observe your acquaintance you will find it to be true. Hungry or not, the Brandons are at dinner, dining frugally and sparely on cold roast beef and cold apple tart. Nothing hot ever figures on the Brandons' Sabbath table, not even potatoes; indeed, unless they boiled themselves, and hopped out of the pot judiciously when they found themselves done, I do not see how they could, as on the Sabbath morn every living soul at Plas Berwyn, every reluctant scullion and recalcitrant housemaid, is trundled off to church, the house-door locked, and the key deposited in Mrs. Brandon's pocket.

All the Brandons hate dining in the middle of the day, consequently they always dine in the middle of the day on Sunday. Everybody knows that there are few things more distinctly unpleasant than to sit in the same room in which you have your meals; to live with the unending smell and steam of departed viands up your nose and eyes and ears: consequently the Brandons always sit in the dining-room on Sunday. Sunday is to them a sort of aggravated Ash Wednesday and Good Friday rolled into one. On Saturday night Miss Bessy Brandon swoops down upon all novels, travels, biographies, magazines, poetry books, that may be lying about, makes a clean sweep of them and consigns them to disgrace and a cupboard till the return of Monday releases them.

The Brandon family at the present moment have got their Sunday faces and their Sunday clothes on, and they misbecome most of them very sorely. Very few men look their best in their Go-to-Meeting clothes. For some unexplained reason, a black coat made by a country tailor shows its shortcomings more plainly than a coloured one. The garment that cases Bob's broad shoulders would draw tears from Mr. Poole's eyes, could he see it. As for Mrs. Brandon, she always has more or less of a Sunday face on—which I do not say in any dispraise, but merely to express a sober, steadfast face, unfurrowed by any violent gust of mirth or blast of anger. She is like Enid and her mother,

"clad all in faded silk,"

and on her breast she has a miniature of the departed Brandon, in Geneva gown and bands, about as big as a teacup, and with two small glutinous curls of the departed's hair at the back. It is so long ago since he died, that she must have forgotten all about him—what he was like, even; but she still wears his effigy, as an old inn continues to hang out the sign of the Saracen's Head, though it is centuries since ever a Saracen has been seen on the earth's face.

Opposite each other, like little bad mirrors of one another, sit the Misses Brandon, in melancholy little gowns of no particular stuff and no particular colour, and little wisps of thin, fine hair well down over their ears, and minute chignons on the napes of their necks—their little, bustless, waistless, hipless figures, long plaintive noses, and meek, dull eyes proclaiming them of that virgin band to whom St. Paul has awarded the palm of excellence. The Sunday literature is scattered about on the hard-bottomed chairs. "Stop the Leak" lies on the pit of its stomach, open at the spot where Miss Bessy abandoned it in favour of the cold beef; the "Saturday Night of the World," with its mouth open, and a paper-knife in it.

"Cut two or three good large slices, Bob, dear; they will be so nice for old John Owen," Mrs. Brandon is saying, in her benignant, cracked, old voice.

"We can leave them as we go by to church; Bob can carry them," says Miss Brandon, with authority.

Robert is silent.

"Bob does not like the idea of being seen carrying a basket; he thinks it would spoil his appearance."

"Hang the appearance!" says Bob, with an easy laugh. "If a man is a gentleman, it does not make him any the less a gentleman even if he were seen wheeling a perambulator down Regent Street; but, to tell the truth, I don't think I shall go to church this afternoon."

"Not go to church! Not go to church!! Not go to church!!!" in three different keys, rising from astonishment to horrified incredulity.

But seldom has Mr. Brandon missed attending divine service from the auspicious day, two and twenty years ago, when, at the tender age of three years, being, Eutychus-like, overcome with sleep, he fell down with much clamour from a high bench, and raised a mountainous red lump on his baby forehead, coming into contact with the hard pew floor:

"And his head, as he tumbled, went knicketty-knock, Like a pebble in Carisbrook well."

Robert feels the weight of public opinion to be heavy, but he sticks like a man to what he said.

22

"Not to-day, mother, I think. Esther said she would be coming in by-and-by to say good-bye to you all, and, as it is her last day, I thought I might as well have as much as I could of her."

"What *do* you mean, Bob? Is the girl going to die to-night?" inquires Miss Brandon, perking up her little tow-coloured head sharply.

"God forbid!" he cries, with a hasty shudder; "don't suggest anything so frightful; but she is off to-morrow for a week or ten days on a visit to some friends."

"Going away without mentioning a word about it!"

"Going away *now!*"

These two sentences shoot out with simultaneous velocity from two mouths.

"Are you surprised at her not telling *us* where she is going? Does she ever tell *us* anything? Does she make *us* her confidants!" subjoins Miss Bessy, with mild spite.

Spite is permissible on the Sabbath, though hot potatoes and novels are not.

"She did not know herself till yesterday," says Bob, briefly, cutting away rather viciously at the beef.

"But who are these sudden friends that have sprung up all at once? What are their names? Where do they live? Tell us all about them, dear boy," says the old woman, gently, seeing that her son is chafed.

"Their names are Sir Thomas and Lady Gerard; they are old friends of the Cravens' father, and they live in ——shire; that is all I know about them."

"A steady-going old couple, I suppose? Will not that be rather dull for a little gay thing like Esther?"

"There is a girl of about her own age, I believe, a ward of Sir Thomas's."

"A ward!—oh!"

"And also a son."

"A son! o—h!"

"Well, why should not there be a son? What harm is there in that?" asks Robert, raising his voice a little in irritation.

"No harm whatever! Much better thing than a daughter! Can push his own way in the world. Not that I know in the least what you are talking about," cries a young, saucy voice, which, with the little sleek, dark head it belongs to, appears uninvited at the door at this juncture. "Oh! I see you are all at dinner, so I'll stay outside till you have finished; it is so horrible to be watched when one is eating, isn't it? I hate it myself." And the head and the voice disappear again as quickly as they came.

A ruddier tinge rushes into Robert's already ruddy cheek—ruddy as King David's when he tended his few sheep in the Syrian pastures, before the weight of the heavy Israelitish crown, and of his own wars and murders had blanched it. Down go the carving knife and fork with a clatter, and, "like a doting mallard," he flies after the little vision, banging the door behind him with an impetus that makes his sisters bound up from their horsehair chairs like two small parched peas. Presently he brings her back in triumph.

"So you are going to run away from us, my love?" says Mrs. Brandon, holding Esther's young white hand in her old veiny one.

"Yes, I'm afraid so; it is a great bore, isn't it?" answers Esther, trying her best to lengthen her round face and look miserable.

"If it is a bore, why do you go?" inquires Miss Bessy, drily.

"Because I think I ought to make some friends for myself; I never met anybody before that had no friends, as Jack and I have not; we literally have not one—except all of you, of course," she ends with a happy after-thought.

"When you come to my age, my dear," says Mrs. Brandon, shaking her head, and all the innumerous stiff frillings of her cap, and bringing to bear on Esther's sanguine youth the weight of her own gloomy experiences, in the infuriating way that old people do, "you will have found out that a few good friends are worth more than a great many indifferent ones."

"But why should not these people be good friends?" asks the girl, a little incredulously. "Who knows? Surely there must be more good people in the world than bad ones; so the chances are in favour of them."

"We are expressly forbidden to judge," begins Miss Bessy, charitably; "otherwise—— There's the first bell beginning; we had better go and put on our things, Jane."

CHAPTER VII.

Five minutes more, and three large brown parasols, a large black poke bonnet and two little dirt-coloured ones, are seen slowly pacing down the hill to the House of Prayer. The lovers have Plas Berwyn to themselves. Bob has gained his point, despite a parting fleer from Bessy as to the undesirability of neglecting the Creator for the creature.

"Tim Dowler! Tim Dowler! Tim Dowler!" cries Esther, joyously, jumping about the room like a child, and mimicking the one church bell which is heard clearly tinkling through the valley. "Listen, Bob! Does it not say 'Tim Dowler' just exactly as if it were speaking it? Oh! look here: I'll lose all their places for them in their good books, and I bet anything they'll never find them again." So saying, she proceeds to remove the paper-knife from the "Saturday Night of the World," and carefully closes "Stop the Leak."

"What spirits you are in to-day, Essie!" says Bob, balancing himself on the window-sill, with his long legs dangling lugubriously, and following her about the room with his eyes, as a child does a butterfly. "I believe it is because you are going to be rid of me for a fortnight."

"Partly, I think," replies Esther, nonchalantly. "It seems as if all my life I had seen and heard of nothing but Glan-yr-Afon and Plas Berwyn, Plas Berwyn and Glan-yr-Afon, and now I'm going to see and hear something fresh; it may be better and it may be worse; but, at all events, it will be something different. Perhaps I shall come back as the country mouse did, more in love than ever with my own cheeseparings and tallow-candle ends; perhaps"—swinging her Sunday bonnet by the strings and looking up maliciously—"perhaps I shall see some one I like better than you, and not come back at all."

"Hush!" he cries, hurriedly, putting up his hand before her mouth. "Don't say that; it is bad luck. I should not mind your saying it if it were not so horribly probable."

Esther subsides into gravity.

"I wish to Heaven you were not so fond of me!" she says, hastily; "please do try not to be: it makes me feel as if I were cheating all the time—having things and not paying for them."

"I could have given you up *at first*, if you had told me it must be so positively; I'm sure I could have made shift to do without you, as I have made shift to do without many a thing that other fellows consider necessaries of life; but now——"

He has seized her two hands, and now holds her standing there before him. To hold her hand is the one familiarity Robert is permitted; not once in all his life has he kissed his betrothed.

"It was a foolish, silly custom," she said one day, pettishly—"no sensibler than rubbing noses together, as the Feejee islanders did; for her part, she hated it, &c."

"But now, what? finish your sentence, please," says the little captive, gaily.

"Esther, I wish these people had not got a son."

"What people?"

"These Gerards."

"Why so? Do you think that they would have left you their money if they had not?"

"No, not that," smiling against his will. "But, Essie, you'll promise to write and tell me what he is like?"

"Yes."

"What sort of age?"

"Yes."

"Whether you see much of him?"

"Yes."

"What he says to you?"

"Come, I cannot promise that," says Esther, bursting out laughing. "Oh you dear old goose! are you jealous of a name, a shade, an imagination?"

"I *am* jealous," he answers, reddening. "I can no more help it than a man in the gout can help having twinges. I shall always be jealous until you are really mine past stealing or taking back again: after that I never shall."

"I should hope not," retorts she, with levity: "if you were, I should think it my duty to try and give you some cause."

The church bell has ceased; there is no sound in the quiet room but that of one fat-bodied bluebottle, labouring and buzzing up the pane, and then tumbling back again. Robert has abandoned the window-sill, finding it a painful and not luxurious seat: he is walking up and down, up and down; one stride and a half of his long legs taking him from end to end of the little room. Esther has thrown herself into an American rocking chair, and is rocking violently backwards and forwards, trying her best to tip herself over.

"Promise me, Essie," says the young man, coming to a sudden standstill beside her—"promise me that you'll talk seriously of—you know what—when you come home; I give you till then? Good heavens! what sort of stuff could Jacob have been made of to have held out all those fourteen years!"

"'The   little   maid   replied,
Some   say   a   little   sighed,

And what shall we have for to eat, eat, eat?
Will the love that you're so rich in
Make a fire in the kitchen,
Or the little god of love turn the spit, spit, spit?'"

answers Esther, evading her lover's urgency by a quotation.

"If I could get an Adjutancy of Volunteers," pursues he, resuming his walk, with his eyes bent on the ground, and frowning away in the intensity of his thinking, "or, better still, a Militia one, or a Chief Constableship, or the Governorship of a gaol: there are always some of those sort of things going about. Why should I not come in for one as well as another fellow? We want so little——"

"Want so little?" interrupts Esther, briskly. "Speak for yourself, please: I want a great deal; only, as far as I can see, want is likely to be my master."

"You are no fine lady," pursues he, talking more to himself than to her, "that requires to be waited on; you can make your own bonnets and gowns, cannot you? My sisters always do."

"So I should imagine," says Esther, drily.

"What do you mean? Are not they all right? is there anything the matter with them?" inquires he, stopping short and looking surprised, as if the idea of there being any deficiency in his sisters' costumes was an entirely new light to him. But Miss Craven purses up her pretty mouth in a silence more damnatory of the Misses Brandon's toilettes than any words could be.

"If we had not a large enough income to live by ourselves," says he, beginning again his tramp, tramp, "we might join housekeeping with mother and the girls; they would not object, I'm sure."

"But I should, *strongly*," cries Esther, springing up, and getting crimson with vexation. "Why, we should all be by the ears in a week. Robert, how many times will you make me tell you that I like you well enough to go sailing along beside you on the sea of life as long as it is nice and smooth, but I really do not love you enough to go bumping over rocks and into breakers with you? I would do it for Jack, and welcome, but for no other human being on the face of the earth."

"Will you never like me as well as you do Jack?" he inquires, sadly, looking at her with eyes so loving, that one would think her own must catch the infection. But, no; they remain coldly bright, with the cold brightness of friendship.

"Never."

"Not after ten years?"

"No."

"Nor twenty?"

"No."

"Nor thirty?"

"No, nor a thousand. Cannot you see what a different thing it is? If one loses a lover one can get a hundred more just as good as, if not better than, the one lost; but if I were to lose Jack—oh, God! how can I suggest anything so awful—who could give me another brother?"

"So be it, then, since it must be that I am to play second fiddle all my life (sighing); but, Essie, you'll promise to write to me every day, won't you?"

"Certainly not."

"Every second day, then?"

"Certainly not."

"Twice a week, then?"

"Per—haps; if I have anything to say."

"And you'll be sure not to stay beyond the fortnight?"

"That depends. If they are *fine*, and inclined to 'country cousin' me, I shall probably be back the day after to-morrow: if they make a great fuss with me, and if Mr. Gerard is young and handsome and civil-spoken, I dare say you will not see me again under two months."

He looks so sincerely pained that her conscience smites her.

"There," she says, "I have teased you enough for one day; let us kiss and make friends,—that is, figuratively. Come," putting out her hand to draw him along with her, "let us go to the kitchen garden and see if the wasps have left us any apricots. If Bessy were here, she would tell us some pleasing anecdote of how some people went and picked apricots on the Sabbath, and got stung in the throat and swelled, and died in great agonies; but I'm willing to run the risk if you are."

Nine o'clock! The maid-servants are at evening church, combining the double advantage of *making their souls* and meeting their sweethearts. Esther, happily rid of hers, is sitting on the ground at the French window of the study, beside her brother. The rooks that blackened the meadow awhile ago have flapped heavily home to the mile-off rookery. It is such a great, still world; who would fancy that there were so many noisy men, barking dogs, snorting steam-engines in it? It seems a world of stars and flowers, as one would imagine it after reading one of Mrs. Heman's poems.

Jack is smoking; now and then Esther takes the pipe out of his mouth, gives a little puff, coughs and chokes, and puts it back again. Oh, blessed state of intimacy, when you may sit by a person for hours and never utter to them! Esther is thinking what a pretty, pleasant Idyllic life hers is; like an Arcadian shepherdess's in this lovely valley, far away from smoky towns and vulgar cares and sordid toils. Young and beautiful (what pretty woman is mock-modest to her own thoughts?), living with a brother who is to her what father, mother, brothers, sisters, husband, children, are to other women; a brother who is only three years older than herself, consequently not likely to die much before her. She is thinking, a little regretfully, that, fair and poetic as this life is, it is passing, and that as it passes she does not feel its beauty as acutely as she ought—does not suck out all its sweetness, as a man swallows a delicious draught hastily, carelessly, without tasting and dwelling upon its rare flavour. It is the same *sort* of thought (only much weaker) as those that torment us as we sit alone by the hearth mourning our dead, and reproach ourselves, with a yearning pain, that while they were yet with us we did not draw our chairs half close enough to theirs—did not take hold of their hands and kiss their faces half often enough—did not half often enough tell them, with eager lips, how preciouser than life they were to us.

"What will you be doing this time to-morrow, Essie?" asks Jack, breaking in upon her reverie; and has not he a right, for is not he king and hero of it?

"Wishing myself back again, to a dead certainty," answers Essie, emphatically. "Jack" (rubbing her cheek up and down softly against his shoulder—Jack is but a young, slight stripling), "I do believe that if I were in heaven, and saw you sitting all alone here smoking your pipe, I should have to throw away my harp and crown, and come down to keep you company."

"If you were in heaven," returns Jack, gravely, "I think you would be so surprised and pleased to find yourself there that you would be in no hurry to come out again for me or anybody else."

"Perhaps so, but I think not," she answers, sighing, and thrusting her arm gently through his.

"Have you got any money, Essie?"

"Plenty."

"How much?"

"Plenty."

"But how much?"

"Never you mind."

"But I do mind."

"Enough to take me there and bring me back again, and I don't suppose they'll charge me for board and lodging."

"Servants at those sort of swell places expect such a lot of tipping," says Jack, pensively, knocking the ash out of his pipe.

"They may expect, then; a little disappointment is very wholesome for us all. They are much better able to tip me than I them."

"There are sure to be charity sermons, too," continues the boy, with a forethought worthy of riper years. "I don't know how it is, but I never went to a strange place in my life without there being a collection for the Kaffirs or the Jews or the Additional Curates or something the very first Sunday after I got there."

"I would pretend I had forgotten my purse."

Jack puts his pipe in his pocket, rises, retires into his sanctum, lights a candle, rummages in a drawer, and presently returns with a five-pound note. Bank notes grew but in scanty crops at Glan-yr-Afon.

"Here, Essie."

"No! *no!* NO!" cries Essie, volubly, jumping up and clasping her hands behind her back.

"Yes! *yes!* YES!"

"No! no! You won't have enough money to pay the men on Saturday night."

"Talk about what you understand," says Jack, gruffly. "Do you think I'm going to let my sister go about like a beggar and whine for halfpence?"

"Oh, Jack, Jack!" throwing herself about his neck, and burying her face in his sunburnt throat. "How bitter it is always to take, and never to give! Oh! if I had but something to give you; but you know I have got nothing in the world."

"You have got Bob."

"Ah! so I have" (making a little grimace); "and if he would do you any good, you might have him, and welcome, to make mincemeat of, if you liked."

CHAPTER VIII.

The 2.25 train from Brainton is due at Felton at 5.30. It is drawing near Hither now, escorted by a vanguard, bodyguard, and rearguard of dust-clouds; it rushes along, with the sun beating down on the roofs of the carriages, making them like little compartments of Hades. If the devil took a hint from the Coldbath Fields cells for "improving the prisons of Hell," he certainly might take a hint from the Brainton train for improving the travelling conveyances of the same locality.

In one of the first-class carriages there is a baby: it has got a cold, and seems rather inclined to be sick; so both the nurse, on whose lap it lies gaping and blowing bubbles, and the idolising mother, who sits over against it, insist on keeping its window tight up. There is a rusty old divine, in gilt-rimmed spectacles and a jowl, reading the *Guardian;* a commercial traveller, with his hat off, his legs up, and a gaudy cap on his head, fast asleep; and, lastly, a little young lady, sitting facing the engine, with the dusty blast driving hot and full in her face, blinking, coughing, choking, with the utmost patience. On her lap lies a huge bunch of red and yellow roses and heavy-scented double-stocks, all limp and drooping and soiled. Bob gave them to her when he came down to the station to see her off—and very kind of him too, and very nice they are; but all the same, as she has already a bag, a box, and a parasol to carry, she thinks (though she barely owns it to herself) that she would almost as soon have been without them.

The dusty blast blows gentler, moderates to a dusty zephyr; the train is slackening speed. "Fel—ton!" "Fel—ton!" cry a row of green-fustianed porters, as the long bulk draws up at the platform.

"Please 'm, are you Miss Craven?" inquires a tall footman in powder and a cockade, touching his hat to Esther, as she stands all by herself, trying to take several beams out of her own eye.

"Yes."

"The carriage is here for you, 'm. Would you please to show me which is your maid and luggage?"

"I have no maid, and there's my luggage," responds Esther, pointing with one grimy kid finger to a small trunk standing on its head, and looking half inclined to burst asunder in the midst. She is ashamed of her destitute condition, and ashamed of herself for being ashamed of it.

"Will it change into a pumpkin?" thinks Miss Craven, as she steps into a large yellow barouche, with two fidgety, showy greys, that is waiting for her at the station gate. After the yammering of the baby, the dull rumble-rumble of the train, how delicious! "If it were only my own," she says to herself, throwing herself back with a consequential feeling on the soft cushions, as some country people pass and pull their forelocks to the well-known liveries.

"Well, odder things have happened! *But* for Bob! The Prince fell in love with Cinderella at first sight; why should not Prince Gerard with me? I dare say I'm quite as good-looking as Cinderella was!"

As they pass Lady Gerard's model school, twenty little charity girls come trooping out in the uniformity of their cotton frock and straw bonnet livery, and drop twenty bob courtesies to Esther, who feels as the man in the "Arabian Nights" did who woke and found himself Sultan. Labouring men go stumping heavily home, with their tools over their shoulders and their heads bent earthwards, as is always the case with the tillers of the soil, who must—oh, hard necessity!—be ever looking down.

Park palings, through which the strong brake fern is thrusting itself, slide past; then a red lodge, picked out with blue bricks, where an obsequious old woman rushes out from the washtub, with hands all soapsuds, to open the gates; then a grassy, knolly park; then a great red house, likewise picked out with blue bricks; then stones clattering under an echoing portico; then the pumpkin stops, and Cinderella descends.

"Miss Craven!" announces the butler, opening a tall door; and Miss Craven, plucking up heart, marches into a high, dark library, lined with high, dark books—marches in, looking very much like a chimney sweep. Dust lies in ridges on her once white bonnet; dust, instead of belladonna, in streaks under her eyes; dust on the parting of her hair, on her eyelashes, up her nose (on which there is also, though, happily for her, she does not know it, a large smut), and a double portion of dust on the great, faded, yellow roses, to which she cleaves with as much pertinacity as the idiot in "Excelsior" clave to that senseless banner which he was so determined to run up hill with.

As she enters, a goddess rises like an exhalation (as Pandemonium did), and comes floating on lilac clouds towards her. This is as things seem to her; in reality, a large, fair, young woman comes forward in a long-tailed mauve muslin. Simultaneously a man's two legs are seen disappearing over the window-sill.

"How do you do?" says the goddess, sweetly. "I think the train must have been rather late; we expected you half an hour ago."

"Yes."

A little pause, each taking stock.

"Won't you have some tea?"

"Thanks."

The tea is poured out; it has been standing on the table an hour, and is perfectly cold. The goddess and the little female collier examine each other stealthily.

"Rather alarming," thinks the latter: "talks in such a low voice, and has such a difficulty in pronouncing her *r*'s. So that is the correct thing, is it? Well, I'll always call Robert *Wobert* for the future."

"Might be pretty, if she were not so filthy," thinks the other.

"Same age as I am, indeed! She looks five years older."

"I think, if you don't mind, we had perhaps better be going to dress. Sir Thomas is so very particular as to punctuality."

"Is he? was that Sir Thomas that got out of the window just as I came in?"

"Oh no! that was St. John."

("St. John! What a pretty name! How much prettier than Bob!")

Sir Thomas Gerard is walking up and down the library, with his watch in his hand, prepared the instant the clock strikes to ring the bell violently, and inquire what is the meaning of dinner being so late. Sir Thomas is a big man, who affects the country squire, the good, old English gentleman—plain Sir Thomas, without any nonsense about him; dresses to the character, and succeeds in looking not unlike the Frenchman's idea of an English *milord*, as depicted in *Punch* some years ago, where he is represented in low-crowned hat and breeches, with the face of a truculent butcher, cracking a whip, and exclaiming, with equal coherency and elegance, "Rosbif! I send my wife to Smiffel! God dam!"

Sir Thomas does not use such strong language when speaking of Lady Gerard, but in other respects the portrait is not unfaithful. Lady Gerard is lying in an arm-chair. She is fat to make you shudder; she has a short, turn-up nose, short legs, a red skin, and next to no hair—all very good points in a pig, but hardly so good in a lady. The clock strikes, and at the same instant the butler opens the door, and announces "Dinner!"

"Come along, Conny!" says Sir Thomas, sticking out his elbow to his ward.

"Are not you going to wait for Miss Craven? And St. John is not down, either," suggests Lady Gerard, who is hoisting herself slowly up out of her chair.

"Wait for 'em? Not I," responds Sir Roger de Coverley. "If people don't choose to conform to the rules of my house, they may go without their dinner for all I care, and serve 'em right, too. Come along, Conny!"

The soup is nearly ended when two people, who have come together by a fortuitous concourse of atoms at the door, make a simultaneous entry into the dining-room.

"Companions in iniquity!" says St. John, with a sarcastic look at his father, bowing to Esther, as he seats himself beside Miss Blessington.

"How do?" says Sir Thomas, putting out his left hand (his right is still grasping his spoon). "Never wait for anybody here; would not let the soup get cold for the Queen nor the Lord Chancellor either."

"Miss Craven mistook you for Sir Thomas before dinner," says Miss Blessington, in her sweet, smooth way to her neighbour.

"Did she? Unintentional compliments are always the most flattering," replies Mr. Gerard, quietly.

Then he looks across through the partition wall of great bigonias in silver pots, and sees a little face peeping at him under and over the broad crimson leaves.

No one would ever call Esther's a Madonna face. No artist would ever ask her to sit for St. Catherine, or St. Cecilia, or St. Anybody else; hers is essentially *beauté du diable*—one of those little, sparkling, provoking, petulant faces that have a fresh dress of smiles or tears, or dimples or blushes, for every trivial, passing question; one of those little faces that have been at the bottom of half the mischiefs the world has seen.

"I only saw a pair of legs," replies the face, exculpating itself; "how could I tell whether they were young or old legs?"

Miss Blessington looks rather shocked, as if she thought that Esther's modes of expression were somewhat *libre;* and indeed at the rate of purity at which we are advancing, *legs* will soon walk off into the limbo of silence and unmentionableness; *arms* will probably follow them, and then perhaps noses.

Although Miss Blessington looks shocked, St. John only laughs. He looks pleasant when he laughs; he did not look pleasant just now, when he was turning up his nose at his cold soup. When he is in an ill-humour he has a decided look of his father, though it puts him into an awful rage to tell him so. He is not handsome, certainly; not a straight-nosed, pink-cheeked, flaxen-curled, fairy prince at all; neither is he very young—not a boy, that is to say—five-and-thirty, or thereabouts; his face has a weather-beaten look, as of one that has felt many an icy wind and many a tropic sun beat against it. No lily-handed, curled woman's darling.

"What do you mean?" cries Sir Thomas, raising his voice, and turning round in a fury (with his stiff grey hair standing upright, and the veins in his forehead swelling) upon an unlucky footman, who has had the *maladresse* to drop three spoons that he was carrying upon a tray. "You stupid hound, mind what you are about, or else keep out of the room, one or the other!"

Esther's mouth opens; she feels a sensation of shamefaced aghastness; but the rest of the company sit with the composure induced by long familiarity with the good old English gentleman's courtesies. Only one little flash of indignant contempt shoots from St. John's grey eyes. "How I hate my father!" would be his reading of the great statesman's dying ejaculation, "How I love my country!"

Nobody ever speaks much at dinner at Felton. St. John because he knows, if he trusted himself to speak at all, it would be to contradict his father flat *whatever* he said, for the mere pleasure of contradicting him; Lady Gerard because she has heard that it is impossible to do two things well at the same time, and as she is quite resolved upon doing the eating part well, she thinks she will leave the talking alone; Miss Blessington because, having contributed her hard, cold beauty to the entertainment, she thinks she has done enough.

The company being rather silent, Esther turns her eyes round the room, and scans the pictures. Two or three Gerards, by Sir Thomas Lawrence, in very full dress; a large copper-coloured woman by Rubens, in no dress at all; "Susanna and the Elders;" "Jupiter and Leda" (twice life-size); a "Venus Sleeping, surprised by Satyrs" (a great gem); and many other like subjects, such as one mostly meets with in the dining-rooms of English nobles and gentles—subjects pleasant and profitable, to employ the eyes and minds of their daughters while engaged in eating their dinners. Esther is staring hard at Susanna's fat, coy face, when her attention is recalled by Mr. Gerard's voice addressing her. She starts and blushes furiously, like a child whose fingers have been found straying among the jam-pots. He looks amused at her confusion.

"I have just been thinking, Miss Craven, how pleasant your first impressions of us must be. What a well-mannered, courteous family you must think us!—I tumbling out of the window at the risk of breaking my neck to avoid you, and my father and mother going to dinner without you."

"If you had been a little quicker in your movements, I should have known nothing about you," responds she, the carmine called forth by her detection dying slowly out of her cheeks, and noticing only the half of his sentence that refers to himself.

"Ah! I am not so young as I was" (with a sigh); "but, to tell the truth, we had just been dragging the pool, like Boodles in 'Happy Thoughts,' and I was such a mass of mud that I had not moral courage to face you."

"We should have met on equal terms. I was as black as a coal, was not I?"

"Railroads do make one wonderfully dusty," replies Miss Blessington, with a polite, evasive platitude.

"I had a worse infliction than any dust to bear," says Esther, stretching her long throat around the bigonia to get a fuller view of her *vis-à-vis.*

"A baby, of course?" replies he, stretching his neck too for a like purpose.

"An aggravated case of baby—a baby that had something odd the matter with it."

"Not so bad as a man drinking sherry," says he, his grey eyes and a bit of his nose laughing through the leaves; "a woman eating gingerbread is bad enough. I travelled once with a woman who ate gingerbread from London to Holyhead without stopping."

"And did not offer you any?"

"Good heavens, no! What a prodigious suggestion!—that would have been adding insult to injury."

"If I had been travelling with you I should undoubtedly have offered you some. I should have judged you by myself, and I am very fond of gingerbread."

"Indeed!"

"And" (with a mischievous look) "fonder still of peppermint lozenges, particularly in church on hot Sunday afternoons."

They were getting quite voluble, chatting and chirping like a nest of magpies—like children playing and laughing in a garden, unmindful that in a cave in a corner is a great old bear who may pounce out on them at any moment. The Felton bear pounces.

"What the devil do you mean leaving that door open? Morris! John! George! Here, some of you! there's a door open somewhere between here and the kitchen. Don't contradict me, sir! I say there is; if I catch you propping those swing doors open," &c. &c.

The birds have gone to bed, and the slugs come out to walk on the damp garden paths. Now and then a little wind gets up, whispers a word or two to the polished laurel leaves, and lies down again. There is a carpet of thin, smoke-grey clouds over heaven's blue floor. The two girls are strolling up and down the terrace walk. Esther has got a red cloak thrown about her shoulders; she is not in the least afraid of taking cold, and declined the offer of it in the first instance; but on second thoughts, reflecting that the dining-room windows look on the terrace, and that the fairy prince may see and like the combination of black eyes and red cloth (fairy princes being always partial to gay colours), accepted it.

I have called Esther "little," and Miss Blessington "large" but the truth is they are much of a height. The difference between them is, that one is a young, slight sapling that has been so busy shooting up skywards, that it has had no leisure to grow broad, and that the other is a full-grown, spreading, stately forest tree. And yet they are the same age; but some women develop, mind and body, much quicker than others.

From the unshuttered dining-room windows comes a great square of yellow lamplight, and lies smooth upon the gravel. Looking in you see rifled fruit dishes, half-filled wine-glasses, moths flying round and round the lamp globes, trying their best to find an entrance to fiery death.

Sir Thomas, in his red velvet easy chair, with his white duck legs stretched out before him—duck trousers and a blue coat and brass buttons are, I need hardly say, the fine old English gentleman's dinner costume—with his head thrown back, till you can see either up into his brains or down his throat, whichever you choose. St. John, with his elbow resting on the shining oak table, which reflects it as a mirror would, and his head on his hand, in a brown study.

"Do you always walk up and down here, Miss Blessington?" inquires Esther, who is getting rather tired of pacing along, along, along monotonously, with her gown sweeping a little avalanche of pebbles behind her.

"Generally" (with a pretty smile).

Miss Blessington has a very pretty smile—an "angelic smile"—people say who see her only once; but it is only one, and is aired every hour of the day—comes out for Sir Thomas, for Lady Gerard, for servants, for dogs, for callers, for old almswomen, for St. John—so that none can take it personally, can they?

"By yourself?"

"Not generally."

The pretty smile is dashed with a faint complacency.

("H'm! That means with St. John—

"'Walking   in   a   shady   grove With my Juliana.'

"Pleasant look-out for me! A bad third! What a pity that Bob is not here! we should be a *partie carrée*, and might change partners every now and then; Miss Blessington should have Bob, and I would have St. John!")

Below the terrace spreads a large square of grass, uninvaded by flower-bed or shrub, mowed and rolled, rolled and mowed, into the similitude of a pancake for flatness. There croquet-hoops glance whitely in the soft half-light; mallets lie strewn like dead soldiers after a battle; balls red, blue, and yellow, like great ripe fruit tumbled among the grass.

"Is this your croquet-ground?"

"Yes."

"Nice and level?"

"Yes."

"Like a billiard table, only a prettier green?"

"Yes; would you like a game?"

"Better than doing nothing, isn't it?" answers Esther, cheerily; she being a young woman to whom the words *rest* and *enjoyment* are not synonymous, as they mostly grow to be to people in later years.

From the dining-room comes the faint melody of the trombone, played with the skill of much practice by Sir Thomas's nose. Some one comes to the window, looks out, puts a hand on the sill, and jumps down. St. John apparently has an aversion from going out and coming in by the authorised modes of exit and entrance. Now that one can see him without any bigonia interposing, one notices that he has kind, eager eyes—eyes that seem to be looking, looking for something that they have not found yet—and rather a long nose, that the sun has got hold of and browned, as a cook browns mashed potatoes.

"Won't you join us, St. John?" asks Miss Blessington, stooping to reinstate a fallen hoop, and looking calm invitation at him out of her great, fine, passionless, cow eyes.

St. John hesitates, and looks towards Esther to see whether she is not going to second the invitation; but she is balancing herself with her two feet on a croquet-mallet, and does not appear to see him.

"Gooseberry I may be," she thinks, "but, at all events, I won't be instrumental in making myself so."

"Do I ever play?" asks he, with petulance, walking off in a huff.

"He did not accept your invitation with the exultant gratitude one would have expected, did he?" says Miss Craven, maliciously.

"He hates the game," replies Miss Blessington, rather sharplier than is her wont— "particularly playing with odd numbers."

"Oh!"

The match begins; it is about as fair as a foot race between Deerfoot and a lame baby. Esther has played about six times in the course of her life; Miss Blessington about six thousand. Miss Blessington makes the round of the hoops in triumphant solitude, while poor Essie struggles feebly, ignorantly, unscientifically, to ring a bell that refuses to emit the faintest tinkle.

"Hare and tortoise!" cries she, laughing at her own discomfiture; "you'll go to sleep presently, and I shall crawl in and win."

"Since you wish me, I don't mind taking a mallet," says St. John, appearing suddenly round a big Wellingtonia, and looking confusedly conscious of being seen descending very awkwardly from his high horse.

"How do you know we wish you to take one?—we never said so," says Essie, flashing at him with her wicked, laughing, half-lowered eyes. ("Since I am another's and he is another's, I don't see why we should not try to amuse each other," she says to herself.)

"It is your turn to play, Miss Craven," interposes Constance, coldly.

"Come to my rescue, won't you?" says Esther, making her seventy-second careless, abortive attempt at the bell, and throwing twice as much *empressement* into her voice from the amiable motive that she thinks such *empressement* is displeasing to Miss Blessington.

"You snubbed me so just now that I don't think I will. I'll leave you to perish miserably," answers he, looking at her as he speaks with an intentness only excusable by the dim light, and the indistinctness of all objects in it.

"Constance, if you don't mind I'll take one of Miss Craven's balls."

"If you remember, I asked you to join us half an hour ago," replies Constance, in her measured way.

"I make one stipulation before we start," cries Esther, gaily, "and that is, that you make no remarks upon my play except such as are of a laudatory nature."

"I'll make no stipulation of the kind," answers he, gaily too; "if I see anything reprehensible I shall testify."

Fate does not smile upon the union of St. John and Esther. Disgrace and disaster attend their arms; in ignorance, unskilfulness, and general incapacity, St. John is no whit inferior to his partner.

"Why, you play worse than I do," cries she, delighted at the discovery.

"I know I do," he answers, not too amiably; "I should be ashamed of myself if I did not; it is the vilest, stupidest game ever any idiot invented; no play in it whatever. All luck! all chance! Look there!" pointing with a sort of ill-tempered resignation to Constance, who, with dress delicately lifted with one hand, and foot gracefully poised, is inflicting heavy chastisement, with a calm, satisfied vindictiveness, on his ball.

"Take that, you fool you!" (this is addressed to the ball, not to Miss Blessington) hurling his mallet at it as it scuds swiftly over the sward and lodges in the pink and purple breast of an aster bed. The head and handle of the mallet fly asunder from the violence of their passage through the air, and Mr. Gerard is reduced to the ignominy of picking up the *disjecta membra* and hammering them together again.

"You must make a sensation when you go to a croquet party," remarks Esther, sarcastically.

"Do you think so badly of me as to suppose I ever do? is thy servant a curate that he should do this thing?" he answers, coming over and standing close to her.

"Please attend to the game, St. John! It is you to play!" exclaims Constance, with suppressed, lady-like irritation, from the other end of the ground, where she stands in majestic solitude.

It is the penalty of greatness to be lonely. A few more egregious blunders on the part of the firm of Gerard and Craven, a few more masterstrokes by Miss Blessington, and the game draws to a conclusion.

"It is ridiculous playing against such luck as yours, Constance," cries St. John, flinging down his weapon in an unjust, unreasonable fury. "It is always the same; it does not matter what—whist, billiards, anything—always the same story. Take my advice" (turning to Essie, and speaking eagerly), "never play at anything, or do anything, or be anything with me, or you'll be sure to be a loser. I am the most unlucky devil under the sun." Then he feels that he is making a fool of himself, and walks off in a rage.

"Why, he is *really* cross," says Esther, opening her great eyes and looking a little blankly after him.

"He is rather odd-tempered," answers Miss Blessington, composedly; "and the most singular thing is, that it is always the people he is fondest of with whom he is most easily irritated."

"How fond he must be of you!" says Esther, internally.

CHAPTER IX.

Death and the sun are very much alike in one respect, and that is, their utter impartiality and stupid want of discernment. They make no difference between those who love them and those who hate. They pay their visits equally to those who are longing for and lifting up eager hands towards them, and those who would much prefer to be without them.

I will drop the parallel, which cannot be carried much farther, and talk of the sun only. He certainly shows very little judgment, and less taste, in these matters. He gives his great, warm light just as readily to a scullery as a boudoir, to an ill-smelling dunghill as to a bed of mignonette; kisses with just as much relish the raddled cheeks of an old fish-wife as the fresh scarlet lips of a young countess.

This present August morning he is blazing full and hot on that very grievous daub of Mrs. Brandon in a no-waisted black satin, out of which she appears to be bursting, like a chrysalis from its sheath, in the Plas Berwyn dining-room, and not a whit more fully or more hotly on the exquisite "Monna Lisa" of Da Vinci, which is the chief jewel of the Gerard collection.

The same sunbeam that brings out with such clearness Monna Lisa's faint, weird smile, takes in also within its compass Esther's small, swart head, round the back of which coils a great, loose, careless twist of burnished hair, like a black snake. She is standing outside the dining-room door, with her lithe, *svelte* figure stooped forward a little. The family are at prayers, as she ascertained by applying her ear to the key-hole, and hearing a harsh, elderly voice going at a good round trot through a variety of petitions, for himself, his children (he has only one, and hates him), his friends, his enemies, his queen, his bishops and curates, his black brethren, &c., all without the vestige of a comma between them.

"What! eavesdropping?" asks St. John, coming down the handsome, shallow stairs in knickerbockers and heather-mixture stockings that his old mother made him.

"Hush!" holding up her forefinger; "they are at prayers."

St. John listens too, and a sneer comes and settles on his mouth.

"Isn't he a worthy rival for the man who said he would give any one as far as Pontius Pilate in the Creed, and then beat him?"

"You ought not to abuse your own father" (in a whisper).

"I know I ought not" (in another whisper).

"Why do you, then?" casting down her eyes, that he may see how large a portion of downy cheeks her long curly lashes shade.

"I only do for him what I know he would do for me if he had the chance."

"Hush! they are nearly over."

"... be with us all evermore. Amen. Morris!"

"Yes, Sir Thomas."

"What the deuce do you mean sticking the legs of that chair against the wall knocking all the paint off the wainscot?"

"Oh!   blessings   on   his   kindly   voice,
And on his silver hair!"

32

says St. John, in ironical quotation; and then the door opens, and a long string of servants issue out, and the two culprits again, as on the previous evening, together enter.

Lady Gerard never appears at breakfast. About twenty years ago she had an illness, and, on the strength of it, has kept up a character for invalidhood ever since. Miss Blessington takes her place at the head of the table; she is sitting there now. Her shapely hands are busy among the teacups; her white lids drooped over her calm eyes. There is a great gold cross on her breast, that rises and falls in soft, even undulations. Eve, as she was when first she grew into separate entity and embodiment out of Adam's side; Eve, of creamiest flesh, and richest, reddest blood, before a soul—a tormenting, puzzling, intangible, incomprehensible soul—was breathed into her.

When Constance marries, her husband will gaze at her as a man might gaze at Gibson's "Venus," supposing that he had bought for a great price that marvel of modern sculpture, and had set it up in the place of honour in his gallery. He would half-shut his eyes, the better to appreciate the exquisite turn of the cold, stately throat, the modelling of the little rounded wrist; would put his head on one side, and look at it this way and that, to determine whether he liked the tinting.

"Faultily faultless, icily regular, splendidly null,"

as the pithy line that everybody knows, and that next to nobody could have written, hath it. At forty Constance will be a much handsomer woman than Esther. At forty those clean-cut, immovable, expressionless features will be hardly the worse for wear; that colourless marble skin will be hardly less smoothly polished than it is now. At forty Esther (if she live so long) will have cried and laughed, and fretted and teased herself into a mere shadow of her present self.

Every one's letters at Felton are put on their plate for them. As Esther takes her seat, she perceives that there is one for her—one directed in a scrawling, schoolboy hand. The blood rushes to her face, as it does to a turkeycock's wattles when he is excited or angry, and she thrusts it hastily into her pocket. To her guilty imagination it seems that written all over it, in big red letters, legible to every eye, is, "From Bob Brandon, Esther Craven's lover." As her eyes lift themselves shyly, to see whether St. John is observing her, they meet his, looking at her curiously, interestedly, puzzledly.

"We allow people to read their letters at breakfast here," he says, with a friendly smile; "we are not particular as to manners, as I dare say you have found out by this time."

"Oh! thanks, I'm in no hurry; it's of no consequence—it will keep," answers Esther, disjointedly, with would-be indifference, and the turkeycock hue spreading to the edge of her white gown.

The morning hours at Felton are not exciting. Sir Thomas is building a new orchid house, and spends much of his time standing over the bricklayers, like an Egyptian overseer, telling them with his usual courteous candour how much more he knows about their trade than they themselves do, who have been at it all their lives. St. John disappears too, and Constance and Esther are left *tête-à-tête*.

Esther has plenty of time to read Bob's letter, and to understand it, which latter requires some ingenuity, as, from the greater rapidity of his thoughts than of his pen, he omits most of the little words—*tos* and *ands* and *whichs* and *whos* and *hes* and *shes*. There is a good deal about his mother in it: several messages from her; a great many questions as to what Mr. Gerard was like, with solemn adjurations to answer them; a sheet devoted to the exposition of the luxury in which it is possible to live on £300 a year; and, lastly, a sentence or two as to his great loneliness, and his eager longing to have his darling Esther back again—not much on that head, as if he were afraid of marring her enjoyment by intruding upon her the picture of his own disconsolateness. It was not an eloquent letter; in fact, it was rather a stupid one, and had evidently been written with a very nasty scratchy pen; but for all that it was a nice one, and so Esther felt, and wished that it had been less so.

Bob is a dear fellow; and, no doubt, when she goes back to Glan-yr-Afon, she will be very glad to see him, and be very fond of him; but, for the present, she would like to forget him altogether—to have a holiday from him: he seems to come in incongruously now somehow.

"Where's St. John?" grunts miladi, who makes her appearance towards luncheon time, from the arm-chair which is witness to so many gentle dozes on her part.

Miladi likes St. John; he is very good to her, and often stands in the breach between her and Sir Thomas.

"Vanished," answers Miss Blessington, in her slow, sweet drawl. "I think Miss Craven must have frightened him away."

It is very pleasant, is it not? when you think you have been making a highly favourable impression on a person, to hear that they have fled before you in abject fear.

"I had no idea that he was such a timid fawn," answers Essie, nettled.

"He is very peculiar," says Constance, her white fingers flying swiftly in and out among the coloured silks of the smoking cap she is embroidering; "and has a most unfortunate shrinking from strangers."

"The greatest friends must have been strangers once," objects Essie, feeling rather small.

"Quite true, so they must; but he is so very *difficile*, we never can get him to admire any one—can we, aunt?"

But "aunt" has fallen sweetly asleep.

"With the exception of two or three fortunate blondes—I prefer dark people myself infinitely, don't you?"

"Infinitely," replies Esther, with emphasis.

It is not true—she does nothing of the kind; but, after all, what is truth in comparison of the discomfiture of an adversary?

CHAPTER X.

Luncheon comes, but no St. John. After luncheon Sir Thomas, Miss Blessington, and Miss Craven go out riding. Miss Craven's knowledge of horsemanship is confined to her exploits on a small, shaggy, down-hearted Welsh pony, concerning whom it would be difficult to predicate which he was fullest of, years or grass. Miss Blessington has lent her an old habit; it is much too big in the waist and shoulders for her, but a well-made garment always manages to adapt itself more or less to any figure, and she does not look amiss in it. It is a matter of very little consequence to her at the present moment how she looks; she is the arrantest coward in Christendom, and her heart sinks down to the bottom of her boots as she sees three horses that look unnaturally tall and depressingly cheerful issue through the great folding-doors that open into the stable-yard.

"Oh, Sir Thomas! it is a chesnut, is it? Don't they say that chesnuts always have very uncertain tempers? Oh! please—I'm rather frightened. I think, if you don't mind, I'd almost as soon——"

"Fiddlesticks!" answers Sir Thomas, roughly. "Cannot have my horses saddled and unsaddled every half-hour because you don't know your own mind. God bless my soul, child! Don't look as if you were going to be hanged! Why, you might ride her with a bit of worsted. Here, Simpson, look sharp, and put Miss Craven up."

After two abortive attempts, in the first of which she springs short, and glides ignobly to earth again, and in the second takes a bound that goes near to carrying her clean over her steed, after having given Simpson a kick in the face, and torn a hole in her borrowed habit, Miss Craven is at length settled in her seat.

It is a hot afternoon; after all, I think that miladi has the best of it, sitting in a garden-chair under a tulip tree, eating apricots. The deer, with dappled sides and heavy-horned heads, are herding about the rough, knotted feet of the great trees that stand here and there in solitary kingship about the park. They spread their ancient, outstretched arms between earth and heaven, and man and beast rejoice in the shade thereof. The dust lies a hand-breadth thick upon the road; the nuts in the hedgerow, the half-ripe blackberries, the rag-wort in the grass—all merge their distinctive colours in one dirty-white mask.

"Is she going to kick, do you think?" asks Esther, in a mysterious whisper of Miss Blessington, across Sir Thomas. "Does not it mean that when they put their ears back?"

"I don't think you need be alarmed," answers Constance, with politely-veiled contempt; "it is only the flies that tease her."

The animal that inspires such alarm in Esther's mind, is a slight, showy thing, nearly thoroughbred; a capital lady's park hack. It is quiet enough, only that the quietness of a young, oats-fed mare, and of an antediluvian Welsh pony blown out with grass, are two different things. She is sidling along now, half across the road, coquetting with her own shadow.

"Oh, Sir Thomas!" (in an agonised voice) "why does not she walk straight? Why does she go like a crab?"

"Pooh!" answers Sir Thomas, in his hard, loud voice; "it's only play!"

"If I'm upset, I don't much care whether it is in play or earnest," rejoins Esther, ruefully.

The glare from the road, the dust and the midges, make people keep their eyes closed as nearly as they can: so that it is not till they are close upon him that they perceive that the man who is dawdling along to meet them on a stout, grey cob, with his hat and coat and whiskers nearly as white as any miller's, is St. John. He looks rather annoyed at the rencontre.

"I have been over to Melford, Sir Thomas, to see that pointer of Burleigh's. It will not do at all; it's not half broken."

"You had better turn back with us, St. John," suggests Constance, graciously.

"No, thanks; much too hot!"

"*Au revoir*, then," nodding her head and her tall hat, and about a million flies that are promenading on it, gracefully.

Esther's fears vanish.

"Three is no company," she says in a low voice, and making rather a plaintive little face as he passes her.

Drawn by the magnet that has succeeded in drawing to itself most things that it wished—viz., a woman's inviting eyes—he turns the cob's head sharp round.

"But four is," he answers, with an eager smile, putting his horse alongside of hers.

She was rather compunctious the moment she had said it. It is reversing the order of things—the woman after the man; "the haystack after the cow;" as the homely old proverb says.

The road is broad, and for a little while they all four jog on abreast, as in a Roman chariot-race or a city omnibus—rather a dreary squadron.

"This is very dull," thinks Esther. "Oh! if I could lose my handkerchief, or my veil, or my gloves! Why cannot I drop my whip?"

No sooner said than done.

"Oh! Mr. Gerard, I am so sorry, I have dropped my whip!"

Mr. Gerard, of course, dismounts and picks it up; Sir Thomas and his ward pass on.

"What a happy thought that was of yours!" says St. John, wiping the little delicate switch before giving it back to her.

"*Happy thought!* What do you mean?" (reddening).

"Oh! it was accident, was it? I quite thought you had dropped it on purpose, and was lost in admiration of your ingenuity."

He looks at her searchingly as he speaks.

"I *did* drop it on purpose," she answers, blushing painfully. "Why do you make me tell the truth, when I did not mean to do so?"

"Don't you always tell truth?" (a little anxiously).

"Does anybody?"

"I hope so. A few men do, I think."

"As I have no pretensions to being a man, you cannot be surprised that my veracity is not my strongest point."

"You are only joking" (looking at her with uneasy intentness). "Please reassure me, by saying that you do not tell any greater number of fibs than every one is compelled to contribute towards the carrying on of society."

"Perhaps I do, and perhaps I do not."

He looks only half-satisfied with this oracular evasion; but does not press the point farther.

"It is not often that my papa and I take the air together; we think we have almost enough of each other's society in-doors."

"He is your father," says Esther, rather snappishly; a little out of humour with him for having put her out of conceit with herself.

"I never could see what claim to respect that was," answers he, gravely; "on the contrary I think that one's parents ought to apologise to one for bringing one, without asking one's leave, into such a disagreeable place as this world is."

"Disagreeable!" cries Esther, turning her eyes, broad open, in childish wonder upon him. "Disagreeable to *you!* Young and——"

"Beautiful, were you going to say?"

"No, certainly not——and with plenty of money to make it pleasant?"

"But I have not plenty of money. I *shall* have, probably, when I'm too old to care about it! *he* is good for thirty years more, you know," nodding respectfully at Sir Thomas's broad, blue back.

"It *must* be tiring, waiting for dead men's shoes," says Esther, a little sardonically.

"*Tiring!* I believe you," says St. John, energetically; "it is worse than tiring—it is degrading. Do you suppose I do not think my own life quite as contemptible as you can? Take my word for it" (emphasising every syllable), "there is no class of men in England so much to be pitied as heirs to properties. We cannot dig; to beg we are ashamed."

"I never was heir to anything, so I cannot tell."

"I should have been a happier fellow, and worth something then, perhaps, if I had been somebody's tenth son, and had had to earn my bread quill-driving, or soap-boiling, or sawbones-ing. I think I see myself pounding away at a pestle and mortar in the surgery" (laughing). "I should have had a chance, then, of being liked for myself too, even if I did smell rather of pills and plaister; whereas now, if anybody looks pleasant at me, or says anything civil to me, I always think it is for love of Felton, not of me."

"You should go about *incognito*, like the Lord of Burleigh."

"He was but a landscape painter, you know. Do you know that once, not a very many years ago, I had a ridiculous notion in my head that one ought to try and do some little good in the world? Thanks to Sir Thomas's assistance and example, I have very nearly succeeded in getting rid of that chimera. If I am asked at the Last Day how I have spent my life, I can say, I have shot a few bears in Norway, and a good many turkeys and grebe in Albania; I have killed several salmon in Connemara: I have made a fool of myself once, and a beast of myself many times."

"How did you make a fool of yourself?" pricking up her ears.

"Oh! never mind; it is a stupid story without any point, and I have not quite come to the pitch of dotage of telling senile anecdotes about myself. Here, let us turn in at this gate, and take a cut across the park: it is cooler, and we can have a nice gallop under the trees, without coming in for the full legacy of Sir Thomas's and Conny's dust, as we are doing now."

"But—but—is not it rather *dangerous?*" objects Esther, demurring. "Don't they sometimes put their feet into rabbit-holes, and tumble down and break their legs?"

"Frequently, I may almost say *invariably*," answers St. John, laughing, and opening the gate with the handle of his whip.

The soft, springy, green turf is certainly pleasanter than the hard, whity-brown turnpike road, and so the horses think as they break into a brisk canter. The quick air freshens the riders' faces—comes to them like comfortable words from Heaven to a soul in Purgatory—as they dash along under the trees, stooping their heads every now and then to avoid coming into contact with the great, low-spreading boughs.

Laughing, flushed, half-fright, half-enjoyment:

"She looked so lovely as she swayed
The rein with dainty finger-tips;
A man had given all other bliss,
And all his worldly worth for this—
To waste his whole heart in one kiss
Upon her perfect lips."

"Delicious! I'm not a bit afraid now; I bid defiance to the rabbit-holes," she cries, with little breathless pauses between the words.

Let no one shout before they are out of the wood. Hardly have the words left her mouth, when all at once, at their very feet almost, from among the seven-foot-high fern, where they have been crouching, rise a score of deer with sudden rustling; and, their slender knees bent, spring away with speedy grace through the mimic forest. Esther's mare, frightened at the sudden apparition (many horses are afraid of deer), swerves violently to the left; then gets her head down, and sets to kicking as if she would kick herself out of her skin.

"Mind! Take care! Hold tight! Keep her head up!" shouts St. John, in an agony.

Next moment the chesnut, with head in the air, nostrils extended, and bridle swinging to and fro against her fore legs, tears riderless past him. In a second he is off, and at the side of the heap of blue cloth that is lying motionless among the buttercups.

"I'm not dead," says the heap, raising itself, and smiling rather a difficult smile up at him, as he leans over it or her, his burnt face whitened with extremest fear. "Don't look so frightened!"

"Thank God!" he says, hardly above his breath, and more devoutly than he is in the habit of saying his prayers. "When I saw you there, lying all shapeless, I half thought—Oh!" (with a shudder) "I don't know what I thought."

"I must be tied on next time, mustn't I?" says Essie, putting up her hand to her head with an uncertain movement, as if she were not quite sure of finding it there. "Oh! Mr. Gerard,"—the colour coming back faintly to her lips and cheeks—"I *do* hate riding! it's horribly dangerous! quite as bad as a battle!"

"Quite!" acquiesces St. John, laughing heartily in his intense relief. "And you are quite sure you are not hurt?"

"Quite!"

"Really?"

"Really!"

To prove how perfectly intact she is, she jumps up; but, as she does so, her face grows slightly distorted with a look of pain, and she sinks back on her buttercup bed.

"Not quite sure, either; I seem to have done something stupid to my foot—turned it or twisted it."

So saying, she thrusts out from under her habit a small foot. It *is* a small—a *very* small—foot; but the boot in which it is cased is country made, and about three times too big for it; so that it might rattle in it, like a pea in a drum. Even at this affecting moment St. John cannot repress a slight feeling of disappointment.

"I'm awfully sorry! Whereabouts does it hurt? There?" putting his fingers gently on the slender, rounded ankle.

"Yes, a little."

"I'm awfully sorry!" (You see there is not much variety in his laments.) "What can I do for it? gallop home as hard as I can, and make them send the carriage?"

"With a doctor, a lawyer, and a parson in it? No, I think not."

"But you cannot sit here all night. Could you *ride* home, do you think?"

"On that dreadful beast?" with a horrified intonation.

"But if I lead her all the way?"

"Very well" (reluctantly); "but (brightening a little) I cannot ride her; she is not here."

"I suppose I must be going to look after her," says St. John, dragging himself up very unwillingly. "Brute! she is as cunning as Old Nick! And you are sure you don't mind being left here by yourself for a minute or two?"

"Not if there are no horses within reach," she answers, with an innocent smile, which he carries away with him through the sunshine and the fern and the grass.

Essie spends full half an hour pushing out, pinching in, smoothing and stroking Miss Blessington's caved-in hat; full a quarter of an hour in picking every grass and sedge and oxeye that grew within reach of her destroying arm; and full another quarter in thinking what a pleasant, manly, straightforward face St. John's is—what a thoroughly terrified face it looked when she met it within an inch of her own nose after her disgraceful *bouleversement*—what a much better height five feet ten is for all practical purposes than six feet four.

At the end of the fourth quarter Mr. Gerard returns, with a fire hardly inferior to St. Anthony's in his face; with his hair cleaving damply to his brows, and without the mare.

"Would not let me get within half a mile of her! far too knowing! Brute! and now she'll be sure to go and knock the saddle to pieces, and then there'll be the devil to pay!"

"I'm so sorry," says Esther, looking up sympathisingly, with her lap full of decapitated oxeyes.

"So am I, for your sake: you'll have to ride the cob home."

"I shall have to turn into a man, then," she says, glancing rather doubtfully at the male saddle.

"No, you won't," (laughing).

He rises, and unfastens the cob from the tree-branch to which he has been tied. He has been indulging a naturally greedy disposition—biting off leaves and eating them—until he has made his bit and his mouth as green as green peas.

"You must let me put you up, I think," says Gerard bending down and looking into his companion's great, sweet eyes, under the rim of her battered, intoxicating-looking hat.

"Must I?" (lowering her eyelids shyly.)

"Yes; do you mind much?"

"No—o."

He stoops and lifts her gently. He is not a Samson or a prize-fighter, and well grown young women of seventeen are not generally feather-weights; but yet it seems to him that the second occupied in raising her from the ground and placing her in the saddle was shorter than other seconds.

A man's arms are not sticks or bits of iron, that they can hold a beautiful woman without feeling it. St. John's blood is giving little quick throbs of pleasure. His arms seem to feel the pressure of that pleasant burden long after they have been emptied of it.

"I think you must let me hold you," he says, gently and very respectfully passing his arm round her waist.

"No, no!" she cries, hastily, pulling herself away—"no need!—no need at all! I shall not fall."

She feels an overpowering shrinking from the enforced, unavoidable familiarity. It does not arise from any distaste for St. John certainly, nor yet from any quixotic loyalty to Bob; it springs from a new, unknown, uncomprehended shyness.

"Very well," he answers, quietly, releasing her instantly, and taking the bridle in his hand. "But I'm afraid you will find that you are mistaken."

They set forward across the park, at a foot's pace and in silence. Esther twists her hands in the cob's mane, and tries to persuade herself that pommelless pigskin does not make a slippery seat. Every two paces she slides down an inch or so, and then recovers herself with an awkward jerk. The sun is hot. Now and then, as the cob puts his foot on a mole-hill, or some other slight inequality in the ground, her ankle bumps against the saddle-flap. She feels turning giddy and sick with the heat and the pain.

"Mr. Gerard! Mr. Gerard! I'm falling!" she calls out loud, stretching out her arms to him, and clutching hold of his shoulder with a violence and tenacity that she herself is not in the least aware of.

He is magnanimous. He does not exult over her; he does not say, "I knew how it would be; I told you so!" He only says, in a kind, anxious voice, and plainlier still with kind, anxious eyes, "I'm afraid you are in great pain?" and replaces the rejected arm in its former obnoxious position.

As they enter the lodge gate, they see Sir Thomas and his ward advancing down the avenue towards them. Miss Blessington is a great favourite of Sir Thomas's. She is good to look at, and hardly ever speaks; or, if she does, it is only to say, "Yea, yea, and Nay, nay."

"Now for an exchange of civilities," says Gerard, rather bitterly; "even at this distance I can see him getting the steam up."

"Miss Craven has had a fall, Sir Thomas, and hurt herself," he remarks, explanatorily, as soon as the two parties come within speaking distance.

"Broken the mare's knees, I suppose?" cries Sir Thomas, loudly, taking no notice whatever of Miss Craven's casualties. "Some fool's play, of course; larking over the palings, I dare say. Well, sir, what have you done with her? where have you left her? out with it!" (lashing himself up into an irrational turkeycock fury.)

"Damn the mare!" answered St. John in a rage, growing rather white, and forgetting his manners.

St. John's rages, when he does get into them, which is not very often, are far worse ones than his papa's, and so the latter knows, and is cowed by the first symptoms of the approach of one.

Miss Blessington looks up shocked. This *jeune personne bien élevée* always is shocked at whatever people ought to be shocked at—Colenso, Swinburne, skittles, &c.

"You are not much hurt, *really*, I hope?" she says, suavely, walking along beside Esther, while Sir Thomas and his heir wrangle in the background. "Which way did you come, and what *has* become of your horse?"

"We came through the park," answers Esther, holding on by her eyelids to the cob's slippery back; "so I suppose the horse is there still. Mr. Gerard tried to catch it, and could not."

"Through the park!" repeats Miss Blessington, with a slight smile of superior intelligence. "Oh! I see; a short cut home! Poor St. John has such a horror of taking a ride for riding's sake, that he always tries to shorten his penance as much as possible!"

CHAPTER XI.

It is the 1st of September, and the seal of impending destruction is set upon many a little plump brown bird; but ignorance is bliss, and the little brown birds do not know it, and are walking about the turnip ridges and amongst the stubble fields as confidently as if there were no such man as Purdey, and no such infernal machine as a gun. St. John and his papa go out shooting together. Sir Thomas knocks up by luncheon time, and returns to his orchid-house, and to the goading the bricklayers, as King Agamemnon did his fellow-chiefs, with bitter words. Esther spends the day in her bedroom, lying in state on a sofa with her ankle bandaged up. It hurts her acutely if she attempts to walk on it; but if she keeps quiet, she is hardly aware of there being anything wrong with it. It is very annoying having to play the invalid for an ailment that is purely local when you feel in riotous health and spirits—to have your dinner sent up to you on a tray when you are so hungry that you could eat double your allotted portion, if it were not that, being an invalid, you are ashamed to say so. One has a sense of shamming, malingering.

Poor Miss Craven passes a very dull day; the red rose on one side the window, and the travellers' joy on the other, look in and say, "Why is this lazy child lying all day on a couch, when we and so many other flowers have been calling to her with our voiceless voices to come out into the breeze and shine?" A bee comes in sometimes, and goes buzz—buzzing about, telling himself how busy he is, and that he has no time to waste now that his honey-harvest is drawing so near to its sweet close. The room is so still that, but for feeling intensely alive, and not having her chin tied up, Esther might almost imagine herself laid out previous to her interment. Now and again Miss Blessington enters noiselessly, says "I hope you are feeling a little easier," in her soft monotone, and then rustles gently away again. She has provided Esther with a novel and a book of acrostics, and thinks she has done her duty by her neighbour amply. The novel is one written with a purpose; a dull one-sided tilt against Ritualism. Esther never found out an acrostic in her life, and has seldom been so completely vacant of employment as to try. She is, therefore, reduced to spending half the day in writing to Bob—half the day! and yet when the letter is finished it only covers three sides of a sheet. She has written, rewritten, and re-rewritten it. All around and about her lie half-covered, quarter-covered, whole-covered sheets, all stamped with the seal of condemnation. Gerard is the stumbling block; his name either will not come in at all, which looks unnatural, or else insists on thrusting itself in every second line. This is the form in which Miss Craven's billetdoux finally presents itself at Plas Berwyn:

"Dear Bob,—Thanks very much for your letter; please put a few stops next time. I had a very disagreeable journey here—bushels of dust and a sick baby. This is a very handsome place, and they are all very kind to me. (H'm! are they? I don't know about that; *one* of them is.) Yesterday I went out riding with Sir Thomas and his ward (so I did; I set out with them), and I stupidly fell from my horse, a sort of thing that nobody but I would have done, and hurt my foot a little; but nothing to speak of. Miss Blessington, the ward, is remarkably handsome, but looks a great deal older than I do. My love to your mother, and thanks for her kind messages; the same to the girls. Tell Bessy that it is hardly worth while sending me 'The Sinfulness of Little Sins,' as I shall have more time for reading when I get home again.

"Yours   affectionately,
"E. C.

"P. S.—Mr. Gerard is not at all good-looking; he seems very fond of shooting; he has been out all to-day."

"The long day wanes: the slow moon climbs."

Dinner is over; nothing to look forward to but bed-time. Yah! How dull! A knock comes at the door. Miss Blessington enters with flowers in her hand—jessamine, heliotrope, everything that smells sweetly and not heavily—unlike Bob's well meaning but annihilating double stocks.

"I hope you are in less pain now" (the usual formula, that comes as regularly and frequently as the doxology in church).

"Oh yes! thanks; I'm very well" (yawning and looking woefully bored.) "What lovely flowers!"

"St. John sent them to you" (rather shortly).

"Mr. Gerard?" (with animation, the bored look vanishing.) "How very kind of him!"

"He always is so good-natured," answers Constance, with a cold generality.

"It is so particularly kind of him, when he has such an overpowering aversion for strangers," continues Essie, with a malicious twinkle in her eyes.

Constance sweeps to the window, slightly discomfited.

"He told me to ask you whether you would like him to come and carry you downstairs for an hour or two?" she says, in a somewhat constrained voice; "but I daresay you would rather be left in peace up here; and I should think that the quieter you kept your foot the better for it."

"On the contrary, I should like it of all things," cries Essie, with perverse alacrity. "In your cheerful company downstairs, I shall be more likely to forget my sufferings, such as they are, than all by my dull self up here; to tell the truth, I was meditating asking your maid to come and talk to me about haberdashery."

Outside Miss Craven's door St. John pauses, as one that is devout hesitates on the threshold of a sanctuary. Chintz curtains rose-lined, white-dressed toilet-table, simple valueless ornaments lying about, two little slippers, that look as if they had been just kicked off—his eye takes in all the details. He feels like Faust in Marguerite's chamber. And Marguerite herself, lying careless, restful on her couch, her two arms flung lazily upwards and backwards, to make a resting-place for her head; the smooth elbows and shoulders gleaming warm, cream-white, through the colder blue-white of her dress; and the up-looking face, childish in its roundness, and blooming down—but oh! most womanish—in the shafts of quick fire that greet him from the laughing, sleepy eyes. Where did she learn that art of shooting? From the pigs and cabbages at Glan-yr-Afon? From old Mrs. Brandon? From Miss Bessie? From—"Stop the Leak?" Deponent sayeth not whence.

"*How* good of you!" she says, with emphasis, stretching out her hand to him, as he stands beside her sofa, looking rather fagged with his day's work. "I had just been calculating how many hours there would be before I could have a decent pretext for going to bed; one gets so tired of oneself."

"Not so tired as one does of one's family," answers St. John, rather ruefully.

"I have no family," she rejoins, simply.

"We Gerards have a particularly happy knack of rubbing each other the wrong way," he says, rather irritably. "I am sometimes tempted to think that we are the most unamiable family God ever put breath into."

"People always think that of their own family," answers Essie, laughing; "they know their own little crookednesses much better than any one else's."

"Has Miss Craven changed her mind, St. John?" asks Miss Blessington from the doorway. St. John starts. "Not that I know of."

He stoops, and lifts her carefully, as a thing most precious; as he does so, a little foolish trembling passes over her, as a baby-breeze passes over some still pool's breast, hardly troubling the sky and the trees that lie far down in the blue mirror. Down the grand staircase he bears her, and Constance follows to see that there is no loitering by the way.

The morning-room at Felton (so called because the family always sit there in the evenings) is very lofty. You have to crane your neck up to see the stucco stalactites, faintly imitative of Staffa and Iona, pendant from the ceiling. There are statuettes in plenty standing about in niches and on pedestals. Venuses and Minervas and Clyties, all with their hair very elaborately dressed, and not a stitch of clothes on. There is a great litter of papers and magazines on the round table: the *Justice of the Peace*, that is Sir Thomas's; the *Field*, that is St. John's; the *Cornhill*, that is everybody's. Sir Thomas and miladi are playing backgammon; miladi is compelled to do so every night as a penance for her sins—four rubbers, and if *he* wins, as she prays and endeavours that he may, five.

"Don't take the dice up in such a hurry, miladi," he says, snappishly; "how the deuce can I see what your throw is?"

"Seizes, Sir Thomas," responds miladi, meekly.

"Seizes! don't believe a word of it! much more like seize ace!"

Miss Blessington, dressed by Elise in Chambéry gauze, and by Nature in her usual panoply of beautiful stupidity, which she wears sleeping and waking, at home and abroad, living and dying, is at work at a little table, a nude Dian, with cold, chaste smile and crinkly hair, on a red velvet shrine just above her head.

"Do they play every evening?" asks Esther, from the recess where she has been deposited by St. John, whose eyes she encounters, considering her attentively over the top of the *Saturday*. Shams, Flunkeyism, Woman's Rights, Dr. Cumming, the Girl of the Period—they have all been passing through his eye into his brain, and, mixed with Esther Craven, make a fine jumble there.

St. John has been rather unlucky in his experiences of women hitherto. He has got rather into the habit of thinking that all good women must be stupid, and that all pleasant women must be bad. Esther is not stupid. Is she bad, then? Those glances of hers, they give a man odd sensations about the midriff; they inspire in him a greedy, covetous desire for more of them; but are they such as Una would have given her Red Cross Knight? Are they such as a man would like to see his wife bestow on his men friends? The wilder a man is or has been himself, the more scrupulously fastidious he is about the almost prudish nicety of the women that belong to him. He likes to see the sheep and the goats as plainly, widely separated as they are in the parable; it moves him to deep wrath when he sees a good woman faintly, poorly imitating a bad one. I do not think that good women believe this half generally enough; or, if they do, they do not act upon it.

"Do they play every evening?"

"Every evening, and Sir Thomas always accuses my mother of cheating."

"And you, what do you do?"

"Read, go to sleep, play cribbage or bézique with Conny."

"Does she live here always?"

"Always."

"You and she are inseparable, I suppose?"

"We get on very well in a quiet way; she is a very good girl, and comes and sits in my smoking-room by the hour with me."

"Wrong, but pleasant, as the monkey said when he kissed the cat," remarks Esther, flippantly. "You are very fond of her, I suppose?"

"H'm!" shrugging his shoulders. "I have a cat-like propensity for getting fond of anything that I live and eat and breathe with—like the fellow in the Bastille, don't you know, that got so fond of a spider. I never should have grown fond of a spider, though; they have got such a monstrous lot of long legs; but the principle is the same."

"Why are not you fond of Sir Thomas then?"

"So I am, I suppose, *in a way;* if he were to tumble into the pool, I suppose I should hop in and fish him out again; I'm not quite sure about that, either."

"We'll have another rubber, miladi?" shouts Sir Thomas's stentor voice, elate with victory; "that is the ninth game I have beat you to-night; you'll never win as long as you leave so many blots—I have told you so a score of times."

Poor miladi, strangling a gigantic yawn, begins to set her men again; she had hoped that her punishment was ended for the night, and that she might be dismissed to the *otium cum dignitate* of her armchair and nap.

St. John jumps up and walks over to the players; there are few things in life he hates so much as playing backgammon with his father, but he hates seeing his mother bullied even more. If a man is cursed with a necessity for loving something, the chances are that he will love his mother, even if she bear more resemblance to a porpoise than to a Christian lady.

"I'll have a rubber with you, Sir Thomas; my mother is tired."

"Fiddlesticks!" growls Sir Thomas. "Tired! what the devil has she been doing to tire herself?—fiddle-faddled about the garden, picking off half a dozen dead roses. Very good thing for her if she is."

But the man's will is stronger than the turkey-cock's, and the latter yields.

CHAPTER XII.

A sprained ankle takes mostly a tedious weary time in getting mended. Esther's, however, is but a slight sprain, and entails only a week's lying on a thoroughly comfortable, well-stuffed sofa close to one of the library's windows, where mignonette sends up continual presents of the strongest and sweetest of all flower-perfumes to her grateful nostrils—entails also being made a fuss with. If Miss Blessington had had her will, the sofa would have been upstairs, and the being made a fuss with, save by a compassionate lady's maid, dispensed with. Miss Blessington desires sincerely, in her affectionate solicitude for her welfare, to keep the young patient in a graceful and pleasing solitude upstairs. The young patient, being of a gregarious turn of mind, desires sincerely to be brought down: and the son of the house, although not particularly young, and in general not particularly gregarious, desires sincerely to bring her down. It is a case of Pull, Devil; Pull, Baker!—Baker being represented by Constance, Devil by St. John and Esther. But two pull stronger than one, and they gain their point.

"Is Miss Craven ready to come down?" asks St. John, one morning, addressing the question to Miss Blessington as they stand together after breakfast.

"I don't know, I'm sure. St. John?"

"Well!"

"If," she says, giving a little factitious cough, and speaking with her usual amiable smile, "it is any object to Miss Craven to get well——"

"I should imagine that there could be no doubt on that point," he answers, picking up the *Pall Mall.*

"I don't know," she rejoins, with a certain air of doubtful reserve.

"It is generally considered pleasanter to have two legs to go upon than one, isn't it? It is not many people that, like Cleopatra, can 'hop forty paces through the public streets.' Have you any reason for imputing to Miss Craven a morbid taste for invalidhood?"

"No; but she is hardly an invalid, and to be made so much of as you, with your usual good-nature to the waifs and strays of humanity, make of her, must be a sensation as pleasant as novel."

"I *am* wonderfully good-natured, aren't I?" he says, laughing broadly to himself behind the little yellowy sheets of the *Pall Mall.* "There is not one man in a hundred that, in my place, would do the same, is there?"

She is silent; the resentment of a slow nature, that has a suspicion of being laughed at, but is not sure of it, smouldering within her.

"Come, Conny, you began a sentence just now which you left unfinished, like a pig with one ear. 'If it is really an object to Miss Craven to get well'—what then?"

"If it is really an object to Miss Craven to get well, I should think that she would be more likely to attain it by lying quietly upstairs than by being continually moved from place to place; *that* is what I was going to say."

"I am sorry you think me such an Orson as to rush up and downstairs with such tremendous violence as to run the risk of dislocating her limbs."

Miss Blessington turns away pettishly.

"I wonder the girl likes to give you the trouble of perpetually carrying her about the house."

"She is well aware that trouble is a pleasure."

"Fully half her day is spent on the staircase and in the passages in your arms."

"What a horribly immoral picture—vice stalking rampant through the Felton corridors in the shape of me carrying a poor lame child that cannot carry herself!"

"It may be a pleasure to you," says Constance, harking back to her former speech, "but it can hardly be so to her—to be haled about like a bale of goods by a total stranger like yourself. If you were her brother, I grant you, it would be different."

"If I were her brother it *would* be different," assents Gerard, blandly.

The sentence is Miss Blessington's own, and yet, by fresh accentuation, it is made exactly to contradict itself.

"You mean it good-naturedly, I don't doubt, but I am not at all sure that it is not mistaken kindness."

"That *what* is not mistaken kindness?"

"You are very dull of comprehension this morning, St. John."

"I always am at these untimely hours; it requires the flame of evening to light up the torch of my intellect. Be lenient to my infirmities, and explain; I am all attention."

"My meaning is sufficiently clear, I should imagine," she retorts, with lady-like, gentle exasperation. "If you had left the girl in her original obscurity, it would have been all very well; but to be taken up and dropped again——"

"Like a hot chesnut!"

"Pshaw! to be taken up and dropped again is hardly pleasant."

"Hardly."

"And when you drop her——"

"Literally or metaphorically?—on the stone floor, or out of the light of my favour?"

"When you drop her" (disdaining to notice the interruption)——

"Well, what then?" he says, laying down the paper, and turning his face, kindled by a certain honest self-contempt, towards her—"To be dropped by me! what a prodigious calamity! Hitherto, Conny, your sex has made, with regard to me, more use of the active than the passive voice of the verb to drop."

"Nonsense!" she says, scornfully; "that *is* the pride that apes humility. Of course, so much notice as you lavish on her is likely to turn the head of a girl who has hitherto probably received no attentions more flattering than those of some Welsh grazier; and when you drop her——"

"When I drop her," he repeats, impatiently, tired of the subject, and of the repetition of the phrase—"she will be no worse off than she was before that misfortune happened to her."

So Esther lies all day long in lazy contentment upon the sofa, looking out at the garden, and at the fountain where four bronze dolphins spout continual showers of spray in the autumn sunlight; dips into Owen Meredith's last poems; peeps between the crisp uncut leaves of new magazine or novel; and looks forward towards the ante-dinner hour, when St. John will come in from the day's amusement or occupation, and passive content will be exchanged for active enjoyment.

Esther has, as you know, made but light of her accident in her letters to her lover; fearing lest, in his eager anxiety on her account, he might get into the train, and give her the unexpected pleasure of seeing him arrive at Felton—seeing him arrive in his threadbare shooting jacket, through whose sleeves he always appears to have thrust his long arms too far, and his patched, creaking, Naullan boots. Imagine St. John introduced to those boots! A cold shiver runs down her spine at the bare idea. St. John is no dandy, it is true, but coats from Poole's are as much a matter of course to him as a knife and fork to eat his dinner with, or a bed to lie upon.

On the afternoon of the day on which the above-reported short dialogue took place, St. John and his father, converging from different points of the compass to one centre, enter almost at the same moment the library. Two canary-coloured Colossi have just deposited tea on a small table. St. John has neither neckerchief nor collar; his brown throat is bared in a *négligé* as becoming to most men as the *à quatre épingles* exactitude of their park get-up is unbecoming. A man in the loose carelessness of his every-day country clothes is a man: in the prim tightness of his Pall Mall toilette he is a little, stiff, jointless figure out of Noah's ark.

"Slops again!" says Paterfamilias, very gruffly. "I never come into this room at any hour of the day or night without finding you women drinking tea! Why on earth, if you are thirsty, cannot you drink beer or water, instead of ruining your insides with all that wash?"

At this courteous speech a silence falls on the company. Sir Thomas mostly brings silence with him; he is half-conscious that at his entry voices are choked and laughter quenched, and it serves to exasperate him the more.

"You sit with your knees into the fire in air-tight rooms all day long," pursues he, in his loud, hectoring voice, "and destroy your digestions with gallons of hot tea, and then you are surprised at having tallow in your cheeks, instead of lilies and roses, as your grandmothers had!"

"Perhaps," says St. John, drily, "the ladies deny the justice of your conclusions; Sir Thomas; perhaps they do not own the soft impeachment of tallowy cheeks which you so gallantly ascribe to them."

42

As he speaks, his eyes involuntarily rest on the clear, rose brilliance of the young stranger's happy, beautiful child-face.

"I don't mind being called 'tallow face,'" says Esther, with a low laugh—"Juliet was; her father said to her, 'Out, you baggage! you tallow face!'"

"He must have been an ancestor of Sir Thomas's in direct male line, must not he?" says the young man, gaily stooping over her and whispering.

Seeing them so familiarly and joyously whisper together, Constance looks up with an air of astonished displeasure, which Gerard perceiving, instantly turns towards her.

"What are you making, Conny?"

"Braces."

"For me, no doubt? With your usual thoughtfulness, you recollected that my birthday falls next week, and you were preparing a little surprise for me. Well, never mind; though I have made the discovery rather prematurely, I'll be as much surprised as ever when the day of presentation arrives."

"They are not for you, St. John; they are for the bazaar."

"The bazaar!" he repeats, a little testily. "For the last month all your thoughts have tended bazaarwards; you neither eat, nor sleep, nor speak, nor hear, nor smell, without some reference to the bazaar."

"Bazaar! Humbug!" growls Sir Thomas, rising and walking towards the door. "A parcel of idle women getting together to sell trash and make asses of themselves!"

Then he goes out, and bangs the door.

"I would not for worlds have given him the satisfaction of agreeing with him while he was in the room," says St. John, insensibly speaking in a louder key now that the autocrat before whom all voices sink has removed himself; "but, for once in my life, I must confess to coinciding in opinion with aged P.: to be pestered with unfeminine, unladylike importunity to buy things that one would far rather be without—to be lavishly generous, and get no credit for it—to be swindled without any hope of legal redress; this is the essence of a charitable bazaar!"

"Dear me!" says Esther, with a crestfallen sigh. "And I had been looking forward to it so much!"

He sits down on a low chair beside her sofa. "Looking forward to a bazaar!" he echoes, with a half-incredulous smile. "My dear Miss Craven, what a revelation as to your past history that one sentence is! Why, I should as soon think of looking forward to a visit to the dentist, or to my mother's funeral!"

"No one expects to *enjoy* it; it is a necessary evil," says Miss Blessington, with resignation.

"Like dancing with married men, or going to church?"

"Conny! Conny!" shouts Sir Thomas from somewhere in the unseen distance.

Conny rises, though reluctantly, and leaves the other two *tête-à-tête*.

"Miss Blessington is going to have a stall," says Esther, presently, for the sake of saying something, catching a little nervously at the first remark that occurred to her.

"Yes."

"And I am to help her."

"Yes."

"But I will promise not to pester you with unfeminine, unladylike importunity to buy my wares."

"I am sorry to hear it."

"Miss Blessington has two friends coming to stay with her for it."

"Yes."

"Are you glad or sorry?"

"Glad is a weak word to express my feelings; I am in ecstasies!"

"They are beautiful, I suppose—refined, witty, as I always picture the women of your world?" she says, a little enviously.

"On the contrary, it would be impossible to find two more faded, negative specimens of Belgravian womanhood: they have not a single angle in either of their characters."

"Do you think *that* a recommendation?"

"I did not say so."

"But you implied it, by expressing such exaggerated joy at their coming."

"So I did—so I do: and if they were to rise in number from two to fifty, like Falstaff's highwaymen, I should express greater joy still."

"And why?" raising herself from her cushions to get a straighter, truer look into his bright, grave eyes.

"Because," he says, lowering his voice a little, and leaning closelier over her, "the larger the party the better chance there is of undisturbed *tête-à-têtes* between congenial spirits. Do you see?"

And Esther *does* see, and thinking on Robert Brandon, is uneasily joyful.

Ere the arrival of the looked-for bazaar, Miss Craven's cure is complete. On the day preceding the one appointed for that philanthropic festivity, she has been walking in the late evening about the moon-coloured garden, free from any remaining lameness, leaning on St. John's arm. She does not need the slight stay, but it pleases him to give and her to receive it. It does not please Miss Blessington, however, watching them from an upper chamber—watching Esther dabble her small hands in the opal water in the great bronze water-lily leaf that makes the basin of the fountain—watching St. John, rapt and absorbed in her pretty foolish chatter. And yet their talk, if she could but hear it, holds nothing obnoxiously fond or *flirtatious;* it might be proclaimed by the bellman in the streets.

"How nice it is to be no longer a devil upon two sticks!" the young girl is saying, joyfully; and the man makes answer, "You will be up to another gallop across the park to-morrow?"

"Never, *never!*" she cries, bringing together emphatically her two gleaming, wet hands. "You have witnessed my first and last equestrian feat; with my own free-will I will mount never a horse again, unless it is the rocking-horse at the end of the north gallery: it is frisky, yet safe; gallops and plunges, yet stands still: that is the horse for me."

He laughs, and then they are silent.

A star falls, hurling itself mysteriously down the sky, and into the dark; two bats glide past, dusky, noiseless. Bats always seem to me like the ghosts of dead birds, that haunt the green gardens and copses they used to love.

St. John speaks presently. "One forms mistaken estimates of people's characters; I should not have imagined you a coward."

"But I am one, physically and morally," she answers, sighing.

As the ladies retire to bed, Miss Blessington enters Esther's room—a familiarity which somewhat surprises that virgin, as it is the first time that it has been accorded to her.

"I have come to congratulate you!" Constance says, civilly; "you have made a wonderful recovery."

"Yes, wonderful!"

"You can walk perfectly well without assistance, cannot you?"

"Perfectly" (turning away her head, in the guilty consciousness of having, despite her soundness of limb, not walked without assistance).

"St. John is very useful as a walking-stick, isn't he?" (playfully.)

"He thought it would tire me less," replies the other, flushing; "he has been most kind!"

"He always is," answers Miss Blessington, quickly: "it is his nature; old beggarwomen, dogs, cats, dirty children in the gutter—it is all one to him."

"Really!"

"That universal geniality amounts almost to a weakness, though an amiable one; it has often been the cause of exciting hopes that, of course, he had neither the wish nor the power to gratify."

"What! in old beggarwomen, dogs, cats, and dirty children in the gutter?" says Esther, smiling merrily, yet with scorn.

"If I did not take an interest in you," continued Constance, leaning in a graceful artistic pose against the mantelpiece, "I should, of course, not take the trouble to mention the subject; but, as I do, I thought it the kindest thing I could do to you to set you on your guard against attentions to which you, who do not know him, might, without vanity, attribute some importance, but which I, who know him so thoroughly, know to mean absolutely nothing, beyond a sort of general *bonhomie* towards the whole of the human race."

"I am deeply grateful," answers the young girl, with sarcastic emphasis; "but in my part of the world, girls are not in the habit of cherishing vague hopes because a man has the civility to offer them his arm when they are disabled by an accident from walking by themselves."

"Well, forewarned is forearmed, you know" (nodding and smiling); "and from some careless, slighting remarks that St. John let fall the other day, I thought I should not be acting the part of a friend by you if I did not warn you against a snare into which I have seen others older, and knowing more of the world than you do, fall. Good night!"

"Stay!" cries Esther, springing up, and catching hold of her companion's gauzy dress in detention. "It is unfair to tell a person half, and not the whole. What were the slighting remarks that Mr. Gerard made *à propos* of me?"

"Really, I—I—don't remember exactly," replies Constance, with reluctance, half-feigned, half-real; "I did not pay much attention at the time; it was an admission that slipped out without my intending it."

"But now that it has slipped out," cries the other, authoritatively, "you must explain it fully, please."

"Well, really—please don't look so tragic, it can be of so very little consequence to you what he said or did not say about you——"

"Infinitesimally little! but still I mean to hear it."

"Well" (with rather an awkward laugh), "the situation is hardly worth such Mrs. Siddons' airs: it was only that, when I was remonstrating with him the other day on his manner to you, he said, in his off-hand, abrupt way, something to the effect that *when* he threw you over—never for a moment denying that sooner or later he would do so—you would get over it soon, or something of that description. I cannot recall the exact phrase. Good night."

But beautiful Esther, standing there stricken, credulous, with eager, angry eyes, forgets to make the answering greeting.

CHAPTER XIII.

The Bazaar day has arrived; so likewise have Constance's chosen friends, the Misses De Grey; so likewise has their brother, commonly called Dick De Grey, for no other reason that we wot of but that at his baptism he received the name of Charles. The large open carriage which had so impressed Esther on her first arrival at Brainton station, and St. John's smart T.-cart, with his big, black horse, at whose head, or rather at some distance below whose nose, a cockaded infant stands trim and tidy, are at the door.

"How are we to divide?" says Miss Blessington, coming out under the portico and unfurling her white Honiton parasol. "How many of us are there? Adeline, Georgina, Miss Craven, and myself, four, and you two gentlemen six. St. John, will you drive Miss De Grey?"

"I should be delighted," he answers, slowly and tardily, not looking up from the gardenia which he is fastening on his coat; "but I believe I am under an old engagement to drive Miss Craven. You have never been in a T.-cart, have you?" (looking at her imploringly, to back him up in the ready lie to which, for love of her, he has just given vent.)

"Never!" she answers, smiling coldly. "And now that I see to what a height one has to climb, and in what close proximity one must be to that huge quadruped's heels, I am in no hurry to make the experiment. I release you from your engagement, Mr. Gerard, if it ever existed; if it is all the same to everybody, I prefer the—I never can recollect the names of carriages—barouche, sociable, landau, which is it?"

He stares at her for an instant in blank astonishment; then, turning away quickly to hide the mortification which he knows to be legible on his face, without a word or a groan helps the oldest, plainest, languidest of the Misses De Grey into the T.-cart and drives off with her. And Esther steps into the sociable, and tries to feel triumphant and dignified, contemplating, for a dozen miles, Miss Georgina De Grey's gold-dusted hair and featureless face, and submitting meekly to having the modest proportions of her own toilette covered up and smothered in the abundance and volume of her *vis-à-vis'* laces and frillings.

"Since he means to throw me over, it is as well to be beforehand with him," she says to herself, her eyes fixed pensively on the revolving black and yellow wheel; "in such cases it is always best to take the initiative. It would have been very pleasant, so high up out of the dust; but what have I to do with aristocratic vehicles? A gig, a wheelbarrow, a pig-tub—such are the only conveyances I am likely to have experience of in after-life; why then inoculate myself with a taste for luxuries that are for my betters?"

And meanwhile St. John holds dreary converse with himself, while a river of sound, on which the words Nilsson, Romeo e Giulietta, Schneider, drums, Holland House, garden party float, pours into his ear from the direction of his companion. "She is honest, at all events; does not relish my society, and does not affect to do so; tolerated me only as long as I was useful, like a dog, in fetching and carrying. Why am I so unpopular with women? Is it what I do, what I say, or what I am, that makes me so? Is it anything mendable or unmendable?"

Precisely seventeen minutes past two of the clock, the Melford town-hall clock, and visitors are beginning to arrive pretty thickly; three or four barouches, seven or eight waggonettes, and nine or ten pony-carriages, are trotting and walking and crawling up the steep Melford street. Climbing the side of a house is child's play to the ascent of that most perpendicular of high streets. The doctor's house, red, and with redder berries thick about its plate-glass windows, stands on your right as you go up the town. The Doctor and the Doctress are issuing from the brass-knockered hall door—she in a grey moire antique, that old Mrs. Evans' quinsy paid for, and gold bracelets that took their rise from Mr. Watkin's decline and fall.

The town-hall stands in its grey limestone respectability in the market place, over against the Bell Inn; it has an arched doorway, and under this arch man, woman, and child go pacing in little, smart tulle bonnets and black hats, with their purses full of small change, and their hearts of that most excellent virtue—Christian charity. Round the hall counters are ranged, and behind these counters stand a phalanx of young women, prepared to exert their little abilities in overreaching and circumventing their fathers, lovers, and brothers, to the utmost.

Miss Blessington's stall is next-door neighbour to poor Mrs. Tomkins', the Felton curate's fat, childridden wife—as, in some foreign city, they tell us that you may see marble palaces and mud hovels cheek by jowl; for, as is a mud hovel to a marble palace, so is poor Mrs. Tomkins in the Melford table of valuation to Miss Blessington.

Mrs. Tomkins' main hope is in her sister, pretty, second-rate, pert Miss Smith, who, with a dog-collar round her waist, to demonstrate its tenuity, and two long, uncurled curls, vulgarly known as "Follow me, lads!" floating over her fat shoulders, has been kissing strawberries and rose-buds, and selling them at half-a-crown apiece, to such attorneys' clerks and doctors' assistants of weak intellect as inhabit Melford town.

On Miss Blessington's other side the Misses Denzil hold sway—daughters of a neighbour baronet, whom for twenty years past Sir Thomas has hated with the hate of hell, because he once beat him in a contest for the county. Belinda Denzil, an elderly young lady, tall and yellow and stately; likest to a dandelion among the flowers of the field; and Priscilla, a beady-eyed, brisk brune, of whom her admirers predicate that she could talk the hind leg off a mule!

Mr. Gerard and Mr. De Grey are strolling about together arm in arm; criticising the wares a little and the saleswomen a good deal. They are not particularly fond of one another; but no more was Alexander Selkirk, I dare say, of his next-door neighbour, when he lived in town, if he ever did. All the same, if the said next-door neighbour had happened to land on that most irreligious of desert islands, where the benighted valleys and rocks never heard the sound of the church-going bell, don't you suppose that he would have rushed into his arms? So in this desert island of Melford, St. John and Dick, the only two respectable fellows, as they think, among a savage horde of squireens, march about, hooked on together for mutual defence against the barbarians.

"You seem to be driving a thriving trade," remarks St. John, who, after his wanderings, has at length come to anchor at Miss Blessington's stall, addressing Esther, but addressing her diffidently, as one that, after the severe and uncalled-for snubbing he had this morning received, was by no means sure of the reception his civilities might meet with, while three old women and a parson squeeze in beside himself and his friend.

"Perhaps you will kindly contribute towards making it more thriving, by buying something;" replies Miss Craven, coolly and drily. "Let me recommend this cigar case to your notice; it is rather ugly, and very dear, but one must not mind trifling drawbacks of that kind on an occasion like the present."

"Did you make it?"

"Yes; but please don't be so polite as to buy it on that account, as, upon the same grounds, you would have to buy a large proportion of the beautiful works of art before you."

So speaking, she turns away from him to another customer, as if glad to be rid of him.

"May I ask what the price of this is?" asks Mr. De Grey, leaning with languid familiarity over Miss Smith's counter (everybody is familiar with Miss Smith; that is one of her great charms), and holding up a gorgeously-embroidered smoking cap between his finger and thumb.

"One pound eleven and sixpence halfpenny," replies the young lady, with glib obsequiousness, all a-twitter with excitement at being addressed by an august being in a cutaway coat who is known throughout the room to be a visitor at Felton Hall. "But, dear me!" (fussing about with unnecessary *empressement*) "I have got a much more stylish one somewhere, if I could but lay my hands on it—one that I made myself, if that is any recommendation! He! he!" (with a giggle.)

"Can you doubt it?" retorts he, sucking the top of his cane, and staring at her with lazy impertinence.

Meanwhile the room is getting very crowded and stuffy: it is a very small town-hall, and all Melford and the southern half of ——shire are compressed into it—the result being much animal heat, some ill-humour, and infinite grief over rent garments; which is reversing the case of the ancients, who rent their garments in sign of grief. And in and through and about this warm throng, many girls, emissaries from different stalls, go pushing and elbowing to enlist unwilling subscribers to raffles. Philanthropy has gone nigh to unsexing them; it has turned modest, reserved ladies into forward importunate Mænads.

46

Foremost, most energetic, most unrebuffable of these emissaries is Miss Priscilla Denzil. She flies about hither and thither, with her white gown all limp and tumbled, and her rough hair pushing its way resolutely from under the blue ribbons which make a vain show of confining it *à la Grecque*. She is not thinking a bit of how she is looking; her whole soul is intent on doing a good stroke of business, and none can escape her.

Sir Thomas Gerard has just entered the hall. Having ridden into Melford on magisterial business, the idea has struck him of how much better and more cuttingly he will be able to abuse the bazaar at dinner this evening if he has had the advantage of seeing it. With a dog-whip in his hand, and an intense desire to lay it about the shoulders of the company expressed in his cross face, he is pushing his way along when attacked by the dauntless Priscilla.

"Oh! Sir Thomas, please let me put you down in the raffle for a fender-stool; *so* handsome! white arums on a red ground; *do* let me, *so* handsome!"

"A *what*, Miss Priscilla?"

"A fender-stool."

"Humph! the stupidest things that ever were invented," answers the baronet, snarling. "If they had been made expressly to trip people up, and pitch them head-foremost into the fire, they could not have answered the purpose better."

"Did they ever pitch you head-foremost into the fire?" asks Miss Prissy, insinuatingly ("because [aside], if so, I wonder whoever was fool enough to pick you out again!")

"No, and they shall never have the chance as long as I can prevent them," replies the gracious elder, walking off.

For a minute Priscilla stands still, rebuffed; but recovering herself, speedily rushes off again, charges with her fender-stool an old maid who has one already, and a poor little whity-brown curate who has no house to put one in, &c., &c.

"I am afraid I have not done them up very neatly," Esther is saying, as she gives a parcel into Mr. De Grey's hands—Miss Smith having at length frightened that gentleman from her side by the rapid strides to intimacy which she was making with him—"My fingers toil in vain after the nimbleness with which shopmen whisk a parcel into shape and compactness before you have time to look round."

Mr. De Grey has spent a small fortune in pincushions, kettle-holders, dressed dolls, and many other such-like articles which no young man of fashion should be without.

"What have I done to be so neglected, Miss Craven?" asks Gerard, elevating his eyebrows plaintively. "Am I expected to put on these slippers on the spot, that I am given no paper to pack them up in?"

"Oh! I beg your pardon; I thought that Miss De Grey was attending to you," answers Esther, in the most business-like, shop-woman voice, without smiling, or lifting her eyes.

"I thought no one ever gave change at a bazaar," he says, trying to make her look up at him, as she puts a few shillings into his hand.

"I do not approve of such extortion," she answers, demurely; "honesty is the best policy."

"That proverb must have been invented, as Whately justly observed, by some one who had tried the other alternative."

She smiles a little against her will. "I wish you two would go now," she says, addressing both young men indifferently: "you are only making me idle. Look! there are three old maids ready to storm the position, and only deterred by you."

"Rhadamantha, Hebe, and Niobe!" says St. John, laughing.

"Please go; I know you are not thinking of buying anything more."

"Don Ferdinando can do no more than he can do, and at present he is pretty well cleaned out."

At Miss Blessington's stall trade is certainly very brisk; it is considered a fitting mark of respect to the family to buy their goods, and so the honest burgesses of Melford make it a point of honour to buy Miss Blessington's and Miss De Grey's blotting books and babies' socks in preference to anyone else's, however superior in fabric and less exorbitant in price anybody else's might be.

Miss Blessington has just sunk upon a chair, with an affectation of great fatigue, and is saying languidly, "If ever any one deserved the martyr's crown, that person is I; within the last ten minutes I have sold nine cushions and fifteen pairs of muffetees."

"There's plenty of cool tea and warm ices at the other end of the room, if you think they are likely to restore you," suggests Gerard, who is still leaning his elbow on the counter, and has not gone away as commanded.

"It makes one quite hot," pursues Miss Blessington, leaning back and fanning herself vigorously, "merely to look at Prissy Denzil rushing about like a Mænad, worrying every one to put into raffles."

"Providence made a great mistake when it made that girl a lady," says St. John, following, with a look of half-disgust in his fastidious eyes, Priscilla's little dishevelled figure; "she would have been much happier haggling for halfpence at a huckster's stall."

The afternoon draws towards its close; people have come and bought, and raffled and gone again, carrying manifold ill-tied paper parcels with them. The farmeresses and yeomen's wives of the Melford district have departed, carrying with them, in their mind's eye, for imitation against next Sunday, the cut of Miss Blessington's skirt, and the profuse curls and *bandeaux* of Miss De Grey's intricate *coiffure*. The room is emptying, and the day's duty approaching its end.

"I say, old fellow," remarks Mr. De Grey, touching St. John on the shoulder as he leans against the wall, gazing somewhat morosely at his own boots, "don't you think we might as well be saying Ta-ta? I don't know what you have, but *I* have had nearly enough of this gay and festive scene."

"All right," answers the other, shaking off dull care; "I have put into exactly twenty-five raffles, and only got a christening robe and a squirt, so I think I may be supposed to have done my duty."

At the door there is a little confusion—carriages driving up, carriages driving away; a small crowd gathered to see the smart ladies; two policemen.

The Felton equipage and Mr. Gerard's T.-cart stand at some little distance down the street. St. John offers Esther his arm, and she, having no decent excuse for declining, takes it. As they walk along, he speaks to her hurriedly and not without temper. "If you have no special ground of quarrel against me—and Heaven knows why you should have—but feel only that weariness to which most women seem, in my society, to be more or less subject, be unselfish, and let me drive you home. I will not speak, neither need you, if you will have it so; there are many things more unsociable than absolute silence."

"Why cannot you be satisfied with this morning's arrangements?" she asks, demurring; the recollection of his reported insult rankling in her mind.

He shrugs his shoulders expressively. "If you had had three fourths of 'Le Follet' and half the *Morning Post* poured into your reluctant ears, as I have, you would not have asked that question."

"If you have heard *half* the *Morning Post*, is it not a thousand pities that you should not hear the other half?" she inquires, drily.

They have reached the T.-cart, the big black horse, the baby-tiger; in the low, red sun the new harness shines brightly.

"I almost wish you could sprain your other ankle," Gerard says, recovering his good humour. "As long as you were lame, you were much more amiable."

Ten minutes more, and the Melford steep street and railway bridge are left behind them, they are trotting with smooth briskness between the nutty, briary hedgerows. At first the silence which Gerard had guaranteed threatens to remain unbroken; it is infringed at last by Esther, out of whose heart the fair late breeze, the happy yellow stillness, and lastly, the proximity to and solitude with the beloved one, are smoothing all angry creases. ("If he did speak lightly of me," she thinks, sorrowfully, "we shall not have the chance of many more drives together; whether he think ill or well, highly or meanly, of me, let me be happy with him while I may!")

"What a pleasant vehicle this would be to make a driving tour in!"

"A tour of all the cathedral towns throughout England, as the Heir of Redclyffe proposed spending his honeymoon in making!"

She laughs.

"I remember long ago the *Saturday Review* saying of some she-novelist's men, that they were like old governesses in trousers: it was not a bad simile, was it?"

Silence falls on them again; broken this time by Gerard, who, turning abruptly towards his companion, says, "You are *not* bored by my society, Miss Craven? Unless you are cast in a mould different from the rest of humanity, you *must* be bored by the society of the Misses De Grey. Why, then, were you so resolute this morning in rejecting the one and accepting the other? This is the problem that has been puzzling me for the last half mile."

She hangs her head like a scolded school-child.

"What *was* your motive?"

"A prudential one, partly," she answers, rallying her spirits. "I knew that in after life I should have small experience of T.-carts and such rich man's luxuries, so I thought it wiser not to run the risk of contracting a taste for them."

"How do you know what the experience of your after life may be?"

"One may argue from the known to the unknown; I can give a pretty shrewd guess."

"And was that your sole motive?"

"What does it matter to you whether it was or not?"

"Nothing; except that, to a philosophical mind like mine, woman and her caprices are an interesting psychological study. Did you ever hear of an essay of Addison's entitled 'Dissection of a Coquette's Heart?'"

"I am not a coquette," she cries, indignantly, answering the indirect accusation directly.

"I did not say you were. I hope you are not—I hope to God you are not!" he answers, with more vehemence than the occasion seems to demand.

"And yet," she says, feeling oppressed by the solemnity of his manner and trying to speak lightly, "I have heard it said that no woman can be thoroughly attractive who is not something of a flirt."

"I had rather that she should be thoroughly *un*attractive then," he answers, shortly and grimly.

"Men always wish to have a monopoly of all pleasant sins," she retorts, a little cynically.

"If you think that the reason why I wish you not to flirt is that I want a monopoly of that occupation, you are mistaken," he says, gravely; "it is an art that I have not either the will or the power to practise."

"Really?"

"Really."

"Seriously?"

"Seriously. Confess that, after that admission, your opinion of me is considerably lowered."

No answer but a smile.

"Confess that you feel for me as sovereign a contempt as the ladies of the last century felt for a man that never got drunk."

"I feel," she says, averting her head and speaking under an impulse that kindles her cheeks and makes her voice falter—"I feel a surprise that the words you say and the words you are reported to say do *not* tally better together."

"What am I reported to say?" (a little impatiently.) "A *réchauffé* of one's own stale speeches is not an appetising dish, but may be wholesome as an exhortation to consistency."

"A person—I was told—" begins Esther, floundering in confusion among different forms of speech—"I was told—by a person that ought to have known—that you had spoken in a slighting, disparaging way of—of—of—a person."

"Who told you so?" (breathlessly.)

"That can be of no consequence."

"Without your telling me I know," he says, his face growing hot with the red of indignant anger, not guilt. "God forgive her for such a lie!"

"It was not true, then?" she asks, eagerly, lifting her eyes, brimful of joyful relief, to his.

"Such an accusation is not worth rebutting," he answers, contemptuously. "Is a man likely to speak slightingly of——" He stops abruptly. ("Not yet! not yet! it is impossible that she can like me yet. Am I an Antinous, to be loved as soon as seen? Let me be patient—be patient!")

CHAPTER XIV.

"I am afraid that their names will not convey much idea to your minds, as you do not know our part of the world, but you may have met some of them in London: Sir Charles and Lady Bolton; Mr. and Mrs. Tredegar; Mr., Mrs., and Miss Annesley; the Misses Denzil (by-the-by, you saw them at the bazaar yesterday); and two or three stray men."

This remark is addressed by Miss Blessington to her two friends on the afternoon following the bazaar, and contains a list of the guests expected at dinner at Felton that evening.

"So there's to be a party?" says Esther, from a window recess, where, hidden by a drooped curtain, she has been lying *perdue* up to the present moment, deeply buried in the unwonted luxury of a French novel.

Constance gives a little start. "I did not know that you were there! Yes; there are a few people coming to dine!"

"Don't you like parties?" asks Miss De Grey, half turning round her head, and a coquettish little lace morning cap, in the direction whence Esther's voice proceeds.

"I—I—think so; I hardly know."

"I suppose that you have only just left the schoolroom?"

Esther laughs. "I can hardly be said to have left it, for I was never in it."

"Did you never have a governess, do you mean? What a fortunate person!"

"Never."

"I am not sure that the other alternative, going to school, is not worse."

"I never went to school."

"Is it possible? Do you mean (raising herself, and opening her eyes) that you have never had any education at all?"

"I suppose not," answers Esther, reluctantly; regretting having made an admission which evidently tells so much against her.

"How very odd!"

"What's very odd?" asks her brother, who, with St. John, lounges in from the billiard-room, where they have been knocking the balls about and getting tired of one another.

"Miss Craven has just been telling us that she has had no education," answers Constance, in her even voice—perhaps not sorry of an opportunity to let Gerard know his *protégée's* deficiencies. "I am sure (civilly) that we should never have found it out if she had not told us."

The *protégée* droops her black eyes in mortification over her book, in which she has already found several things that amuse, several things that startle, and several other things that profoundly puzzle her innocent mind.

How unnecessary to make the admission of her own illiterateness, and how needless for Constance to be in such a hurry to repeat the confession!

"What an awful sensation it must be being such an ignoramus!" says Gerard's voice, low and laughing, as he sits down on the window-seat beside her. "What does it feel like?"

She looks up with a re-assured smile.

"At all events," continues he, glancing at her book, "you are doing your best to supply your deficiencies, *however late in life.*"

She colours a little, and involuntarily puts her hand over the title.

"What is it? May I see?"

She hesitates, and her other hand goes hastily to its fellow's help; then, changing her mind, she offers the book boldly to him.

He looks at the title, and a slightly shocked expression dawns on his features: men are always shocked that women should *read about* the things that *they do.*

"Where did you get this?" (quickly).

"I climbed up the ladder in the library; pleasant books always rise to top shelves, as the cream rises to the top of the milk."

"Will you oblige me by putting it back where you took it from?"

"When I have read it? Of course."

"*Before* you have read it."

"Why should I?" (rather snappishly).

"Why should you," he repeats, impatiently—not much fonder of opposition than are most of his masterful sex. "Why, because it is not a fit book for a—a *child*like you to read."

"A *child* like me!" (sitting bolt up and reddening). "Do you know what age I am?"

"I have not an idea; forty, perhaps."

She laughs.

"Don't you know that all women are children till they are twenty-one; and you are particularly childish for your age."

"I am, am I?"

"Child or no child, this is a book that no modest woman ought to read."

"But that all modest *men* may, with pleasure and profit for themselves," rejoins she, ironically. "Well, when I have finished it I shall be better able to tell you whether I agree with you or not."

"Do you mean to say that, after what I have told you, you are still bent on reading it?" he asks, astonishment and displeasure fighting together for the mastery in his voice.

"Certainly!" (looking rather frightened, but speaking with a sort of timid bravado). "Do you suppose that Eve would have cared to taste the apple if it had been specially recommended to her notice as a particularly good, juicy Ribstone pippin? Give it me, please!"

"Take it!" he says, throwing it with hasty impoliteness into her lap. "Read, mark, learn, and inwardly digest every word of it; and since you have a taste for such literature, I can lend you a dozen more like it."

So speaking, he rises abruptly, and leaves her side and the room at almost the same moment.

When he is gone, finding that the rest of the company have likewise slipped away in different directions, Esther relieves her feelings by flinging the disputed volume on the floor; sits for a quarter of an hour staring uncertainly at it; then, pocketing her pride, picks it up, sneaks off with it to the library, and, climbing the high, steep ladder, deposits it in the hole whence she had ravished it, between two of its fellows, as agreeably lax and delicately indelicate as itself. Half an hour later, passing through the hall, she sees the door of Gerard's sanctum ajar, and hears some one walking to and fro within. To one so praise-loving, the temptation to trumpet forth her own excellence is irresistible. She knocks timidly.

"Come in!"

"I don't want to come in," she answers, standing in beautiful, bashful awkwardness in the aperture.

"Is there anything that I can do for you?" he asks, advancing towards her, looking slightly surprised.

"No, nothing; I—I—only came to tell you that I had put—*it* back."

At the end of her sentence her eyes, downcast at first, raise themselves to his with the innocent, eager expectancy of a child that waits for approbation of some infantile good action.

"You have, have you?" he cries, joyfully, catching both her hands; "and was it because I asked you?"

"I don't know for what other reason," she answers, unwillingly.

"And have not read a word more of it?"

"Not a word."

"Not even looked at the end?"

"No."

"Well, you *are* a good child!"

"*Child! child!*—always *child!*" she cries, puckering up her low forehead into the semblance of a frown. "I have a good mind to go and fetch it down again!"

"A good old woman, then! a good old lady!—which is best? which is most respectful? Don't go!" (seeing that she is about to withdraw.)

"It is dressing-time!"

"Not for half an hour yet," pulling her gently in, and closing the door.

"See!" she says, half embarrassed by this *tête-à-tête* that she has herself invited, holding up a bunch of scarlet geraniums that she has lately reft from one of the garden's dazzling squares—"I have been stealing! I hope Sir Thomas won't prosecute me; but as a new dress is with me a biennial occurrence, these are the only contributions I can make to the evening's festivity."

"*Red*, of course!" he answers, smiling. "I never saw you that you had not something red or yellow about you. But why scarlet geraniums? Don't you know that the least imaginable shake (suiting the action to the word, and gently jogging the hand that holds the flowers)—there!" as a little scarlet shower confirms his prognostications.

She stoops to pick up the scattered blossoms.

"If I had some gum, I would drop a little into the centre of each flower; *that* keeps the petals quite firm; I have often done it at home," she says, kneeling on one knee, and looking up gravely for advice and assistance into his friendly, dark face: "but I have no gum."

"Haven't you? I have—somebody has" (ringing the bell). "Please sit down" (drawing an armchair forwards for her). "This is Constance's chair: and don't look as if you were racking your brains for a decent excuse to get away from the only comfortable room in the house."

She obeys, and her eyes wander curiously round. Pipes, whips, saloon pistols, prints of Derby winners; photographs of Nilsson tricked out in water-weeds as "Ophelia;" of Patti gazing up, as "Marguerite," into Mario's fortunate eyes; a table strewn with books—two or three yellow-paper backed, with enticing Gallic titles, similar to the one she has just so heroically foregone. Looking up from these latter, she involuntarily catches his eye.

"You are thinking that what is sauce for the goose is sauce for the gander," he says, laughing rather consciously; "but I assure you that it is not so. The gander is not nearly such a delicate bird, and takes much stronger seasoning."

The gum arrives. She holds the flowers, while he with a paint-brush delicately insinuates one drop into the scarlet heart of each. Their heads are bent so close together that his crisp brown locks brush against the silk-smooth sweep of hers.

"Gently, gently!" cries Esther, pleasantly excited by the consciousness of doing something rather *hors de règle* in that prim household, in having this impromptu *tête-à-tête* with its heir—"not so much! the least *soupçon* imaginable—there! does not it look like a sticky dewdrop?"

"These people that are coming ought to be very much flattered by the efforts you are making in their honour," says Gerard, half jealously.

"Are they worth making efforts for?"

"*You* must tell *me* that to-morrow."

"Who will take me in to dinner, do you think?" she asks, confidentially, looking up at him with childish inquisitiveness.

"I have not an idea; but make your mind easy; it won't be Sir Thomas or me."

"Hardly; but I am sorry that you do not know who it will be, as you might have told me what to talk about."

"Do you always get up your subject beforehand, like Belinda Denzil, out of the *Saturday* or *Echoes of the Clubs*?"

"Oh no! but—"

"St. John! St. John!" shouts Sir Thomas, banging a swing-door, behind him, and coming heavy-footed through the hall.

"It's Sir Thomas!" says Esther growing suddenly pale: and if she had said, and had had reason to say, "It's the Devil!" she could not have made the communication in a more tragic whisper: then, not waiting for any advice as to her conduct, snatching up her bouquet, she flies as if shot from a crossbow, out of the window and into the garden.

Was not it Lord Chesterfield who said that the guests at a dinner party should never be less than the Graces or more than the Muses? Kant preferred the Grace number, and had daily two friends, never more, to dine with him. The guests at the Felton banquet greatly exceed the Chesterfieldian limits. Those who have come only to dinner have been bemoaning themselves heavily, as they came along, on the hardship of being forced away from garden and croquet-ground, and obliged to drive three, four, five miles bare-necked and bare-backed—and a woman nowadays in full dress is verily and indeed bare-necked and bare-backed—through the mellow crimson evening.

To even these grumblers, however, destiny now appears kinder—now, I say, that the too candid daylight is shut out, that the amber champagne—

"With beaded bubbles winking at the brim—"

is creaming gently in every glass, and the *entrées* are making their savoury rounds.

Esther has fallen to the lot of one of the stray men of whom Miss Blessington spoke—a man who, when bidden to dinner, complies with the letter of his invitation, and *dines* chiefly and firstly; looks upon the lady whom he escorts to the social board as a mere adjunct—an agreeable or disagreeable one, as the case may be, but as merely an adjunct, as the flowers in the vases, or the silver Cupids that uphold the fruit baskets. In the intervals of the courses he has no objection to being amused: it is too much exertion to be very amusing himself, but he is not unwilling to smile and lend an indulgent ear to his companion's prattle, so as that prattle does not infringe upon the succulent programme that he has, by diligent study of the *menu*, laid out for himself.

Baffled on her left hand, Miss Craven turns to her right, to be baffled there also. Not that this right-hand neighbour labours under any excessive *gourmandise*—he is willing, on the contrary, that the unknown, black-eyed innocent and the turtle cutlet should share and share alike in his regards; but ere a quarter of an hour their conversation has come to a shipwreck. In it he takes too much for granted: as, for example, that she has been to London this season; that she has seen Faed's last picture; that she has been at Lady ——'s ball; that, by having seen both, she is in a position to judge of the comparative merits of Mademoiselle Nilsson's and Madame Carvalho's rendering of "Marguerite." Tired at length of saying, "I was not there," "I have not seen it," "I never heard of her," she relapses into a mortified silence; thinking, what an impostor must I be to have thrust myself in among all these fine people—I, who cannot even catch their jargon for five minutes!

Foiled in her own little conversational ventures, she tries to listen to other people's. In vain: if, above the general hum, she catches the beginning of one sentence, it is immediately joined on to the end of another. As well, listening to the sultry buzz of a swarm of bees, might one try to distinguish each separate voice. But the dumb show, at least, is left her: the waggling heads, the moving jaws—poor jaws, that have to talk and eat both at once! To put a history to each of these heads—to pick out characters by watching the delicate shades of difference with which each person sits; says, "No, thank you;" laughs—this is not unamusing. Yes, to study the faces, and find similitudes for them: one nut-cracker; several flowers; one plum-pudding; one horse, one vulture, one door-knocker. She is puzzled to find a resemblance for all; for Belinda Denzil, for instance, who, virginally clad in white muslin, that seems to mock her thirty celibate years, is apparently forcing the suave yet weary De Grey into an up-hill, one-sided flirtation. No man has hired Belinda, and it is, with her, the eleventh hour. What fowl, or fish, or quadruped, or article of furniture is she most like? Before Esther can decide this point quite to her mind, the signal of retirement is given, and each maid and wife rises obedient and vanishes.

It is the general complaint in the Felton neighbourhood that at that house the men sit unfashionably, wearisomely long over their wine. Sir Thomas belongs to that excellent school that in their hearts regret the good old days, when a man never rejoined the ladies without seeing double their real number. Half an hour, three-quarters of an hour, an hour and a quarter have passed. Several girls are beginning to yawn behind their fans; the Misses De Grey are driving heavily through a long duet, with never a squire to turn over the leaves (in the wrong place) for them. The door opens, and a fat, bald head appears; the most uninteresting always come first, but, like Noah's dove, he is the harbinger of better things. Five minutes more, and the room is as full of broadcloth as of silk and satin. The younger men are still hovering about uncertainly, unfixed as yet in their minds as to which elaborate fair one they shall come to final anchor by.

The epicure, now that there is nothing to eat, casts his eyes round in search of the finest woman and the comfortablest chair to be found in the great gilded room. Both requisites he finds united in Esther's neighbourhood. Accordingly he is moving towards her, when his attention is happily arrested by a remark that he overhears as to the best method of dressing *beccaficos*. Instantly Miss Craven's white, silky shoulders and red-pouted lips go out of his head. White shoulders and red lips are good things in their way, but what are they to *beccaficos!* Esther draws a long breath of relief. What an escape! In a minute more suspense is ended, and the low armchair beside her is occupied by the person for whom it was intended—for whom, indeed, she has been slyly keeping it half-covered by her dress.

"Well! and how are you getting on?" says Gerard, asking a silly question for want of a wiser one occurring to him, and looking rather affectionate.

St. John is not in the very least degree elevated; but it is useless to deny that the best and fondest of men are still fonder after dinner than before: it must be a very,*very* deep love that cannot be a little deepened by champagne.

"Better than I thought I should be a few seconds ago, when that odious gourmand seemed to be steering this way," she answers, not taking any great trouble to hide her pleasure in his neighbourhood.

"Poor devil! he must not come to you for a character, I see."

"I could forgive a man *most* sins," she says, rather viciously, "but I *never* could forgive him the making me feel in his estimation I stood on a lower level than red mullet and ortolans."

"Well, you know, they *are* very good things," answers Gerard, chiefly to tease her, but partly also because he really thinks so. "Don't look so disgusted," he continues, laughing. "I was afraid you were bored at dinner: you looked absent; I tried to catch your eye once or twice, but you would not let me."

"I was not bored," she answers, simply; "I was quite happy. You see I did not know who was who, and I amused myself pairing the people: I find that I paired them all wrong, though."

"Gave every man his neighbour's wife, did you? I dare say that some of them would not have objected to the arrangement."

"I married *that* old man" (indicating with the slightest possible motion of her head the persons alluded to) "to *that* old woman; I wish it was not ill-manners to point. They both looked so red and pursy and consequential, as if they had been telling each other for the last thirty years what swells they were!"

"*Which* old man to *which* old woman? Oh! I see."

"They are rather like one another, too," she continues, gravely; "and you know people say that, however unlike they may be at starting, merely by dint of living together, man and wife grow alike."

"Do they?" he says, a transient thought flashing through his mind as to whether, after twenty years of wedlock, that blooming peach face would have gained any likeness to his hard, mahogany one. "But how did you find out your mistake?"

"He put down her cup for her so politely just now, that I knew he could not be her husband."

He looks amused. "You are rather young to be so severe upon wedded bliss."

"Was I severe?" she asks, naïvely; "I did not know it; but, you know, a man may be fond of his wife, may be kind to her, but can hardly be said to be *polite*: politeness implies distance."

"Does it?" he says, involuntarily drawing his chair closer to hers, and leaning forward under pretence of looking at the flowers that make a scarlet fire in her hair. "By-the-by, how does the gum answer?"

She forgets to reply to his harmless question, while her eyes fall troubled, half-frightened: the eyes that cannot, without a theft upon a third person, give him back his tender looks—the eyes in whose pupils Brandon is to see himself reflected for the next forty, fifty, sixty years.

There is a little stir and flutter among the company: Belinda Denzil moving to the piano; a music-stool screwed up and down; gloves taken off; then a polite hush, infringed only by a country gentleman in the distance saying something rather loud about guano, while Belinda informs her assembled friends in a faint soprano that "He will return; she knows he will." She has made the same asseveration any time the last ten years; but he has not returned yet, and her relatives begin to be afraid that he never will.

During the song Gerard falls into a reverie. At the end, coming out of it, he asks with an abrupt change of subject: "What did you say the name of your place was?"

53

"Glan-yr-Afon."

"Glan Ravvon?" (following her pronunciation.)

"Yes; you would never guess that it was sounded *Glan Ravvon* if you were to see it written: it is spelt quite differently."

"What does it mean? or does it mean anything?"

"It means 'Bank of the River;' so called, because it is not near the bank of any river."

"What part of the world is it in?—Europe, Asia, Africa, America, or the Polynesian Islands?"

"It is three miles from Naullan, if you are any the wiser."

"Naullan! Naullan!" he repeats, as if trying to overtake a recollection that eludes him. "Of course it does: why I was *at* Naullan once."

"Were you?" (eagerly.) "When?"

"Two years ago; no, three. I was staying in the neighbourhood with some people for fishing. No doubt you know them—the Fitz-Maurices?"

Esther's countenance falls a little. "I—I—have heard of them," she says, uncertainly.

"Why, they must be neighbours of yours."

"They are rather beyond a drive, I think," she replies, doubtfully.

"If you are three miles from Naullan, and they are only four, I don't see how that can be."

She does not answer for a moment, but only furls and unfurls her fan uneasily; then, looking up with a sudden, honest impulse, speaks, colouring up to the eyes the while. "Why should I be ashamed of what there is no reason to be ashamed of? They *are* within calling distance, and I do know them in a way; that is to say, Lady Fitz-Maurice bows to me whenever she recollects that she knows me; but, you see, they are great people, and we are small ones."

He looks thoroughly annoyed. The idea that the woman of his choice is by her own confession not *exactly* on his own level, grates upon his pride.

"Nonsense!" he says, brusquely, "one gentleman is as good as another, all the world over; and it must be the same with ladies."

"St. John, you are wanted to make up a rubber," interrupts Constance, sweeping up to them, resplendent but severe, in green satin and seaweed, like a nineteenth century Nereid, if such an anachronism could exist.

"Am I?" looking rather sulky, and not offering to move.

"We have got one already, but Sir Charles and Mrs. Annesley wish for another.'

"Let them play double-dummy!" settling himself resolutely in his chair, and looking defiantly at her out of his quick, cross eyes.

"Absurd!"

"If you are so anxious to oblige them, why cannot you take a hand yourself?"

"You know how I detest cards!"

"And you know how I detest Mrs. Annesley." (Mrs. Annesley is the vulture of Esther's lively imagination.)

Too dignified to descend to wrangling, Miss Blessington desists, and moves away, casting only one small glance of suppressed resentment at the innocent cause of Mr. Gerard's contumacy.

"How *could* you be so disobliging?" cries Esther, reproachfully, in childish irritation with him at having drawn her into undeserved disgrace.

"Why shouldn't I?" he asks, placidly. "Believe me, it is the worst plan possible to encourage the idea that you are good-natured among your own people; it subjects you to endless impositions. For the last thirty years I have been struggling to establish a character for never doing what I am asked; would you have me undo all my work at one blow?"

"St. John is impracticable," says Constance, returning from her fruitless quest, and stooping over the card-table her golden head and the sea-tang twisted with careless care about it. "You must accept of me as his substitute, please; he is good-naturedly devoting himself to my little friend. Did you happen to notice her, Lady Bolton? She is really looking quite pretty to-night. She does not know anybody, poor child! and he was afraid she might feel neglected."

CHAPTER XV.

The world's life is shorter by a fortnight than it was on that last day I told you of, and during that fortnight the ordinary amount of things have happened. The usual number of people have had their bodies knocked to atoms and their souls into eternity by express trains; the usual number of men and maids have come together in the *Times* column in holy matrimony; and the usual number of unwelcome babies have been consigned to the canals. A great many players have laid down their cards, risen up, and gone away from the game of life; but whether winners or losers, they tell us not, neither shall we know awhile; and other players have taken their places, and have sat down with the zest of ignorance.

"Nature takes no notice of those that are coming or going."

She is briskly occupied at her old business—the business that seems to us so purposeless, progressless, bootless—the making only to unmake; the beautifying only to make hideous; the magnifying only to debase. Oh life! life! Oh clueless labyrinth! Oh answerless riddle!

September is waning mellowly into death, like a holy man to whom an easy passage has been vouchsafed; the land has been noisy with guns, and many partridges have been turned into small bundles of ruffled feathers—little round, brown corpses. Bob Brandon walks stoutly up the furzy hill sides and along the stony levels after the shy, scarce birds; he is out and about all day, but you do not hear him whistling or humming so often as you used to do. "He goeth heavily, as one that mourneth." The fortnight is past, and yet another week, and still Esther holds no speech of returning; her letters have waxed fewer, shorter, colder. Since that first one, mention of Gerard's name is there in them none. Bob is not of a suspicious nature, but he can add two and two together. He has been doing that little dreary sum all the last ten days, till his head aches. But though he can do this sum himself, he will not suffer any one else to do it—at least in his presence.

One day at dinner, when Bessy was beginning a little sour adaptation of the text, "The lust of the flesh, the lust of the eye," &c., to Esther, he interrupted her with downright outspoken anger and rebuke; and, though he apologised to her afterwards, and begged her pardon for having spoken rudely to her, yet she felt that that theme must not be dealt with again. He had promised to love her always in all loyalty, and whether she were loyal or disloyal to him made no difference. He will let no man, woman, or child speak evil of her in his hearing:

".....   love   is   not   love
That   alters   when   it   alteration   finds,
Or bends with the remover to remove."

Jack Craven, too, is beginning to wonder a little when Esther is going to return to the old farmhouse—beginning to feel rather lonely as he sits by himself on the window-ledge of an evening, smoking his pipe, with no one to take it out of his mouth now, and thinking on his unpaid for steam ploughs and sterile mountain-fields, with no one to speak comfortably to him, or console him with sweet illogical logic.

"All is not gold that glitters." Care gets up behind the man, however fine a horse he may be riding. Care is sitting *en croupe* behind Miss Craven, and she cannot unseat him. It strikes her sometimes with a shock of fear that she is succeeding *too* well; that the admiration and liking and love she had hankered so greedily after, had striven unfairly for, had made wicked lightnings from her eyes to obtain, was ready to be poured out lavishly, eagerly, honestly at her feet, and she dare not put out a finger to take them up. She had been walking miles and miles of nights, up and down her bedroom, from door to window, from window to door, when all the rest of the house are abed and asleep.

"What *shall* I do?—what *shall* I do?" she cries out to her own heart, while her hands clasp one another hotly, and the candles, so tall at dressing time, burn short and low. "Oh! if I had some one to advise me!—not that I would take their advice, if it were to give up St. John! Give him up! How can I give up what I have not got? Oh Bob, Bob, if you only knew how I hate you!—Only less than I hate myself! Oh! why was not my tongue cut out before that unlucky day when I said I would *try* to like you? Try, indeed! If there is need for trying, one may know how the trial will end. Shall I tell St. John? What! volunteer an unasked confession? Warn him off Robert's territory when he is not thinking of trespassing? And if I were to tell him—oh Heaven! I had sooner put my hand into a lion's mouth—what *would* he think of me? He, with his fastidious, strict ideas of what a woman should be and do and look? Shall I write and ask Bob to let me off? It would not break his heart; he is too good; only bad people ever break their hearts, as I shall do some day, I dare say. Oh! poor Bob, how badly I am treating you! Poor Bob! and his yellow roses that St. John made such fun of! How I wish that the thoughts of your long legs and your little sour Puritan sisters did not make me feel so sick! Oh! if you would but be good enough to jilt me! What *shall* I do?—what *shall* I do? Wait, wait, go on waiting for what will never come, probably, and when I have degraded myself by waiting till hope is quite dead, go back whence I came, and jig-jog through life alongside of Bob in a poke bonnet like his mamma's. Ah Jack, Jack! why did I ever leave you? How I wish that all Bobs and St. Johns and other worries were at the bottom of the Red Sea, and you and I king and queen of some desert island, where there was nothing nearer humanity than monkeys and macaws, and where there was no rent nor workmen's wages nor lovers to torment us!"

One must go to bed at some time or other, however puzzled and pondering one may be; and in furtherance of this end, Esther, having reached this turn in her reflections, begins to undress. In so doing she misses a locket containing Jack's picture, which she always wears round her neck. She must have dropped it downstairs, where perhaps some housemaid's clumsy foot may tread upon it, and mar the dear, ugly young face within. She must go and look for it, though the clock is striking one. She takes up her candle, and runs lightly downstairs. The gas is out. Great shadows from behind come up alongside, and then stretch ahead of her; the statues glimmer ghostly chill from their dark pedestals. With a shock of frightened surprise she sees a stream of light issuing through the half-open door of the morning-room. Is it burglars, or are the flowers giving a ball, as in Andersen's fair, fanciful tale? She creeps gently up, and peeps in. The lamp still burns on the centre table, and pacing up and down, up and down, as she has been doing overhead, is a man buried in deepest thought. Fear gives place to a great, pleasant shyness. "I—I—I have lost my locket," she stammers.

He gives a tremendous start. "You up still!" he says, in astonishment. "Lost your locket, have you? Oh! by-the-by, I found it just now; here it is. Do you know (with a smile) I could not resist the temptation of looking to see who you had got inside it. Are you very angry?"

"Very!" she answers, drooping her eyes under his. She could sit and stare into Bob's eyes by the hour together, if she liked, only that it would be rather a dull amusement; with St. John it is different.

"Don't go; stay and talk a minute. It is so pleasant to think that we are the only conscious, sentient beings in the house—all the others sleeping like so many pigs," he says, coming over to her with an excited look on his face, such as calm, slow-pulsed English gentlemen are not wont to wear.

"No, no, I cannot—I must not."

She has taken the bracelets off her arms, and the rose from her hair: there she stands in her ripe, fresh beauty, with only the night and St. John to look at her.

"Five minutes," he says, with pleading humility, but putting his back against the door as he speaks.

"If you *prevent* my going, of course I cannot help myself," she answers, putting on a little air of offended dignity to hide her tremulous embarrassment.

"Don't be offended! Do you know" (leaving his post of defence to follow her)—"do you know what I have been doing ever since you went—*not* to bed apparently?"

"Drinking brandy and soda-water, probably" (looking rather surly, and affecting to yawn).

"That would have been hardly worth mentioning. I have been wondering whether my luck is on the turn. I have been da——I mean very unlucky all my life. I never put any money on a horse that he was not sure to be nowhere. Luck does turn, sometimes, doesn't it? Do you think mine is turning?"

"How can I tell?"

"You don't ask in what way I have been so unlucky. Why don't you? Have you no curiosity?"

"I never like to seem inquisitive," answers Esther, coldly, hoping that he does not notice how the white hands that lie on her lap are trembling.

"Do you recollect my telling you that I had made a great fool of myself once?"

"Yes."

"Do you care to hear about it, or do you not?" pulling at his drooping moustache, in some irritation at her feigned indifference.

"Yes, I care," she answers, lighting up an eager, mobile face—fear, shyness, and the sense of the impropriety of the situation all ceding to strong curiosity.

"Well, it was about a woman, of course. *Cela va sans dire;* a man never can get into a scrape without a woman to help him, any more than he can be born, or learn his A B C."

"Was she handsome?" looking up, and speaking quickly.

That is always the first question a woman asks about a rival. I do not know why, I am sure, as many of the greatest mischiefs that have been done on earth have been done by ugly women. Rousseau's Madame d'Houdetot squinted ferociously.

"Pretty well. She had a thundering good figure, and knew how to use her eyes. By-the-by" (with an anxious discontent in his tone), "so do you. I often wish you did not; I hate being able to trace one point of resemblance between you and her."

"Did she refuse you?" asks Esther, hastily, too anxious for the sequel of the story to think of resenting the accusation made against her eyes.

"Not she! I should not have been the one to blame her if she had; one cannot quarrel with people for their tastes. She swore she liked me better than any one else in the world; that she would go down to Erebus with me, be flayed alive for me—all the protestations usual in such cases, in fact, I suppose," he ends bitterly.

"And threw you over?" says Essie, leaning forward with lips half apart, and her breast rising and falling in short, quick undulations.

"Exactly; had meant nothing else all along. I filled only the pleasant and honourable situation of decoy duck to lure on shyer game, and when the bird was limed—such a bird, too! a great, heavy, haw-haw brute in the Carabineers, with a face like a horse—she pitched me away as coolly as you would pitch an old shoe—or as you would pitch *me*, I dare say, if you had the chance."

"And what did you do?" asks Essie, breathlessly, her great eyes, black as death, fastened on his face.

St. John smiles—a smile half fierce, half amused.

"Run him through the body, do you suppose?—spitted him like a lark or a woodcock?—cut out his heart and made her eat it, as the man did to his wife in that fine old Norman story? No; I could have done any of them with pleasure if I had had the chance; with all our veneering and French polish, I think the tiger is only half dead in any of us; but I did not; I did none of them: I—prepare for bathos, please—I went out hunting; it was in winter, and, as misfortunes never come singly, I staked one of the best horses I ever was outside of: that diverted the current of my grief a little, I think."

He speaks in a jeering, bantering tone, scourging himself with the rod of his own ridicule, as men are apt to do when they are conscious of having made signal asses of themselves in order to be beforehand with the world.

"And she told you she was fond of you?" ejaculates Essie, raising her sweet face, sympathetic, indignant, glowing, towards him.

"Scores of times—swore it. I suppose it is no harder to tell a lie a hundred times than once; *ce n'est que le premier pas qui coûte*. Tell me," he says, vehemently, leaning over her, and taking hold of her hand, as if hardly conscious of what he was doing—"you are a woman, you must know—tell me, is there no difference between truth and lies? have they both *exactly* the same face? How is a man to tell them apart?"

They are both speaking in a low key, almost under their breath, for fear of drawing down upon themselves the apparition of Sir Thomas in *déshabille* and a blunderbuss. Their faces are close together; she can see the lines that climate and grief and passion have drawn about his eyes and mouth—can see the wild, honest anxiety looking through his soul's clear windows.

"I—I—don't know," she answers, stammering, and shivering a little, half with fear at his vehemence, half with the strong contagion of his passion.

"Do you ever tell untruths?" he asks, hurriedly, scanning her face with anxious eyes, that try to look through the mask of fair, white flesh, and see the heart underneath. "Don't be angry with me, but I sometimes fancy that you might."

"*I!* what do you mean?" snatching away her hand, and the angry blood rushing headlong to her cheeks.

"Is thy servant a dog that he should do this thing?" Hazael was only the first of a long string who have asked that virtuously irate question.

His countenance clears a little. "You must forgive me," he says, repentantly. "I suppose it is my own unlucky experience that has made me so suspicious; because my own day has been cloudy, I have wisely concluded upon the non-existence of the sun. But, come" (smiling a little), "one good turn deserves another: have you nothing to tell me in return for the long list of successes I have been confiding to you?"

He watches her changing, flushing, paling face, with a keen solicitude which surprises himself. What can this downy, baby-faced rustic have to confess? Now for Bob! Now is the time—now or never! Sing, oh goddess, the destructive wrath of St. John, the son of Thomas! What time, place, situation, can be suitabler for such a tale? It is an hour and a half past midnight; they love one another madly, and they are alone.

Are they alone, though? Is this one of the statues stepped down from its pedestal in the hall that is coming in at the door, severely, chilly, fair, with a candle in its hand?

"Miss Craven!" ejaculates Constance (for it is she), stopping suddenly short, while a look of surprised displeasure ripples over her calm, smooth face.

Silence for a second on the part of everybody.

"It is a pity, St. John," says Miss Blessington, drawing herself up, and looking an impersonation of rigid, aggressive, pitiless virtue, "that you and Miss Craven should choose such a very unseasonable time for your interviews; it is not a very good example for the servants, if any of them should happen to find you here."

"The servants have something better to do than to come prying and eavesdropping upon their betters," retorts St. John, flushing angry-red to the roots of his hair, and not taking the most conciliatory line of defence.

"You are mistaken if you think I have been eavesdropping," says Constance, with dignified composure, her grave face looking out chastely cold from the down-fallen veil of her yellow hair. "I could not sleep, and came down to look for a book. Pray don't let me disturb your *tête-à-tête!*" making a movement towards going.

"Don't be a fool, Conny!" cries St. John, hastily, in bitter fear of having compromised Esther by his ill-advised detention of her: "it is the purest accident your having found Miss Craven and me together here!"

"I am well aware of that," she answers, with a little smiling sneer.

"You know what I mean, perfectly well: it is the purest accident our *being* here. Miss Craven lost her locket, and——"

"And" (smiling still)—"and you have been helping her to look for it. Yes, I see. Well, I—hope you will find it. Good-night!" going out and closing the door behind her.

"What did she say?—what does she mean?" cries Essie, panting, and with a face hardly less white than her dress.

"What does it matter what she means? She's a fool!" answers St. John, wrathfully. "Go to bed, and don't think about her; who cares?"

But he looks as if he did care a good deal.

CHAPTER XVI.

The weekly clearance of mundane books has been made at Plas Berwyn; the skimp drab gowns, and the ill-made frock coat, whose flaps lap over one another so painfully behind, have been endured by the Misses Brandon and their brother respectively. At church has been all the Brandon household: son and daughters, man-servant and maid-servant, ox and sheep, camel and ass. I need hardly say that the last quartette have been introduced merely for the sake of euphony, and to give a fuller rhythm to the close of the sentence. The Misses Brandon always stand as stiff as pokers during the creed, with their backs to the altar. It amuses them, and it does not do anybody else any harm, so why should not they, poor women? Bob truckles to the Scarlet Woman; he bows, and turns his honest, serious face to the east. The service is in Welsh, of which he does not understand a word. He can pick his way pretty well through the prayers, however, by the help of a Welsh and English prayer book. There are several landmarks that he knows, whose friendly faces beam upon him now and again when he is beginning to flounder hopelessly among uncouth words of seven consonants and a vowel. These are his chief finger-posts: "Gogoniant ir Tad, ac ir Mab, ac ir Yspryd Glan;" that is, "Glory be to the Father, and to the Son, and to the Holy Ghost." "Gwared ni, Arglywd daionus!" "Good Lord, deliver us!" "Na Ladratta!" "Thou shalt not steal!"

Jack Craven has been to church too, and has, as he always does, been reading the inscriptions on the coffin-plates, nailed up, Welsh fashion, against the dilapidated, whitewashed walls, in lieu of monumental tablets. Esther has also been to church; has been in state in a great, close carriage, in company with Sir Thomas, Miladi, and Miss Blessington. Sir Thomas has been storming the whole way about a gap he detected in a hedge that they passed, through which some cattle have broken, so that they all arrive at the church door in that calmly devout state of quietude which is the fittest frame of mind for the reception of Divine truth.

The Gerard pew in Felton church is as large as a moderate-sized room, and is furnished with arm-chairs and a fire-place. In winter, Sir Thomas spends fully half the service time in poking the fire noisily and raking out the ashes. There is no fire now, and he misses it. A high red curtain runs round the sacred enclosure, and through it the farmers' wives and daughters strain their eyes to catch a glimpse of Miladi's marabout feathers, and Miss Blessington's big, golden chignon, and little green aerophane bonnet. St. John generally pulls the brass rings of his bit of curtain aside along the brass rods, to make a peep-hole for himself over the congregation. The shape and size of the pew do away with the necessity for any wearisome conformity of attitude among the inmates. During the prayers, Sir Thomas stands bolt upright, with one bent knee resting on his chair; his bristling grey head, shaggy brows, and fierce spectacles looming above the red curtain, to the admiration and terror of the row of little charity girls beneath. Constance kneels forward on a hassock, with a large, ivory prayer book, gold-crossed, red-edged, in one hand, and a turquoise and gold-topped double scent-bottle and cobweb cambric handkerchief in the other. She confesses in confidence to her pale lavender gloves that she has done that which she ought not to have done, and has left undone that which she ought to have done; making graceful little salaams and undulations of head and body every two minutes. Miladi confesses that she has gone to sleep. St. John makes no pretence of kneeling at all: he leans, elbow on knee and head on hand, and looks broken-hearted, as men have a way of doing in church.

In the afternoon, no one at Felton thinks of attending Divine service. It is a fiat of Sir Thomas's that no carriage, horses, or servants are to be taken out more than once a day, and the two miles' walk is an insuperable impediment to Lady Gerard, and hardly less so to Constance.

After luncheon the three ladies are sitting in the garden, with the prospect of four unbroken hours of each other's companionship before them. Masses of calceolarias, geraniums, lobelias, are flaring and flaunting around them—masses in which the perverted eye of modern horticulture sees its ideal of beauty. Nature, in her gardening, never plants great, gaudy squares and ovals and rounds of red and blue and yellow, without many shades of tenderest grey and green to soften and relieve them. Across the grass St. John comes lounging; his Sunday frock coat sitting creaseless to his spare, sinewy figure. Esther hates the sight of that coat: it reminds her so painfully, by its very unlikeness, of the singular garment that forms the head and crown of her betrothed's scant wardrobe.

"Do you know, I have half a mind to go to Radley church this afternoon. Will any one come with me?—will you, Conny?" turning, mindful of last night, with a conciliatory smile to Miss Blessington.

"How far is it?" she asks, indolently, divided between her hatred of walking and her desire to frustrate the *tête-à-tête* she sees impending between St. John and Esther.

"Three or four miles; four, I suppose."

She lifts her large blue eyes languidly, "Four miles there, and four miles back! Are you mad, St. John? What do you suppose one is made of?"

"Will *you* take pity on me then, Miss Craven?" turning eagerly to Esther.

She tilts her hat low down over her little, straight, Greek nose, looks up at him with shy coquetry under the brim, but answers not.

"A man who delights in solitude must be either a wild beast or a god, don't you know? I have no pretence to be either: I hate my own society cordially. Come" (with a persuasive ring in his pleasant voice); "you had much better."

"Don't be so absurd, St. John!" cries Miss Blessington, pettishly. "Miss Craven would far rather be left in peace."

"Would you?" (appealing to her.)

"No—o; that is—I mean—I think I should like the walk, if I may. May I, Lady Gerard? do you mind?" (turning sweet red cheeks and quick eyes towards her hostess.)

"I, my dear! Why should I mind?" responds Miladi, leaning back and fanning herself with a large fan (I believe that fat women often suffer a foretaste of the torments of the damned in the matter of heat)—"so as you don't ask me to go with you (with a fat smile). And, St. John, be sure that you are back in time for dinner, there's a good boy! You know what a fuss Sir Thomas is always in on Sunday evening?"

"I know that Sir Thomas is digging his grave with his teeth as fast as he can," answers St. John disrespectfully.

"Shall not we be rather late for church if we have four miles to go?" asks Esther, as she steps out briskly beside her companion, while heart and conscience keep up a quarrelsome dialogue within her.

"It is not four miles; it is only three."

"You told Miss Blessington four?"

"So I did; but I drew for the extra mile upon the rich stores of my imagination."

"Why did you?" she asks, turning a wondering rosy face set in the frame of a minute white bonnet towards him.

"Did you ever hear of the invitations that the Chinese give one another?" he asks, laughing, and switching off a fern-head with a baby umbrella—"which, however pressing they may be, are always expected by the giver to be declined. My invitation to Conny was a Chinese one: I was not quite sure that she would understand it as such, and I was so afraid that she would yield to my importunities, that I had to embroider a little in the matter of distance; do you see?"

There has been rain in the morning; now the clouds have rent themselves asunder, and broken up into great glistering rocks, peaks, and spires, such as no fuller on earth could white:

"Blue isles of heaven laugh between."

The breeze comes more freshly over the wet grasses and flowers, and blows in little fickle puffs against St. John's bronzed cheeks and Esther's carnation ones. The girl's heart is pulsing with a keen, sharp joy; all the keener, as the heaven's blue is deeper for the clouds that hover about it.

"I shall have him all to myself for three hours," she is saying inwardly; "he will speak to no one but me; he will hear no one else's voice (she forgets the parson and the clerk). Surely Bob may spare me these three hours, and just a few more, out of the great long life during which I shall tramp-tramp at his side! Three hours:

59

> "Then   let   come   what   come   may
> No   matter   if   I   go   mad,
> I shall have had my day."

"Let me carry your prayer book?"

"No, thanks; it is not heavy" (retaining it, mindful of a certain inscription in the fly-leaf).

"I am like a retriever; I like to have something to carry" (taking it from her with gentle violence).

"'*Esther Craven* from *Robert Brandon*.' Who *is* Robert Brandon when he is at home?" (speaking rather shortly.)

Esther's heart leaps into her mouth. Shall she tell him *now*, this minute, without giving herself time for second thoughts, which are not by any means always best? Shall she lift off the weight of compunction, anxiety, shame, that has been pressing upon her for the last fortnight?— let it fall down, as the dead albatross fell from the Ancient Mariner's neck—

"Like lead into the sea?"

The subject has introduced itself naturally, easily, without any of the dragging in by the head and shoulders of the officiously-volunteered confessions that she had salved her conscience by deprecating. Shall she, with strong, brave hand, push away all hope of the fine house and the broad lands, of the carriages and horses, the roses and pine-apples, the down pillows and fragrances of life? Shall she courageously, nobly, and yet in mere bare duty, turn away from the fairy prince and return to her hovel and scullionship? Shall she, or shall she not?

"Who *is* Robert Brandon?" repeats St. John, rather crossly.

In the second that follows Esther's life destiny is settled. She refuses the good and chooses the evil. ("He is the man I am engaged to," that is what she ought to have said.)

"He is in the ——th foot." This is what she does say, blushing till the tears come into her eyes, turning away her head, and feeling stabbed through and through with shame.

"An ally of yours?" (quickly.)

"I have known him all my life," she answers, evasively.

"I thought he was a very young child, from this specimen of his caligraphy," remarks Gerard, superciliously, examining Bob's sprawly, slanty characters. "He would be none the worse for a few writing lessons."

Esther is a mean young woman: she feels ashamed of her poor lover, and his pothooks and hangers, and yet vexed with St. John for sneering at them.

"It was a fact worth inscribing, I must say," continues he, ironically—"the making of such a very handsome present," holding the poor little volume between his lavender kid finger and thumb, and surveying it with a disparaging smile. "He must have had a great deal of change out of sixpence, I should think."

"If you have nothing better to do than abuse my property," cries Esther, impulsively, snatching it out of his hand, "you may give it me back," looking half disposed to whimper.

"I apologise," responds St. John, gravely. "I did not mean to offend you; I give you *carte blanche* to insult mine" (holding out a very minute Russia leather one). "But may I ask, is Mr. Robert Blandon, or Brandon, or what's his name, your godfather?"

"No; why?"

"Because I never heard of any one being given a prayer book except as a wedding present, or by their godfathers and godmothers at their baptism. As you are not married, I know it could not have been the first case, and so I concluded it must be the last."

"Robert is not old enough to be my godfather," says Essie, overcoming by a great effort the repugnance to pronouncing the fateful name: "he is quite young; a great deal younger than you," she ends, rather spitefully.

"He might easily be that," replies St. John, coldly. "Once, not so very many years ago, in whatever company I was, I always was the youngest present; now, on the contrary, in whatever company I am, I always feel the eldest present. I don't suppose I always am, but I always feel as if I were."

"I believe old people have the best of it, after all," says Esther, recovering a little of her equanimity: "they have certainly fewer troubles than young ones. I should say that Sir Thomas was decidedly a happier man than you are."

"A man's happiness is proportioned to the simplicity of his tastes, I suppose," answers St. John, sardonically. "Sir Thomas's happiness lies in a nutshell: he has two ruling passions—eating and bullying; he has a very fair cook to satisfy the one, and my mother always at hand for the gratification of the other."

"We have all our ruling passions," rejoins Esther, with a light laugh, "only very often we will not own them. Mine is burnt almonds; what is yours?"

"Going to church," he replies, in the same tone; "as you may perceive by the strenuous efforts I have made to get there this afternoon."

Radley church stands on a knoll. Radley parishioners have to go upwards to be buried—a happy omen, it is to be hoped, for the destination of their souls. The church has a little grey tower, pretty, old, and squat, and a peal of bells—these are its claim to distinction—a merry peal, as people say; but to me it seems that in all the gamut of sad sounds there is nothing sadder, sorrowfuller, than bells chiming out sweetly and solemnly across the summer air.

Rung in by the grave music of their invitation, St. John and Esther enter. Verger or pew-opener is there none, so they slip into the first of the open sittings that presents itself. The clergyman is young and energetic: he has rooted up the tall, worm-eaten, oak pews—disfiguring compromises between cattle-pen and witness-box—has clothed several

"Dear   little   souls
In nice white stoles,—"

and is trying to teach himself intoning. He produces at present only prolonged whining groans, but it is a step in the right direction.

Rest is good after exertion, and so Essie thinks. The south wind has been playing tricks with the dusk riches of her hair. Nature has been laying on her bistre under the great liquid eyes, and emptying a whole potful of her rouge on the rose velvet round of her cheeks. She is not in apple-pie order at all, and yet

"She   was   most   beautiful   to   see,
Like a lady from a far countree."

If Esther were to murder any one, and her guilt were to be brought home to her as plainly as the eye of day shines in the sky at noon, judge and jury would combine to acquit her.

"Blessed be God, who has made beautiful women!" says the Bedouin, and Gerard echoes the benediction, as he stands with his big lavender thumb on one side of the hymn book, and her small, lavender thumb on the other, while the "dear little souls" are singing sweetly and quickly:

"There   God   for   ever   sitteth,
Himself   of   all   the   Crown;
The   Lamb,   the   Light   that   shineth,
And goeth never down."

Grand words, that make one feel almost good and almost happy merely to say them!

There is only one hymn-book in the pew, and St. John is glad of it. There is something pleasant in the sense of union and partnership, though it be only a three minutes' partnership in a dog's-eared psalter.

"Is not there some different way of going home?" asks Essie, as they stand side by side, after service, in the high churchyard, looking down on the straggling damson trees, the grey smoke spiring northwards under the south wind's faint blowing, the dark-blue green of the turnip fields. "I hate going back the same way one came; it shows such a want of invention!"

"There is another way," answers St. John, scooping out a little plump green moss from a chink in the wall with the point of his umbrella, while the parson and the parson's sister, on their homeward way, turn their heads to look at them—the parson at Esther, the parson's sister at St. John—Jack at Jill, and Jill at Jack as is the way of the world; "but it is a good deal longer and a great deal muddier than the one we came by."

"I like mud," says Essie, gaily, stooping and picking a daisy from a little child's grave at her feet; "it is my native element; at home we are up to our knees in mud in winter, and over our ankles in summer."

So they chose the longer and the muddier way. It is its length that is its recommendation to them both, I think.

Down the village street, past the Loggerheads and the Forge, and along a long country lane, paved unevenly with round stones after a way our forefathers in some of the northern counties had of paving, in imperfect prophetic vision of MacAdam. To-day no broad waggon-wheel groans, nor hoofed foot clatters along; only a few cottagers and smart-bonneted servant girls trudge along to the Primitive Wesleyan Methodist Chapel, built A.D. 1789, that stands in simple, dissenting ugliness at the hill-foot, while over its newly-painted, gingerbread-coloured door stands this modest announcement: "This is the Gate of Heaven."

"It strikes me," says St. John, rousing himself out of a reverie which has lasted a quarter of an hour—"it strikes me as one of the few instances in which one's experience tallies with what one reads in novels, the awkward knack people have of interrupting one at the wrong moment."

"How do you mean?" asks Essie, coming out of a reverie, too.

"I never," pursues he, taking off his hat, and passing his hand over the broad red mark it has made on his forehead—"I never read aloud to any one in my life—I was rather fond of reading poetry at one period of my history, I leave you to guess which—not that she cared about

61

it—she did not know Milton from Tommy Moore; but I never read to her in the course of my life without the footman coming in to put coals on at the most affecting passages—Arthur's parting from Guinevere, say, or Medora's death—and clattering down the tongs and shovel, making the devil's own row."

Esther laughs.

"These reflections are *à propos* of—what?"

"Of Conny's most ill-timed entry last night," he answers, with energy. "I don't suppose she makes such a midnight raid once in five years, and she certainly could not have found you and me *tête-à-tête* at two in the morning more than once in fifty years. Why could not she leave us in peace that once? We did not grudge her any amount of pleasant dreams; why need she grudge us our pleasant wakefulness?"

"Do you think she came on purpose, then?" asks Essie, her eyes opening as round in alarmed surprise as a baby's when a grown-up person makes ugly faces at it.

He shrugs his shoulders slightly. "Cannot say, I'm sure. Conny is not much in the habit of burning the midnight oil in the pursuit of knowledge generally. If it *was* accident, she came in at a wonderfully *à propos*, or rather *mal à propos*, moment. Tell me," he says, crossing over to her side of the road, and fixing frankly-asking eyes upon her; "I may be mistaken—it is a misfortune to which I am often incident—but I could not help thinking that, just as that unlucky candle appeared round the corner last night, you were going to tell me something—something about yourself? I thought I saw it in your face. I think I deserved some little reward for raking up for your behoof the ashes of that old fire that I burnt my fingers at so badly once."

Esther still remains silent, but turns her long neck from one side to the other with a restless, uneasy motion.

"Are lamplight and the small hours indispensable accessories?" he asks, with gentle pleading in look and words—"or could not you tell me as well now?"

"Tell you what?" she says, turning round sharp upon him, and snapping, as a little cross dog snaps at the heels of the passer-by—"must I invent something?"

"Are you sure that it is *necessary* to invent?" he asks, scanning the fair, troubled face with searching gaze.

She pulls a bunch of nuts out of the hedge from among their rough-ribbed green leaves, and begins to pick them out of their sheath. "What am I to tell you?" she says, petulantly, a suspicion that he may have heard a rumour of her engagement crossing her mind: "that I live in an old farmhouse with my brother Jack, and that we are very hard up—you know already; that 'Su dry da chi' is Welsh for 'How do you do?' and that our asparagus has answered very badly this year?"

"Of course, I cannot force your confidence," he answers, rather coldly.

"Why do you insist upon my having something to confide? What reason have you for supposing that I have?" she cries, with increased irritation.

"None whatever, but what you yourself have given me!"

"*I!*"

"Yes, *you;* not your words, but your face now and then. Don't think me impertinent. You know what unhappy reason I have had to be suspicious. But tell me" (trying his best to get a look round the corner into the averted, perturbed face of his companion)—"tell me whether there is not something between you and—and—that fellow that gave you the prayer-book?"

Esther's heart gives one great bounding throb; the thin muslin of her dress but poorly conceals its hard, quick pulsings.

One more chance for her! Fate generally gives us two or three chances before it allows us to consign ourselves irrecoverably to the dogs. One more choice between loyalty and disloyalty—a plain question, to be answered plainly, unequivocally—Yes or No; Robert or St. John. The man whose conversation bores her, whose proximity and whose gaze leave her colder than snow on an alp's high top an hour before sunrise, and with whom she has promised to live till death do them part; or the man, no whit better or handsomer, whose coming, felt, though unseen, makes her whole frame vibrate, as a harp's strings vibrate under the player's hands—beneath whose eyes hers sink down bashful, yet passionate—the man whom, after this week, she must see never again until death do them unite. Woman-like, she tries to avoid the alternative.

"What is that to you?" she retorts, abruptly, endeavouring to be playful, and succeeding only in being rude.

"Nothing whatever," he replies, flushing angrily; and then they walk on for some distance in silence.

"Are you angry?" asks Esther, presently, with a smile, half saucy, half frightened.

"*I?* not in the least," he replies, with an air of ostentatious indifference, but with a complexion undoubtedly florider than nature made his.

"You look excessively cross, and have not uttered a word for the last half mile," she says, pouting out her full red under-lip, and then looking (a little alarmed at her own audacity) to see in what spirit he takes her impertinence.

"When I do not get civil answers to civil questions, I think it best to hold my tongue," he says, stalking along with his head up, and hitting viciously with his umbrella at the tall, yellow mulleins in the hedge.

"People's ideas differ as to what *are* civil questions," says Essie, trying to stalk too, and to elevate nose and chin in emulation of his. "Suppose that I had asked you how many times you had been refused, would you have answered me?"

"Undoubtedly I should," he replies, gravely.

"How many times have you?" she asks, coming down from her elevation of offended dignity with a jump, and looking up at him with naïve, eager curiosity.

"Questions should be answered in the order of priority in which they are asked," he replies, with a smile of amusement at her simplicity, but with a good deal of dissatisfied doubt underlying the smile. "Answer my question, and I'll answer yours."

Esther turns away, and passes her hand along the hedge, catching idly at any grasses or flowers that come in her way, to the great detriment of her Sunday gloves. His anxiety overcomes his hurt pride.

"Give me an answer one way or another," he says, breathing rather short. "Is there not something between you and him?"

Esther is silent. "No" is a plain downright lie, at which conscience demurs, and "Yes" a cannon-ball that will knock her away from St. John's side out into the drear, great world for ever.

"For God's sake answer me!" he says again, in great agitation at a dumbness that seems to him ominous.

Hearing the sharp pain and angry fear in his voice, she hesitates no longer. Lie or no lie, she takes the plunge.

"Nothing!" she says, faintly, turning first milk-white, then red as a rose in her burning prime.

"Why do you turn away your face? Are you quite certain?" he asks, quickly, only half convinced by her weak negation.

"Certain," she replies, indistinctly, as if just able to echo his words, but not to frame any of her own.

"Why do you stammer and blush, then, whenever his name is mentioned?" he asks, with jealous impatience.

"I won't stand being catechised in this way," she cries, blazing out angrily, and stopping short, while sparks of fire, half quenched in tears of vexation, dart from the splendid night of her eyes. "I have answered a question which you ought never to have asked; you must be a person of very little observation," she continues, sharply, "not to have discovered during the three weeks that I have been with you that I blush at everything and nothing; I should be as likely as not to blush when Sir Thomas's name was mentioned, or—or——"

"Or mine," suggests St. John, ironically; "put it as strongly as you can."

"Or yours, if you like," she answers, hardily, but crimsoning painfully meanwhile in confirmation of her words.

At a little distance farther on, their path forsakes the road and leads across a line of grass fields. St. John crosses the first stile, and waits politely on the other side to help Esther over.

"No, no!" she cries, petulantly, withdrawing her foot from the first rung—"I hate being helped over stiles. Go on, please."

He obeys, and walks on. Her dignity does not allow her to hurry her pace to overtake him, nor does his permit him to slacken his steps till she come up with him; and they walk on in single file, goose-fashion, through two fields and a half.

Dividing and watering the third field, as the four ancient rivers divided and watered the rose gardens and asphodel fields of Paradise, a little beck, with many turns and bends and doublings back upon itself, strays babbling, like a silver ribbon twisted among the meadow's green hair. It is not like the Welsh brooks, fretful and brawling, making little waterfalls and whirlpools and eddies over and about every water-worn stone; smoothly it flows on, as a holy, eventless life flows towards the broad sea whose tides wash the shores of Time. In dry weather it is slow-paced enough, and crystal clear; now the late heavy rains have quickened its current, and rolled it along, turbid and muddy. Even though swollen, however, it is still but a narrow thread, and St. John clears it at a jump.

"Shall I go on still?" he asks, with a malicious smile from the other side, addressing Esther, who stands looking down rather ruefully at the quick, brown water at her feet.

63

"I believe you knew of this, and brought me here on purpose to make a fool of me," she cries, reproachfully.

"I did nothing of the kind," he answers, quietly. "Last time I was here there was a plank thrown across; but you see the stream has been higher than it is now" (pointing to the drenched grass and little deposit of sticks and leaves on the bank), "and has probably carried it away."

"How *am* I to get over?" she asks, hopelessly, with a look of childish distress on her face.

"I'll carry you," he answers, springing back to her side; "the brook is shallower farther down; I can lift you over with the greatest ease imaginable."

"*That* you shan't!" answers Esther, civilly turning her back upon him.

"May I ask why?" he asks, coolly. "After the number of times I have carried you up and down stairs at Felton, you can hardly be afraid of my letting you fall?"

"The very fact of my having already had so many obligations to you makes me resolved not to add to their number," she replies, stiffly, with an effort to look dignified, which her laughing, *débonnaire*, seductive style of beauty renders peculiarly unsuccessful.

"If you can suggest any better plan, I shall be delighted to assist you in carrying it out," rejoins he, smothering a smile.

"I'll jump!" she says, desperately, eyeing meanwhile the hurrying stream and space between bank and bank with calculating look.

"You cannot," he cries, hastily; "you'll get a ducking as sure as I stand here. Don't be so silly!"

The word "silly" acts as a whip and spur to Essie's flagging courage. She retreats a few yards from the edge, in order to get a little run to give her a better spring.

"As headstrong as an allegory on the banks of the Nile!" remarks Gerard, resignedly, quoting Mrs. Malaprop and folding his arms.

Neither the preparatory run, nor the tremendous bound she takes, avail to save Miss Craven from the fate which her obstinacy and the comparative shortness of her legs render unavoidable. She jumps short, and falls forward on the wet bank; her lavender kid gloves digging convulsively into it, and her legs disporting themselves fish-like in the brook.

He is at her side in an instant, raises gently and lifts her on to the grass, unmindful of the pollution caused to his coat by the muddy contact.

"What a fool I was!" she cries, passionately, sinking down among a grove of huge burdock leaves, smothered in shame and angry blushes.

St. John thinks it rude to disagree with her, so holds his peace.

"Why don't you laugh at me? why don't you jeer me?" she continues, vehemently; "why don't you tell me you are very glad of it, and that I richly deserve it, as I see you are longing to do? Anything would be better than standing there like a stock or a stone!"

"It is not of much consequence how I stand or how I look," he replies, coldly. "It would be more to the purpose to know how you are to get home!"

"I will walk as I am," she cries impulsively, springing to her feet; "it will be a fit penance for my idiocy, and you shall go on ahead. I don't want you to be disgraced by being seen in company with such an object."

"That is very probable, isn't it?" he answers, laughing good-humouredly. "No, I have a better proposition than that, I think. It has just occurred to me that an old servant of ours lives at no great distance from here, her cottage is not more than three or four fields off. If you can manage to get there she would dry your clothes for you in a minute."

Rendered docile by her late disaster, feeling very small, and hanging her head, Esther acquiesces. Her gown, from which every particle of starch or stiffness has fled, clings to her limbs and defines their form; the water drips down from her in a thousand little spouts and rivulets: bang, bang, go her soaked petticoats against her ankles at every step she takes.

"You have had almost enough of taking me out to walk, I expect," she remarks presently, rather grimly.

"You have had almost enough of jumping brooks, I expect," he retorts, drily; and then they walk on in silence till they reach a little whitewashed cottage, with its slip of potato ground and plot of pinks and marigolds and lark-spurs—an oasis of tilled ground among the wilderness of pasturage.

St. John knocks at the half-open door and puts his head in. "Are you at home, Mrs. Brown? How are you?" says he, in that frank, friendly voice that goes far to make the Felton tenants wish that Sir St. John reigned in Sir Thomas's stead.

"Quite well, thank you, Mr. St. John; I hope I see you the same," replies the person addressed, coming to the door with a jolly red face and a voluminous widow's cap that contradict one another; "it's a long time since we've seen you come our way."

"So it is, Mrs. Brown; but, you see, I have been after the partridges."

64

"And Sir Thomas, I hope he keeps pretty well, Mr. St. John?"

"Yes, thanks."

"And Miladi, I hope she has her health."

"Yes, thanks."

"And Miss Bl——?"

"Yes, thanks," interrupts St. John, rather impatiently, breaking through the thread of her interrogatories. "Do you see, Mrs. Brown, that this young lady has met with an accident: she has tumbled into the brook. Do you think you could let her dry herself at your fire a bit?"

"Eh dear, Miss, you *are* in a mess!" ejaculates Mrs. Brown, walking round Esther, and surveying her curiously, as she stands close behind Gerard, dripping still, with a hang-dog air and chattering teeth. "Why, you have not a dry stitch upon you; you are one *mask* of mud! Would you please to step in?"

Mrs. Brown and Essie retire into an inner chamber for the purpose of removing the wet clothes and replacing them temporarily with some of the contents of Mrs. Brown's wardrobe.

St. John remains in the outer room, looks at the clock, behind whose dial-plate a round china-moon-face peeps out; takes up the mugs on the dresser: "For a Good Boy," "A Keepsake from Melford," "A Present from Manchester," hiding amongst numberless gilt flourishes; chivies the tabby cat; counts the flitches of bacon hanging from the rafters; walks to the door, and watches the bees crawling in and out of the low door of their straw houses, and the maroon velvet nasturtiums trailing along the borders, and lifting their round leaves and dark faces up to the knees of the standard rose.

As he so stands, whistling softly and musing, some one joins him in the doorway. He turns and beholds Esther, bashful, shame-faced, metamorphosed. To Mrs. Brown's surprise, she has declined the magnanimous offer of her best black silk. There is nothing coquettish or picturesque, as she is aware, about an ill-made dress that tries to follow the fashion and fails—destined, too, for a woman treble her size. She has chosen in preference, a short, dark, linsey petticoat and lilac cotton bedgown, which, by its looseness, can adapt itself to the round slenderness of her tall, lissom figure. Her bonnet was not included in the ruin of her other garments, but she has taken it off, as destructive to the harmony of her costume.

St. John surveys her for some moments: looks upward from petticoat to bedgown, and downward from bedgown to petticoat, but observes a discreet silence.

"Does it become me?" she asks at last, with shy vanity. "Why do not you say something?"

"I have been so unlucky in two or three of my remarks lately," replies he, with a concluding glance at the round, bare arms that emerge whitely from the short cotton sleeves, "that I have become chary of making any more."

"You need not be afraid of offending me by telling me that it is unbecoming," she says, gravely—"quite the contrary!"—she continues rather discontentedly—"think that it suits me *too well*, as if it were a dress that I ought to have been born to. Upon Miss Blessington now such a costume would look utterly incongruous."

St. John bursts out laughing. "A goddess in a bedgown! Diana of the Ephesians in a linsey petticoat! Perish the thought!"

Esther looks mortified, and turns away.

The cleansing of Miss Craven's garments is a lengthy operation. Mrs. Brown retreats into her back kitchen, draws forward a washtub, kneels down beside it, turns up her sleeves, and with much splashing of hot water and s lathering of soap, rubs and scrubs, wrings out, dries, and irons the luckless gown and petticoat.

It is latish and duskish by the time that St. John and his companion set out on their homeward way. Two or three starflowers have already stolen out, and are blossoming, infinitely distant, in the meadows of the sky. They are not loquacious: it is the little shallow rivulet that brawls; the great deep river runs still. Silently they walk along; her little feet trip softly through the rustling grass beside him: the evening wind blows her light garments against him. He has taken her little gloveless hand as he helps her over a stile (adversity has made her abject, and she no longer spurns his assistance), and now retains it, half absently. Bare palm to bare palm, they saunter through the rich, dim land. It is dusk, but not so dusk but that they can see their dark eyes flashing into one another: sharp, stinging pleasure shoots along their young, full veins. The vocabularies of pain and of delight are so meagre, that each has to borrow from the other to express its own highest height and deepest depth. As they pass along a lane, whose high grass banks and overgrown hawthorn hedges make the coming night already come, Esther's foot stumbles over a stone. The next moment she is in his arms, and he is kissing her repeatedly.

"Esther, will you marry me?" he asks, in a passionate whisper, forgetting to make any graceful periphrasis to explain his meaning, using the plain words as they rise in his heart.

No answer. Emotions as complicated as intense check the passage of her voice. Even here, on this highest pinnacle of bliss—pinnacle so high that she had hardly dared hope ever to climb there—the thought of Bob and his despair flashes before her: her own remarks about the senselessness of kissing—about its being a custom suited only to savages, and her own great aversion to it—recur to her with a stab of remorse.

"You won't?" cries St. John, mistaking the cause of her silence, in a voice in which extreme surprise and profound alarm and pain are mixed in equal quantities.

Still no answer.

"If you have been making a fool of me all this time, you might, at least, have the civility to tell me so," he says, in a voice so sternly cold that remorse, coyness, and all other feelings merge into womanish fear.

"Don't blame me before I deserve it," she says, with a faint smile. "I will mar——"

She finishes her sentence on his breast.

Perfect happiness never lasts more than two seconds in this world; at the end of that time St. John's doubts return. He puts her a little way from him, that she may be a freer agent. "Esther," he says, "I half believe that you said 'yes' out of sheer fright; you thought I was going to upbraid you; and I am aware" (with a half smile) "that there are few things you would not do or leave undone to avoid a scolding; you did not say it readily, as if you were glad of it. I know that you have only known me three weeks, that I am not particularly likeable, especially by women, and that I always show to the worst possible advantage at home. All I beg of you is, tell me the truth: Do you like me, or do you not?"

"I do like you."

"Like is such a comprehensive word," he says, with a slight, impatient contracting of his straight brows. "You *like* Mrs. Brown, I suppose, for washing your clothes?"

"I like you better than Mrs. Brown."

"I did not doubt that," he answers, laughing; "probably you like me better than Sir Thomas, than my mother, than Constance, perhaps; but such liking as that I would not stoop to pick off the ground. I must be first or nowhere. Am I first?"

"No, you are not," she answers firmly.

His countenance falls, as Cain's did.

"I am not!" he repeats, in a constrained voice. "Who is then, may I ask?"

"Jack, my brother—he is, and always will be!"

"Bah!" cries Gerard, laughing, and looking immensely relieved. "How you frightened me! I believe you did it on purpose, as you said to me about the brook this afternoon. After him, am I first?"

"Yes."

"Before——what's his name?—the fellow that writes such a remarkably good hand—before Brandon?"

"Why do you always worry me about him?" she exclaims, angrily, turning away.

"Why do you so strongly resent being worried about him?" retorts St. John suspiciously.

"It is wearisome to hear a person always harping on one string," she answers coldly. "Believe me or not, as you choose; but please spare me the trouble of these repeated and useless asseverations."

"I beg your pardon!" he says, his countenance clearing, and passing his arm round her half-shrinking, half-yielding form. "I will never dig him up as long as I live. Peace to his ashes! Oh darling!" he continues, his voice changing to an emphatic, eager, impassioned key—"I have been so little used to having things go as I wish, that I can hardly believe it is I that am standing here. Pinch me, that I may be sure that I am awake! Oh Esther! is it really true? Can you possibly be fond of me? So few people are! Not a soul in the wide world, I do believe, except my old mother. The girl that I told you about last night lay in my arms, and let me kiss her as you are doing; she kissed me back again, as you do not; I looked into her eyes, and they seemed true as truth itself, and all the while she was *lying* to me: my very touch must have been hateful to her, as it is to you, perhaps?"

"You are always referring to that—that *person*," says Esther, lifting great jealous eyes, and a mouth like a ripe cleft cherry, through the misty twilight towards him. "I perceive that I am only a *pis aller* after all. If you had ceased to care for her, you would have forgiven her long ago, and have given up measuring everybody else by her standard."

"I have forgiven her fully and freely," he answers, magnanimously, and standing heart to heart with a woman

"...... fairer than the evening air, Clad in the beauty of a thousand stars;

66

> More lovely than the monarch of the sky,
> In wanton Arethusa's azured arms."

He may afford to be magnanimous. "I not only forgive her, but hale down blessings on her own and her plunger's ugly head. To be candid," he ends, laughing, "I forgave her a year ago, when I met her at Brainton Station, grown fat, with a red nose, and a tribe of squinting children, who, but for the finger of Providence interposing, might have been mine."

Speaking, he lays his lips upon the blossom of her sweet red mouth; but she, pricked with the sudden smart of recollected treachery, draws away from him.

"Come," she says, with a slight shiver, "let us go home. We shall get into dreadful disgrace as it is; what will Sir Thomas say?"

"I can tell you beforehand," says St. John, gaily; "he will say, with his usual charming candour, that, if we ask his opinion, we are a couple of fools to go gadding about to strange churches just to see a parcel of lighted candles and squeaking little boys and popish mummeries; that, for his part, he has stuck to his parish church for the last fifty years, and means to do so to the end of the chapter; and that, if we don't choose to conform to the rules of his house, &c."

"Does he always say the same?" asks Esther, smiling.

"Always. A long and affectionate study of his character has enabled me to predicate with exactness what he will say on any great subject, Esther."

"How do you know that my name is Esther?" she asks naïvely. "You have never heard any one call me so."

"Do you forget the flyleaf of the Prayer-book that——Hang it! I was on the point of uttering the forbidden name!"

Smiling, he looks for an answering smile from her, but finds none.

"I have heard of you as Esther Craven from my youth up," he continues. "Before you came we speculated as to what 'Esther' Craven would be like; it was only when you arrived *in propriâ personâ* that you rose into the dignity of 'Miss' Craven."

"I hate being called Esther," she says, plaintively, with eyes down-drooped to the lush-green grasses that bow and make obeisance beneath her quick feet; "it always makes me feel as if I were in disgrace. Jack never calls me Esther unless he is vexed with me. Call me *Essie*, please."

"Essie, then."

"Well?"

"I think it right to warn you" (putting an arm of resolute possession, bolder than ever poor Brandon's had been, round her supple figure—for who is there in these grey evening fields to witness the embrace?)—"I think it right to warn you that I may very possibly grow like Sir Thomas in time; they tell me that I have a look of him already. I do not see that myself; but, even if that does come to pass, can you promise to like me even then?"

"Even then."

"I may very probably d——n the servants, and be upset for a whole evening if there are lumps in the melted butter; I may very probably insist on your playing backgammon with me every evening, and insist, likewise, on your being invariably beaten. Can you bear even that?"

"Even that."

They both laugh; but in Esther's laugh there is a ring of bitterness, which she herself hears, and wonders that he does not.

As they near the house, they see thin slits of crimson light through the dining-room shutters. Esther involuntarily quickens her pace.

"Why are you in such a hurry?" he asks, his eyes shining eager with reproachful passion in the passionless white starlight. "Who knows? to-morrow we may be dead; to-day we are as gods, knowing good and evil. This walk has not been to you what it has to me, or you would be in no haste to end it."

"I don't suppose it has," she answers, half-absently, with a sigh.

He had expected an eager disclaimer, and is disappointed.

"There can be but one explanation of that," he says, angrily.

"If you only knew——," begins Esther, with an uncertain half-inclination to confess, though late.

"If you are going to tell me anything disagreeable," he says, quickly putting his hand before her mouth, "stop! Tell me to-morrow, or the day after, but not now—not now! Let there be one day of my life on which I may look back and say, as God said when he looked back upon His new world, 'Behold, it is very good!'"

She is silent.

"And yet, perhaps, it would be better if I knew the end of your sentence; if I only knew—what?—how little you care about me?"

"You are mistaken," she answers, roused into vehemence. "I love you so well, that I have grown hateful to myself!" and having spoken thus oracularly, she raises herself on tiptoe, lifts two shy burning lips to his, and kisses him voluntarily. Then, amazed at her own audacity, clothed with shame as with a garment, she tears herself out of his arms, as in delightful surprise he catches her to his heart, and flies with frenzied haste into the house.

CHAPTER XVII.

The sweetness of September is that of the last few days spent with a friend that goeth on a very long journey; and we know not whether, when he returneth, we shall go to meet him with outstretched arms, or shall smile up at him only through the eyes of the daisies that flower upon our straight green graves.

"Our sweetest songs are those that tell of saddest thought,"

and our sweetest seasons are, to my thinking, those in which the ecstasies of possession are mixed with the soft pain of expected parting. A September sun—such a one as warmly kissed the quiet faces of our young dead heroes, as they lay thick together on Alma's hill-side—is shining down with even mildness upon the just and the unjust, upon Constance Blessington's grass-green gown as she sits at breakfast, and on the hair crown of yellow gold with which Providence has seen fit to circle her dull fair brows.

"I think that you must have regretted being in such a hurry to run away from the garden and us," she is saying, with a gentle smile of lady-like malice, to Esther, à propos of her yesterday's misadventure.

"Sitting in the shade eating nectarines is certainly pleasanter occupation than grovelling on your hands and knees on a mud-bank," replies Esther, demurely.

"St. John is so terribly energetic!" says Miss Blessington, rather lackadaisically; "he would have walked me off the face of the earth long ago if I had let him."

Remembering the Chinese invitation, Esther cannot repress an involuntary smile.

"What about St. John?" says the young man, entering; having caught his own name, with that wonderful acuteness of hearing with which every one is endowed when themselves are in question.

"Much better have stuck to your parish church," says Sir Thomas, brandishing a large red and yellow bandanna, which is part of the old English costume, "than gone scrambling heigh-go-mad over hedges and ditches after new-fangled Puseyite mummeries!"

Gerard and his betrothed exchange a glance of intelligence. Gerard is looking slightly sentimental; his head is a little on one side; but on his discovering that he is an object of attention to Constance, it returns rather suddenly to the perpendicular.

Esther's eyes are brillianter than their wont; her cheeks are flushed with a deeper hue than the crimson lips of a foreign shell, but it is not the flush of a newly-departed sleep. The angel of slumber has passed by the portals of her brain, as the destroying angel passed by the blood-painted lintels of Israel. Thoughts sweeter than virgin honey, thoughts bitterer than gall, have kept her wakeful. Ere she went to bed, she spent three hours in writing letters of dismissal to Brandon, and at the end left him undismissed. "I *cannot* write it to him!" she cries, sitting up in bed in the dark, and flinging out blind arms into the black nothingness around her; "anything written sounds so harsh, so abrupt, so hard. I must tell him myself very gradually and gently, and tell him how sorry I am, and beg him to forgive me, and cry—go down on my knees, perhaps. No; I should look such a fool if I did that! After all, no one cries long over spilt milk—least of all any one so sensible and utterly unimaginative as poor dear Bob." And with that, thinking in a disparaging, hold-cheap way of him and his love, she turns the pillow over to try and find a cooler place on the under side for her burning face to rest on.

"Two dissyllabic names now passing many mouths by three dissyllabic names are here expressed," reads Miss Blessington, with distinct gravity, after breakfast that morning, out of an acrostic book that lies on the work-table before her, while Esther sits opposite with pencil and paper, ready to write down the products of the joint wisdom of their two minds. But the top of the pencil is being bitten by the young scribe's short white teeth, and her eyes are straying away absently—away through the open window and out to the sunshiny sward, where two of St. John's dogs, forbidden by Sir Thomas on pain of death, to set paw within the house, are rolling over one another, making abortive bites at each other's hind legs, and waggishly, with much growling and mumbling, taking each other's heads into their mouths.

"That is the whole," continues Constance. "These are the proofs; a woman, a wise man, a king, a poet, a beauty!"

Silence.

"A woman!" says Miss Blessington, cogitatively, resting her smooth chin on her hand, and looking vaguely round at the cabinets and busts for inspiration.

Esther makes no suggestion.

"A woman!" repeats Miss Blessington, raising her voice a little.

Esther comes back to consciousness with a little jump. "Oh! I beg your pardon; I don't think I was attending. A——what did you say?"

"A woman!" repeats Miss Blessington, for the third and last time.

"A woman!" echoes Esther, vacantly; "that is rather vague, is it not? There have been a good many women, one way or another."

"Let us try the next, then," says Constance, obligingly: "A wise man."

"Solomon!" answers Esther, glibly.

"I said a *dis*syllable name," remarks Constance, with gentle asperity.

The door opens, and St. John enters.

"Tell us a wise man's name?" "Who was a wise man?" cry they both in a breath.

"Solomon!" replies St. John, brilliantly.

"So I said," says Esther, smiling; "but, unluckily, it must be a *two*-syllabled wise man. I'm afraid that it would be disrespectful to abbreviate him into *Solmon*, wouldn't it?"

"One ought to be provided with a Bible, a Lemprière, and an encyclopædia before one attempts to grapple with these devices of Satan," says Gerard, sitting down on the arm of the sofa beside Constance and looking over her shoulder.

"A woman! Who is the woman?"

"We have not found out yet."

"A king! Who is the king?"

"We have not found out yet."

"You seem to be on the highroad to success," says he, laughing, and throwing himself back lazily.

"We have only just begun," says Miss Blessington, a little reproachfully. "You and Miss Craven are always so impatient."

"There are a great many two-syllabled kings' names," says Esther, with a prodigious effort to look intelligent and interested: "Edward, Henry, Louis, Ahab, Alfred, Joash!"

"I daresay it is one of those Jewish kings," says Constance, reflectively; "they are always fond of introducing Bible names into acrostics. Is there a Bible anywhere about, St. John?"

St. John walks slowly round the well-laden tables; looks over photograph books, Doré's "Elaine," Flaxman's "Dante;" but in vain. He comes back, and shakes his head.

"I will go and fetch one," says Constance, rising with noiseless grace, and rustling softly away among the console tables.

"May she long be occupied in searching the Scriptures for a dissyllabic king!" cries Gerard, drawing a long breath, and yawning as the door closes behind her.

"I am glad she is gone," says Esther, looking rather embarrassed, "as I have something to say to you."

"Say on."

"I must go home to-morrow," she continues, drawing hideous faces and wooden-legged cows on her bit of paper.

"Are you beginning to try experiments on me already?" he asks, incredulously, leaning his folded arms on the little table which forms a barrier between them.

"No; but I have received a letter from Jack this morning, which——"

"Which you are going to read to me?"

"Oh, no—no!" she answers, hastily, putting her hand in involuntary protection over her pocket; "it—it—wouldn't interest you." (It would have interested him rather too much.) "He seems to be missing me a good deal."

"Be honest," says St. John, stretching out his hand and taking hers captive, pencil and all. "Does he miss you as much as I shall?"

"More, a good deal, I should say," she replies, looking up with an arch smile; "I don't make your tea, and order your dinner, and darn your socks. One, two, three, four weeks," continues she, marking each number with her slender fingers on the table. "I have actually been here nearly a month, and" (with a half-absent sigh), "do you know, the very day I left home I told them——"

"Who's them?"

She blushes furiously. "Them—did I say them? Oh! I meant *him*, of course—Jack."

"Does he always speak of himself in the plural, like a king, or a reviewer?"

"Nonsense!" cries Esther, pulling away her hand rather impatiently. "Do you never make slips of the tongue?"

"Frequently. Well, you must write and tell *them*" (with a laughing emphasis on the *them*) "that they must get some one else to darn their socks, for that you have found something better to do."

"I could not have anything better," she answers, reddening with indignation. "You don't understand about Jack, or you would not make jokes!"

"It is a fault I'm not often guilty of; being funny never was my besetting sin," he answers, drily. "Essie, whenever you do go home, I have a great mind to go with you—if you will invite me."

"Oh, no, don't!" she cries, with involuntary eagerness, the pencil dropping from between her fingers.

"I believe you are ashamed of me," he says, angrily, walking off to the window to hide the flush of vexation which is invading his weather-worn cheeks.

"Ashamed of myself more likely," she cries, jumping up suddenly and following him.

"Why?"

"You fine gentlemen do not understand the

"'short and simple annals of the poor,'"

she answers, with a forced laugh. "You would probably be in the position of Mother Hubbard's singularly ill-used dog;

"'When   you   came   there,
The cupboard was bare.'"

"You think that gluttony, like gout, must be hereditary," says Gerard, laughing again, and yet looking very tender withal—not with the puling, milk-and-water tenderness of a green love-sick boy, but with the condensed, strong passion of a world-worn, world-tainted, half world-weary-grown man.

"There are other reasons too," says Essie, drooping her eyelids, over which the small blue veins—

"'wandering, leave a tender stain—'"

with a maiden's shyness, under the new-known fire of a lover's gaze.

"What other reasons?"

"I have never mentioned anything about you to Jack!" she answers, twisting her one paltry ring round her finger. "I don't suppose he is aware of your existence, unless he has bought a new 'Baronetage' since I left home—a piece of extravagance that I do not think he is likely to have been guilty of: and he would think it so odd if I were to appear suddenly on the scene, dragging you in tow."

"That would be easily explained," replies St. John, gravely, drawing himself up, and looking rather too conscious of the eight centuries of Norman blood in his strong veins. "I suppose that a man may be allowed to travel for a few hours in company with his future wife without any one being straightlaced enough or behind the world enough to call it *odd!*"

"Your future wife!" she repeats, with a dreamy, mournful smile. "Am I that? I think not. I shall *never* be your wife," she says, a look of melancholy inspiration crossing and darkening, as a travelling cloud crosses and darkens the blue eyes of a June brook, the sweet red and sweeter white of her little piquante face.

"Do you know any just cause or impediment why you should not be?" he asks, gaily.

"None," she answers, shuddering a little, as she has got into the habit of doing lately—"except" (throwing herself impulsively into his glad arms) "that it would make me so intolerably happy!"

There is a pause—a little brief pause—in which that shyest, fleetest-winged of earth's visitants—Happiness—folds her pinions and settles down for a little minute on two beating, trembling human hearts.

"Do you know," continues Essie, after awhile—raising herself, and looking up, with tears glistening, like dew on the autumn grass, upon her long swart lashes—"Do you know that in a book I was reading the other day I met this sentence: 'Le bonheur sur terre est un crime puni de mort comme le génie, comme la divinité'? It has haunted me ever since yesterday."

"As far as that goes," he answers, thoughtfully, "there is nothing in this world that is not punished with death, except Death himself. Well" (smiling fondly, and stroking her ruffled, scented love-locks), "may I come? may I be Mother Hubbard's dog?"

"Why do you want to come *now*, particularly?" she asks, in rather a troubled voice.

"Because I am a coward," he answers, laughing—"because I like a quiet life, and I imagine that there will be squally weather here when I announce my intention of taking you as a helpmeet for me."

"I *am* a *mésalliance*, I suppose?" she answers, rather sadly. "What will Sir Thomas say? Anything very bad?"

70

"Oh, nothing out of the way," answers Gerard, with a careless shrug. "He will call me an ass, and tell me that I always was, from a boy, the biggest fool he ever came across; and that, for his part, he'll wash his hands of me: and he'll probably conclude with a threat of cutting me off with a shilling."

"And will he?" asks Esther, quickly, looking up eager-eyed, parted-lipped.

"Why do you ask?" said the young man, sharply.

"Do you think that I want to marry a *beggar?*" inquires she, playfully, not detecting his suspicion.

"You need not be alarmed," he replies, coldly, and his arms slacken their fond hold a little. "He will not, for the very excellent reason that he cannot."

The door handle, turning, rattles. With one spring, Esther returns to her seat—to her deserted cows and impossible profiles. St. John looks out of the window. No transformation scene at Drury Lane could be more complete.

"Ahab—Jehu—Zimri—Omri—Joash!" recites Miss Blessington, entering, with an open Bible in her hand.

CHAPTER XVIII.

"I am afraid you must think it very rude of us, leaving you alone on the last evening of your visit," says Miss Blessington next day to Esther, as the two girls stand together in the conservatory, picking bits of heliotrope and maidenhair, and regardless of the ten and twenty little pots that their long gowns have knocked down; "but, you see, it is such a long-standing engagement, and we can so seldom induce Sir Thomas to go to a ball, that we really could hardly get out of it."

She speaks politely, with that friendly suavity that one feels on the ultimate and penultimate days of their stay to a guest that one is glad to be rid of.

"Oh, never mind me," says Essie, lightly; "I can always amuse myself: and, besides, it will be very nearly bedtime by the time you go."

"They intend me to go with them," St. John had said to her overnight, *à propos* of this ball, "and of course I intend it too; only some prophetic instinct tells me that my head will begin to ache prodigiously towards dressing-time. I am half divided between that and toothache, only I suppose that the latter necessitates the simulating of acute bodily torture, and subjects one to unlimited offers of boiled figs, hopbags, laudanum, and the Lord knows what."

Gerard had found his betrothed stubborner than he had expected as to her expressed resolution of departure. Looking at the childish roundness of her soft face, at the dewy meekness of her heavenly eyes, he had fancied her malleable by his hand, as clay by the potter's; and so, in most things, she would have been. In most things, it was to her easier to yield than to resist—less trouble—and, besides, it pleased people; but in the one prime passion of her life, her love for her brother, you might as well try to move the Tower of London with your finger and thumb as to stir her. After half an hour of arguments, persuasions, caresses, St. John is constrained vexedly to own to himself that in that young faithful heart *lover*-love holds as yet only the second place. The sole concession he could win from her was that of one day, the day of the ball.

"We may imagine the clock put on thirty years, and ourselves already in possession," he says, laughing—"only minus the gout and wrinkles and spectacles we shall also have come into possession of by then."

"What the devil do people mean," says Sir Thomas, entering the morning-room that evening after dinner, with his hair brushed up into a stiff cockatoo, and tugging away at a huge pair of white kid gloves, off which he has already succeeded in bursting both buttons, "dragging a man away from his own fireside to see a lot of fools cutting capers, and flourishing their heels in each other's faces?"

From Sir Thomas's description one would imagine that the Cancan was habitually danced at the balls he frequents.

The door opens, and Miss Blessington makes her appearance; looking, not vain or conscious, but calmly defiant of any one to make a better—a triumph of lace and tulle and flowers, and milk-white flesh, and grand, cold curves and contours.

"Oh, how beautiful!" cries Essie, clasping her little hands, with the unaffected admiration of one handsome woman for another. "I know it is rude to make personal remarks; but is not she, Lady Gerard?"

"It is a pretty dress," replies miladi, whose unwieldy bulk not even the cunningest of Parisian *couturières* has been able to fashion into anything nearer than an approximation to any shape at all; "but I never think that Elise's taste is as good as Jane Clarke's used to be."

Constance has walked to a pier-glass, and is examining with anxiety a bite that a gnat has been savage enough to inflict on her face, a little under the lower lip, and which has been disturbing her wonted composed serenity ever since 3 p.m., when the catastrophe took place.

"Does it show much?" she asks, turning with a concerned, serious look to Esther.

"Oh no! hardly at all."

"I think I will put a little bit of sticking-plaster on it," she continues, gravely. "It will only look like a patch; and patches are always so becoming."

"Let me go and get you a bit!" cries Essie, good-naturedly, running off.

When she returns Sir Thomas is saying, fussily: "Now, why is not that boy dressed? Always the same! Always late! Never in time for anything!"

"He is not coming, Sir Thomas; he has got a headache, and is gone to lie down—at least he said so," replies Constance, coldly, but casting a scrutinising glance at Esther (who is deftly, with a small pair of scissors, cutting out a little circle of sticking-plaster) as she speaks.

"Stuff and nonsense!" cries "that boy's" papa, angrily—"a pack of lies! A fine Miss Molly you have made of your son, miladi! He'll be afraid of going out shooting next year for fear of getting his feet wet!"

"Is that about the right size?" inquires Esther, timidly, raising a pair of guilty pink cheeks, and exhibiting the result of her labours on the point of the scissors.

"Good God! miladi, do take that plaguy long tail of yours up! How the devil can I help treading on it?"

These are the last sweet words of Sir Thomas, as he follows wife and ward into the carriage. They are gone, and Essie sits down in the large empty room to await the resurrection of her lover. The sort of shy half-fear which always assails her at his expected approach comes over her more strongly than ever. A distant door bangs faintly somewhere about the house; then another nearer. "He is coming!" she says to herself, and the quick blood rushes tingling to her fingers' ends.

It is a hot night, and the tall French windows stand unshuttered and open. Some impulse of timid coquetry urges her to flee from before him: she is ashamed that he should see the plain letters of joy written on her face at his coming: she would fain have yet a few moments of the happiness of expectancy, to whose delights those of reality are but seldom comparable. From the terrace a flight of stone steps leads down, with many a twist, to the mere. In a minute Essie has run lightly down, and is standing by the water's edge.

The dahlias are nodding their round drowsy heads, and the sentinel hollyhocks stand up stiff and pompous with their clustered flower-spikes—rulers and law-givers among the flower-people; the little ripples are biting with playful tooth the low sedge-banks, and the tall bulrush forest, whence the coot and the waterhen families sailed out into life in the warm spring weather. To and fro rock the heavy, lazy, water-lily leaves, whose bloom-time is past two months ago. Through her garden, the sky, the high moon walks stately, holding her silver lamp, in whose light all things shine deliciously.

Essie stands entranced. It seems to her like the intermediate residence of some happy soul, freed from the world's toil and moil, shrived from sin, emancipated from life, where it should dwell in tempered bliss till that last day when heaven's brighter glories, stronger raptures, should burst upon and clothe it for aye. She strolls along the narrow gravel path, bathing her hands with childish delight in the moonbeams, and then stoops and picks up two or three little stones that the night's sweet alchemy has gifted with a bright short glory not their own. So stooping, she hears a man's quick firm foot running down the garden steps. She raises herself, and goes to meet him with "a moonlight-coloured smile" on her face. "Aren't they lovely?" she asks, holding up her pebbly treasures for him to look at.

Not speaking, he takes the little pink palm, stones and all, into his hand, and looks into her face; and then, as if yielding to a temptation that he hates, that he would fain resist, and to which, being over-strong, he must yet succumb, he snatches her to his breast, and kisses her fiercely—eyelids, lips, and neck—with a violence he is himself hardly conscious of.

"Stop!" she cries, surprised, half-shocked, pushing him away from her. "What do you mean? You frighten me!"

He recollects himself instantly, and releases her. "It *is* alarming being kissed, especially when you are not used to it," he answers, with a sneer.

She looks up at him in blank astonishment. Has he gone mad? Is it the moonlight that has given him that white wrathy look?

"Something has happened!" she says, quickly. "What is it? tell me!"

"Oh! nothing—a mere bagatelle!" he replies, with a little bitter laugh. "It is only that I have been hearing a pleasant piece of news."

"What is it?"

"Only that an acquaintance of mine is going to be married!"

"Is it an acquaintance of mine too?"

"About the most intimate you have, I should say: yourself, in fact!"

"Is that news?" she asks, trying to smile. "I *am* going to be married, am not I, to you?"

"I am not aware that my name is—Brandon," he answers, coldly, while his sorrowful, fierce eyes go through her heart like poisoned arrows.

She turns her head aside and groans. A great vague darkness blots out the broad moon, and the stars' thick cohorts; the bright water beside her grows black as hell's sluggish rivers.

He had not known how much he had been buoyed up by hope till that mute gesture of hers bid him despair.

"It's true, then?" he asks in a voice of sharp rage and anguish, catching hold of the white wonder of her arm, on which his fingers, unwittingly cruel, leave crimson prints.

"Is *what* true?" she asks, faintly, trying for yet a little longer to stave off Fate, to push away Nemesis, with her weak woman-fingers.

"That you are—God! am I choking?—engaged to Brandon?"

"I was once," she falters under her breath.

"How long ago?"

"When first I came here."

"And since then you have written to break it off?" he asks, while a tone of joyful hope vibrates in his deep voice.

"No, I have not," she answers, in a frightened whisper.

St. John's face gathers blackness. "I am to understand, then," he resumes, in a constrained voice, out of which the man's strong will keeps the pent passion from bursting forth, "that you belonged to him at the time when I kept you out of bed one night to listen to an interesting chapter in my own autobiography?"

"Yes."

"And when, in reply to my inquiries, you denied having any connection beyond common acquaintance with—with him?"

"Yes."

"And when you were good enough to overlook all trifling obstacles, and to consent to marry me?"

"Yes."

The little catechism ended, the last cobweb of doubt torn away, they stand dumb. Esther's guilty head sinks down on her breast as a flower's head sinks overladen with rain. Suddenly she looks up and stretches out her arms. "Speak to me!" she says, huskily. "Curse me! strike me! call me some bad name—only speak!"

"I wish to God you were a man!" he answers, in a hard, low voice; while his straight brows draw together into one dark line across his face, and his lips look white and thin under his moustache.

"That you might *kill* me!" she says, incoherent with excitement. "Well, kill me now! If revenge is so pleasant to you, I give you leave!"

"Let us have no heroics, please," says he, contemptuously; "you don't appear to be aware that it is not the fashion for English gentlemen to murder women who make fools of them. It may be a sensible practice, but it is at present confined to the *tiers état*."

Having spoken, he makes a slight movement to depart.

"Are you going to give me up?" she cries, smiting her hands together, and forgetting in her great dismay to reflect whether the remonstrance accorded well with her dignity or not.

"I have no claim upon you," he answers, icily.

"What do you mean?" she cries, passionately. "You are unjust. There could be nothing too bad for *him* to say of me, but what injury have I done you? You ought to thank me and praise me for having been wicked and dishonourable and double-dealing for your sake."

"For my sake!" he repeats, with a sardonic smile. "I am hardly so conceited as to take it personally."

"What do you mean?" she asks, quickly. "If I did not do it for your sake, for whose did I?"

He is silent.

"Do you mean," she inquires, slowly, her cheeks paling to the whiteness of snowdrops blowing, "that you think I gave him up because I wanted to be a grand lady—because I wanted to have all these fine things" (looking round at the flowering gardens, at the broad lake, at the stately house shimmering in the moonshine) "belonging to me?"

Still he holds his peace.

"Is that what you meant?" she repeats, urgently.

"I meant," he says, looking up, his eyes flashing with a hard, metallic gleam, "that you thought a rich man a better investment than a poor one, and, being equally and conveniently indifferent to both, you thought it wisest to select the former."

"If such is your opinion of me," she says, turning away indignantly, "I don't wonder at your being in such a hurry to be rid of me!"

He looks askance at her out of the corners of his eyes. She has hidden her face in her hands, but by the panting breast and heaved white shoulder he sees that she is weeping—that a storm of sobs is shaking her childish frame.

"I am in a hurry to be rid of you!" he says, harshly, steeling himself against her. "From a woman who could throw a man over with the deliberate, cold-blooded artlessness you have done, one may well sing 'Te Deum' for being rescued in time."

She flings up her little head proudly, and the dusk splendour of her eyes blazes through great tears. "Listen to me!" she says, laying hold of his arm with one small burning hand. "I am a bad girl, I know, but I am not the calculating, mercenary wretch you take me for. I tell you honestly that the first day I came here—I had never been staying at a great house before—I thought it must be pleasant to live in large rooms, and have gilt and ormolu and fine pictures about one, and to have carriages and horses and servants, and not to be obliged to think twice before one spent sixpence; and I thought, too" (her long neck droops, and she blushes painfully as she makes the confession), "what a pity it was that I was already engaged, for that otherwise, as I was pretty, you might have taken a fancy to me——" She stops, choked with maiden shame. Upon her averted face an enduring flush, like a hectic autumn leaf's, burns red and angry.

"But as soon as I saw you, almost," she continues, commanding her tears with great difficulty—"as soon as you spoke to me, all such thoughts went out of my head. I don't know why they did," she says, simply. "You were not particularly pleasant or civil; I did not think you good-looking, and you gave me the idea of being ill-tempered; but" (with a sigh) "one cannot reason about those sort of things. I began to think so much about what you *were*, that I forgot to remember what you had."

He makes no comment upon her confession.

"Do you believe me?" she asks, eagerly, her little fingers tightening their clasp upon his coat-sleeve.

Still he is dumb.

"Do you?" she repeats, excitedly, the quick breath passing to and fro pantingly across the threshold of her crimson lips.

"Why do you insist on making me uncivil?" he says, with a sarcastic smile. "I do *not* believe you. I dare say you fancy you are telling truth; but if another man were to come on the scene with a few thousands a-year more, and a higher position in the social scale, you would enact the same part over again. Women must be true to their instincts. Those who are bent on rising must kick down the ladder by which they have climbed: it is an irreversible law."

"You are mistaken," she says, eagerly. "I have no desire to climb; if I came here with any silly, childish idea that rich people were happier than poor ones, I have been quite disillusioned. Bob" (how oddly the little unromantic name comes in among her heroics!)—"Bob is a happier man than you are, though he is only a lieutenant in a foot regiment, and has next to nothing to live upon."

"I have no doubt that *Bob*" (with a little sneering emphasis on the monosyllable) "is in all respects a very superior person to me," says St. John, with a bitter pale smile, like a gleam of wrathful sunlight on a day of east wind and clouds and driving sleet.

"I quite agree with you," she answers eagerly, her great eyes flashing angry, like unwonted meteors that blaze fitful in the winter sky, "and I wish to Heaven I had never left him!"

Over Gerard's features a spasm, contracting and puckering them, passes ugly and painful; his hands clench themselves in the mightiness of his effort to govern his smitten soul. "That is easily remedied," he answers, after a little pause, in a clear cold voice. "Why should not you go back to him as you came? There is no reason why he should ever hear of this—this *episode*, this *interlude*, this *farce*."

"And you think that I am to be bandied about like a bale of goods!" she cries, scornfully, voice trembling and lip quivering with passion. "You are like the woman in the Judgment of Solomon, who said, 'Let it be neither mine nor thine, but divide it!' *You* love me! You never did!"

"Perhaps not," he answers, with slow difficulty; "perhaps what I loved was my ideal that I fancied I had found in you, and when I found I was mistaken, perhaps the love went too! My God, I wish it had!"

Through the proud calmness of his voice penetrates a tone of bitter, unwilling tenderness. Hearing it, her whole soul is melted into fresh, quick tears.

74

"It is not my ideal, or any one else's, that I love in you!" she cries, stretching out eager white arms towards him; "it is yourself—your very self! Oh, if I could but tear out my heart, and show it you! Oh! why won't you believe me?"

He looks at her—looks at the innocently-wooing arms, at the tear-stained, dimpled, tremulous face—and feels his resolution wasting away like wax before the fire, as Samson's wasted away in Delilah's lap. He turns his eyes away across the cool silvered flood, and hardens his heart against her.

"Why cannot you?" she repeats, in her sweet, vibrating voice.

"Because I have not the faith that removes mountains," he answers, harshly; "because a thing must be probable, or at least possible, before I can give credit to it; because I am unable to understand how, for a man whom you confess to having thought ill-looking, ill-tempered, and ill-mannered, you could, out of pure disinterested love, throw over one to whom you must, at least, have pretended to be sincerely attached."

"I never pretended anything of the kind," she answers, vehemently. "If you don't believe me, ask him. I was engaged to him because he seemed unhappy, and because I did not see any particular reason why I should not, and because he asked me."

Through all his bitter, surging wrath, St. John can hardly forbear a smile. "And you became engaged to me because I asked you?" he says, drily. "At that rate, there is no reason why the number of your aspirants should not be increased *ad infinitum*.

"And were you going to play the play out to the end, may I ask, and *marry* us both?" he inquires, in the same cutting key.

No woman can stand being sneered at; she much prefers having the tables and chairs flung at her head.

"Do you think it manly or witty to jeer at me," cries Essie, stung almost to madness by his taunts, "because I have been fool enough to desert for you a man worth a hundred of you?"

Gerard stands motionless in the moonlight, with folded arms, and a chill, painful smile on his stern mouth. "I have already announced my conviction of his superiority, and have advised you to return to him," he says.

"Do you mean *really?*" asks Essie, her wild, wide eyes flaming in half-incredulous fear on his face.

"I do," he answers, with icy steadiness.

"And you have done with me altogether?" she says, brokenly, her tears forcing their way through her slight shielding fingers, and falling one after another, slow and heavy, on the stones at her feet. "Serve me right!—Serve me right!"

Once again, intoxicated by her great fairness, he goes nigh to pardoning her; once again his obstinate will comes to his aid. "If I were to marry you now," he says, resolutely, "my life would be one long suspicion: I should love you madly, and should disbelieve in you."

With that, and his saying he should love her madly, a little creeping hope steals warmly about her heart. "Why should you disbelieve in me?" she asks, putting out a timid peace-making hand.

"Because a faith once broken can never be mended," he answers, sternly—"it may be patched up, but a patched faith will not do to go through life with; because a woman who has deceived a man once for one object may deceive him a second time for another. I should never," he says (words coming quicker and emotion deepening as he proceeds), "look in your sweet eyes without thinking I read some treachery in them; I should never press your heart against mine without fearing that it was beating for some one else."

She withdraws her rejected hand, and falls to weeping sorelier than ever, but very mutely.

"What madness induced you to tell me so many lies?" he cries, passionately, with mournful severity. "Were you bent on putting a gulf, that could never be bridged through all eternity, between us? Did not you know that that is the one sin I could never forget or forgive?"

She looks down humbled and crestfallen, and says, sobbingly, "I was afraid of you. I thought that, if I told you, I should lose you as I have done now, without telling you. I was on the point of speaking two or three times, but you looked so angry that my courage failed, and I *dared* not."

"Afraid of me!" he says, reproachfully. "By your own showing, then, you could not have loved me perfectly, for 'perfect love casteth out fear,' If you are afraid of me, it is indeed time for us to part."

"I see you are bent on misconstruing every word I say," she says, hopelessly, and yet with a little petulant movement of shoulder and head, "and so I'll hold my tongue."

He looks at her, not relentingly, but with infinite sadness. "I almost wish that Constance had left me in my Fool's Paradise!" he says.

"Constance!" exclaims Esther, quickly. "Was it she that told you?"

"It was," he answers, quietly: "she heard it this morning; she was annoyed with me for not going to the ball, and chose this ingenious and, I must say, complete mode of revenge."

"What *had* I done to her?" says Essie, bringing her two hands together sharply, and looking upwards to Heaven's great black, blue floor above her,

"Thick inlaid with patines of bright gold."

"What *had* I done to her," she says, in a sort of wonder, "that she should do me such a mischief?"

Looking at her as she stands with upturned eyes, like some sweet prayerful saint or penitent Magdalen, drawn by a cunning hand that has been resolved three centuries back into elemental dust—dust that has stopped a bunghole perhaps, like Alexander's—Gerard's resolution breaks a little; not his resolution of parting from her—*that* remains firm as ever—but his power of so parting with nonchalant coldness. "Child!" he cries, a little roughly, and yet with a half-groan, placing a hand heavily on each of her shoulders—"Child! why are you so pretty? If it was your nature to be deceitful and underhand, why could not you be ugly too? Your beauty is the one thing about you that I believe in, and it drives me distracted!"

"And yet," she answers, with a melancholy smile, "you told me just now, very calmly, to go back to—to *him:* you seemed to contemplate with great equanimity the prospect of seeing me and my *distracting beauty*" (with a bitter emphasis) "in another man's possession."

"You are mistaken," he answers, with quick violence. "By God's help, I'll never see you again after to-night."

Hearing that heavy sentence, her knees tremble beneath her a little; a momentary dimness comes over her eyes; voice, breath, and heart seem to suspend their functions. No word of protest, of lamentation, of entreaty, crosses her whitened lips.

"What right have I to be with you?" he asks, indignantly—"I, who cannot see you without coveting you? What right have I to steal another man's wife, any more than his horse or his money?"

"Let me go, then," she answers, with a low, moaning sigh—"since it must be so. You know what is right better than I do. Good-bye!"

"Good-bye!" he answers, very shortly, and turns away his head sharply, that only the lake and the stars may see the distortion that the passion of that parting is working on his face.

"Say you forgive me before I go!" says the tender, tremulous voice, that might unman a hero—might unsaint an anchorite—as she lingers yet a little minute beside him.

"Why should I say what is not true?" he asks, turning round roughly upon her. "I don't forgive you, and never shall, either in this world or the next."

"You must!" she says, sobbingly, the words coming a little wildly through a tempest of tears. "I cannot go unless you do; if I went now, I should remember you all my life as you are to-day; to-day would blot out all the happy hours we have been together!"

For all answer he turns away from her, and buries his face in his hands.

"Look at me kindly once again!" she says, calmness growing out of her strong emotion, putting up her two small hands and trying to draw his away from before his hidden face. "I may be very wicked; I suppose I am—as you say so—mean, underhand, deceitful; but yet, for the sake of what is gone, look at me kindly once again: that won't hurt you, as it is for the very last time!"

Still Gerard remains speechless—not from obstinacy, but because he cannot command his voice: and his pride revolts from speaking shakily, quaveringly, like an hysterical woman or paralytic old man.

"If I were a thief, or a murderer!" she says, indignantly, withdrawing her hands, "you could not turn from me with greater loathing!"

"You are a murderer!" he answers, with fierce vehemence, looking at her once again as she had asked him—looking at her with wrathful, reluctant passion, but not kindly. "You have murdered my whole future—my hope, my belief in women, in truth—my everything of life but what is merely animal. If you had murdered my body I could have forgiven you much more easily. Time or disease must have done that sooner or later, but now—" He stops abruptly.

"If I am a murderer, I am a suicide too," she replies, with a smile more tearful than her tears. "St. John," she says, earnestly, "don't you know that people always attend to dying requests, however foolish and unreasonable they may be? This of mine is a dying request, for after to-night I shall be dead to you. Say, 'Essie, I forgive you.'"

"What is it to you whether I forgive you or not?" he inquires, sullenly, with a certain savage pulling and biting of his moustache. "Are you mistaking me for Brandon again? Why should two indifferent acquaintances like us go through the farce of begging each other's pardons? What are we to one another?"

76

"Nothing," she answers, calmly; "you need not be so eager to remind me of that; my memory needs no refreshing; but we *have been* something—do what you will you cannot take that away from me—so for the sake of that 'have been,' say you forgive me!"

"Falsehoods don't pass my lips so glibly as they do yours," he answers, doggedly. "If I were to say, 'I forgive you' a thousand times, I should be no nearer the doing it. Good-bye!" he says again, abruptly, putting out his hand; feeling that the strain is too great for him, and that if it last much longer, he, being but human, will break under it. Her answering farewell is to fling herself upon his breast.

"I can no more say 'good-bye,'" she says, desperately, in a passionate whisper, "than you can say 'I forgive you.' St. John, take me back, try me once again! I know I ought not to say it—that it is undignified, unwomanly, perhaps—but I cannot see my everything going away from me without reaching out a hand to stop it. Oh, my darling! give me one more trial!"

Her arms cling about his brown throat close as the bindweed clings about the hedges in sultry August; her white warm breast heaves and pants against his, as the sea heaves and pants against the shore's tawny sides; her eyes, impassioned as only dark eyes can be—alluring, despairing—flame into his eyes, and down through his eyes into his heart. Prisoned in those sweet, frail fetters, he feels strength and name and fame ebbing from him, as Merlin's ebbed under Vivien's wily charm.

"Is not it better to be tricked by such a woman," Passion whispers, "than to spend long æons of unswerving fidelity with one less maddeningly fair? Were not such moments of ecstasy very cheaply purchased, even by years of suspicion and deceit?" But Will and Honour push her back with their strong right hands. "She has deceived you once, and therefore she will deceive you twice. She is enacting *this* melodrama on *your* breast: she may enact the next on another man's. Put her away!—put her away!"

Hearkening to them, he, with a groan as of one that teareth out his right eye, with relentless fingers unfastens her arms from about his neck. "*Your* darling!" he says, contemptuously; "you are forgetting whom you are addressing!"

"I am, indeed," she answers, with a sudden revulsion of feeling; "but it is a mistake that one does not make twice in a lifetime."

"I hope not," he answers, taking refuge in surly rudeness from the almost overpowering temptation to fall at her feet and say, "Essie, come to me! deceive me! outwit me! overreach me; do what you please, I cannot help it! If there were a thousand Brandons and ten thousand treacheries between us, I *must* be yours, and you *must* be mine!"

"I have degraded myself once to the dust before you," rejoins Essie, in a voice that tries to be angry, but is only trembling; "but there is no fear of my doing it again. And yet," she continues, after a pause, her soft nature making it more difficult for her to part from him in anger than to incur his contempt by again descending to supplication—"and yet, since I have confessed to having been wicked, you might as well forgive me. How much the better will you be for going through life with the consciousness that you have made one wretched woman even more unhappy than she would otherwise have been? You forgave that other girl who deceived you because she did not love you. Forgive me, who deceived you, because I loved you too well!"

"I forgave her," he answers, sternly, "because I had ceased to care about her—because what she stole from me had lost its value. Perhaps at some future period I may be in the same frame of mind towards you; at present I am some way off it. I neither forgive you, nor have I the slightest wish to do so!"

Seeing that she is abasing herself in vain, she refrains. "Well, then, since you wish it, so it must be," she answers, with meek despair; and catching suddenly his hand before he has time to prevent her, she kisses it very humbly and sorrowfully. Then, unforgiven, unrecalled, she passes away. And Gerard, the battle over, the victory won, sits down on a garden-seat, and cries like a child for his pretty lost plaything.

CHAPTER XIX.

And so that act of the play is finished: all the actors have strutted and fumed and fretted through their little parts, and now the curtain has fallen. When next it rises, the principal actress in this tragic drama is discovered lying full-dressed on her bed; her pretty face buried—eyes, nose, and mouth—in the tumbled pillow; her little neat-shod feet hanging over the bedside. She looks as if she had been thrown there, an inert, passive mass, by some spiteful giant. Six miles away, at Lord ——'s ball, the fiddles are squeaking, and the pink-and-green Chinese lanterns swinging to and fro among the orange boughs in the slight wind made by the rustling dresses and passing men and women. Sir Thomas, with his hands in their burst white gloves under his coat tails, and his blue-cloth back leaning against a marble mantel-piece, is talking sweetly, in his hard, rasping voice, of scab and foot-rot. Miladi is gone down to supper for the sixth time on the sixth devoted married man's arm; she is eating game pie, and drinking sherry and champagne and moselle in turns. Miss Blessington, sweeping about on the arm of a small white gentleman, whose estate is as large as his person is minute, is responding a little superciliously to a presumptuous younger son, who, annihilated by her Greek profile and Juno bust, has invited her to tread a measure with him.

"No, tha—anks; I never da—ance round da—ances."

Meanwhile Esther lies stretched upon the counterpane, while a gloomy pageant of all that she has lost passes before her eyes. Greedier than the dog in the fable, she had tried to keep shadow and substance: Gerard's love, Brandon's liking. Now, lo! both have fallen into the water. There are a few circles, a few rising bubbles; then all is over—gone, sunk to the bottom, to come up again never more. Vanished from her grasp is the great house—are the buhl and marqueterie cabinets—are the "Venus surprised by Satyrs" and the "Susanna and the Elders"—are the vineries, pineries, peacheries. Did they ever exist? or were they only a mirage, such as the sky presents to us sometimes—a mirage of ships shocking together, of armed men meeting in fight?

"Go back to your pigstye!" said the magic fish to Ilsabil, the fisherman's wife, when she modestly requested to be made lord of the sun and moon. "Go back to your pigstye!" cries Fate to Esther. At any other time the subsiding from the prospect of being rather a great lady into the certainty of being a very small one would have caused considerable annoyance to Esther's aspiring soul. *Now*, the *things* she has lost merge and lose themselves in the *person* she has lost. But is he lost necessarily, irrecoverably? Despite the forlorn attitude, the tear-swollen face, trying to suffocate itself in down, Hope is busy whispering, "You will see him again to-morrow: men in real life are not like men in novels—changeless of purpose, hard as iron or adamant. What they are one half-hour, they are the exact reverse of the next; what they swear to-night they will unswear to-morrow." As Hope, the deceiver, thus murmurs, there comes to her ear the sound of wheels briskly rolling to the door. "Is the ball over so early? are they come back already? or——?" She does not give herself time to speculate on any other hypothesis, but, springing from the bed, runs to the window, draws aside curtain and blind, and looks out. The hall-door is open; a vehicle stands before it. The moonlight and the light shed from the hanging-lamp in the portico are fighting together, struggling for possession of a horse and dog-cart, of two footmen's floured heads, and of a portmanteau and hat-box that they are carrying out. "Thud! thud!" she hears the portmanteau go in at the back of the cart. Then a man comes out—a man in hat and overcoat—drawing on dogskin gloves, and saying, "John, go and look for my box of cigar-lights; I left it on the smoking-room table." It is St. John, speaking in much his usual voice. He is going away! going away! and he can think of his cigar-lights! Her heart stops pulsing for a second, then sets off galloping at the rate of a hundred and twenty a minute. Going without making any sign! She leans further out of the window, and rests her white arms, that look whiter than any lilies in the moonlight, on the sill. He is so close beneath her, if the servants were not there, she might call to him; as it is, he will never know that she has watched his departure. A sudden impulse prompts her to throw up the window higher, to rustle her dress, to cough, in order to attract his attention. At the unexpected noise John and Thomas turn their heads and look up, but their master does not. He gives a slight start, but, instantly recovering himself, walks steadily to the cart and gets in. Then she knows that he knows that she is looking at him—knows that he is resolute to part from her—

"taking no farewell—"

as Lancelot took none of Elaine.

The horse is a little fidgety at starting. "Wo-o-o! Gently, old lass!" This is the affecting form that St. John's last words take. She cranes her neck out of the window; she leans out her lithe body, reckless of the danger of losing her balance and tumbling on the hard gravel drive below, in her eagerness to catch the last glimpse of the lessening, dwindling bulk; then, forgetting to shut the window, careless of any cold or stock of rheumatism that she might be laying up for herself, she returns to her former position, flings herself again prone on her bed, again buries her face in the pillow; but this time no beguiling hope sits and whispers pleasant falsities to her. Hope got up upon the dog-cart, and drove away with Gerard.

The night wanes; morning dreams, that they say come true, invade many sleepers' brains. At Lord ——'s ball people are still dancing with the fury produced by champagne and supper; but Sir Thomas, Miladi, and Miss Blessington, are at home again, and in bed. Constance is not one of those hard dancers who think that one after-supper galop is worth ten ante-coenal ones. Not for all the entrancing valses Strauss ever composed would she run the risk of damaging the freshness of her toilette, nor the still more serious risk of exchanging the marble coolness of her cheeks for the unsightly flush of heat or the ugly pallor of exhaustion.

Dawn is just beginning stealthily to unlatch the eastern gate; her torch, new-lit, makes but a puny opponent for the night's one great and myriad lesser lamps. Esther has fallen into an uneasy doze, her damp brow and loosened hair resting on her bare, outflung arm. Suddenly a knock at her door makes her start up in a vague, confused horror. Is it St. John come back? Is it some one come to murder her? A thousand impossibilities flash across her bewildered brain. Without waiting for permission, the person who knocked enters; not St. John, nor a murderer— only a dishevelled housemaid, who has evidently just thrown a gown over her night attire, and endeavoured abortively to gather up the straggling hair out of her sleepy eyes under a muslin cap put on awry.

"A tallygraph for you, miss!" says she, coming forward, holding in one hand a blue envelope, and in the other a tall, solemn tallow candle, as sleepy as herself.

A telegraphic message! Oh hateful telegraph! Cruellest of modern inventions! Oh hastener of evil tidings, that, without you, come all too speedily! Oh maker of sick hearts and blanched cheeks and arrested pulses!

Esther snatches it, while a sudden, awful cold grasps her heart, and reads by the wavering, feeble light these words, in a scrawly clerk's hand:

"Robert Brandon to Esther Craven. Come home instantly; Jack is very ill."

With how few pen-strokes can a death-warrant be written! For a moment she sits bolt upright, void of breath or motion, as a white dead woman, from the house of whose fair body the spirit departed an hour ago; the telegram grasped in a stiff hand that knows not of it. Then consciousness returns, brought back by a huge, tearing, killing agony; then even the agony yields to one intense, consuming longing—one all-dominating purpose—the longing to slay time and space; to be with him *now*, this instant; to be beside Jack dying, not Jack dead.

"Can I see Sir Thomas?" she asks collectedly, but in a rough, deep voice. "I have had bad news from home: my brother is very ill."

"Indeed, 'm, you don't say so;" replies the servant, growing broadly awake under the delightful excitement of a calamity having happened to somebody, and of herself being the first recipient of the news.

"I *must* see Sir Thomas!" Esther says, putting her hand up in a bewildered way to her head, and then springing off the bed and walking quickly towards the door.

"See Sir Thomas," repeats the woman, the most unfeigned alarm painting itself on her broad face—"*now!* Indeed, ma'am, you must be mad to think of such a thing! It would be as much as all our places are worth if he were to be disturbed before his usual time."

Esther turns and clutches her arm, while her great eyes brimful of despair, burn on her face. "I tell you my brother is *dying!*" she says, hoarsely—"I know he is; I must go to him *this minute;* for God's sake help me to get to the station!"

"Indeed, 'm, I'm sorry to see you in such trouble, *that* I am!" answers her companion, moved to compassion by the terrible, haggard misery of the young, round face, that she, in company with her fellow-servants, had often admired in its happy, dewy rosiness at prayers on Sunday evenings; "but, you see, all the men are in bed, and Simpson 'ud cut off his own 'ead afore he'd venture to take out the carriage without Sir Thomas's orders."

The tall, yellow candle flares between them: lights up the tortured beauty of the one woman, the placid stolidity of the other. Esther groans, and smites her hands together.

"Is there *no* vehicle I can have?" she asks in impatient agony—"no cart?—no anything? I'd give all I have in the world to any one who would take me. Oh God! how many minutes I am wasting."

The housemaid puts down her flat candlestick on the table, and rubs her forehead with her rough fore-finger to aid her thinking powers. "There's the dog-cart that the under-servants goes to church in," she says, presently, with an uncertain suggestion: "if we could knock the men up, you might have *it*, perhaps."

"Knock them up this instant, then!" cries Esther, with passionate urgency—"*now, this minute!* Go, for God's sake!"

So saying, she almost pushes the woman out of the room, and herself follows her. Through long passages and corridors, full of emptiness and darkness—darkness utter and complete, save where through the gallery's high-stained east window the chilly, chilly dawn comes peeping, with a grey glimmer, about the black frames, never closing eyes, and stiff, prim simpers of the family portraits—down to the lower regions, where the huge kitchen-grate yawns, black as Erebus—up steep back-stairs along other passages. In one of these passages Esther stands, her frame trembling and teeth chattering with cold and nervous excitement, while her companion raps with broad, hard knuckles on a door, and loudly calls on Simpson to awake. But hard workers are hard sleepers, and it is some time before the coachman can be induced to leave the country of slumber. When at length he is aroused, and has come out to them, in all the yawning sulkiness of disturbed sleep, it is a still longer time before he can be induced to admit the possibility of *any* vehicle whatever being put at Esther's disposal: with so righteous a fear of his wrath has Sir Thomas succeeded in inspiring his subordinates.

It is not without the aid of all her remaining money, with the exception of what is needed for the purchase of her railway ticket—not without the aid of all that is left of poor Jack's hardly-spared five-pound note—that she is able at length to induce him to consent to the getting ready of the dog-cart "in which the under-servants goes to church." Fully three-quarters of an hour more elapse before one of the helpers can be knocked up, can dress himself, can harness the oldest and screwiest horse in the stables, and put him, with many a muttered grumble, into the cart. Wretched Esther follows the man and his lanthorn to the stable-yard, with the vain idea that her presence may hurry his movements. During most of the three-quarters of an hour she walks quickly up and down over the hard, round stones with which the yard is paved, or stands watching, with greedy eyes, every step in the harnessing process; while her hands clench themselves, as his are clenched who is dead by some very cruel, violent death, and a pain like a red-hot, two-bladed knife keeps running through her heart. Before the horse is well between the shafts, she has climbed into the cart and taken her seat.

"The luggage is not in yet, 'm," suggests the groom, respectfully.

"Oh! never mind the luggage," cries Esther, feverishly; "I don't want it! I don't want anything! I'm ready! Get in, please, and set off this minute!"

Dawn is breaking, slowly, coldly, greyly, without any of the rose-coloured splendours that mostly gild the day's childhood, as the glorious delusions of youth gild our morning. There has not been a positive, actual frost in the night—not frost enough to congeal the wayside pools or to kill the dahlias—but the air has, for all that, a frosty crispness, as of the first breath of coming winter. The trees and hedgerow holly-bushes loom gigantic, formless, treble and quadruple their real size, folded round and round in a mantle of mist; the meadows are like lakes of mist; sheets of vapour steaming damply up to the shapeless, colourless, low-stooping heavens. Esther has forgotten to take any wrap: through the poor protection of her thin cotton dress and jacket the mist creeps slowly, searchingly, making her limbs shake and shudder; but she herself is unconscious of it—she could not have told you afterwards whether she had been warm or cold.

At the turnpike gate a sleepy old man comes hobbling out (men at toll-gates are mostly one-legged), in his hand a candle, to which the white morning is beginning to give a very sickly, yellow look: it seems to Esther that he will never have done fumbling in his breeches-pocket for the sixpence of change that eludes his search.

"Why do you stop? Cannot you go a little quicker?" asks Esther, hoarsely, her teeth chattering with cold and misery, as the groom allows his horse to walk up a long, gentle incline.

"Sir Tummas allus gives pertikler horders as we should walk the 'orses up this 'ill," replies the man; "you see, 'm, it's collar-work pretty nigh all the way from our place to Brainton."

"But it is such a little hill, and Sir Thomas need never know," pleads Esther, imploringly. "I have not got any money now, but if you'll take me quicker—a good deal quicker—I will send you five shillings—ten shillings—by post, when I get home."

"Much obliged to you, ma'am," answers the man, touching his hat, and giving another instance of the influence of filthy lucre by whipping up his horse.

"When is the next train to Berwyn?" cries Esther, almost before they had pulled up at the station, to a porter, who stands waiting to receive any arriving passengers.

"7.20," replies the man, briefly.

"And what time is it now?"

"6.15."

"Is not there one before 7.20?"

"None; you are just too late for the 6.10 one; it has been gone about five minutes."

Unmindful of the presence of the careless, indifferent onlookers, Esther clasps her cold hands together and groans. In a great despair, as in a great bodily agony, we do not much mind who sees or hears us.

"Too late!" she says, with a heavy, tearless sob—"five minutes too late! Oh God, it *is* hard!"

"Any luggage, Miss?" asks the porter, in his civil, matter-of-fact voice.

The common-place question brings her back to life. "No, none," she answers, collecting herself; and so saying walks into the station, and, taking refuge in the waiting-room, sinks down upon a green Utrecht velvet chair.

Owing to the earliness of the hour, other occupant of the room is there none; neither is there any fire (a fire always looks in good spirits; it never has the blues). Alongside of the empty fire-place stands a stiff, green Utrecht velvet sofa, and round the bare table more green Utrecht velvet chairs. Opposite to Esther, against the wall, hangs a roll of texts. Involuntarily her haggard eyes lift themselves to them, and light upon this one—which, under the slightly inappropriate title of "Encouragements to Repentance," heads the list: "Woe to me, for I am undone!" She shudders, "Is it an omen?" turns away her head quickly, and tries to look out of window, but the wire-blind hinders her gaze. Once again, "Woe is me, for I am undone!" standing out clear and black in large type from the white paper, greets her eyes. She can bear it no longer, but rising hastily, runs out, and begins to walk swiftly up and down the platform.

Brainton is a large station—a junction of many lines. Engines are snorting and puffing about; boilers letting off steam, with a noise calculated to break the drum of any ear; tarpaulin-covered waggons standing shunted on side lines. A train has just come in, and is disgorging its human load; a man with a hammer is walking along by the side of it, stooping and tapping the wheels; porters are driving luggage-piled trucks before them, and shouting out, "By your leave!" to any unwary traveller who may cross the relentless path of their Juggernaut: other parties are enduring and answering, with angelic patience and *bonhomie*, the agitated and incoherent questions of unprotected females in waterproof cloaks and turn-down hats. Everybody and everything is rampantly *alive;* even to his handiwork, man seems to have imparted some of his own intense vitality; to the engines he has given motion and voice—motion and voice ten thousandfold stronger than his own.

In her hurried walks, Esther suddenly comes face to face with a fair-haired youth, who, followed by a porter carrying a gun-case, is walking lightly along with his hands in his pockets, whistling for very lightheartedness,

"I paddle my own canoe."

Jack's tune! What business has he to whistle it? All fair-haired youths, with nothing very prominent in any of their features, are more or less alike; and this amount of resemblance the unknown bears to her boy. Long after he has passed her, amid the shrieking of the engines, the shouts of the porters—"Take your seats for Wolverhampton, Birmingham!" "All here for Chester, Warrington, and Manchester?"—the well-known tune echos faintly back to her ears. An overpowering, blinding, deafening rush of feeling comes over her; she sits down hastily on a bench that is near at hand, in close proximity to an Irish labourer, with a blue-spotted bundle, and, careless of the contaminating contact, buries her head in her hands, and rocks to and fro in a paroxysm of despair.

It is one of those incontrovertible facts that we all know to be true, and that we all feel to be false, that every hour is of the same length; that in an hour of Elysium there are sixty whole minutes, and that in an hour of Hades there are only sixty. In Esther's hour of waiting there are, however, seventy-five minutes, as the train is a quarter of an hour late.

"Is it a fast train?" she asks eagerly of the bearded guard, who, with the politeness inborn in guards, opens the carriage-door for her.

"No, miss," he answers, with suavity—"slow train, miss; stops at every station; 6.10 was the fast train, miss!"

Off at last, sliding slowly at first past platform, officials, trucks, book-stalls, dowdy women and dusty men; then the wind comes beating with a strong rush against Esther's cheeks, blowing back her hair, as they fly through the air at the rate of fifty miles an hour.

The transit from Brainton to Berwyn occupies three hours, and during the greater part of that time Miss Craven maintains almost exactly the same attitude; with her greedy eyes devouring every field and tree and homestead as they run past—each village spire and bridge a finger-post to tell her that she is so much nearer her boy. She does not cry at all, or groan. Even had she wished to do so, conventionality—that makes us laugh when we would fain weep, makes us weep when we would fain laugh—would have forbidden her, for she is not alone in the carriage. Two other travellers share it with her—two extremely cheerful young men, to whom it is a matter of supreme indifference how many hedges and meadows are before, how many behind them. They are not exactly gentlemen: and indeed it is a matter of almost as curious inquiry as what becomes of all the pins that are made and lost, in what part of the train, if it be not in the guard's van, gentlemen and ladies travel, as assuredly they are but seldom to be met with in first-class carriages. The two youths have made themselves and their hat-boxes, rugs, &c., luxuriously comfortable, and seem rather disposed to be funny—to "show off," as children say, for the benefit of the lovely girl, who looks so disconsolate and dishevelled, who seems so unflatteringly unaware of their presence. They eat sandwiches and drink sherry; they are provided with a large stock of all the morning papers, and by-and-by the eldest and boldest of them proffers *Punch, Fun,* and half-a-dozen other dreary comicalities to Esther. She looks at him for a second with her large wistful eyes as she declines the offered civility, and then resumes her watch. Having obtained that one short glance, he ceases from his witticisms, half-conscious of being in the company of a great sorrow—as we involuntarily hush our voices and speak softly in the presence of our great master and owner—Death. Perhaps, cowardly slaves as we are, we fear lest, if we should speak loudly, he might be reminded of our existence—might lay his heavy hand on our shoulders also.

Another hour of waiting at Berwyn—another hour before there is any train for the branch line that leads to Glan-yr-Afon—any train, at least, that stops at so insignificant a station. Another hour of tramping in forlorn, impotent impatience up and down the platform, hustled by a hurrying crowd, who know nothing, and care, if possible, less about her and her grief. Well, if every one in England wept for every one else's sorrows, the noise of tears and sobbings would drown the whirring of all the mills in Leeds and Manchester—the booming of all the cannon at Shoeburyness. It is half an hour past noon, when, almost before the train has stopped at the little wayside station, Esther springs out. She is the only passenger for Glan-yr-Afon; and the man who unites in himself the functions of station-master and porter looks at her with a recognising eye. He must know whether Jack is alive or dead. He looks much as usual, but so he would whether Jack were alive or dead. Feeling an overmastering sense of fear of and repugnance from the news he may have to give her, she runs to the little wicket that leads out into the road.

"Your ticket, please, miss!" cries the man, following her.

She had forgotten it; it takes a minute to extricate it from her glove; she thinks that he looks as if he were going to speak; and, in a blind terror of what he might say, turns from him and rushes down the road. Any suspense is better than some certainties.

CHAPTER XX.

The mountains stand still and drowsy in the sleepiness of midday. Through the mistiness of the air, the russet glories of the dying bracken blaze on their breasts: the oak-woods still keep their deep dusk green, but the sycamore has felt the kiss of winter, and is growing red and sere beneath it. The sun is reigning, sole despot of the sky, having banished every rebel cloud beyond the horizon's limits. It is almost always fine weather when we are most miserable. Whatever poets say to the contrary, Nature is not sympathetic: rather is she very insolent to us in her triumphant, durable beauty. She loves to say to us, "Though you are weeping, my eyes are dry: though you are very sick and feeble, I am strong and fair: though you are most short-lived, here to-day and gone to-morrow, I am eternal, I *endure*."

In the meadow below the house, Jack's sheep are browsing—the Cheviots that he was so proud of: down the stony, steep back-road the cart-horses come jogging, to be watered at the pool at the hill-foot. With shortened breath and straining muscles, Esther runs fleetly past them, not daring to look into the carter's face. Through the gate, by the stables, and then the familiar little old house comes in sight, with its high-pitched roof and its old-fashioned chimney-pots. White pigeons are walking about on the gravelled sweep, bowing and scraping, and making love, with a formal solemnity worthy of Sir Charles Grandison. The Virginia creeper's scarlet banners wave from the wall; the hall-window is open; on the ledge lies a tabby cat, with one eye open and the other shut; two cocks are crowing in emulous rivalry in the farmyard. Everything looks peaceful, happy, *alive*. Gathering a little feeble hope from these signs, Esther collects her small remnant of breath, and runs towards the door. She has nearly reached it, when, stepping hastily out from the porch, one comes to meet her: *one*, but not *the* one: he will pass through that porch but once again, and then not of his own accord, but borne heavily on others' shoulders. Unable to frame any speech, Esther looks up mutely in Brandon's face (for it is he), and there reads her doom. "He is dead—he is dead!" she sees written wetly on either eye.

"He is better off than we are," says the young man, brokenly, taking hold of both her hands.

She sits down heavily on the bench in the porch: what hurry is there now? After all, it is but a poor shabby remnant of us that Death gets when he makes his final claim upon us; in most of us the greater, better part has died long before. Of Esther, three-fourths died as she sat on the oak bench in the porch that autumn morning: breath remained, and blood still circulated through veins and arteries, and speech and hearing were left; but youth, and hope, and heart, died very suddenly and utterly, to come back to life again never any more. She sits staring vacantly at the seat opposite her for several minutes, and then speaks distinctly, almost loudly: "How long ago?"

"About eight," answers Brandon, briefly and sadly, turning away his head to hide his womanish tears for the young fellow that fell asleep so gently in his arms, in the early morning, when other folks were waking.

"What was it killed him?" asks the girl, in the same hard, clear voice.

Bob looks at her in astonishment: he had been steeling himself against faintings, hysterics, a terrible scene of shrieks and waitings, but this conscious stony collectedness fills him with a fearful surprise.

"It was diphtheria," he answers, sorrowfully taking her hand again, and stroking it, while his hot tears fall thick upon it.

She leaves it in his, passive as the hand of a statue, unknowing, indifferent, whether he held it or not.

"Did he suffer much?" she inquires, lifting her lovely, hopeless eyes piteously to his face.

"Not at the last," answers Brandon, evasively, almost under his breath.

Silence for a few seconds: the cocks are still crowing, the pigeons courting, the cat purring on the window-sill: Nature is fond of these horrible contrasts.

Presently she speaks again: "Why was not I sent for before?" she asks in a rough, harsh whisper.

"We telegraphed for you yesterday morning, the instant that we found there was any danger," he replies, speaking very gently, but wincing a little under the reproach implied in her question.

"And it did not reach me till this morning. If I had had it when I ought, I suppose I should have been in time to see him," she says, with apathy, looking away towards the misty hill.

"He sent you his love," says Brandon, struggling again with that same breaking in his voice. "Dear fellow! he was quite happy!"

"Was he?" she says, with the same vacant look. "I'll go to him." As she speaks, she rises and moves towards the door.

"You had better not," he says hastily, laying his hand on her arm.

"Why?" inquires she, looking at him with perfect calmness; "are you afraid of my fainting or going into hysterics? You need not be; it is only that I am not the least sorry that Jack is dead, and that I want to be."

"It is not that," he answers, earnestly; "but—but—you know, dear, that it is a terribly infectious complaint."

"Is it?" she answers, a ray of animation lighting up her haggard face. "I'm glad; perhaps God will let me catch it!"

Seeing that she is resolute, he ceases trying to dissuade her. In the small dark hall, old Luath is lying on the rug; seeing Esther enter, he raises himself quickly, and goes to meet her, with heavy tail wagging and affectionate eyes, on which age is written in blue dimness. Now that the master's sister has come home, he is sure that the master cannot be far behind. He is waiting for him, waiting to walk round the farm; he has been waiting this long time, thinking that he has gone upon a journey; and so he has. But oh! Luath, it is a journey on which man may take neither horse nor dog, neither wife, nor sister, nor friend; a journey on which some man, woman, or child is setting off every minute that beats; and whence no explorers return, with maps and charts, and wondrous tales, to vaunt themselves of their exploits, and be extolled and praised as benefactors to their race. Let us hope that it is because they find that country most pleasant that they come not again. In the drawing-room a canary is shrilling his loud, sharp song: they have thrown a shawl over his cage to keep him quiet; but through the shawl the sun pierces, and the bird's keen clear jubilation goes up to meet it. How can he sing so very gaily now Jack is dead? At the room-door they pause.

"Don't come in! I'd rather have him to myself, please," Esther says, in a steady whisper.

"Promise not to kiss him, Essie!" Brandon rejoins, very earnestly; also in a whisper, "We cannot spare you too."

She takes no notice of his request, but, opening the door gently, enters the chamber, where the king of kings, and lord of lords, almighty Death—before whom we all grovelling do unwilling obeisance—is holding one of his myriad courts. It is but a small, slightly furnished room in which he is holding this one, but that concerns him but little. His majesty is so great that he can afford to dispense with the adventitious adjuncts of pomp and circumstance. Without his crown and sceptre, without his courtiers—Plague, Pestilence, and Famine—he is still very king and emperor.

The window is open, but the white curtains drawn—

"While through the lattice ivy shadows creep."

On the table stand physic-bottles—puny foils with which we fence with death—and an open Bible, out of which Brandon, with shaking voice, and a weak, dying hand held in his strong tender one, read the old comfortable words that have soothed many a transit, to the young traveller who was setting out meekly, and not fearfully, in the autumn morning. Over the bed spreads a white sheet, and beneath it a formless form!

Can that be Jack? Can that be Jack, lying still and idle in the bright midday?—Jack, to whom the shelter of a house was ever irksome, who was up and about at cock-crow, to whom all weathers were the same, and the bracing wind blowing about the heathery hills the very breath of his nostrils? A feeling of incredulity steals over her. She walks to the bed and turns down the sheet from the face, and the incredulity deepens into incredulous awe. Oh, ye liars! all ye that say that sleep and death are alike! what kinship is there between the pliant relaxer of soft limbs, the light brief slumber, that, at any trivial noise, a trumpeting gnat or distant calling voice, flies and is dissolved, and the grave stiff whiteness of that profoundest rest that no thousand booming cannons, no rock-rending earthquake, no earth-riving thunderbolt can break? It is an insult to that strong narcotic to liken any other repose to that he gives. They have crossed the young fellow's hands upon his unheaving breast, meekly, as the hands of one that prayeth; and laid sprigs of grey-flowered rosemary in them. She looks at him steadfastly, a great, awful amazement in her dilated eyes. Is *this* the boy that whistled "I paddle my own canoe"—whose step, glad and noisy, echoed about the stairs?—the boy that sat and smoked at the study window, with her fond head resting on his young slight shoulder?—the boy that was worried about failing crops and barren land?—the boy whose laugh had a sincerer ring in it than any one else's, who made so many jokes, and had such a light heart? Can *this* be he—this white, awful, beautiful statue? Was ever crowned king, in purple and minever, half so majestical as he, as he lies on his narrow bed in the scant poor room, with that serene stern smile that only dead mouths wear on his solemn changed face?—that smile that seems to say, "I have overcome! I *know!*"

Esther's love for Jack is great as love can be—greater than Jonathan's for David, greater than David's for Absalom; and this pale, prone figure is unearthly fair and grand; but can she connect the two ideas? What have they to say to one another? Can she realise that if this form be not her brother, neither will she find him again on the earth's face, though she seek him carefully with tears. For one instant it comes home to her; for one instant light darts into her soul—light keen and cruel as the forked lightning flash that, on some mirk night, glares blinding bright into a dark room, illumining every object as with the furnace-fires of hell! She sinks on her trembling knees by the bedside, and says, with dumb, heart-wrung entreaty—"God! God! give him back to me, or let me go where he is."

But the great Lord that said once, "Lazarus, come forth!" has said "Come forth!" to never another since him. "Lie thou still, till I call thee!" He says; and none durst move hand or foot. But since he cannot come to her, why should not she go to him? Has the disease that slew him spent all its force on that one slight frame? Is not there enough of it left to kill her too? It was Juliet's thought when she spake reproachfully to her dead Romeo, as she looked into the empty poison-cup—

"Oh,   churl!   drink   all   and   leave   no   friendly   drop, To help me after——."

Suddenly Brandon's beseeching words recur to her: "Promise not to kiss him, Essie!" If she kiss him, he may give her the boon of death. Instantly she rises, and stooping over him, lays her tremulous warm lips on his still cheek. The unearthly awful cold of the contact between the dead and the living strikes a chilly shrinking along her veins and limbs; but not for that shrinking does she desist. Again and again she kisses him, driven on by that strong drear hope, saying moaningly, "My boy,! my boy!—give it me! give it me!" Then unbelief comes back. This is not Jack: he is somewhere else. She will find him by-and-by. This is very terrible, this present experience, but she catches herself thinking she will tell Jack all about it when she sees him. To the incredulity succeeds a stupid apathy. She sinks down upon her knees again, with her elbows resting on the counterpane, and fixes her stony eyes upon the dead stripling; watches him; looks at him steadfastly, without intermission; looks at "the shell of a flown bird," as the old philosopher very grandly said. She does not know how long she means to stay there; she does not know how long she has already staid there; when some one entering, lays his hand upon her shoulder, and says, with kindly gravity, "Come away, dear!"

"I am doing no harm!" she answers dully, not moving her eyes.

"Come, darling!" he says, not attempting to reason with her, but speaking in the coaxing tone one would use to a fractious sickly child.

She answers neither "Ay" nor "Nay;" she neither resists nor consents, and so, half carrying, half leading, he takes her from the room, and they leave poor Jack lying all alone in his shroud, smiling sternly sweet.

CHAPTER XXI.

So the blinds are drawn down; a sort of notice that people put in their windows, saying, "Do not look in, or you will see Death!" and the few neighbours round drive up and inquire how Miss Craven is, and are informed that she is pretty well. And the servants each do the other's work; and there is a general interesting*bouleversement* in the household, and much chattering and crying and a stream of visitors in the kitchen. And Brandon goes hither and thither, taking upon himself all the drear work of arranging Jack's final departure from his home among the mountains, and keeping at bay his mothers and sisters, who, armed with bibles, hymnals, and "Reflections for a Mourner," are prepared to sally forth in proselytising ardour upon the conquest of Esther's soul. And Esther herself is, for the time, soulless as the fair marble mask in the quiet room upstairs.

"His lips are very mild and meek;
Though one should smite him on the cheek,
Or on the mouth, he will not speak."

If any one were to smite her on lip or cheek, neither would she resent it or complain; she sits in an armchair, in the drawing-room, with her hands folded in her lap, and the servants bring her tea every half-hour (incessant tea being supposed to be the necessary accompaniment of great grief), and request her to "keep up." So she sits in the armchair all day long—trying to be sorry, trying to weep. She has had Sarah in, and has made her tell her all the particulars of her brother's last hours; has listened attentively while the woman—the easy tears streaming down her cheeks—relates how "Mr. Brandon was with poor master all along, from the very first, and if he had been his own born brother, he could not have been kinder," and how he lifted him up in his arms, and laid his head on his shoulder—"Master could breathe easier so, poor dear young gentleman!"—and he (master) had been so pleasant-spoken to the last, and had said, said he, 'God bless you, old fellow! I'd have done as much for you, if I had had the chance;' and how, about seven o'clock, he had asked what o'clock it was—we all knew what that meant—and had then seemed to fall asleep in Mr. Brandon's arms, and just as the clock struck eight, he gave a sigh—like that—and a sort of pleasant bit of a smile, and was gone all in a minute!" It is very touching, but it does not touch Esther. She rises and walks into the hall, and looks at his greatcoat and his hat, and kisses his gloves, that seem to retain somewhat of the shape of the kind hands that once filled them. She thinks resolutely of how he has been her one friend throughout life; thinks of the presents he gave her, and of how seldom he went to any town without bringing her some little remembrance back from it; thinks of that last five-pound note, so hardly spared, and yet so very gladly given; thinks of how poor he was, how slight, how young. But it is all no good; it seems to her like some pathetic tale about a stranger that she is telling herself. And the days pass, and she grows weak from inanition, but refuses all food. If she can be unnatural, horrible enough to feel hunger and thirst now Jack is dead, at all events she will not indulge her low nature; and so she eats not, and her pulse grows feeble,

"And all the wheels of being slow!"

So it comes to pass that she falls sick and is carried up to bed, and lies there half in sleep, half in insensibility. And the mornings and the evenings go by, and Jack's burial-day comes. They had hoped that it would have passed without her knowing, but it was not so. Now that he is leaving his home for this last time, he does not go light-springing down the stairs, as at other times, but with much tramping of strange feet, with purposed muffling of strange voices. How can she fail to hear,

"The steps of the bearers heavy and slow?"

Through all her trance it breaks; from her little latticed window, with her sick limbs trembling beneath her, and her miserable eyes nailed to the gaoler coffin, in whose strait custody her dead lies prisoned, she sees the drooped pall and the black-scarfed mourners. These mourners are but few, for Jack—though now awfuller than any absolutest monarch—was, in life, poor and of little consequence: the gap made by the extinction of that one young life is but narrow. Standing there, she feels a pang of bitter regret and anguish that there are not more people to be sorry for Jack. And so, being weak, the fountains of her soul are broken up within her, and she falls to weeping mightily; and, but for that weeping, she would, perchance, have died, some say; but I think not—for why should grief, being our natural element, kill us any more than water the fish, or air the bird?

CHAPTER XXII.

Thus the grave yawns for another victim, and having swallowed him, and a million more that same day, returns to its former state of insatiable famished greed. It is a law—natural, wise, and comprehensible by the feeblest understanding—that all created beings, in which there is progressive life, must come forth, ripen, decay, and fall. But why, oh! why, in too many cases does the decay and fall forerun the ripening? Why is so many a worm permitted to gnaw out so many a closed bud's green heart? Why is the canker death allowed to pasture on so many an unblown life? Why are so many little toddling children, not yet come into the heritage of reason to which we are all by our human birth entitled, borne from their mother's emptied arms to their small short graves? Is it, as Hartley Coleridge very nobly, whether truly or untruly, said—

"God only made them for his Christ to save?"

Very wasteful is the mighty mother, knowing that her materials are inexhaustible. And so they lay Jack down in the wormy grave.

"Bear, bear him along, With his few faults shut up like dead flow'rets."

No one will ever abuse him or say anything ill-natured of him again; for to speak evil of the helpless, speechless, answerless dead, requires a heart as bad, a nature as cowardly vile, as his must be that foully murders a young child. And the mourners go home, and take off their hatbands and scarves, and give them to their wives to make aprons of. And old Luath lies in the hall, watching still, with ears attentively pricked at any incoming footstep, and hope drooping, as day droops too, begins to howl dismally towards sun-down.

And Esther—"You ought not to grieve for him; it is a happy change for him; he is in Heaven!" So they had said to her weepingly, as people do say to us, when the desire of our eyes has left us; but even as they spake them, she felt that they were but words, hollow and empty as the greetings in the market-place with which we salute our indifferent acquaintance. Was she so sure that the change had been a happy one? It was a change from the known to the unknown, from moderate certain evils, and moderate probable good, to infinite possibilities of horror or blessedness. Where lay this heaven, this promised land, where we so confidently lodge our dead? Was it up above that highest bluest arch that looks in truth pure enough, and solid enough, to be the floor of some sweet elysium? Ah! no! Human knowledge, that like a naughty, prying child, has found out at once so infinitely too much and too little, tells us that that skyey vault is but thin air. She thinks, shuddering—"What if heaven itself be but thin air? *Is it anywhere?* What if its existence at all be but the fine-spun fancy of poor human hearts, that must needs frame for themselves some blessed definite hope, since *real* hope have they none? Is it a beautiful tender fraud practised by themselves upon themselves, to save them from the despair of the black vagueness into which they must send out their departed ones, and go out themselves when life's little day is over? Oh, light! light! When the great God said, 'Let there be light!' in the material world, why did not He say so too in the world of spirits? I know that my soul shall live for ever! I know that there is that within me over which the most insatiable of monsters, insatiabler than any slain in classic tale—a monster that turns beauty to unsightliness, whose handmaid is corruption, and whose drink is tears—has no power. But alas! alas! can I rejoice in my immortality, when I know not where, or under what conditions, those endless, endless æons will roll themselves away into the past?"

"We must bow beneath the rod," says old Mrs. Brandon, nodding her head and her poke bonnet. It is the identical poke bonnet, and not another, in which she once paid her congratulatory visit. The summer sun had browned it a little, but otherwise it is in a state of high efficiency. "We must bow beneath the rod, knowing that it is a *tender Father's* hand that wields it."

"I suppose so," answers Esther, listlessly. To her it seems a matter of indifference whose hand it was that inflicted such an immedicable hurt, seeing that it has been inflicted by some one, and now yawns, a gaping rift in her soul, never to be assuaged by any balsam.

"Suppose!" cries Miss Bessy, her long, uncertain nose reddening a little in her righteous zeal, at the slackness of Esther's faith. "Surely, surely, if we are *Believers*, there can be no '*suppose*' in such a case."

"I did not mean to express any doubt," Esther says, gently, but wearily.

"*Suppose* will not do us much good at the *Last Day*," continues Miss Bessy, rather venomously. "Unless we can lay fast hold upon Jesus" (*laying hold of a roll of paper to exemplify the tenacity of her own grasp*[1]), "unless we have assurance that we are *Elect*, where are we?"

"If it is any comfort to you, love, you know that you have our prayers," says Mrs. Brandon, squeezing Esther's hand.

"We have set apart a special day with several Christian friends," says Bessy, with animation, "to wrestle in prayer for you, that this searching dispensation may be blessed to your conversion—that you may find the Lord."

"Thanks," answers Esther, meekly, too broken-down to resent even the indignity of being set up on a metaphorical stool of repentance, amid a select circle of Miss Bessy's Christian friends.

"If we could send you anything from Plas Berwyn—" begins Mrs. Brandon.

"Any books or leaflets," interrupts Bessy.

"Any eatables, or anything of that kind," amends her mother. "I daresay you have not been thinking much about housekeeping lately, my poor child; and you know whenever you feel inclined to come to us *for good*, you will always find open hearts and open arms," concludes the good old woman, suiting her action to her words, and folding Esther in a black bombazine embrace.

86

"Thank you very much," replies the girl, gratefully, her low, sad voice almost smothered by her mamma-in-law's bonnet strings, amongst which her little disconsolate head is lying *perdue.*

"We are only broken cisterns, you should remember, mamma," says Bessy, a little reprovingly of her parent's carnal materialism; "leaky vessels, all of us! You should direct Esther to the one *Ebenezer.*"

The race of Eliphaz the Temanite, Bildad the Shuhite, and Zophar the Naamathite, is by no means extinct: if not in the male line, at all events in the female, it still survives in the person of many a Miss Bessy Brandon.

Brandon has been busy all day with Jack's lawyer: returning in the afternoon, he finds Esther sitting on the study window-ledge, on which she and Jack used to sit on summer nights, and watch the little feathery, plumy clouds sail along the sky's sapphire sea; used to watch

"The large white stars rise one by one,"

and speculate who lived in them, and what they were made of. Jack has entered into the ranks of the initiated, but she still sits and wonders.

"Come out for a stroll, Essie," says the young man, stooping over her till his yellow beard, curly as a bull's forehead, almost touches her dark, drooped head.

"If you like," she answers, indifferently; and so drags herself slowly up, and walks away heavily to get ready.

"Where shall we go?" inquires he, as they stand at the farmyard gate. The callow Cochin chickens have grown up, and are stalking about, in all the dignity of long, yellow legs and adolescence, under the frames of the corn-ricks, "Where shall we go?—to see my mother?"

"That would be returning her visit almost too promptly," answers the young girl, with a weary smile; "it is not more than half an hour since they left this house."

"*They!* Were my sisters here too, then?" inquires Bob, quickly; his confidence in his sisters' infallibility as to words and actions not being so perfect as in his mamma's. "I hope their coming did not worry you much."

"Nothing worries me now," she answers, calmly; "I defy anything to worry, or anger, or frighten me. Do you remember a line of Mrs. Barrett Browning's? Oh no, by-the-bye, you never read poetry—

"'Fallen too low for special fear.'

"That is exactly my case."

"I never know the right sort of thing to say, don't you know," remarks Brandon, rather awkwardly, looking down, and poking about little pebbles with the end of his stick. "But I had hoped that mother might have hit upon something that would have comforted you a little."

"She meant to, I am sure," replies Esther, gravely. "She was very kind, and so were the girls, I suppose; only some of Bessy's speeches rather reminded me of Eliphaz the Temanite's, 'Remember, I pray thee, who ever perished, being innocent? or where were the righteous cut off?'"

"I wish to heaven that Bessy could be possessed with a dumb devil!" says that young lady's brother, looking up, red with sudden anger. "No one should ever have my leave to try and cast it out."

"Let us go to the common," Esther says, abruptly, not heeding him.

|1|A fact.

CHAPTER XXIII.

The common stretches, long and stony, at the top of the hill that backs Glan-yr-Afon. To reach it they have to climb through the waving woods, where the beeches and sycamores emulously cast down their crimson and amber leaves to strew the path before their feet. To reach it, they have to pass the woodman's stone cottage, his pigstye, and his little yap-yapping rude dog. From the common you may look upwards or downwards—northwards, to the valley-head; southwards, to the sea.

From among the scant brown mountain-grass, the limestone crops frequent, in peaks, and slabs, and riven rock-fragments. Far down in chinks and crevices little black-stemmed ferns grow darkling, and over the rock's rough face, the lichens, drab and yellow, make their little plans and charts. One may fancy some former people of strong giants sleeping very sweetly beneath those unchiselled tombstones, with their epitaphs written out fairly in Nature's hand in green mosses and rain furrows. In spring the hill's harsh front is crowned with a yellow splendour of gorse-flowers, but now a single blossom blows here and there desolate, just to hinder the old saying from being quite a lie. Below, in the valley, the mists roll greyly; and out above them

Naullan church spire rises, pointing heavenwards, as if showing the way to the dead flock gathered round its feet; points heavenwards, like the finger of some sculptured saint.

The autumn winds are piping bleakly, singing an ugly peevish dirge for the gone summer, bending the frost-seared brake-fern all one way, and with rough hands pushing back Robert and Esther, saying, "This is *our* territory; what brings you here?"

Esther shivers.

"You are cold, I'm afraid," says Brandon, anxiously, putting his head on one side, not out of sentimentality, but in the endeavour to keep his hat on.

"Yes," she answers, rapidly; "and I'm glad of it. I should *hate* to feel warm and comfortable; I want to be cold, and faint, and miserable *always*. Do you know," she continues, excitedly, laying her hand on his arm, "yesterday I *laughed?*—yes! I actually *laughed!* and it is only a fortnight since—wasn't it horrible of me? I want the days and the weeks to go by quickly: I want it to be a long time since Jack died!"

Brandon makes no answer—partly because he is utterly at a loss for a reply, partly because he is still wrestling with his hat. Presently they come to a disused quarry, where the quarrymen have hewn out rock-ledges into comfortable seats for them. The wind howls above them, angry and sad, and flings hither and thither the flowerless broom-pikes that look over the cliffs, but it cannot reach them.

"Esther," says Bob, taking up a sharp stone, and beginning to draw white lines on the rock's smooth surface, "it seems as if I had no other occupation nowadays than to say disagreeable things to you, but I cannot help it: do you think you can bear to leave Glan-yr-Afon in three weeks or so?"

"Bear!" she repeats, bitterly; "I can bear anything—I have proved that already, I think. Any one that had had any feeling would have died of *this;* but I—I sleep and eat as well as ever: I am like the baker who refused Christ the loaf—I *cannot* die!"

"Hush!" he says, eagerly; "don't want to go before your time, or perhaps the Almighty might take you at your word."

There is silence for a moment or two, then Brandon speaks again: "At the end of three weeks you will come to us then?"

No answer.

Thinking that the wind has carried away his words, he repeats his question: "At the end of three weeks you will come to us, then?"

She turns her head round slowly. "Could not I live in some hovel by myself?"

He shakes his head. "Impossible! You see," he says, speaking with slow reluctance, "he— poor dear fellow!—laid out a great deal of money on all the latest improvements in farming implements, and things of that kind, and they did not bring him anything back; they would have done, no doubt, if he had been given time," he adds, quickly, afraid of seeming to cast the faintest slur upon the dead boy.

"You mean to say that I have no money—that I am a beggar," she says, fixing her clear, steadfast eyes upon him: and in them is none of that dismay which her words seem to imply.

"I mean to say," he answers, heartily, "that henceforth you are to be one of us, and that we are very, *very* glad of it."

She does not say "Thank you;" she neither assents nor refuses; she only looks away, and watches the distant trees tossing violent arms, in riotous fight with the wind.

Something in her manner makes Brandon uneasy. "It is agreed, then?" he asks, eagerly.

No reply.

"Why don't you answer me, Esther?" (with a slight natural impatience in his tone).

She turns her face slowly round towards him—a face paled by her late agonies, thinned by long fastings, and by thousands of great tears. "Because," she replies, "I have one friend in the world now; and when I have answered you, I shall have none!"

"What *do* you mean?"

"If I were to come to you, I should come as your supposed future wife, shouldn't I? Well, I should be an impostor."

A great sickening fear whitens his brown face, but he contains himself, and speaks quietly: "Do you think I meant to *bargain* with you? Do you think I meant to make a profit for myself out of your troubles? What have I ever done to make you think me so mean?" he asks, reproachfully.

She draws a heavy sighing breath. "Why am I beating about the bush?" she says, chiding herself; "it must out, sooner or later! Oh, Bob! Bob! if I had it in me to be sorry about anything, I should be sorry about this!"

"About what?" he asks, cruelly excited. "Look this way, Esther. Is it—is it what I have been afraid of all along?"

88

Her head sinks in shamed dejection on her breast. "Yes, it is," she answers, faintly.

There will be a great storm at sea to-night; the gulls are circling about, calling wildly to one another—here, twenty miles inland.

"Who is it?" asks Bob, in a husky whisper, presently.

She sighs again, profoundly. "Do you remember," she says, "before I went to the Gerards'—how many hundred years ago was that?—your saying one day that you wished they had not got a son, and my laughing at you about it? Well! you were right!—it is he!"

Brandon turns away his head, speaks not, nor gives any sign. It is in silence that a good brave man meetliest takes his deathblow.

"I don't think he would have cared much about me, if I had let him alone," says Esther, taking a sort of gloomy pleasure in painting herself as black as possible.

There is a pause—a pause, during which Brandon is fighting one of those duels in which most men have to engage at least once in their lives—the duel with a mortal agony, that says, tauntingly, "I am your master! I have conquered you!" to which one that is valiant makes answer, "You are strong, you are terrible; but you are *not* my master. I will keep you under!"

"You will go to him then, of course, instead of coming to us?" he says, presently, speaking in some one else's voice (for it certainly is not his own), and keeping his head turned away; for no one is willing to parade their death-pangs before others' eyes.

She laughs derisively. "Go to him! Hardly! I should get but an indifferent welcome if I did. You know I never told him a word about you—ladylike and honourable of me, wasn't it?—but some one else did him that good office; and now, if he were to see me falling over the edge of that cliff, he would not put out a finger to save me. That is his sort of love!" She ends, bitterly, "And I think he is right."

Another longer silence. Brandon is wrestling with that adversary of his, that deadly anger and pain; that riotous, tigerish jealousy, that makes us all murderers for the time, in thought at least; that mad, wild longing—madder, wilder than any love ardour, than any paroxysm of religious zeal—to have his hands, for one moment of strong ecstasy, about the throat of the rich man that has robbed him of his one ewe lamb. The sweat of that combat stands cold upon his brow, but he overcomes. After a while he speaks gently, as one would speak to a little sick child: "Were you very fond of him, Esther?"

"I suppose so," she answers with reflective calmness, looking straight before her. "I must have been, or I should not have said and done the mean things I did. I should not have degraded myself into begging him to take me back again, when I might as well have begged of this rock" (thrusting her soft hand against it) "to turn to grass and flowers. He told me that he would never forgive me, either in this world or the next! I thought it very dreadful at the time, but I don't much care now whether he forgives me or not."

"Have you forgotten him so completely already?" asks Bob, forgetting his own misery for the moment, in sheer blank amazement.

"Forgotten him!" she repeats thoughtfully. "No, not that! not that! I might as well try to forget myself. I remember every line of his face, his voice, and his ways, and every word he said almost; but if I were to see him standing close to us here, I should not feel the slightest inclination to go to him, or to call him to come to me. I feel all dead everywhere." They remain in the same attitude for several minutes, neither of them stirring nor uttering a word. Then Esther speaks, with a certain uneasy abruptness. "Well!" she says, "I am waiting!—waiting for you to call me a murderess and a bad woman, and all the other names that St. John gave me, on much less provocation. Make haste!" she says, with a nervous forced laugh; "I am in a hurry to hear that I have succeeded in getting rid of my last friend. Quick! quick!—tell me that you hate me, and have done with it!"

"*Hate* you!" he repeats, tenderly; his brave voice trembling a little in spite of himself, and the meekness of a great heroism ennobling his face. "You, poor soul! Why should I hate you because another man is better and more loveable than I, and because you have eyes to see it?"

The eyes he speaks of turn upon him, wide and startled, in astonished disbelief of his great generosity.

"You don't understand!" she says, quickly. "You don't take it in. I was *engaged* to him; I was going to marry him, and all the time I never once mentioned your name to him, of my own accord; and when he asked me about you, I said you were only a common acquaintance. You *must* hate me!" she ends, vehemently; "don't pretend that you don't!"

"Hush!" he answers sorrowfully, but very gently, "that is nonsense! I don't even hate him; at least" (pausing a moment, to thrust down and trample under foot one more spasm of that intolerable burning jealousy)—"at least, I try not. It was my own fault. I knew all along that I was poor, and stupid, and awkward, that I had nothing but sheer love to give you, and I hoped against hope that that might win you at last. We all set our affections upon some one thing, I suppose," he says, with a patient, pitiful smile, "and I daresay it is all the better for us in the end that we don't often get it: but oh, love! love! you might have told me!" Then his resolution breaks a little, and, covering his face with his hands, he groans aloud, in a man's dry-eyed agony—how much awfuller to see than a woman's little tears, that flow indifferently for a dead pet dog, or a dead husband! Esther sits looking at him during several minutes, awestruck, as a child that has made a grown-up person cry; then one of those quick impulses that carry some women away seizes her.

"Bob!" she says, putting her sweet mouth close to his ear, while her gentle, vibrating voice thrills down to his stricken soul, "I have been very bad to you, but I will make up for it!"

"Will you?" he says, looking up with a mournful, sceptical smile; "how?"

"I'll marry you, if you'll have me, and make a very good wife to you," she says, simply, with unblushing calmness, eyelids unlowered, and voice unwavering.

"Child!" he cries, "you are very generous, but do you think I cannot be generous too?"

"It is not generosity," she says, eagerly; "I *wish* to marry you!"

He shakes his head sadly. "You don't know what you are saying," he answers, taking her little hand between both his—holding it almost fatherly, in a tender prison. "You don't know what marriage is. You don't understand that a union so close with a person you don't love would be infinitely worse than being tied to a dead body; the one could not last very long, the other might for years."

She looks at him silently, with her grave, innocent eyes, for an instant or two while she tries to get down to the depth of her own heart—tries to feel something besides that numb vague indifference to everything. "If I don't love you," she says, doubtfully, "I love nobody; I like you better than anyone else in the world! Didn't Jack die in your arms?" she says, breaking out into sudden and violent tears. "Wasn't his head resting on your shoulder when he went away? Oh, dear, dear shoulder!" she cries, kissing it passionately. "How can I help loving you for that?"

At the touch of her soft mouth, that has been to him hitherto, despite his nominal betrothal, a sealed book, his steadfast heart begins to pulse frantically fast: if a river of flame instead of blood were poured through his veins, they could not have throbbed with an insaner heat: his sober head swims as one that is dizzy with strong drink; reels in the overpowering passion of a man that has not frittered away his heart in little bits, after our nineteenth-century fashion, but has cast it down,*whole*, unscarred by any other smallest wound, at one woman's feet. Oh, if he might but take her at her word! Or, if there must be no marriage between them, why may not there be a brief sweet marriage of the lips? It would do her no harm—since kisses, happily for the reputation of ninety-nine hundredths of the female world, leave no mark—and it would set him for an instant on a pinnacle of bliss that would equal him with the high gods.

But the paroxysm is short. Before she who has caused it has guessed at its existence, it is put down, held down strongly. Women are very often like naughty children, putting a lighted match to a train of gunpowder, and then surprised and frightened because there is an explosion.

"You are deceiving yourself," he says, speaking almost coldly. "You think you like me, because I happened to be the last person that was with the dear fellow that's gone—because you knew that I was grieved about him too: but think of me as you thought of me when you were at the Gerards', and you'll know how much you love me for myself."

"Love!" she repeats, dreamily—"love! love!" saying over and over again the familiar, common word, until by very dint of frequent repetition it grows unfamiliar, odd, void of meaning. "I have used up all I ever had of that: perhaps I never had much, but I think you the very best man that ever lived. Is not that enough to go upon?"

He shakes his head with a slight smile. "Worse and worse! that would be a difficult character to live up to. No!" he says, looking at her, with the nobility of an utter self-abnegation in his sorrowful blue eyes. "I will *never* marry you, Essie! never!—I swear it! If you were to go down on your knees to me, I would not: I should deserve that God should strike me dead if I could be guilty of such unmanly selfishness!"

"You refuse me then?" she says, with a sigh of half-unconscious relief. "Was ever such a thing heard of? And I have not even the satisfaction of being able to be angry with you."

"I refuse you!" he answers, steadily, taking her two little hands in his. "But—look at me, dear, and believe me—as I said to you before, so I say now, I shall love you to-day, and to-morrow, and always!"

The two young people sit silent; each looking down, as it were with inner eyes, on the wreck of their own destiny—wrecked already! though their ships have so lately left the port. The vapours still curl about the dun hills: the clouds stoop low, as if to mingle with their sister mists. With many a sigh, and with many a shiver, the trees shower down the ruddy rain of their leaves; earth is stripping her fair body for the winter sleep. Then Brandon speaks:

"Promise me one thing, Essie!"

"*Anything* almost."

"That this—this—*talk* we have had shall make no difference as to your coming to us!"

"What!" she cries, suddenly springing to her feet, tears of remorse and mortification rushing to her eyes. "After having done you the worst injury a woman can do a man, am I to be indebted to you for daily bread—for food, and clothes, and firing? How much lower do you wish me to fall? Have you *no* pity on me?"

"You are misstating the case," he says, quietly, his downcast eyes fixed on a little fern that, with his stick, he is up-digging from its strait home between two neighbour rocks: "you will be indebted to *me* for nothing; I shall not even be there; I shall have gone back to Bermuda."

"Gone!" she repeats, blankly. "Are *you* going too? Is everybody going away from me? And do you think," she continues, passionately, "that it will be easier for me to lie under such an obligation to your mother and sisters than to you? Is not it always harder to say 'Thank you!' to a woman than to a man? And would not I immeasurably rather sell matches, or hot potatoes at the street-corners, than do either?"

He smiles slightly, yet very ruefully withal. "My darling!" he says, looking wistfully at her noble head and delicate, thoroughbred face, "you are a great deal too pretty to sell hot potatoes, or matches either; bread-winners should not have faces like yours!"

"That is bad reasoning," she answers, trying to laugh; "if I am pretty, people will be more likely to buy my wares. Oh, Heavens!" she cries, throwing up her eyes to the dark wrack driving over head, "what business have people to bring children into the world only to starve, or to sponge upon others? There ought to be an Act of Parliament against it! Oh, why—why is not one allowed to have a look into life before one is born—to have one's choice whether one will come into it at all or no? But, if one had, who *would* come?—who would?"

"I would," answers Bob, stoutly. "I don't think the world is half a bad place, though it is the fashion to abuse it now-a-days, and though it does do one some curiously dirty turns now and then. But after all," he adds, very gravely, "bad or good no one can accuse it of lasting long, and there's a better at the other end of it."

"Or a worse," says Esther, gloomily. "Who knows? One cannot fancy the world without one, can one?" she continues, following out her own ideas. "One knows that, not long ago, there *was*, and not long hence there *will be*, no I; but one cannot realize it!"

"Why should one bother one's head trying?" says Bob, with philosophy.

"The leaves seem to come out in the spring," she continues musingly, without heeding him, "the winds to blow, and the birds to sing, all with some reference to *oneself*: one cannot understand their all going on when oneself has stopped!"

Reflections of this character are not much in Bob's way. Pensive musings upon the caducity of the human race are, generally, rather feminine than masculine. A woman dreams over the shortness of life, while a man crowds it with doings that make it, in effect, long. Brandon turns the conversation back into a more practical channel.

"Have you any friends that you have known longer than you have us, Essie?"

"None."

"Any to whom it would be less irksome to you to lie under an obligation, as you call it?"

"None."

"Any that you like better, in short?"

"None," she answers, with a little impatience, as if, in a way, ashamed of her own destitution. "Good or bad, I have *no* friends, *none*, and you know it."

He looks at her with a sort of shocked amazement. "Good God! what is to become of you, then?" he asks, bluntly.

"I don't know."

"How are you to live?"

"I don't know."

"Have you never once thought about it?"

"Never. I thought that we," she says, her lips beginning to quiver piteously, and her faithful thoughts, that never wander far from it, straying back to the new bare grave, where one half of that "*we*" lies sleeping—"I thought that we should have lived to be old together: most people live to be old!"

A great yearning pity—purer, nobler, with less of the satyr and more of the god in it, than in any access of human passion between man and woman—seizes him as he looks at her, sitting there so forlorn, with one thin hand lifted to shield her weary purple-lidded eyes, that have grown dim with weeping for "her boy."

"Poor little soul!" he says, compassionately; and he takes, with brotherly intimacy, the other hand, that lies listless in her lap, and lays fond lips upon it.

When one is on the verge of a burst of crying, a harsh word may avert the catastrophe, but a kind one inevitably precipitates it. With how unjust, unreasonable a hatred does one often regard the person who ill-advisedly speaks that kind word! As for Esther, she buries her face on his shoulder and begins to sob hysterically. Her hat falls off, and her bare, defenceless head leans on his breast, while the autumn wind wafts one long lock of her scented hair against his face. She has forgotten that he *was* her lover, has forgotten that he is a man; she remembers only that he is a friend, which is a sexless thing—that he is the one being who cares about her, in all the great, full, crowded world. Despite the utter abandonment of her attitude, despite the clinging closeness of her soft supple form to his, he feels none of the painful stings of passion that so lately beset him. They are tamed, for the moment, by a nobler emotion: they dare as little assail him now, as they dare assail the holy saints in Paradise. With any other man such abandonment might have been dangerous: with him she is safe. He lays his kind broad hand on her ruffled head, and strokes it, just as Jack used to do, in the pleasant days before he went.

"Come to us, Essie!" he says, with persuasive tenderness; "we'll be good to you; we won't plague you; you would have come to us as my wife, why won't you come as my sister?"

"Because I like buying things better than being given them!" she answers, vehemently, though still incoherent from her tears. "If I had come as your wife, I should have given you something in exchange,—*myself*, body and soul, my whole life. It would have been of no value *really*, but you would have thought it something; as your sister, I shall give you absolutely nothing!"

"Child! child! why are you so proud?" he asks, with mournful reproachfulness. "Why are you so bent on standing alone? Which of us *can* stand alone in this world? We all have to lean upon one another, more or less, and the strongest of us upon God!"

"Yes, I know that!—I know that!" she answers, hastily; "but I would far rather beg, and have to be obliged to any common stranger that I had never seen before, and that most probably I should never see again, than to you. With them I should, at all events, start fair: I should have no old debts to weigh me down; but to you I owe so much already, that I am racking my brain to think how I can pay some part of it, instead of contracting new ones."

"You would contract no new ones," he rejoins, earnestly; "on the contrary. Essie, you told me just now that you would be very glad to be able to make up to me for any pain you may have made me suffer: *now* is your time!—*now* is your opportunity!"

"How?" she sobs, lifting up her head, and speaking with a slow, plaintive intonation. "You will be at the other side of the world, thousands of miles away! How will it affect *you*?"

"I *shall* be at the other side of the world," he answers, steadily; "better that I should be so! better so! But do you think that my being so far away will make it pleasanter for me to think of the one creature I love above all others on the face of the earth, starving, or worse than starving, at home?"

"Worse than starving!" she repeats, opening her great, wide eyes in astonishment. "What *can* be worse than starving? Oh! I see what you mean" (a light breaking in upon her, and the colour flushing faintly into her face). "You think I should go to the bad—do something disgraceful, if I had nobody to look after me: I am sorry you have such a bad opinion of me, but I don't wonder at it," she ends, with resigned depression.

"I have no bad opinion of you!" he answers, eagerly; "but I know the end that women, originally as pure and good as you, have come to before now. I know how hard it is for a beautiful poor girl to live *honestly* in this world, how frightfully easy to live *dis*honestly!"

"Well!" she says, recklessly; "and if I did live dishonestly, what matter? Whom have I got to be ashamed of? Whom have I got to disgrace?"

Brandon looks inexpressibly shocked. "Hush!" he says, putting his hand before her mouth; "you don't know what you are saying! For Heaven's sake, talk in that strain to no one but me! Any one that knew you less well than I do might misunderstand you."

She looks up at him, half-frightened. "One does say dreadful things without intending it," she says, apologetically; "but I only meant to express, as forcibly as possible, how little consequence it was what happened to me."

"For God's sake, word it differently then!" he says, almost sternly; "or, better still, don't say it or think it at all! It is morbid, and it is not true. If it is of no consequence to any one else what becomes of you, it is of intense, unspeakable consequence to me: how many times must I tell you that before you mean to believe it?"

"To *you!* in *Bermuda?*" she says, with a little doubting sigh.

"Yes, to *me*, in *Bermuda*," he answers, firmly. "Perhaps you think that it was only because I looked upon you as my own, my *property*, that I took so great an interest in you: it was not as *mine*, it was as *yourself*, that I cared about you. You are *yourself* still, though you are not nor ever will be mine."

Then, like Guinevere's, "his voice brake suddenly."

"Then, as a stream, that spouting from a cliff
Fails in mid-air, but gathering at the base,
Remakes itself and flashes down the vale,
Went on in passionate utterance."

"Essie! they say that women are more capable of self-sacrifice than men. Prove it to me now! Sacrifice this pride of yours; consent to the one thing that would make me leave England with almost a light, instead of *such* a heavy heart!"

She is silent for a minute or two, halting between two opinions; hesitating, struggling with herself: then she speaks, rapidly, but not easily—

"I cannot, Bob—I cannot! Ask me anything, not quite so hard, and I'll do it! Just think how young I am, seventeen last birthday, I have probably forty or fifty more years to live; do you wish me to promise to be a pensioner for *half a century* on your mother's charity?"

He does not answer.

"Don't be angry with me for having a little self-respect!" she cries, passionately, snatching his hand. "I will go and stay with your people till I have found something to do, if they will have me. I will get your mother to help me in looking for work; I will take her advice in *everything*, do whatever she tells me; I will do anything—anything in life to please you, except——"

"Except the one thing I wish," he answers, sadly and coldly.

"If you speak in that tone I shall have to promise you *anything*," she says, despairingly; "but it will only be perjury, for I shall infallibly break my promise again. Why should not I work?" she goes on, in a sort of indignation at his silence. "Am I a cripple, or an idiot? Let me wait till I am either the one or the other, before I *come upon the parish!*" she says, with the bitter pride of poverty; "at all events, let us call things by their right names."

"As you will," he answers, deeply wounded. "If you take it as a great indignity to be offered a home with the oldest friends you have in the world, of course I can say no more; but oh, child! you are wrong—you are wrong!"

CHAPTER XXIV.

It is Sunday evening. Miss Craven has been to church for the first time since her *bereavement*, as people call it. She has displayed her crape in all its crisp funeral newness before the eyes of the Plas Berwyn congregation. Also, she has been made the subject of conversation, over their early dinner, between the imbecile rector and his vinegar-faced, bob-curled wife; the latter remarking how unfortunately unbecoming black was to poor Miss Craven—really impossible to tell where her bonnet ended and her hair began; and how lucky it was for her that people did not wear mourning for as long a time as they used—three months being *ample* nowadays, *ample* for a brother! Esther has sat in their pew for the first time alone: she has looked at Jack's prayer-book, at his vacant corner under the dusty cobwebbed window, with eyes dryly stoic; she has walked firmly after service down the church-path, past a grassless hillock, where he who was her brother lies, dumbly submitting to the one terrific, changeless law of decay—the law that not one of us can face, as applying to ourselves, without our brains reeling at the horror of it. Oh! thrifty, harsh Nature! that, without a pang of relenting, unmixes again those cunningest compounds that we call our bodies—making the freed elements that formed them pass into new forms of life—makes us, who erewhile walked upright, godlike, fronting the sun, communing with the high stars—makes *us*, I say, creep many-legged in the beetle, crawl blind in the worm!

It is evening now, and Esther sits, in her red armchair, beside the drawing-room fire, *alone* again. The wind comes *banging* every minute against the shuttered French window, as one that boisterously asks to be let in; the ivy leaves are dashed against the pane, as one that sighingly begs for admittance. Every now and then the young girl looks round timidly over her shoulder, in the chill expectation of seeing a death-pale spirit-face gazing at her from some corner of the room; every now and then she starts nervously, as a hot cinder drops from the grate, or as the small feet of some restless mouse make a hurry-skurrying noise behind the wainscot. As often as she can frame the smallest excuse, she rings the bell, in order to gather a little courage from the live human face, the live human voice, of the servant that answers it.

Around Plas Berwyn also the wind thunders—against Plas Berwyn windows also the ivy-leaves fling themselves plaintively; but there the resemblance ends. The steady light from the lamp outblazes the uncertain, fitful fire-gleams: at Plas Berwyn there are no ghost-faces of the lately dead to haunt the inmates of that cheerful room. They are all sitting round the table on straight-backed chairs—no lolling in armchairs, no stealing of furtive naps on the Sabbath—sitting rather primly, rather Puritanically, reading severely good books. To Bob's palate, the *Hedley Vicarsian* type of literature is as distasteful as to any other young man of sound head and good

93

digestion, but he succumbs to it meekly, to please his mother; if Sunday came *twice* a week, I think he would be constrained to rebel. From the kitchen, the servants' voices sound faintly audible above the howling wind, singing psalms. The family are divided between prose and poetry. Miss Brandon is reading a sermon; her sister a hymn. Here it is:—

THE FIRM BANK.[1]

"I have a never-failing bank,
A more than golden store;
No earthly bank is half so rich,
How can I then be poor?

"'Tis when my stock is spent and gone,
And I without a groat,
I'm glad to hasten to my bank,
And beg a little note.

"Sometimes my banker, smiling, says,
'Why don't you oftener come?
And when you draw a little note,
Why not a larger sum?

"'Why live so niggardly and poor?—
Your bank contains a plenty?
Why come and take a one-pound note
When you might have a twenty?

"'Yea, twenty thousand, ten times told,
Is but a trifling sum
To what your Father hath laid up,
Secure in God his Son.'

"Since, then, my banker is so rich,
I have no cause to borrow:
I'll live upon my cash to-day,
And draw again to-morrow.

"I've been a thousand times before,
And never was rejected;
Sometimes my banker gives me more
Than asked for or expected.

"Sometimes I've felt a little proud,
I've managed things so clever:
But, ah! before the day was done
I've felt as poor as ever!

"Sometimes with blushes on my face
Just at the door I stand;
I know if Moses kept me back,
I surely must be damned.

"I know my bank will never break—
No! it can never fall!
The Firm—Three Persons in one God!
Jehovah—Lord of All!"

A charming mixture of the jocose and familiar, isn't it?

"Mother," says Bob, rather abruptly, looking up from a civil-spoken, pleasant little work, entitled "Thou Fool!" which he is perusing (it is generally an understood thing that conversation is not to be included among the Sabbath evening diversions at Plas Berwyn)—"Mother, do you know I don't think I shall try for extension, after all?"

The gold-rimmed spectacles make a hasty descent from their elevation upon Mrs. Brandon's high thin nose.

"Dear Bob! why not?"

"Because I don't see why I should," he answers, frankly. "I'm perfectly well: why should I shirk work any more than any other fellow? I might say that I prefer a cool climate to a hot vapour-bath, English winds to oily calms, but I don't suppose that I am singular in that!"

"My dear boy!" says the old woman, tremulously, stretching out her withered hand across the table to him,—"why did you ever go into that dreadful profession? Why did not you enter the ministry, like your dear father, as I so much wished you to do?"

"I'm very glad I didn't, mother!" replies the young man, bluntly; "I should have been a fish sadly out of water, and, after all, I hope that Heaven will not be quite so full of black coats that there will not be room for one or two of our colour."

"Have you told Essie?" inquires his eldest sister, joining in the conversation.

"Yes, she knows."

"Will she be ready to go with you on such short notice?"

"No."

"You'll leave her behind, then?"

"Yes."

"I thought you always had such a horror of long engagements?"

"So I have, but—but" (involuntarily lowering his voice, and lifting "Thou Fool!" to be a partial shade for his face)—"there is no engagement between us now!"

Six startled eyes fix themselves upon his face. "What!" cry three simultaneously shrill female voices. "No engagement! Has she thrown you over?"

"No."

"Have *you* thrown *her* over?" (with an astonished emphasis on the pronouns).

"No."

"Have you quarrelled, then?" "No, we haven't," answers Bob, wincing. "Poor little child! one would hardly choose such a time as this to quarrel with her. Cannot you understand two people coming to the conclusion that they are better apart; better as friends than as—as anything else?"

His three comforters stare at one another in bewilderment; then his parent speaks, shaking her head oracularly:

"I'm afraid I see how it is, Bob; you have found out that this unfortunate girl is, in some way, unworthy of you, and you are too generous to confess it, even to us."

Bob dashes down "Thou Fool!" in a fury, and his blue eyes shine with quick fire.

"Mother, do you call that the 'charity that thinketh no evil?' I tell you, Essie is willing to marry me to-morrow, but I—"

"But you are *not* willing!" interrupts the domestic pack, bursting again into full cry.

"Tell us something a *little* more probable, Bob, and we'll try and believe it," subjoins Bessy, with a small curling smile.

"It is a matter of perfect indifference to me whether you believe me or not," replies the young man, sternly; keeping under, with great difficulty, an unmanly longing to box Miss Bessy's ears. "I only tell you, *upon my honour*, that Essie is willing to marry me, and that I—solely for her own sake, solely because I know that an inferior being cannot make a superior one happy— am *not* willing."

"And a very good thing too," cries Bessy, viciously. "I always thought you were singularly ill-suited to one another; I always said so to mamma and Jane. Didn't I, mamma?—didn't I, Jane? 'Can two walk together except they be agreed?' you know."

"Girls," says poor Bob, harried almost beyond endurance, and addressing his sisters by the conveniently broad appelative which covers everything virgin between the ages of six and a hundred—"Girls, would you mind going into the dining-room for a few minutes? I want to speak to mother alone."

The "girls" look rebellious, but their rebellion does not break into open mutiny. Rising, they comply with his request.

"Of course, what *most nearly* concerns our *only* brother cannot be supposed to have any interest for *us*," says Bessy, leaving her sting behind, like a wasp, and shutting the door with as near an approach to a bang as her conscience will admit.

As soon as they are well out of the room, Bob comes and sits at his mother's feet, and lays his head on her lap, as he used to do when he was a very little boy. She passes her fingers fondly through his curly hair.

"This is a severe trial, my dear boy," she says, a little tritely; "but take an old woman's word for it; look for comfort in the right direction, and you'll *surely, surely* find it!"

"*I* don't want comfort," answers Bob, pluckily; he having by no means exiled his sisters in order to pule and whimper over his own woes. "*I* do very well."

"I thought you had come to your old mother for consolation," answers his parent, a little aggrievedly: naturally somewhat disappointed at being balked of the office of Paraclete, so dear to every woman's heart; "if not, what was it that you wanted to talk to me about that you did not wish your sisters to hear?"

"About *her!*" he answers, emphatically, lifting up his head, and reading her face earnestly. "I didn't wish her to be the mark for any more of Bessy's sneers. I wonder," he says, a little bitterly, "that she who is always talking about '*our Great Exemplar*' does not recollect that *He* never sneered at any one."

"Did you say that it was Esther Craven that you wished to speak to me about?" inquires Mrs. Brandon, rather coldly.

"Mother," he says, passionately, "she has not a farthing in the world! What *is* to become of her?"

"Any one that my dear son takes an interest in will always be welcome to a home with me, for as long as they like to avail themselves of it," says the old lady, primly.

He shakes his head.

"She would not come," he says, despondently; "she is too proud: she hates to be beholden to any one: she is bent on working for her own living."

"And a very proper resolution, too," replies his mother, stoutly, her heart being steeled against Esther by a latent conviction that that fair false maid has dealt unhandsomely by her son. "Providence is always more willing to help those that help themselves."

"How *can* she help herself?" cries Esther's champion, indignantly. "What sort of work are those little weak hands, that little inexperienced head, fitted for?"

"Women with hands as weak and heads as inexperienced have toiled for their daily bread before now, I suppose," rejoins Mrs. Brandon, with a certain hardness, foreign to her nature, and arising from that spirit of contradiction, innate in us all, which makes us look coldly upon any object that some one else is making a fuss over.

Bob springs to his feet in great wrath, and speaks low and quick: "Mother! I'm sorry I ever broached this subject to you; one takes a long time, I see, to get acquainted with one's nearest relatives' characters. If you can see the child of one of your oldest friends working her poor little fingers to the bone for the bare necessaries of life without stretching out a finger to help her, *I* cannot!"

Speaking thus disrespectfully, he walks towards the door.

"A   spaniel,   a   woman,   and   a   walnut   tree, The more you beat 'em, the better they be."

says the rude old saw. Every woman, from a mother to a mistress, enjoys, rather than otherwise, being bullied.

The old woman half rises, and stretching out her hand to her son, says, "My boy! come back! let us talk rationally: don't quarrel with your old mother about a person that will never be so good a friend to you as she is."

He turns, half hesitating: anger's red ensign still aflame on his honest face.

"Shall I tell you, Bob, why I cannot feel common compassion for—for this girl?"

"Why?"

"Because," says the old lady, with emotion, Mr. Brandon's image heaving up and down rather quicklier than usual upon her ample breast,—"because some instinct tells me that she has not had common compassion upon you."

"'An eye for an eye, and a tooth for a tooth;' in fact," answers Bob, with a sarcasm unusual to him, "you are forgetting, mother, how often you have impressed upon me that we are no longer under the Mosaic dispensation! But why should she have compassion on me, may I ask? In what way do I stand in need of it? *I'm* not a woman, thank God!"

She looks at him, intently, with a steadiness that disconcerts him. "Bob, can you look me in the face and tell me that you have not been unhappier since you knew Esther Craven than ever you were before in all your life?"

"I have," he answers, simply, "and happier too; so that makes it square."

Foiled in this direction, she varies her point of attack a little: "Can you look me in the face, and tell me that since your engagement she has behaved to you as a modest, honourable woman should behave to the man she has promised to marry?"

He casts his eyes down troubled, and begins to fidget with a dilapidated little Chelsea Cupid on the mantelshelf, too truthful to say "Yes," too generous to say "No."

"She is ready to fulfil her promise," he answers, evasively. "She is willing to marry me whenever I like, as I told you before—to-morrow! to-night! this instant, if I wish!"

"For a home, of course; one can understand that, in her situation," says his mother, in a tone of slighting pity.

Bob perceives, and is stung by it.

"No, not for a home!" he answers, indignantly. "Poor soul! she may have that without paying such a heavy toll for it."

"To what motive, then, do you ascribe her willingness?"

"She told me that she liked me better than any one else in the world," he answers, with the reluctance of one who is making a statement that he believes will not be credited by the auditor to whom it is addressed.

"My poor simple boy! and you believed her?" (with a sort of compassionate scorn).

He hesitates. "I believe that she meant what she said at the moment," he replies, doubtfully.

"If there was such perfect harmony of opinion between you, why was the engagement broken, may I ask?" she inquires, a little sharply.

No answer, except quickened breathing, and a frown slightly contracting his climate-bronzed forehead.

"Was it—oh, my dear boy! if it was so, no one can respect your scruples more than I do—was it because you were not quite sure that she was one of the Lord's people?"

"Oh, dear, no," answers the young man, quickly, with scarcely repressed impatience in his tone—"nothing of the kind. God forbid my being so presumptuously uncharitable! How am I to know who is, or who is not? All I know is that if she is not, neither am I; and I trust, mother, that you will find, by-and-bye, that they are not quite such, a scanty nation as you seem to imagine."

"A higher authority than I am has expressly designated them 'a little flock,'" says the old woman, sententiously, pursing up her mouth; "but far be it from me to wish to judge, whatever you may imply. But I am still waiting to hear what your motive was for breaking your engagement, a motive which you seem to have such an unaccountable difficulty in telling me."

He looks down, for an instant or two, biting his lips, then speaks petulantly:

"Why should I tell you, mother?—why should I tell any one? A man's *motives* are his own concern, whatever his actions may be; if mine are strong enough to satisfy myself and her, surely that is enough."

"Oh, of course," answers his mother, rather nettled at what she considers a want of confidence; "only that, unless I am put in possession of the circumstances of the case, I really don't see how I can be expected to give advice——"

"I don't want advice," interrupts the young man, eagerly. "I want a much better thing—assistance."

"Assistance in what?"

"Why, in hindering that poor girl," he says, with warmth, "from being thrown upon the world penniless, helpless, and without a friend, as she will be after the sale at Glan-yr-Afon."

"Not without a friend, as long as you are alive, Bob; one can answer for that!" rejoins his mother, rather tartly.

"I count for nothing," says Bob, quietly. "A man's friendship can be of no service to a woman, unless he is in some authorised position of relationship or connection with her; otherwise he does her more harm than good. What she needs, and what I hoped she would have found in you, mother, is a woman-friend."

"If," replies his mother, drawing herself up and looking very stiff—"If she is, as you say, *too proud* to avail herself of the home that I am, *for your sake,* willing to offer her, she is likely to be *too proud* to consent to be befriended in any other way."

Brandon looks at her for a moment with something akin to indignant scorn in his face, dutiful son as he usually is; then, repenting, throws himself on his knees beside her, and clasping his arms about her withered neck, says, entreatingly: "Mother, why are you so hard upon her?—what has she done to you? Just think, how would you have liked Jane or Bessy, when they were her age, to have been driven out into the world to make their own way, without a single soul to say a kind word to them, or give them a helping hand; and," he continues, musingly, "they never could have been exposed to the temptations she will be—they never were beautiful, like her!"

He had never spoken truer words in all his life, but the truth is not always the best to be spoken.

"At all events," says the old lady, with emphasis, freeing herself from his arms, and getting rather red in the face—"At all events, Bob, however disparagingly you may speak of them, they were and are good, modest, pious girls, that would not trifle with an honest man's affection for their own amusement, as handsomer ones have done before now."

"I never heard of any honest man having given them the chance," retorts Bob, sarcastically, quitting his caressing posture, with a revulsion of feeling as sudden as it was complete.

"The servants are assembled," says the youngest, best, modestest, piousest of the girls, opening the door, and putting in her little drab face. "Must I tell them to go back to the kitchen for a quarter of an hour, or has Bob nearly finished his *private communication?*"

"Quite!" replies Bob, emphatically.

He is standing leaning against the chimneypiece, his colour heightened, and a sorely angered look on his open simple face.

"You need not wait for me, mother," he continues, seeing his parent look inquiringly towards him, as she moves with the slowness of age and portliness to the door; "I shall not come to prayers to-night. When one prays, one ought to be in charity with all the world, ought not one? And I am not."

[1]A real Revivalist hymn.

CHAPTER XXV.

The rough winds and the spiteful rains have wellnigh stripped all their red-and-yellow clothing off the trees: upon the oaks alone some leaves still hang persistent, though withered and crackly. The apples and pears are all gathered and stored for the winter; even the dark-blue Orleans plums, that require the crisping frost to ripen them, are eaten and gone.

The sale at Glan-yr-Afon is over; it is enrolled among that countless array of unrecallable events, great and little, that is past. The new tenant, an ordinary Welsh farmer, with an overfull quiver of sprouting Welshmen and Welshwomen, has entered into possession. No one has taken the trouble to "redd up" the garden for the winter; flowers do not help to pay the rent—they give back nothing but their beauty and perfume; and so, over Esther's trim flower-beds, sheep-dogs gallop, and children, boisterous with health and spirits, run races. The rustic seat under the old cherry-tree—the seat that Jack fashioned in the summer evenings—has been broken up for firewood; and in Jack's chair in the dining-room, the father of the family reposes his plethoric bulk of an evening, when he does not happen to be getting drunk at the "Punch Bowl," and snores euphoniously.

And Bob, pursued by blessings, prayers, lamentations, and strong wishes for his safe back-coming, is gone—gone away in a smoky steamer, over the mist-mantled grey sea. Not a few of the tears that fell for him came from Esther's eyes—not love-tears, shed privily, secretly, dashed away with hasty care at the sound of any approaching footsteps, but poured out openly, publicly, in the presence of his mother and sisters—mingled with theirs, indeed, as of no different quality. Not more openly, not more publicly, had she wept for old Luath, when, on the day before the sale, the old dog, who had ailed and moped ever since his master's (to him) unaccountable disappearance, crawled weakly to her feet, and, looking up dimly wistful into her face for the last time, died licking her tender hand. On the day before his departure, Brandon came to say "Good-bye" to her.

"I have told mother *nothing*," he says, with some embarrassment, in allusion to their late engagement—"nothing, except that I was sure that I could not make you happy. I have given her no reason, Esther—give her none either! She will not ask you point-blank, and it is always easy to evade indirect questions; there are some things that it is of no use being confidential about."

"I see," she answers, with a faint smile. "I understand, neatly as you have gilded the pill, you are afraid that she would turn me out-of-doors if she knew what a treacherous, black-hearted wretch I have been; that I should have to take refuge even sooner than I must otherwise do in the workhouse, to which I always look forward as my final destination."

Then, bidding God bless her, he wrings her hand, strongly, and so takes his last farewell of her, nor ever sees her fair face and great gentle stag eyes again.

And now he is gone—gone with a difficult smile on his face, and very little money in his pocket. He never has much, but he has less than usual now; having spent his few last sovereigns on the erecting a plain white cross at the head of Jack's low grave, that, when this generation has passed, his place of sleeping may not be quite undistinguished from that of his neighbour dust. He has gone, with his heart's strongest longing balked, his prime hope death-smitten; but yet not despairing—not cursing his day, nor arraigning High God, saying, "Why do I, undeserving, thus suffer?" He carries away with him no heavy seething load of revenge, no man-slaying ardour of hatred against the woman that has wronged him, and the man for whose sake she did it. Life is full, interesting, complex—not all on one string, whatever morbid women and moody rhymers may say; not all sexual love—all of it, that is, that is not devoted to drinking, as Anacreon, Catullus, and Moore have dulcetly told us. And therefore, though poor, disappointed, and heart-wrung, Brandon is not all unhappy. He has been greatly sinned against, and has forgiven, thus exercising the function that raises us nearest to a level with the Godhead.

And meanwhile Esther, left behind in wintry Wales, takes his emptied place at *triste* Plas Berwyn. Despite all her resolves, despite her high talk that a morsel of Mrs. Brandon's bread would choke her—that it would be better to starve than to be under any obligation to the family of the man she has betrayed—she is now eating that suffocating bread, now lying under those annihilating obligations.

Want makes us swallow our dignity—makes us do many mean things. One *must* live; one must keep in that breath that perhaps is only spent in sighs: and Mr. James Greenwood has made us all out of love with the workhouse. So she sits down three times a day at Mrs. Brandon's table, the unwillingest guest that ever sat at any board, and eats the bread of charity, and the roast mutton and apple-tart of charity, when the conclusion of the long Puritan grace gives her permission to do so.

There is plenty of time for thinking at Plas Berwyn, for in that still household talk is not rife. When people never leave their own little one earth-nook, rarely see any one beyond their immediate family circle, and rarelier still read any reviews, papers, books, that treat of any subject but one, they have not much to talk about. There are few minds original enough, copious enough, to suffice to themselves—to be able to do without supplies derived from external objects. Our thoughts are generally our own, merely by right of immediate possession; mostly they are the thoughts of others, more or less digested, more or less amalgamated with thought-matter of our own.

They are not unkind to her, these chill faded women. Not loving her—for, as Bessy appositely quoted, "Can two walk together except they be agreed?"—and Esther and they are most surely in nothing agreed; mistrusting her, though not knowing, of having dealt falsely by their brother; sincerely, though bigotedly, looking upon her society as unprofitable—nay, almost contaminating; as being one of the unregenerate many—one standing in the cold, outside their little clique of elect, safe souls: despite all this, they are yet willing to give her food and shelter, to give them her for an indefinite number of years, to make her a part of their own dry sapless lives.

But she is not willing—oh, most unwilling! Let me not be mistaken, however: it is not with the dryness and saplessness of the offered life that she quarrels. Life must henceforth be to her, everywhere, dry and sapless; the duller it is, the less it contrasts with her own thoughts. It must be lived, somewhere: it can be lived pleasurably nowhere. Then, why not unpleasurably, greyly, negatively, at Plas Berwyn? Why not, supposing that she had been able to pay for her own cups of tea and slices of mutton, for her own iron bedstead and deal washhand-stand?

But, supposing that she was not able; supposing that she was so destitute as to be glad, even while weeping over his poor rough body, that her old dog had died because she was too poor to be able to keep him; supposing that this life entailed upon her the bitter pain of being daily, hourly grateful to people for whose society she had a strong repugnance, and upon whom, in the person of one of their nearest and dearest, she had inflicted a mortal injury? It is hard to live with people whose every idea runs counter to your own—whose whole tone of thought and conversation is diametrically opposed to what you have been used to all your life—and yet not be able to contradict, to argue with, or differ from them, because you are eating of their bread and drinking of their cup. The mere fact of feeling that you are too deeply indebted to people to be able, without flagrant ingratitude, to quarrel, makes you desire ardently to fall out with them.

"How much better to be a professed beggar at once!" thinks Esther, with a sort of grim humour. "How much better to whine and shuffle along the streets at people's elbows, swearing that you have a husband dying of consumption, and six children all under three years of age starving at home!"

It is only the very basest and the very noblest natures that can accept great favours and not be crushed by them. Esther's is neither. To her it is only the thought that her state of dependence is temporary that makes it supportable. She has lost no time in appealing to Mrs. Brandon for her aid in the search for work—*work*, that vague word, that conveys to her no distinct idea, that stands to her in the place of something to be done by her, in return for which she may be able to obtain food and drink, without saying "Thank you" to any one for them.

On the afternoon of the day of Bob's departure Esther has been sitting for an hour or more, in listless sadness, on the fender-stool before the fire, her eyes staring vacantly at the battered Michaelmas daisies and discoloured chrysanthemums in the wintry, darkening garden outside. Mrs. Brandon's steel knitting-pins click gently, as she knits round and round, round and round, in the monotonous eternity of a long-ribbed knickerbocker stocking. The fire-gleams flicker dully red on the sombre, large-patterned flock-paper, which makes the room look twice as small and twice as dark as it need otherwise do. Esther is roused from her reverie by the entrance of the servant with the moderator lamp.

"Mrs. Brandon!" she says, addressing her hostess.

"Yes, my dear!" The "my dear" is a concession to Bob's memory.

"Bob told me," says the young girl, with some diffidence, "that you were good enough to say that you would help me in looking for—for—something to do!"

The old lady looks scrutinizingly at her over the tops of her spectacles. "My dear son expressed such great, such *surprising* anxiety, considering that your connection with him is at an end, about your future, that I *did* promise."

"And you will?" asks the other, timidly.

"*I* always keep *my* promises, Esther, I hope" (with a slight expressive accent on the *I* and *my*).

"When will you begin?—soon?—at once? to-morrow?" cries the girl, eagerly.

Mrs. Brandon hesitates: "I must first know for what sort of employment you wish—for what sort you are best suited?"

"I am suited for nothing," she answers, despondently; "but that must not deter me. If nobody did any work but what they were fitted for, three quarters of the world would be idle."

"Would you be inclined to take a situation as governess, if one could be found for you in a respectable pious family?"

She shakes her head. "I don't know enough, and I have no accomplishments. I can read a few pages of 'Racine' or 'Télémaque' without applying *very* often to the dictionary; modern French, with its colloquialisms and slang, baffles me; and I can play a few 'Etudes' and 'Morceaux de Salon' in a slipshod, boarding-school fashion; but these extensive requirements would hardly be enough."

Mrs. Brandon pauses in consideration. "There are so few occupations open to *ladies*," she remarks, with an emphasis on the word. "Most professions are closed up by our sex, and all *trades* by our birth and breeding."

"When one is a pauper, one must endeavour to forget that one ever was a lady," answers Esther, rather grimly; "my gentility would not stand in the way of my being a shoeblack, if women ever were shoeblacks, and if they paid one tolerably for it."

"Would you like to try *dressmaking?*" inquires her companion, rather doubtfully.

Esther gives an involuntary gasp. It is not a pleasant sensation when the consciousness that one is about to descend from the station that one has been born and has grown up in is first brought stingingly home to one. Happiness, they say, is to be found equally in all ranks, but no one ever yet started the idea that it was sweet to go down. Quick as lightning there flashed before her mind the recollection of a slighting remark made by Miss Blessington, *à propos* of two very second-rate young ladies, who had come to call at Felton one day during her visit there, that "they looked like little milliners!" Was she going to be a "*little milliner?*"

"I'm afraid I don't sew well enough," she answers, gently, wondering meanwhile that the idea has never before struck her what a singularly inefficient, incapable member of society she is. "I cannot cut out: I can make a bonnet, and I can mend stockings in a boggling, amateur kind of way, and that is all!"

Recollecting whose stockings it was that she had been used to mend in the boggling way she speaks of, a knife passes through her quivering heart.

"The same objection would apply to your attempting a lady's-maid's place, I suppose?"

"Yes, of course" (bending down her long white neck in a despondent attitude); "but" (with regathered animation in eye and tone)—"but that objection would not apply to any other branch of domestic service—a housemaid, for instance; it cannot require much native genius, or a very long apprenticeship, to know how to empty baths, and make beds, and clean grates: I ought to be able to learn how in a week."

Mrs. Brandon's eyes travel involuntarily to the small, idle, white hands that lie on Esther's lap—the blue-veined, patrician hands that she is so calmly destining to spend their existence in trundling mops and scouring floors.

"My dear child," she says, with compelled compassion in her voice, "you talk very lightly of these things; but you can have no conception, till you make the experiment, of what the trial would be of being thrown on terms of equality among a class of persons so immensely your inferiors in education and refinement."

"I believe it is a well-authenticated fact," answers Esther, firmly, "that in some town in one of the midland counties a baronet's wife is, or was, earning her living by going out charing. What right have I to be more squeamish than she?"

"It is unchristian," pursues Mrs. Brandon—unconvinced by Esther's anecdote, which indeed she treats as apocryphal—"to call anyone common or unclean, and God forbid that I should ever do so! But imagine a lady, born and bred like yourself, exposed to the coarse witticisms of the footman and the intimate friendship of the cook!"

Esther's little face seems to catch some of the deep fire-glow—her breast heaves up and down in angry, quick pants.

100

"Mrs. Brandon, do you suppose that they would be so *impertinent*——?" she begins, fiercely; then breaks off, ashamed. "I forgot; it would be no impertinence then! Well!" (with a long low sigh) "I am tough: I have borne worse things! This is but a little thing, after all; I can bear this!"

"I think, Esther, that if, as I fear, you are leaning on your own strength, and not on an *Unseen Arm*, you are overrating your powers of endurance."

"Perhaps; I can but try."

"Impossible!" answers Mrs. Brandon, with cool, common sense. "Who would hire you? Ridiculous!—childish! No, Esther; we must try and find something more eligible for you, if you are still foolishly bent on declining the *happy*, and respectable, and (I humbly hope I may say) *pious* home that I am so willing—that we are all so willing—to offer you."

"Oh yes! yes! yes!" cries the child, passionately. "I *am* bent on it! It is less degrading even to be exposed, as you say, to the witticisms of the footman and the friendship of the cook, than to live upon people on whom you have no claim beyond that of having been already most ungrateful to them—than to impose on their generosity, to sponge upon them!"

"As you will, Esther," answers Mrs. Brandon, loving her too little, and respecting her independence of spirit too much, to reason further with her.

There is a pause—a pause broken presently by Esther, who speaks diffidently: "Mrs. Brandon, don't you think that if I could get into one of those large shops in London, or one of our great towns, I could try on cloaks, and measure yards of ribbon, without requiring any great amount of knowledge of any kind, theoretical or practical?"

Mrs. Brandon looks doubtful. "It is not so easy as you may imagine, my dear, to obtain admission into one of those shops: a friend of mine made great efforts to get a situation for a *protégée* of hers at Marshal & Snelgrove's, or Lewis & Allenby's, and after waiting a long time, was obliged to give it up as hopeless."

"Perhaps she was not tall?" suggests Esther, rather timidly.

"I really never inquired."

"They like them tall!" says the girl, involuntarily drawing up her slight *élancé* figure; "and I'm tall, am I not?"

"I should imagine that that qualification alone would hardly suffice," answers the old lady, drily; "and indeed," she continues, pursing up her mouth rather primly, "even if it would, I should hardly think a situation in a shop, or other place of public resort, desirable for a girl so young, and of so—so—so *peculiar* an appearance as you."

"Peculiar!" repeats Esther, rather resentfully, raising her great eyes in unfeigned, displeased surprise to her companion's face. "Am I so very *odd-looking*, Mrs. Brandon? I don't think I can be, for no one ever told me so before!"

"I did not say *odd-looking*, my dear," returns Mrs. Brandon, sharply; "please don't put words into my mouth."

"If people came to buy cloaks, they would surely be thinking of how *they* were looking, not how *I* looked," says Esther, not yet quite recovered from her annoyed astonishment; "*my* appearance, beyond the mere fact of my being tall, could not be of much consequence one way or another."

Mrs. Brandon takes off and lays down her spectacles the better to point the rebuke she is about to administer.

"Esther," she says, severely, "since you insist on my explaining myself more clearly, I must tell you that I think a girl should be steadier in conduct, and more decidedly imbued with religious principles than I have any reason for supposing you to be, before she is exposed to the temptations to which a young and handsome woman is liable in one of those sinks of iniquity, our great towns."

Esther flings up her head with an angry gesture. "I really don't see what temptations a person even as unsteady and irreligious as I am," she says, contemptuously, "could be exposed to in a haberdasher's shop. Temptation, in a woman's mouth, always implies something about *men;* and in a place specially devoted to woman's dress, one would be less likely to see them than in any other spot on the face of the earth."

"If you are so much better informed on the subject than a person of *treble* your years and experience," says Mrs. Brandon, resuming her spectacles, and beginning to knit faster than ever, "I have, of course, no more to say."

An apposite retort rises prompt and saucy to Esther's lips, clamouring for egress through those sweet red gates; but the recollection of Mrs. Brandon's weak tea and legs of mutton, and the obligations thereto hanging, drives it back again. She leans her elbow on her knee, and elevates her straight dark brows.

"The question is," she says, gravely, "can you suggest anything better? When one has no money, and none of the acquirements that command money, one must take what one can get, and be thankful."

But Mrs. Brandon is silent, counting her stitches, buried in calculations as to whether her stocking-leg has attained the length and breadth suited to the dimensions of one of her son's large limbs.

The wind shakes the shutter as if, in its lonely coldness outside, it coveted the fire and lamp-light. The old grey cat sits on the fender-stool beside Esther, yawning prodigiously every now and then; her round fore-paws gathered trimly under her, and the sleepy benignity of her face half-contradicting the fierce stiffness of her whiskers, and the tigerish upward curve of her lips.

"What is done in haste is always ill-done, my dear!" says Mrs. Brandon, presently, having satisfactorily calculated that five more rows will conduct her to Bob's large heel—giving utterance to her little trite saw with a certain air of complacency. Original remarks come forth doubtfully, questioningly, feeling their way: it is only a well aired platitude that can strut and swagger forwards in the certainty of a good reception. "We will think over the subject seriously and prayerfully: we will take it with us to the Throne of Grace, and make it the subject of *special* intercession of worship this evening."

"Oh no, no! please not!—*please* not!" cries Esther, the lilies in her fair cheek turning quickly to deepest, angriest carnations. "I should not like it: I could not come to prayers if you did. Why cannot we talk it over *now*, this instant? There's no time like the present."

"I see no hurry, Esther," answers Mrs. Brandon, coldly.

"But there is a hurry!—*every* hurry!" exclaims the girl, passionately, throwing herself on the floor beside Mrs. Brandon, too much in earnest to be chilled by the frosty cold of her manner; her whole soul thrown, in bright entreaty, into the great clear pupils of her superb, up-looking eyes. "I don't think I ever knew what the words meant till now. I don't believe I ever could have been in a real hurry in my life before! Put yourself in my position, Mrs. Brandon," she says, laying her little eager hand on her companion's rusty-black-coburg knee; "imagine how you would like to be wholly dependent, not only for luxuries and comforts—one might well do without them—but for bare bread and water, on people that are neither kith nor kin to you, and that have taken you in out of Christian charity, and because they think it right—not in the least because they love you!"

"If I were exposed to such a trial, Esther," replied Mrs. Brandon, deliberately rubbing her spectacles gently with her pocket-handkerchief, "I hope that I should bear it meekly; that I should kiss the rod, knowing that it was an Allwise Hand that brandished it, and that I was so chastened in order to lower the pride of a too carnal heart."

"Then God forbid that my carnal heart may ever be so lowered!" cries the other, springing impetuously to her feet, and drawing up her head haughtily. "Why," she continues, beginning to walk up and down the little room with agitated steps and fingers hotly interlaced—"why did God implant such an instinct as self-respect in us, if supinely submitting to what destroys all self-respect is a passport to heaven? Who would bow beneath any rod if they could get from under it? It is a metaphor that always reminds me of a naughty child, or a broken-spirited cur."

Mrs. Brandon deposits her knitting on the table; rises slowly—old people's joints, like wooden dolls, decline to bend on short notice (it is a pity, is it not, that our machinery is not calculated to remain in a state of efficiency, even through our paltry seventy years?)—dismounts from the footstool, on which her feet have been perched, walks to the door, there stands, and, shaking her stiff, grey curls, speaks with trembling severity:

"Esther, until you can discuss this subject with less irreverent violence, I must beg to decline any further conversation upon it."

CHAPTER XXVI.

"Wanted, by a young person, aged 17, a situation as companion to an invalid or elderly lady. Salary not so much an object as a comfortable home in a pious family. Address, A. B., Post Office, Naullan, N.W."

This is the modest form in which Miss Craven's desire for work comes before the public. She had begged earnestly for the expunging of the "pious family."

"It is not true, Mrs. Brandon," she says, with vexed tears in her eyes; "it is nothing to me whether they are pious or not—the salary is far the greatest object."

"If it is, my dear, it ought not to be," answers promptly Mrs. Brandon, who, having paid for the insertion of the advertisement, thinks that she has a right to word it as she wishes.

And now it has gone forth through the length and breadth of the civilized world, from the Arctic to the Antarctic Poles—has found its way into clubs and cafés, hotels and private houses, numerous as the sea-sand grains, in the overgrown advertisement sheet of the *Times*. To not one in ten thousand of that journal's millions of readers is it more interesting than any other announcement in the long columns of—

"Wanted, a cook."

"Wanted, a cook."

"Wanted, a good plain cook."

"Wanted, a footman."

"Wanted, a footman."

A companionship, then, is what has been decided upon as the vocation to which Esther is best suited: it requires neither French nor German, neither astronomy nor the use of the globes: it demands only a patience out-Jobing Job, a meekness out-Mosesing Moses, a capacity for eating dirt greater than that of any *parvenu* struggling into society, health and spirits more aggressively strong than a schoolboy's, and a pliability greater than an osier's. These qualities being supposed to be more quickly acquirable than music, drawing, and languages, Esther has decided upon entering on the office that will call for the exercise of them all.

Besides the printed advertisement above quoted, Mrs. Brandon has been advertising largely in private, by means of many long-winded epistles; has been seeking far and wide among the circle of her acquaintance for some grey maid, wife, or widow, in the tending of whose haggard, peevish age Esther may waste her sweet, ripe youth, unassailed by wicked men, in safe, respectable misery. And meanwhile Esther waits—waits through the fog-shrouded, sun-forgotten November days, through the eternal black November nights,—waits, straying lonely along the steaming tree-caverned wood-paths—the solemn charnels of the dead summer nations of leaves and flowers.

Preachers are fond of drawing a parallel between us and those forest leaves; telling us that, as in the autumn they fall, rot, are dissolved, and mingle together, stamped down and shapeless, in brown confusion, and yet in the spring come forth again, fresh as ever; so shall we—who, in our autumn, die, rot, and are not—come forth again in our distant spring, in lordly beauty and gladness. So speaking, whether thinkingly or unthinkingly, they equivocate—they lie! It is not the *same* leaves that reappear; others *like* them burst from their sappy buds, and burgeon in the "green-haired woods;" but *not* they—*not* they! They stir not, nor is there any movement among the sodden earth-mass that was *them*. If the parallel be complete, others like us—others as good, as fair, as we! but yet *not we*—other than us, shall break forth in lusty youth, in their strong May-time; *but we* shall rot on!

"Oh touching, patient earth,
That weepest in thy glee;
Whom God created very good,
And very mournful we!"

how much longer can you bear the weight of all your dead children, that lie so heavy on your mother breast!

One morning, on joining the Brandon family before prayers, Esther finds Mrs. Brandon reading aloud a letter; but on Esther's entrance she desists. Hearing her voice stop, the young girl comes forward eagerly.

"Is it about me?" she asks, panting, forgetting her morning salutations.

"Yes, Esther," replies Mrs. Brandon, laconically, continuing to read, but this time to herself.

Esther walks to the window, drums on the rain-beaten pane, returns to the table; takes up the bread-knife, and begins to chip bits of crust off the loaf; sits down, gets up again; then, unable to contain herself any longer, cries out, hastily, "Will it do?—will it do?"

"If you will give me time, my dear, to finish this letter in peace, I shall have a better chance of being able to tell you," answers the old lady, drily.

Esther sits down again, snubbed; and then the door opens, and the three middle-aged, quakerish maid-servants make their sober entry, each with bible and hymnal in her hand; and the long exposition, the eight-versed hymn, and extempore prayer set in. To Esther's ears, all the words of exposition, hymn, and prayer seem to be, "Will it do?—will it do?"

"I have received a letter," begins Mrs. Brandon, slowly addressing Esther, when the "exercise" is ended, "from a valued Christian friend of mine, who has lately met with a lady and gentleman considerably advanced in life, who are on the look-out for a——"

"Companion?" interrupted Esther, breathlessly.

"For a young person who may supply the place of their failing sight, by reading to them, writing letters for them—may arrange the old lady's work, and make herself a generally useful, agreeable, and ladylike companion."

"That does not sound hard, does it?" says Esther, with a nearer approach to hopefulness in her face than has been seen there since her brother's death. "Neither reading, writing, nor being ladylike are very difficult accomplishments, are they? Oh, Mrs. Brandon, I hope they'll take me, don't you? What is their name?"

"Blessington!"

"Blessington!" repeats Essie, her lips parting in some dismay. "I wonder are they—can they be—any relation to Miss Blessington, Sir Thomas Gerard's ward?"

"I really cannot tell you, my dear. You have given us so very little information as to your visit to the Gerards, that I was not even aware that Blessington was the name of Sir Thomas's ward."

Esther passes by the small reproach in silence.

"Perhaps they may be her father and mother," suggests Bessy.

"She has no father nor mother."

"Her grandfather and grandmother?"

"She has no grandfather nor grandmother."

"Her great-uncle and great-aunt?"

"Possibly."

"Very likely the same family," remarks Mrs. Brandon, intending to say something rather agreeable than otherwise. "Blessington is not a common name."

"I recollect," Esther says, contracting her forehead in the effort to recall all that was said upon a subject which at the time interested her too little to have made much impression—"I recollect her mentioning one day having some old relations in ——shire, whom it was a great bore to have to go and visit."

"These people live in ——shire."

"Then it must be the same," cries Essie, a look of acute chagrin passing over her features. "Oh, Mrs. Brandon, what a disappointment! I'm afraid we shall have to look out again! I'm afraid this won't do!"

"And why not, pray?" inquires the other, staring in displeased astonishment from under her thick white eyebrows at her young *protégée*.

Silence.

"Did you," inquires the old lady, looking rather suspiciously at her, "have any quarrel or disagreement with the Gerards during your visit which could render you unwilling to meet any one in any way connected with their family?"

"Oh no! no!—certainly not!" answers Essie, vehemently, blushing scarlet as any June poppy.

The elder woman's sharp ancient eyes pass like a gimlet through and through the younger one. They fasten with the pitiless fixedness of one who has passed the age for blushing, and has consequently no compassion for that infirmity upon the betraying red of her sweet bright cheeks.

"Are you *quite* sure, Esther?"

"Quite," replies Esther, with steady slowness. "I don't like them, as a family. In fact, I *hate* them all; but I have had no quarrel with them."

"I wonder that you cared to spend a whole month and more with people that you hated," says Miss Bessy, with a sprightly smile.

"So do I, Bessy," answers Esther, bitterly, turning away her head; "but that's neither here nor there."

"Am I to understand, then," says Mrs. Brandon, with an inquisitorial elevation of nose and spectacles, "that an apparently *groundless* and, as far as I can judge, *ungrateful* feeling of dislike towards people who, from the little you have told us of them, seem always to have treated you with indulgent kindness, is your sole motive for wishing to decline this very desirable situation?"

"When one has seen better days," answered the poor proud child, sighing, "one wishes to keep as far as possible from any of those who have known one formerly."

"Tut!" answers Mrs. Brandon, chidingly; "it can be a matter of very little consequence to people in the position of the Gerards whether you have a few pounds a year more or less. They can afford to be kind to you, whatever your circumstances may be!"

"I don't *want* them to be kind to me," cries the girl, fiercely, stung into swift anger. "I know nothing I should dislike more. The only wish I have, with regard to the whole family, is that I should never hear their names mentioned again!"

Mrs. Brandon seats herself at the table, and begins to pour out the tea out of a huge, deep-bodied family tea-pot. Miss Bessy divides the small curling rashers of fat bacon into four exactly equal portions. At Plas Berwyn it is generally a case of "Cynegan's Feast; or enough and no waste." That is to say, at the first onslaught *everything* vanishes; and if any one, with fruitless gluttony, craves a second help, he must console himself with the idea that many medical men agree in the opinion that, in order to preserve ourselves in perfect health, we should always rise from table feeling hungry.

"If," says Mrs. Brandon, resuming the conversation, and setting her words to the music of a peculiarly crisp piece of toast, which she eats with a rather infuriating sound of crunching— "If, Esther, you can be deterred by so trivial an obstacle from availing yourself of an opportunity, humanly speaking, so promising—a door, I may say, opened for you in a *special* and *remarkable* manner, in answer to prayer—you cannot expect me to exert myself a second time on your behalf."

Esther stoops her head in silence over her fat bacon, which she has not the heart to eat.

"Esther is more difficult to please than we expected, is not she, mamma," says Bessy, smiling slightly—"considering that she told us yesterday she envied the man who brought the coals, because he earned his own living?"

"And so I did," answers Esther, gloomily.

"I'm afraid, Esther," says Mrs. Brandon, taking another piece of toast, and shaking her head prophetically, "that you will have to pass through a *burning fiery furnace* before the stubborn pride of the unregenerate heart is brought low!"

"Perhaps so," answers the young girl, calmly; but to her own heart she says that she defies any earthly furnace to burn hotlier than the one she has already passed through.

CHAPTER XXVII.

In another week letters have passed, references been asked and given; Esther proved unimpeachably respectable; the amount of her salary agreed upon; the day of her journey into —— ——shire fixed, and all preliminaries settled previous to her undertaking the agreeable, free, and independent office of companion to John Blessington, Esq., of Blessington Court, in the county of ——, aged eighty-nine, and to Harriet Blessington his wife, aged eighty.

Miss Craven has but one good-bye to say, and on the afternoon of the day before her departure she stands in the churchyard ready to say it. It is only to a grave. Huge cloud headlands, great leaden capes and promontories, mournful and heavy with unwept snow-tears, heap and pile themselves up behind the dim mirk hills; it snowed last night, but the snow has nearly all melted; only enough remains to make the old dirty church-tower, from which great patches of whitewash have fallen, look dirtier than ever. Upon the broken headstones, all awry and askew with age and negligence, the lichens flourish dankly. Wet nettles and faded bents overlie, overcross each cold hillock. No one cares to weed in the garden of the dead. Each hillock is the last chapter in some forgotten history.

Oh! why must all stories that are told truly end amongst the worms? Why must death be always at the *end* of life? Oh! if we could but get it over, like some cruelest operation, in the middle or early part of our little day; so that we might have some half a life, some quarter or twentieth part even of one, to live merrily in, to breathe and laugh and be gay in, without, in our cheerfullest moments, experiencing the chilly fear of feeling the black-cloaked skeleton-headed phantom lay his bony finger on us, saying, "Thou art mine!"

Upon the grey flat tombstone near the church-gate the great grave yew has been dropping her scarlet berries, one by one—berries that shine, like little lights, amid the night of her changeless foliage: there they lie like a forgotten rosary, that some holy man, having prayed amongst the unpraying dead, going, has left behind him. Evening is closing in fast; the air is raw and chill; no one that can avoid it is outside a house's sheltering walls: there is no one to disturb Esther's meeting with her brother. What cares she for the cold, or for the six feet of miry earth that part them. She flings herself upon the sodden mound; stretching herself all along upon it, as the prophet stretched himself on the young dead child—hand to hand, heart to heart, mouth to mouth. She lays her lips upon the soaked soil, and whispers moaningly, "Good-bye, Jack—good-bye! Oh! why won't they let you answer me? Why have they buried you so deep that you cannot hear me?"

Lord God! of what stuff can Mary and Martha have been made, to have overlived the awful ecstasy of seeing their dead come forth in warm supple life out of the four-days-holding grave! Their hearts must have been made of tougher fibre than ours, or, in the agony of that terrible rapture, soul and body must have sundered suddenly, and they fallen down into the arms of that tomb whence their brother had just issued in his ghastly cerements, in dazed, astonished gladness!

As Esther lifts her streaming eyes, they fall upon the inscription on the cross at the grave-head:

"HERE LIETH THE BODY
OF
JOHN CRAVEN,
WHO DEPARTED THIS LIFE
SEPT. 24TH, 186-. AGED 21 YEARS."
"Lord, have mercy upon me, a sinner!"

She casts her arms about the base of the holy symbol; she presses her panting breast against the stone. "Lord, have mercy upon me, a sinner!" she cries too; and surely the live sinner needs mercy as much as the dead one? And as she so lies prostrate, with her forehead leant against the white damp marble, a hideous doubt flashes into her heart—sits there, like a little bitter serpent, gnawing it: "What if there be *no* Lord! What if I am praying and weeping to and calling upon nothing!

"............ Let   me   not   go   mad!
Sweet   Heaven,   forgive   weak   thoughts!   If   there   should   be
No   God,   no   heaven,   no   earth   in   the   void   world—
The wide, grave, lampless, deep, unpeopled world."

They tell us—don't they?—in our childhood, that wickedness makes people unhappy: I think the converse is full as often true—that unhappiness makes people wicked.

A little icy wind creeps coldly amongst the strong nettles and weak sapless bents, blowing them all one way—creeps, too, through Esther's mourning weeds, and makes a numbness about her shivering breast. For a moment an angry defiant despair masters her.

"What if this great distant being, who, without any foregone sin of ours, has laid upon us the punishment of *life*—in the hollow of whose hand we lie!—what if He be laughing at us all this while! What if the sight of our writhings, of our unlovely tears and grotesque agonies, be to Him, in His high prosperity, a pleasant diversion!"

So thinking, against her will she involuntarily clasps closer the cross in her straining arms—involuntarily moans a second time, "Lord, have mercy upon me, a sinner!" No—no! it cannot be so! it is one of those things that are too horrible to be believed! There is no justice *here!* none! but it exists *somewhere!* How else could we ever have conceived the idea of it? It is, then, in some other world: we shall find it on the other side of these drenched, nettly charnels—on the other side of corruption's disgrace and abasement:

"............If   this   be   all,
And   other   life   await   us   not,   for   one
I   say,   'tis   a   poor   cheat,   a   stupid   bungle,
A   wretched   failure!   I,   for   one,   protest
Against it—and I hurl it back with scorn!"

Despair never stays long with any one, unless it is specially invited. Struck with sudden horror at the daring blasphemy of her thoughts, wretched Esther, with clasped hands and a flood of penitential tears, sinks upon her trembling knees. God grant that the thoughts that come to us, we know not whence, that stab us in the dark, that we welcome not, neither cherish at all—yea, rather, drive them away rudely, hatingly—may not be counted to us for crimes in His great Day of Reckoning, any more than the sudden-smiting disease that makes the strong man flag in his noonday is counted to him! With a sudden revulsion of feeling, with a paroxysm of devotion, powerfuller than the former one of doubt had been, the desolate child, prone on the grave of her one treasure, lifts quivering lips and emptied arms to Him who

"............For   mankynde's   sake
Justed in Jerusalem, a joye to us all!"—

to Him of whom

"..........They   who   loved   Him   said   'He   wept,'
None ever said 'He smiled!'"

Perhaps the good Lord, who was sorry for Mary and Martha, may be sorry for her too. Perhaps, after all, her boy is well rid of troublesome breath—well rid of his cares, and his farm, and his useless loving sister! Perhaps she is falsely fond to desire him again—to be so famished for one sight more of his grey laughing eyes, of his smooth stripling face! Beyond her sight, he may be in the fruition of extremest good—in the sweet shade, beneath pleasant-fruited trees, beside great cool rivers. Would she tear him back again thence to toil in the broiling sun, because, so toiling, he would be in her sight?

"If   love   were   kind,   why   should   we   doubt
That holy death were kinder?"

The night falls fast; she can scarcely any longer distinguish the clear, new black letters on the cross. Lights are twinkling from the village alehouse; the forge shines like a great dull-red jewel in the surrounding grey; laughing voices of boisterous men are wafted unseemly amongst the graves. Shuddering at the sound, she raises herself up quickly; then, stooping again, kisses yet once more the wet red earth that is now closest neighbour to her brother, and sobbing "Good-bye, my boy, good-bye!—God bless you, Jack!" gathers her dusky cloak about her slight shivering figure, and passes away through the darkness.

CHAPTER XXVIII.

It has snowed all day; an immense white monotony is over all the land. The clouds that piled themselves in sulky threatening last night behind the Welsh hills, and many others like them, have to-day fulfilled their threats, and have been, through all the daylight hours, emptying their flaky load on the patient earth. It is as if a huge white bird had been shaking his pinions somewhere, high up in the air—shaking down millions of little down feathers. Rain always seems in earnest, snow in play—with such delicate leisureliness does it saunter down. The rushing train, that bears Esther to her new distant life, is topped like any twelfth-night cake; so are the wayside stations; so are the houses in the smoky towns; so are the men, sparsely walking about on the country roads; so are the engine drivers and stokers; so are the sheep in the fields.

Miss Craven has been sitting all day long in the narrow *enceinte* of a railway carriage, between the two close-shut, snow-blinded windows—sitting opposite a courteous warrior, who, travelling with all the luxuriousness which his sex think indispensable, is magnanimous enough to share his buffalo-robe and foot-warmer with her. A *tête-à-tête* of so many consecutive hours with a man would, under any other circumstances than a railway journey, have produced an intimacy that would last a life-time; but now, all the result of it is a couple of bows on the platform at Paddington—a look of interested curiosity after his late companion's retreating figure, as she hurries herself and her small properties into a filthy four-wheeler, on the part of the warrior, and total oblivion on the part of Esther. Since that time she has traversed London in her dilapidated shambling *growler*, she has had awful misgiving that the "cabby," with the villany that all women ascribe to all "cabbies," is purposely taking her in a wrong direction—is bearing her away to some dark, policeless slum, there to be robbed and murdered. She has reflected, with cold shivers of terror, as to what would be the wisest course to pursue, supposing such to be the case. Should she look silently out of window till she caught sight of the friendly helmet and tight frock-coat of some delivering "Bobby," and then scream? Should she open the door and jump out on the snowy pavement?

While still undecided, her cab stops, and—all mean back-streets and sorry short-cuts being safely passed—deposits her and her box, bag, and umbrella, beneath the Shoreditch lamps and among the Shoreditch porters. Then an hour's waiting in the crowded general waiting-room, where all the chairs are occupied by fat men, none of whom make a movement towards vacating theirs in favour of the slender weary woman, who, with crape veil thrown back from her sad child-face, is holding her little numb hands over the fire, trying vainly to bring them back to life. Then more train; then a three-miles' drive in a fly, up hill and down dale, along snowy country lanes.

And now her journey is ended: the fly has stopped at the door of a great, vague, snow-whitened bulk, that she takes upon trust as Blessington Court. The driver, having rung the bell, now stands banging his arms, each one against the opposite shoulder, in the rough endeavour to restore circulation. The servants are too comfortable—the butler over his mulled port in the housekeeper's room, and the footmen over their mulled beer in the servants' hall—to be in any hurry to attend to the summons. At length, after five minutes' waiting, a sound of withdrawing bolts and turning keys makes itself heard; the heavy door swings inward, and a footman appears in the aperture, blinking disgustedly at the snow, which drives full into his eyes. Esther immediately descends, and enters with the abrupt haste characteristic of extreme nervousness.

"Will you pay him, please?" she says, with a certain flurry of manner, to the servant. "I—I don't know how much I ought to give him—how many miles it is."

While the man complies with her request, she stands in the huge stone-floored hall, lit only by firelight, shivering with cold and fear. She peers up at the ceiling—of which, by-the-bye, there is none, as the hall runs up to the top of the house; at the walls, from which great life-size figures, dimly naked, glimmer uncomfortably cold. Anxious doubts assail her as to whether there are any rules of which she is ignorant for a "companion's" behaviour and deportment; she is not aware that she has ever seen one of those curious animals hitherto in the course of her life. Ought they to make a reverence on entering a room? Ought they to say "Sir" or "Ma'am" to whoever they address? Ought they to laugh at everybody's jokes?—not sit down unless given leave so to do, and not speak unless spoken to? So wondering, she tremblingly follows the footman as he opens the door of an adjoining apartment, and, announcing "Miss Craven," retires joyfully to the society of his compeers and his beer.

The apartment in which Esther is thus left stranded is as large as the hall that she has just quitted. It seems to her oppressively immense—quite a long walk from the door to the inhabited portion. A very big roasting fire burns on the hearth: and right in front of it, in the very glare of its hot red eyes, sits a very old man, doubled together in an armchair—one hand in his breast, and his aged head sunk upon it, apparently fast asleep. An old lady, wrapped up in a shawl, reposes in another easy-chair, with her eyes likewise closed. A lamp with a green shade burns faintly on a centre table, and beyond lamp and table sits a third person, hidden by the lamp-shade from Esther's eyes.

"Are they all asleep?" thinks the poor girl, advancing with gentle, hesitating steps. "They seem to be. How can I wake them?—or would it be disrespectful?"

While she so speculates, the third person rises and comes forward. "How do you do, Miss Craven? You must have had a cold journey, I'm afraid?" says a bland, unforgotten voice.

It is Miss Blessington. In an instant, Esther seems to have jumped back over the past intervening months—to be just entering on her Felton visit. There is the same voice greeting her—the same tones of polite inquiry; the same words almost, except that *then* it was, "How do you do, Miss Craven? You must have had a hot journey, I'm afraid?" and now it is, "How do you do, Miss Craven? You must have had a cold journey, I'm afraid?"—the same undulating walk; the same effect of lilac evening clouds. Involuntarily she turns her head and glances towards the window, half-expecting to see St. John's legs disappearing through it. Instead, an old woman's voice sounds quavering: "Are you Miss Craven, my dear? Come here!"

Esther does not hear. "It *was* rather cold," she says, answering Constance, in half bewilderment between past and present, her eyes dazed with the light after her long, dark journey.

"Mrs. Blessington is speaking to you," says Constance, in mild reminder.

Esther turns round quickly. "Oh! I beg your pardon—I did not hear—I hope I was not rude," she cries, forgetting the "Ma'am" she had half-purposed employing.

"Who's there?—who's talking?" asks the old man, lifting up his head, and speaking in a voice tremulous indeed, but with a remnant of the power and fire that "youth gone out had left in ashes."

No one answers.

"Who's there, Mrs. Blessington?" he repeats, with querulous anger.

"Miss Craven, uncle—the young lady that we expected to-day—don't you know?" replies Constance, stooping gracefully over him, and putting her lips as close as possible to his withered ear.

"H'm! Tell her to come and speak to me. I want to see what she is like," he rejoins, much as if she had not been in the room.

"Go to him, my dear," says the old lady.

"And speak as loud as you can; he is as deaf as a post," adds Constance, not in the least lowering her voice at the announcement, in perfect confidence of the truth of her assertion, shrugging her handsome shoulders as she speaks.

Esther goes trembling, and lays her small cold hand in the long bony wreck of muscle, vein, and flesh that is stretched out to her. He gazes at her face with the eager intentness of the purblind.

"What is your name?" he asks abruptly.

"Esther," she answers, faltering.

"Cannot hear a word you say—you mumble so," he says, pettishly.

"Go round to the other side; the other ear is the best," suggests Constance, calmly.

Esther obeys. "*Esther,*" she repeats, speaking unnecessarily loud this time—at the top of her voice, in fact, out of sheer nervousness.

"You need not scream at me, my dear, as if I were stone deaf. *Esther* or *Hester*, did you say?"

"Esther."

"And who gave it you, pray?"

"My father and mother, I suppose."

"H'm! Well, you may tell them, with my compliments," he says, with a senile laugh, "that I think they might have found a prettier name to give a young lady, and that the old squire says so. The old squire says so," he repeats, chuckling a little to himself.

"I cannot tell them," answers Esther, half-crying. "They are dead."

"Oh, indeed!"

There his interest in the new comer seems to cease. His white head sinks back on his breast again, and he relapses into slumber.

Esther has had neither luncheon, dinner, nor tea—a fact which none of her companions appear to contemplate as possible. *One* bun has been her sole support throughout the long bitter day—only *one*, because all such buns must be bought with Mrs. Brandon's money.

"I daresay you would like to go to bed, dear, you look tired," says Mrs. Blessington, scanning rather curiously Esther's fagged, woebegone little face. "Travelling is so much more fatiguing than it used to be in former days, when one travelled in one's own carriage, whatever they may say. I remember," she continues, with an old woman's garrulity, "Mr. Blessington and I travelling from London to York by easy stages of twenty miles a day, in our own curricle, with outriders. One never sees a curricle nowadays."

"I *am* rather tired," the girl answers, with a faint smile, "and cravingly hungry," she might have added, but does not.

"Ring the bell for James to light the candles."

Weak from inanition, and with limbs cramped by long remaining in one position, Esther follows Miss Blessington up low flights of uncarpeted stone stairs, through draughty twisting passages, along a broad bare gallery, down more passages, and then into a huge gloomy, mouldy room—frosty, yet cold, despite the fire burning briskly on the old-fashioned-hobbed grate; a vast dark four-poster, hung with ginger-coloured moreen; a couch that looks highly suitable for lying-in-state on; an old-fashioned screen, covered with caricatures of Fox, Burke, the Regent, and Queen Caroline; and on the walls a highly valuable and curious tapestry, which waves pleasantly in the bitter wind that enters freely beneath the ill-fitting old door, giving an air of galvanic motion and false life to the ill-looking Cupids, green with age, that play hide-and-seek amongst vases, broken pillars and wormy blue trees.

"You have plenty of room, you see," says Miss Blessington, with a curve of her suave lips, as she lights the candles on the dressing-table, which, instead of being pink petticoated, white-muslined deal, is bare sturdy oak, with millions of little useless drawers and pigeon-holes in it.

"Plenty," echoes Esther, rather aghast, surveying her premises with some dismay.

"You must not be frightened if you hear odd noises; it's only rats," says her companion, putting one small white-booted foot on the fender.

"I wish that—that stuff would not sway and shake about so," says the young girl, pointing nervously with one timid fore-finger to the tapestry. "Might not some one get behind it very easily and hide, as it does not seem to be fastened down?"

"Possibly," replies Miss Blessington, indifferently. "I never heard of such a thing having happened."

"Am I near any one else—tolerably near, I mean?" asks Esther, her heart sinking.

"Not very."

"Would no one hear me if I screamed?" she inquires, laying her hand unconsciously on the marble round of her companion's firm white arm, while her frightened eyes burn upon Constance's impassive face.

"We will hope that you will not make the experiment," she answers, with a cold smile, and so goes.

CHAPTER XXIX.

I think that people's value, or want of value, is seldom their own: it belongs rather to the circumstances that surround them—to attributes foreign to themselves—outside of them. Had Robinson Crusoe, while walking down Bond Street in flowing wig and lace ruffles, first met his man Friday, he might have tossed him sixpence to avoid his importunities; but would hardly have taken him into intimate friendship—would hardly even have admitted him as a man and a brother. Among the blind the one-eyed is king, and among a crowd of total strangers an acquaintance rises into a friend.

Lonely Esther is half-inclined to effect this metamorphosis in the case of Miss Blessington. The mere fact of having eaten, drank, and slept for a considerable period under the same roof with her—the bare fact of having lived with and disliked her during a whole month and more—was enough recommendation in a house not one of whose inmates had she ever beheld before. Almost as a friend has she greeted her this morning. With admiration most unfeigned, though made a little bitter by mental comparison with her own dimmed, grief-blighted beauty, has she regarded the stately woman, the splendid animal, sleek and white as a sacred Egyptian cow; the brilliancy of whose pale, bright hair, and the perfect smoothness of her great satin throat, are heightened by the sober richness of her creaseless black velvet dress. Voluptuous, yet cold, the passions that her splendid physique provoke are chilled to death by the passionless stupor of her soul. I am not at all sure that impassioned ugliness—supposing the ugliness to be moderate, and the passion immoderate—has not more attraction for the generality of men than iced beauty.

Esther's warmth is thrown away; she might as well expect that the "Venus de Medici" would return the pressure of warm clinging fingers with her freezing, sculptured hand.

"I was so glad to find you here last night: it was so pleasant to see a face one knew," Miss Craven says, with the rash credulity of youth unexpectant of snubs.

Miss Blessington looks slightly surprised. "Tha—anks; it is very good of you to say so, I am sure," she answers, rather drawlingly, and with a small, cold smile that would repress demonstrations much more violent than any that Esther had meditated. It is difficult *always* to remember that one is a "companion."

The Blessington dining-room is, like the other reception-rooms, huge and very nobly proportioned. Did we not know that our seventeenth and eighteenth century ancestors were not giants, we should be prone to imagine that it must have been a race of Anakims that required such great wide spaces to sup, and sip chocolate, and play at ombre in. The furniture is in its dotage; it has, figuratively speaking, like its owners, lost hair and teeth, and all unnecessary etceteras; it is reduced to the bare elements of existence. Three tall windows look out upon a flat lawn, and in the middle of this lawn, exactly opposite Esther's eyes, as she sits at breakfast, is an unique and chaste piece of statuary, entitled "The Rape of the Sabines." The space afforded by the stone pediment is necessarily limited, and consequently Roman and Sabines, gentlemen and lady, are all piled one a-top of another in such inextricable confusion as to demand a good quarter of an hour's close observation to determine which of the muscular writhing legs belong to the Roman ravisher and which to the injured Sabine husband. As the sculptor has given none of his *protégées* any clothing, the snow has been kind enough to throw a modest white mantle over them all.

"Mr. and Mrs. Blessington do not come down to breakfast?" says Esther, interrogatively, as the two girls seat themselves at table.

"No; they breakfast in their own rooms."

"I suppose," says Esther, with some embarrassment, "that they will send for me if they want me for anything, won't they? Perhaps" (with diffidence)—"perhaps you will kindly tell me the sort of things they will want me to do?"

"My uncle will be down presently," answered Miss Blessington, "and he will then expect you to read to him until luncheon."

"To read what? The Bible?" inquired Esther, who has a vague idea that the Bible is the only form in which literature should employ the attention of the aged.

"The Bible? Oh, dear, no!" (with a little laugh). "The papers: the *Times*, *Saturday*, and *Justice of the Peace*, are his favourites; he takes a great, a *remarkable* interest, considering his age, in politics."

"I like reading aloud," says Esther, resolute to look on the bright side.

"Reading aloud to my uncle is very fatiguing," replies Constance, cheeringly: "one has to sustain one's voice at a pitch several octaves higher than the natural one. I attempted reading to him once or twice, but it affected my throat so much that I had to leave off," she ends, with a little lackadaisical cough.

"I daresay it won't affect mine," rejoins the other rather drily.

There is a pause. Talking is a vice to which Miss Blessington is nowise addicted—more especially objectless talking to a little person of the feminine gender who is not one of *nous autres*.

"I hope," says Esther, presently, trusting to the obtuseness of her companion's perceptions not to discover the flagrant hypocrisy of the question—"I hope that Sir Thomas was quite well when you left Felton?"

"Quite—thanks."

"And Lady Gerard?"

"Yes—thanks."

"And—and" (bending down her head in the vain endeavour to screen the red blush that the frosty sun, flaming in through the window opposite, makes obtrusively evident)—"and Mr. Gerard?"

"He is *very* well—thanks," replies Miss Blessington, with the conscious smile that had formerly exasperated Esther, and with an emphasis not common with her.

Miss Blessington does not usually employ emphasis: it is *mezzoceto*, as is enthusiasm of which it is the exponent.

Half an hour later Esther is sitting beside the old squire, as close as possible to his best ear, brandishing the *Times'* giant squares in her unaccustomed hand. The old squire is a superb wreck. Spiteful Time is fond of removing the landmarks that youth sets upon our faces; is fond of changing great, clear, almond eyes into little damp jellies—sweet moist pursemouths into dry bags of wrinkles; but it is a task beyond even *his* power to destroy the shape of that grand old bent head—to deface the outlines of that thin-nostriled, patrician nose.

"What shall I read first?" asks the young girl, timidly, but enunciating each syllable with painstaking slowness and clearness.

"The State of the Funds," replies the old gentleman, promptly, thrusting his hand into his breast, and closing his eyes, in his favourite attitude.

Esther has not the most distant idea where the "State of the Funds" lives: she turns the huge sheets topsy-turvy—inside out, outside in—in the vain search for their habitat, making, meanwhile, the most unjustifiable aggressive rustling and crackling, which she presumptuously trusts to his deafness not to hear.

"Don't make such an infernal crackling, my dear!" he says presently, with some pettishness.

"I thought you could not hear," she unwisely answers, trembling.

"God bless my soul, child! The dead would have heard the noise you were making," he rejoins, snappishly.

Having at length mastered the fact that the "State of the Funds" comes under the head of "Money Market and City Intelligence," Esther gives the desired information. Then follows a leader:

"The position of American politics is at this moment peculiarly perplexing and anomalous; so perplexing that even those English observers who, like ourselves, have given a careful and constant attention to the course of the Transatlantic movement since the first appearance of Secession, can hardly pretend clearly to understand——"

"Pretend clearly to *what?* For God's sake don't gabble so!"

"Can—hardly—pretend—clearly—to—understand—the—full—meaning—of—the—situation,—and—must—feel—that—it—would—be——"

"Is there no medium, may I ask, between gabbling and drawling?"

"And must feel that it would be rash to express a confident opinion thereupon."

Esther now proceeds for a considerable period unchecked—gradually and unconsciously relapsing into the brisk gallop so dear to youth when engaged upon a subject that does not interest it. Suddenly a deep slumberous breath, drawn close to her ear, makes her aware that her hearer has lapsed into sleep.

"I have read him to sleep," she says to herself, with a sort of triumphant feeling at her own prowess, taking furtive glances at the wrinkled profile, sunk, in perfect imbecility of slumber, on his breast.

Not feeling any particular personal interest in the effect of Secession upon American politics, she stops, and gazes vacantly out of window at the "Rape of the Sabines." But the cessation of the sweet monotony that lulled him, arouses the old man.

"Go on—go on!" he cries, fussily, lifting his head and opening his dim eyes. "What are you stopping for? Read that paragraph over again; you read it so fast that I could not quite follow the meaning of it."

She complies, and so, with dozing and waking, waking and dozing, on one side, reading and stopping, stopping and reading on the other, the little drama plays itself out till nearly luncheon-time.

"We are going to drive into Shelford this afternoon; do you feel inclined to come with us, Constance, my dear?" asks the old lady, as they quit the luncheon-table—Esther dutifully bringing up the rear, with air-cushion, footstool, and *couvre-pied*.

"Not to-day, aunt, I think—thanks," answers Constance, with the utmost sweetness; the "Not to-day" seeming to imply that on some future morrow she will gladly avail herself of the invitation to join her elderly relatives in their *triste* airing; but Miss Blessington being in her generation a wise woman, that morrow never comes.

The old family-coach rolls round the frosty sweep to the door; two large horses, sleek and fat with over-many oats and over-little work, draw it.

"The   tails   of   both   hung   down   behind,
Their shoes were on their feet."

"Give me your arm, Miss Craven; one is very apt to fall this frosty weather," says the old lady, appearing at the door, transformed, by the aid of numberless cloaks and shawls, and a huge velvet bonnet, date anno domini, into a large and perfectly shapeless bundle.

Supported on one side by Esther's slender arm, and on the other by the florid and plethoric butler, she is hoisted up the three steps into the body of the ancient machine, which is painted invisible green, and hung marvellous high in air. The same course is pursued with the old gentleman, who, muffled, comfortered, and scarved up to the tip of his venerable nose, follows. Lastly, the young prop steps in, and sits down humbly with her back to the horses—a process which usually ends in making her sick. The windows are shut tight up; a great hot skin of some wild beast is thrown over their knees; in that confined atmosphere it emits a strong furry odour, more powerful than agreeable; striving emulously with it—sometimes mastering it, sometimes mastered by it—is the fusty smell of the cloth lining. The old people do not seem to perceive either; old noses have less keen scent, old lungs require less air to feed on, than young ones.

"Trit-trot, trit-trot, trit-trot," goes the old vehicle along the beaten snow of the broad turnpike-road. As they are jogging a little brisklier than usual down a *very* slight decline, the old gentleman speaks—his strong, shaky old voice loudly audible above the "rumble—rumble—rumble," which, joined to the want of air, is fast making Esther faint and headachy:

"What the deuce does Ruggles mean going at such a pace down these steep hills? Does he think he is to knock my horses' legs all to pieces for his own amusement?"

"I'm sure I don't know, Mr. Blessington," answers the old lady, nervously laying hold of the side of the carriage; "it is not at all safe this slippery weather; I'm sure I hope the horses are roughed."

"Miss Craven, tell him to mind what he is about; tell him to go slower—*much* slower," says the old gentleman, in some excitement.

Miss Craven, having with some difficulty lowered the front window, thrusts her head out of it, and, having taken the opportunity to open mouth and nose and eyes as wide as they will go, to inhale as large a quantity as possible of crisp fresh air, cries: "Ruggles! Ruggles! go slower! *much* slower!"

Ruggles grins, but complies, and subsides into a solemn walk, which continues until they reach Shelford. There smug bareheaded shop-keepers, violet-nosed, scarlet-fingered, standing out in the cold street at the carriage-door, executing with pleased alacrity extensive commissions of half a yard of elastic for Miss Blessington—three ounces of red wool for Mrs. Blessington's knitting—half a dozen blue envelopes for Mr. Blessington. Then, "trit-trot, jig-jog," home again.

Dinner at six: a later hour would be fatal to his digestion, the old gentleman thinks, then, a nice long evening—long as one of those *Veillées du Château*, when Madame la Baronne read aloud some enthralling yet severely moral tale, and Cæsar and Caroline and Pulchérie all sat entranced, unheeding the flight of time, as ticked away by the château clocks. There is only one small lamp in the whole of the grand old room, and that, in deference to the old man's failing eyes, is hung with so large and deep a green shade, that it is impossible to see to do anything by its light. There is nothing for it but to gape, from seven till ten, at the great battle-pieces hung round the walls—to endeavour to make out, by the aid of the fitful firelight, the singularly clean dead bodies, free apparently from the slightest speck of dust, or stain of blood; at the red-nostriled chargers, snorting away their ebbing lives with all four legs in the air. At ten o'clock, James rung for, to light the candles: then Mrs. Blessington, her air-cushion, work-basket, and Shetland shawl, escorted to her room; two long chapters and several psalms read to her; then a frightened rush along dark passages and draughty galleries to the great distant bedroom—to the rats' multifarious noises; to the ingenious tunes played by the wind upon the rattling window-frames; to the ginger-curtained bed and many-folded screen; to *possible* sleep, and *certain* terrors—terrors none the less awful for being totally unreasonable.

CHAPTER XXX.

This first day is a sample of Esther's new life; the other days were like it—not a jot better, not a jot worse. The same thing happened at the same time each day: no two things ever changed places. It was a life that provided all the necessaries of life—that demanded no hard manual labour, no overworking of the brain. The intellectual faculties that it called into play must have been possessed by any moderately intelligent seven-years' child. No one bullies Esther; no one oppresses her; no one troubles their head much about her. So as she performs her monotonous, easy, tiresome little duties towards them, the old people have no sort of objection to her enjoying life, *if she can*. With the aged, comfort and happiness are interchangeable terms: continuous warmth of body, pleasant-tasted meats, a profound stagnant quiet around their arm-chairs, much sleep—these are their *summum bonum*. They have had love, and have outlived it—excitement also, and grief: they have outlived all but the elemental instincts that refuse to be outlived. Looking back from the vantage-ground of dotage on the fought battle of life, they wonder that any one can long to be in the thick of it. In this life of Esther's there are no hardships to be borne—none of those sufferings, the enduring of which with self-conscious complacent heroism almost compensates them. It has none of the elements of tragedy: there is nothing very noble in bearing with respectable patience the trifling annoyance of making yourself hoarse roaring the price of wheat, and the pros and cons of disendowment, into an old man's ear; there is nothing grand in picking up the countless dropped stitches in an old woman's knitting. In it there is nothing to endure, nothing to enjoy; it is essentially negative, flat, stale, sterile. It would be all very well if any end were to be seen to it; if it were not a sort of small Eternity in life; if there were to be distant holidays to be looked forward to, when the few saved pounds might be poured, with the joyful generosity of the very poor, into some stricken parent's lap—might go to buy boots and shoes for needy little brothers and sisters. But

"Fatherly, motherly, sisterly, brotherly Home she has none."

All her life seems crowded into the seventeen years behind her; there seems to be nothing left to happen in the fifty or sixty years ahead. She has nothing to look forward to but huge cycles of newspaper-reading, footstool-carrying, message-running; of lending all her useful organs of sight and hearing and touch to others; of keeping for herself only her suffering, aching, empty heart!

"Every succeeding year will steal something away from her beauty."

People pity her now, because she is so young and pretty—not reflecting that the possession of the two best gifts under heaven makes her so much the less worthy a subject for compassion. Twenty years hence, she will probably be a "companion" still—will be not near so young, nor near so touching, and infinitely more to be pitied.

The snow lies long—longer than it generally does at this time of year. Ordinarily the old Cheshire saying holds good:

"If there's ice in October as 'll hould a duck, All the rest of the winter 'll turn to muck!"

But this October there has been ice enough to hold many ducks; but yet the rest of the winter shows no signs of, as the homely saw phrases it, "turning to muck." In the little flower-garden, round three sides of which the ivied buttressed house is built, only a white heap here, and a white depression there, show where bush or bed were wont to be. Over the fair wide park, with all its mimic hills and valleys, copses and spinneys, God has laid a great sheet—great as the one that was let down by its four corners on the housetop to the fastidious Apostle—a sheet purely, crisply, miserably white. In the park Esther, in the early gloaming, after the daily drive, so literally a promenade *en voiture*, takes long walks; ruins her boots, discolours her petticoats, and makes her crape crimp with snow-water: strolls listless and alone under the old bare trees that have stripped off all their clothing—now at the very time that they seem to need them most; traces the slender footprints of the famished birds—the little delicate tracks crossing and recrossing one another. And always the leading thought—displaced now and then by lesser thoughts, that flit like travelling swallows through her mind, but ever, ever returning—is, "Where is Jack? Where has my boy gone to? Where is he *now, at this moment?*" If some trusty messenger could but come to her, with sure tidings, saying, "It is well with him!" Has she any reason for believing him to be in heaven, beyond the vague confidence that most people seem to feel that their relatives must be there, on the principle, I suppose, of the French Duke, of whom his kindred remarked, that "God would certainly think twice 'avant de damner une personne de sa qualité!'"

Jack's death had been most unlike the deaths of the shining Evangelical lights in Bessy Brandon's books, whose whole lives had been but trifling prologues to the jubilant drama of their death. Death had been to them an ecstasy; they had died with words of confident rapture on their lips, with strains of welcoming music in their ears: he had departed painfully, sadly, almost dumbly; no sound of triumphant clarions greeted him from beyond Death's deep ford. Is he, then, in *hell?* Oh blessed doctrine of cleansing purgatorial pains! if our faith would but admit of you! Which of us does not seem to himself so much too bad for heaven, so much too good for hell?

"Let Faustus live in hell a thousand years, A hundred thousand, and at the last be saved!"

Where is he, then?—where is he? She takes counsel of the mute forces of nature—of the clouds, the snows, and the blasts. But of what use? They knew not of his story; or, if they did, they were forbidden to tell of it: silence was laid like a seal upon their lips.

It is not in the most edifying books that the grandest sayings are to be found. What can be nobler than this of Rousseau's dying Julie: "Qui s'endort dans le sein d'un père, n'est pas en souci du réveil?"

The wearier in body she can return from these long, sad rambles, the better pleased is Esther; for is not weariness the father of sleep—sleep, the one impartial thing under heaven; sleep, the radical; sleep, the leveller, that leaves a king's arms to embrace a tinker? But of what use is it to sleep, if in sleep one hear—

"False voices, feel the kisses of false mouths, And footless sound of perished feet?"

And worse even than such dream-tortured slumber is fear-tortured waking. Constitutionally timid, a weakened body and broken spirit have made Esther pitiably nervous. Jealousy, remorse, and fear run a dreary race for the palm of extremest suffering; and I am not sure that fear does not win. The poor child suffers the torments of the damned in her huge hearse-bed in the far-off, rat-haunted, ghostly old chamber. She dreads falling asleep, for fear of waking to find the low fire playing antics with Burke's long nose and spectacles, with Pitt's maypole figure on the screen; flickering over the malignant fleshy Cupids on the wall; waking to see, looking in upon her through the curtains, Jack's face—not kind, *débonnaire*, smiling, as she used to see it in the study at home (for *that* could frighten no one), but solemn, stiff, with closed eyes and bandaged chin, as she had last seen it. Sometimes she sits up in bed, a cold sweat standing on her brow, as some noise, distincter than usual, sounds through the room; "thud, thud," as of some falling object; an unexplained rustling in the passage; a little clicking in the door-lock—sits up, listening with strained ears, thinking, "Can *that* be rats?" Momently she expects to see some crape-masked burglar enter the door or window. And if such burglar did enter, it would be useless to scream for help; she is too far off from the rest of the household to be heard: it would be of no use to ring the bell, for it rings downstairs, miles away, and everybody is in bed and asleep upstairs. So she lies quaking—her terror now and then rising to such an uncontrollable pitch that she feels as though, if it lasted a moment longer, she must go mad: listening with intense impatience to the leisurely "Tick-tack, tick-tack, tick-tack" of the cuckoo-clock outside; listening with inexpressible longing to hear it say, "Cuckoo, cuckoo, cuckoo, cuckoo!" four times. At four o'clock she will be safe, she thinks; at four o'clock cocks begin to crow, dairymaids to get up, the bodiless dead return to their churchyard homes, night's unutterable horror to pass. What wonder if, after the agony of such vigils—agony causeless, you will say, unreasonable, but none the less real, none the less acute for that—she comes down in the morning wan, nerveless, with haggard cheeks, and great dark streaks under the unrested beauty of her eyes?

"The time is near the birth of Christ."

"Stir-up Sunday" is past; people have bought their raisins, and suet, and citron, and begun to mix their Christmas puddings. Turkeys lie dead, thick as autumn-leaves in Vallambrosa. The snow is gone, but not without leaving Miss Craven the legacy of a very bad cold, derived from countless soaked stockings and neglected wet petticoats. She has had it a fortnight, and her weakened, lowered frame seems incapable of shaking off the trifling ailment. For a week her voice has been almost gone, and she has consumed many sticks of liquorice, many boxes of black currant lozenges, in the endeavour to bring it back to the requisite shouting pitch for the inevitable daily newspaper reading.

It is afternoon: heavy rain, following the thaw, has prevented the invariable drive to Shelford. Mrs. Blessington and the two girls are sitting in the great room hung with battle-pieces, which is old-fashioned named "the saloon." It is a mercy that it is a great room—else the fire, piled halfway up the chimney, and the never-opened windows would render it unendurably close. As it is, the atmosphere, though less stifling than that of the interior of the family-coach, is fustier than is altogether agreeable.

"My dear," says Mrs. Blessington, shivering, "pick up my shawl; I really must have sand-bags to those windows; there comes in a wind at them that positively nearly blows one out of one's chair."

Esther complies, and then resumes her occupation of holding a skein of wool for Miss Blessington to wind. As often as she can do so without positive rudeness, she takes long looks at her companion's face—immovably polished, like a monumental angel's: looks at her, half out of that sheer love of beauty in any form, from a man's to a beetle's, which is innate in some sensuous natures; partly, and much more, because each frosty-fair feature of her face, each trinket almost upon her person, is linked indissolubly in her mind with some look or word of St. John. Association, they say, lies stronger in a smell than in aught else—stronger than in anything seen or heard; and so now the slight subtle scent floating from Constance's perfumed hair recalls to the sad young "companion," with a thrust of sharpest pain, her one day's betrothal; that one day for whose sweet sake she does not regret having endured the calamity of existence; that day when they sowed—

".... Their talk with little kisses, thick As roses in rose harvest."

It is odd how often, when one is musing dumbly on some unspoken name, the people in whose company one is give utterance to that name, without any former conversation having led up to it.

"My dear Constance," says Mrs. Blessington, her slow old thoughts having at length travelled from draughts and sandbags, "do you think St. John has any fancy as to what room he has? Young men are sometimes *faddy*. I depend upon you to tell me, and I will give Franklin orders about it."

St. John's room! He is coming here, then! The wool that she is holding drops forgotten into Esther's lap; the old delicious carmine that used to make her so like a dog-rose springs up suddenly lovely into her face. Love is as hard to kill as any snake:

"Now, at the last gasp of love's latest breath,
When, his pulse failing, passion speechless lies;
When faith is kneeling by his bed of death,
And innocence is closing up his eyes:
Now, if thou wouldst, when all have given him over
From death to life, thou mightst him yet recover."

"Unless you hold the skein differently, Miss Craven, I'm afraid I really cannot wind it," says Constance, a slight shade of contemptuous displeasure in her voice.

Esther jumps back to reality, to find Miss Blessington's icy, unescapable eyes riveted upon her. She cannot turn away her head, nor dive under the table for an imaginary lost handkerchief; she cannot lift her hands to hide her face; her occupation, which keeps both ruthlessly employed, forbids it. She can only sit still, plainly crimson, and be stared at.

"Thanks, very much, aunt," Constance says, in her ladylike, piano voice, beginning again to turn the scarlet ball swiftly through her long pale fingers; "but I don't think he has any fancies. I could not think of letting you spoil him by supposing he has; I'm sure he will be very happy, wherever you put him."

"The blue room, in the west gallery, is one of the warmest in the house," rejoins the old lady, gathering her wraps closelier about her: "it is next but two to Miss Craven's; it has the same aspect. Yours is warm—isn't it, my dear?—and there is a bath-room opening out of it."

"Is Mr. Gerard coming here?" asks Esther, tremulously, resolute to show Miss Blessington that she *can* mention his name.

"Yes, my dear—to-morrow. Do you know him? Oh no! of course you cannot," replies the old lady, looking a little inquisitively at the tender rose-face of the girl.

"Miss Craven met him at Felton, last autumn," Constance answers for her—no faintest gust of feeling apparently agitating the even indifference of her voice. "He was most good-natured to her; riding and walking, and altogether making a martyr of himself. St. John makes himself very useful, flirting with all the young ladies that come to the house: he really is invaluable in that way!"

Esther stoops her head low down, choked with indignation. "Perhaps I don't come under the head of a 'young lady,'" she says, almost in a whisper; "but he certainly did not flirt with me."

"Didn't he?" Constance replies, carelessly. "Oh, if I recollect right, he amused himself a little—he always does. I often take him to task about that manner of his; it might give rise to unlucky mistakes; people who don't know him don't understand it."

Esther bites her lips, but has the sense to allow, with vast difficulty, this last observation to pass unquestioned.

"His horses have arrived already," continues Constance, placidly; "he has actually been unconscionable enough to send four of them: he is evidently going to test uncle's and your patience to the utmost by making a perfect visitation."

"Felton is such a good hunting country, that I wonder Mr. Gerard can bear to leave it now, just as the frost has broken up," remarks Esther, almost composedly; a dim, exquisite hope flashing up in her mind that he has heard of her being at Blessington, and is coming to ask her to forgive him—to forgive her, rather; to ask her to kiss and make friends.

The story-book ending, "Lived happy ever after," is running through her brain, when her reverie is broken, gently, but very effectually, as reveries are apt to be, by a simple speech of Miss Blessington's, spoken with a little smile:

"It is evident that Miss Craven has not heard our news, is not it, aunt?"

"What news?" inquires the girl, eagerly.

"Nothing of much interest to any one but ourselves, I suppose. It is only" (speaking with slow triumph, and narrowly watching the effect of her words) "that St. John and I have made up our minds to marry one another!"

The knife cuts as clean and clear as she could have wished; the divine happy rose-flush slips away suddenly out of the poor blank face opposite her; a grey ashy-white takes its place. She had thought that pain and pleasure were buried with Jack on the slope of Glan-yr-Afon's mountain graveyard; but that moment of raging agony undeceives her. For an instant the table and chairs seem dancing round; a humming buzz sounds dully in her ears; then the faintness passes; the table and chairs stand still again; the buzz ceases; and she is sitting on an old gilt chair: her arms still moving mechanically, with the outstretched wool upon them, while Constance goes winding, winding on—winding away hope and pleasure and joy; while the ball, growing larger under her hands, seems to have stolen its red colour from Esther's heart-blood.

"Our friends have really been very disagreeable to us about it," says Miss Blessington with a subdued laugh; "they tell us that it is the most uninteresting marriage they ever heard of, for that they had all foretold it, heaven knows how many centuries ago!"

"It is very seldom," replies Mrs. Blessington, shaking her head slowly to and fro, "that a young man shows the sense St. John Gerard has done in coming into his parents' views for him: in the present day they are mostly so headstrong and resolute to pick and choose for themselves, which generally ends in their selecting some worthless person utterly unsuited to their rank and fortune."

"How long have you been engaged?" asks Esther, presently, framing her words with as much difficulty as though they had been spoken in some little-known foreign tongue. Worse to her than the loss of St. John is the consciousness that that loss is written in despair's grey colours on her faded face, right under her rival's victorious eyes.

"How long? I really forget," answers Constance, with affected carelessness. "Oh, no! By-the-by, I recollect; it was almost immediately after you left Felton. I daresay" (with a smile) "that you were among the ranks of the prophets; lookers-on proverbially see most of the game."

"Indeed—no!" cries the girl, with a passionate disclaimer, the agony of loss made sharper by the humiliation of defeat. "Nothing ever struck me as more unlikely!"

"Indeed! And why, may I ask?"

The skein is finished; Esther lifts one hand to her face, and feels a slight relief in the partial shade.

"Why, pray?" with a slightly sharpened accent.

"Because—because," she answers, in confusion, "you had been brought up together from children; because Mr. Gerard's manner seemed so much more like a brother's than a—a—lover's."

The word so applied half chokes her.

"We dislike public demonstrations of affection, both of us," rejoins the other, coldly displeased; "we leave those to servants and *savages*."

A footman enters with tea in handleless red dragon cups, costly as age, brittleness, and ingenious ugliness can make them.

Esther leans back in her chair, idle, staring vacantly at the pane, blurred with big rain-drops.

After a pause, "You have not congratulated me, Miss Craven," Constance says, sipping her tea delicately; her madonna smile relaxing the severely correct lines of her Greek mouth.

Esther gives a great start. "I? Oh, I beg your pardon! I—I forgot; I—I—I congratulate you!"

"I was just going to write and tell you the news," says Constance, graciously—"I thought it might interest you, as you had been with us so lately, and seen the whole thing going on—when we heard of your brother's sudden death."

Esther rises abruptly, and walks to the window, with that painful hatred in her heart towards Miss Blessington that we feel towards those who lightly name our sacred dead to us.

"Was he your *only* brother, my dear?" inquires Mrs. Blessington, with languid interest.

"Yes."

"Dear—dear! Very sad—very sad! And what did he die of? Consumption?"

"No—diphtheria."

"Ah! A very fatal complaint, my dear, especially among children. I have always had a great horror of it. In my younger days it used to be called sore throat, but I suppose it killed just as many people then as it does now that it has got a fine long Latin name. I suppose your poor brother suffered a great deal—didn't he, love?"

No answer, except a stifled sob, a rush from the room, and the sound of flying feet upon the hall's stone floor.

There are some things past human endurance; and to hear Jack's parting agonies—agonies whose memory she herself dare as yet hardly contemplate in her heart's low depths—lightly discussed by a gossiping old woman, is one of those things.

CHAPTER XXXI.

"Get me some fresh candles—long ones; longer than these—as long as you possibly can," Esther says that same evening, on going to bed, to the housemaid whom she finds putting coals on her fire.

"I think, 'm, that you will find these will last for to-night," the woman answers, looking at the very respectable dimensions of the unlit candles on Esther's queer old-fashioned toilet-table.

"No—no, they won't!" she answers, nervously; "it is better to be on the safe side."

"Would you like a night-light, miss?"

"Oh no, no! they make the corners of the room blacker than ever, and they cast such odd shadows. I'm *so* afraid of the dark," she ends, shuddering.

"I'm afraid you don't sleep well, 'm?"

"Not very. By-the-by" (with a sudden inspiration), "have you got anything that you could give me to make me sleep—any opiate of any kind?"

"I've got a little laudanum, ma'am, that Mrs. Franklin give me last week when I had a bad face."

"Fetch it me," she cries, eagerly; "that is, if you don't want it yourself. It is very foolish of me," she says, looking rather ashamed, "but I cannot sleep for fright."

The servant goes, and presently returns with a small dark blue bottle.

"About how much ought one to take, I wonder?" Esther says, holding it up between herself and the firelight.

"If you have never been used to take it before, I should think two or three drops would be *hample*, 'm; I hope, 'm" (with a little anxiety in her florid plebeian face), "as you'll be careful not to take a *h*overdose, or you might chance never to wake up again: I knew a young person as took it by mistake for 'black dose'—it was the fault of the chemist's young man—and in an hour she was a corpse; they said as she had took enough to kill ten men."

"It is no wonder that she was a corpse, then," Miss Craven answers, with a slight smile. "I should not think" (scrutinising the little bottle inquisitively), "that there was enough here to kill one woman, let alone ten men. Yes, I'll be careful; thanks, very much. Good night!" (with her pretty courteous smile).

The housemaid being gone, Esther bolts the door—a weakly defensive measure against one class of assailants, the crape-masked burglars; though, as she is aware, utterly impotent against the other and worse class—the intangible, unkeep-outable *revenants*; the rustlers along the passage, the rattlers of the lock. She then seats herself at the dressing-table, flings down her arms among her brushes and combs, and sinks her head upon them, in closest proximity to the candles, whose little spires of flame the wind, thrusting its thin body in between window and frame, drives right against the tumbled plenty of her hair. In this attitude she remains a long time; forgetting even to search under the bed, up the chimney, behind the screen, or in the huge japanned chest, upon which a disconnected but interesting landscape of cocks, pagodas, and junks picks itself out, in tarnished yellow, from the dull black ground.

It is impossible for the most comprehensive mind or body to contain any two distinct, even though not necessarily opposite feelings, in their fullest force, at the same time. If one is famished with hunger, one cannot be consumed by thirst; if one is consumed by thirst, one cannot be famished with hunger. If one is in despair at being forgotten by one's lover, one is indifferent as to the onset of any number of ghosts and murderers; if one is paralyzed by fear of ghosts and murderers, one is tolerably indifferent as to one's lover's lapse of memory. For the first time since his death, Jack is not the leading thought in Esther's mind. Poor dead! How can they be so unreasonable as to expect to be anyone's leading thought? Even we noisy, voiceful, visible living are obliged to keep crying out, "I am here—remember me," in order not to sink into oblivion amongst our neighbours and kinsfolk.

"Wilt   thou   remember   me   when   I   am   gone,
Further   each   day   from   thy   vision   withdrawn—
Thou in the sunset, and I in the dawn?"

Pretty, tender, touching lines; but I think that the answer to them, if given truly, would hardly content the asker: "I will remember thee for a very little while; even till I see some one younger and prettier than thou wert, and then I will forget thee!"

Miss Craven starts up, after awhile, and begins to walk up and down, over the creaky, up-and-downy boards, and to speak vehemently and out loud to the rats, who, numerous and cheerful as usual, are scrabbling, pattering, squeaking under the floor, behind the wainscot, in the japan-chest. "At all events," she says, with a sort of savage satisfaction, "there is one comfort: he'll be miserable—he'll curse the day when he ties himself to that lump of blancmange. Blancmange! white meat! that exactly expresses her; she looks as if she would be good to eat—soft, luscious, ripe. Unfortunately, a man does not contemplate *eating* his wife!"

But even this little angry gleam of comfort has but a short life. Soon, too soon, it occurs to her that men do not look at a woman with women's eyes. Men, being three parts animal themselves, condone any offence to a woman the animal part of whom is perfect and beautiful. How else is it that beauty—mere blank beauty, although destitute of any accessory charms—can always command its price in the market, and that price a high one? In marrying Constance, St. John will have no disappointments to undergo, no discoveries to make. He has known her all her life; has seen her change from a handsome stupid child into a handsomer stupider girl, and bloom, lastly, into a handsomest, stupidest woman. Constance has no antecedents; she is a woman without a history. That also is in her favour. A man likes to write his name on a sheet of white paper better than on one upon which many other men have written theirs. Perfectly virtuous, perfectly healthy, perfectly beautiful, young, rich, not ill-tempered, not fast, not shrew-tongued—surely she is a prize worth any man's drawing. If, in addition to her long list of qualifications, she possessed also Desdemona's heart and Imogen's mind, it would be too hard upon the rest of womankind:

"Why should one woman have all goodly things?"

Want of sympathy with the companion of her life makes a woman embittered, reckless—sends her often trespassing on her neighbours' preserves, in the endeavour to find there that congeniality of spirit which is not to be met with in her own. Want of sympathy with the companion of *his* life sends a man oftener to his club; makes him much pleasanter to other women when he goes into society; makes him sulky and sleepy when he dines at home—that is all. Doubtless St. John will be indifferent to his bride at first; he will dislocate his jaw with yawning during their wedding-tour, but she will bear him children; "selon les us et coutumes Anglaises, elle aura beaucoup d'enfants;" he will like her for that. Year by year they will come here to Blessington, probably. Year by year she (Esther) will see the blossom of a fuller contentment on his wide brow, the quiet of a deeper rest in his restless eyes. And she herself will be here always, for one cannot throw away one's daily bread. Year by year they will find her with ever thinner hair, sharper shoulders, drabber cheeks; and he, looking upon her with the forgiveness of complete indifference, will say to himself, "She is bad, and she is ugly; I was well rid of her!" Than to be so forgiven, how much rather would she have been struck down dead by his hand, lifted in righteous anger and vengeance, on that moonlit September night, beside the glassy rush-brimmed mere at Felton! A sudden rage at her own fatuity fills her, when she looks back on that idiotic hope that had upsprung in her mind, that his object in coming to Blessington was to pardon her, and take her back to himself. Do men ever pardon a sin against themselves?

"...............Worse than despair,
Worse than the bitterness of death, is hope.
It is the only ill which can find place
Upon the giddy, sharp, and narrow hour
Tottering beneath us. Plead with the swift frost,
That it should spare the eldest flower of spring;
Plead with awakening earthquake, o'er whose couch
Even now a city stands, strong, fair and free,
Now stench and blackness yawns like death. Oh! plead
With famine and wind-walking pestilence,
Blind lightning, or the deep sea; not with man—
Cruel, cold formal man—righteous in words,
In deeds a Cain."

She sits down before her looking-glass, and stares desperately, with inner eyes, at the blank ruin of her life; with outer eyes at the ruin mirrored in her sunken, altered face, that the old looking-glass, blurred with rust stains, makes look more sunken and altered still. Involuntarily she lifts her thumb and forefinger, and lays them in the hollows of her cheek, as if seeking for the red carnations that used to flower so fairly there. She has noticed before the decay of her beauty—noticed it with apathy, as who should say, "Everything else is gone, why should not this go too?" But now she observes it with a sick pang, as at the parting with a friend; she would give ten years of her life to reach it back again. "It was only for my beauty he liked me," she says, still speaking aloud; "it was only for my beauty that anybody could like me; there is nothing else to like in me. I never was clever, or said witty things, or sang, or played: I was only pretty. Now that is gone, everything is gone!"

As one shipwrecked, floating about on a plank among the weltering waves of some great plunging, grey-green sea, strains his eyes along the horizon to see some sail-speck, some misty palm-island, that looks as though it were hung midway in air; so she strains her mental eyes to catch sight of some friendly ship that may take her off from this rock of her despair. This world is full of pairs, but some oversight has left a good many odd ones also; Esther is an odd one. Her road has come to a blank wall, and there stopped. Is there no ladder that can overclimb this wall?—no gap in all the thickness of its brick-and-mortar?—no outlet?

She rises and stands by the fire; her eyes down-dropped on the blue-and-white Dutch tiles—on the hobs, and queer brass-inlaid dogs: involuntarily she raises them, and they rest upon

118

the little laudanum-bottle on the chimneypiece. Quick as lightning, an answer to her thought-question seems flashed across her mind. There is a ladder that can overclimb *any* wall; there is a gap that can give egress through the stoutest masonries; there is an outlet from the deepest dungeon; and this ladder, this gap, this outlet, men call *Death*. Over the sea of her memory the housemaid's words float back: "I hope you'll be careful not to take an overdose, 'm, or you might chance never to wake again!" They had been spoken in careful warning; to her they seemed words of persuasive promise. Never to wake again! Never to say again in the evening, "Would God it were morning!" and in the morning, "Would God it were evening!"

To Esther, the great sting of death had always laid in his pain—in his gasping breath, twitched features, writhen unfleshed limbs; but this death that comes in sleep can be no bitterer than a mother that lifts her little slumbering child out of his small bed (he not knowing), and bears him away softly. The idea of self-slaughter, when first suggested, has always something terrific, especially to us, who from our birth have been taught to look upon it as a crime hardly second to murder; to us, to whom Cato's great heroism and Lucretia's chaste martyrdom seem as sins. Some vague idea that suicide is forbidden in the Scriptures runs through Esther's mind. She sits down at the table, and, drawing a Bible towards her, searches long among the partial, temporary, and local prohibitions and commands of the Books of the Law, and still longer among the universal, all-applying prohibitions and commands of Gospel and Epistle. Whether it be that she search ill, or that there is nought therein written on the subject she seeks, she knows not; only she finds nothing; and, closing the book, she leans her pale cheek on her closed white hand. Her brain feels strangely calm, and she even forgets the darkness of the night, musing on a deeper darkness.

What is this death, that we write in such great black letters? After all, what is it that we know about him, for or against? Is it fair to condemn him unheard, unknown? Why should we give him any embodiment?—why should we personify him at all? He is but an ending: what is there in the end of anything more terrifying than in its beginning, or its middle? Death is but the end of life, as birth is its beginning, and as some unnoticed moment in its course is its middle.

Why are the waters in which we set our feet at the last more coldly awful than those out of which we stepped at the first? Both—both, are they not portions of the great sea of Eternity that floweth ever round Time's little island? A clock is wound up for a certain number of hours; when that number of hours has elapsed, it stops. Our more complicated machinery is wound up to go for a certain number of years, months, days; when that number of years, months, and days is elapsed, we stop—that is all. What is this life, about the taking or keeping of which we make such a clamour, as if it were some great, costly, goodly thing?

"It   is   but   a   watch   or   a   vision
Between a sleep and a sleep."

It is cowardly, disloyal, say they, for a soldier to desert the post at which he has been set. Ay, but the galley-slave, chained to an oar, if he can but break his chain and be gone, may flee away, and none blame him. A prisoner that is not on parole, what shall hinder him from escaping? If he can but burst his bars, and draw his strong bolts, may he not out and away into the free air? If, before our birth, in that unknown pre-existence of ours at which backward-reaching memory catches not, we, standing looking into life, had said, "Oh, Master, give me of this life! I know not what it is, but I would fain taste it; and if Thou givest it to me, I swear to Thee to keep and guard it carefully, as long as I may——." But have we ever so asked for it? Has it not been thrust upon us, undesiring, unconsulted, as a gift that is neither of beauty nor of price? Who can chide us, if, laying it down meekly at the everlasting feet, we say, "Oh, Great Builder! take back that house in which, a reluctant tenant, Thou hast placed me. Resume Thy gift; it is a burden too heavy for me! Lay it, I pray Thee, on shoulders that mayhap may bear it stoutlier!"

She lifts the bottle, having uncorked it, to her lips and tastes. It has a deathly, sickly flavour, not enticing. Hesitating, she holds it in her hand, half-frightened, half-allured; while her heart beats loud and hard. "It is the key to all my doubts," she says within herself, looking steadfastly at it; "it is the answer to all my questions. If I do but drink this little draught, I shall have all knowledge; I shall never wonder again! I shall know where Jack is; I shall be with him! But shall I?" Ay, that's the rub! Even in this small world, to be alive at the same time with another person is not necessarily, or even probably, to be *with* him. Wide continents, high mountains, deep rivers often sever those that are closest of kin; and in the world of the dead, which, being so much more populous, must be so much the greater, is it not likely that still wider continents, higher mountains, deeper rivers, may part two that would fain be together? What if, before her time, she incur the abasement of death, the dishonour of corruption, and yet attain not the object for whose sake she is willing desperately to lay her comely head in the dust?

She changes her attitude, puts down the bottle, and again stoops her small flower-face on her bent fingers—her thoughts varying their channel a little: "If I go, I shall leave no gap behind me, any more than a teacupful of water taken out of a great pool leaves a gap behind. If it is disgraceful to go willingly out of the world, instead of being dragged unwillingly out of it, my disgrace is my own. I involve no one else in it; there is no one of my name left to be ashamed of me. I leave no work undone in the world. Hundreds of others can carry air-cushions, and read to a deaf old man far more patiently than I have done. My fifty pounds a year will go to put daily bread into some other poor woman's mouth, to whom it may perhaps taste sweeter than it has done to me." Her head sinks forward again on her outstretched arms.... "It is awful to go out into the dark all by oneself," she thinks, with a pang of intense self-pity, as she feels the warm, gentle life throbbing in her round, tender limbs: "and I, that hate the dark so——, is it very wicked of me to think of this thing? People will say so, but I will not hear them. Where shall I be to-morrow at even?"

"You will be at Blessington, and feeling a good deal ashamed of your absurd paroxysm of cowardly despair," answers plain common sense, who, in the shape of an untold multitude of rats, begins rushing and gnawing, hundred-toothed, scampering hundred-footed behind the walls.

Esther lifts her foolish prone head, and listens. "Skurry—skurry!" go the rats; "Crack!" go the beams; "Thud!" goes some unexplained bulk, in the dining-room underneath! As the tide, at flood, creeps up and over the sands, so the child's old fear creeps up and over her new mad scheme of suicide. "Rustle—rustle!" come the ghostly dresses along the China gallery; "Click, rattle—rattle, click!" goes the door-lock. Down goes the laudanum bottle on the table, and Esther, springing to her feet, begins to unfasten, with fingers rendered nervous by extreme haste, her dress and the belt round her slim waist. "Crack—crack—crack!" goes something close to the bed-head; "Bang!" goes a distant door. There is no wind; what or who can have executed that bang? The fire, which has been burning hollow for some time, collapses, and falls in suddenly with a clear, loud noise. In one leap Miss Craven is in bed and beneath the sheltering bed-clothes.

All very well pensively to contemplate, in half-earnest, the conveying oneself out of a world that has been a most harsh step-mother to one, but by no means well to have one's graceful farewells to existence broken in upon by a nation tailed and whiskered—by the spirits of old reprobates in flowered dressing-gowns, and of ladies, who nightly carry their patched and powdered heads like parcels under their arms.

Good night, wicked woman! May the rats career all night over your small face, as a punishment for your great idiocy!

CHAPTER XXXII.

St. John has arrived; he has jumped down from the dog-cart that brought him from the station, wrapped up in a huge greatcoat lined with otter-skin, that makes him look like "three single gentlemen rolled into one." His nose, always rather a salient point in his face, is reddened by the east winds, and his eyelids purple with want of sleep, as he has been travelling night and day—not from any violent hurry to reach his destination, but because boats and mail-trains suited—from the South of Ireland, where for the last ten days he has been daily shooting the wily woodcock, and nightly putting into practice the excellent resolution expressed in the song of "not going home till morning," with some rather fast bachelor-friends, who, like himself, are as yet destitute of household angels, to bring heaven to their hearths, to take away their cues, blow out their cigars, and reduce the number of their brandies and sodas. Neither a good-looking nor a good-tempered young man does he look as he makes his descent. The first he cannot help—the second he can. His ill-humour is owing partly to a violent headache; partly to the information, just imparted to him by the butler, that "the family dines at six o'clock now *reg'lar*—no difference made whatever company there may be—on account of the old squire's 'ealth."

Perhaps, had St. John known that a woman was watching his arrival, he might have endeavoured to smooth his features into an expression of greater amiability. Had he known that that woman was Esther Craven, the look of bored annoyance would certainly have given way to a stronger one, whether of pleasure or pain. Crouched on one of the paintless window-seats in the China gallery, she watches his coming, as she had watched his going; only that now she makes no smallest effort to attract his attention—cowers away rather in the dark, while he stands, unconscious and grumbling, in the patch of red light that comes through the open hall-door. He has been here half an hour now—half an hour spent in the hot airtight saloon, where the giant fire draws a strong woolly smell from Miss Blessington's winter dress, as she sits right into the fire—a practice not permitted by the autocrat of Felton, and consequently largely indulged in by his subjects when away from his master-eye.

The old squire has requested St. John to come round to his other side—to draw his chair closer to his—to speak more distinctly. The old lady has explained to him the exact manner in which the draught comes through the middle window, and catches her just at the back of the neck, so that when she wakes in the morning it is so stiff that she can hardly turn it a quarter of an inch one way or another. Miss Blessington has expressed one fear that he had had a cold journey down, and another that he had not been able to get a foot-warmer at Shoreditch; there were always so shamefully few there, particularly these afternoon trains, that all the business-men came down from their offices by. Constance had certainly never spoken a truer word, than in saying that she and her lover were not fond of public demonstrations; the question that their acquaintance asked each other was, whether they were any fonder of private ones.

As the clock strikes half-past five, Miss Blessington rises and floats away lightly, and without noise, to dress. Not for a kingdom would she rob one second from the sacred half-hour—all too short already—though the toilette to be made is only for the benefit of two purblind old people, who cannot see it, and of a young man who does not know gingham from "gaze de Chambéry," and who has seen her in short frock and trousers, in long dress and chignon, in court-dress, in ball-dress, in walking-dress, in driving-dress, in staying-at-home dress, any thousand number of times during the last seventeen years.

Momently the hot close atmosphere is making Gerard's headache worse; momently the prospect of the six-o'clock dinner becomes more intolerable to him. Heroically, however, he enters into conversation with his great aunt-in-law elect.

"So you have been trying an experiment, I hear," he says, scratching the cat's ear and cheek and chin as she successively lifts them to him for titillation,—"set up a 'companion,' haven't you? Do you find it work well?"

"You must ask grandpapa," replies the old lady, looking towards her husband, who, with head sunk on chest, lips protruded, and eyes closed, seems at the present moment hardly in a condition to be put through a catechism on any subject; "he has more to say to her than I have. You see it was too great a strain on dear Constance's strength reading to him every day, and he dislikes Gurney's reading" (Gurney is the valet): "he says he never minds his stops, and *bawls* at him; and so we thought it better to get a person of more education, who would be always on the spot, and——"

"And whose strength," interrupts St. John, a little ironically, "unlike Constance's, would be warranted *un-overworkable?*"

"Exactly," answers the old lady, innocently.

"And she is a satisfactory beast of burden, I hope?" says Gerard, yawning till the tears come into his eyes; "fetches and carries well?"

"She seems a nice, quiet, ladylike person enough," replies Mrs. Blessington, leaning back placidly in her chair, with her hands, in black kid half-gloves, lying folded in her lap—"only, unfortunately, over-sensitive: those sort of people always are. Why, it was only yesterday that she rushed from this room with such violence that she nearly shook Constance and me out of our chairs, because I made some slight observation about a brother of hers who died lately, and to whom, it seems, she was much attached. I'm sure I had no intention of hurting her feelings, poor girl!"

"Girl!" repeats St. John, laughing; "that means a gushing thing of fifty, I suppose?"

"More like fifteen. By-the-by, she said something the other day about having known *you.*"

"Known me!" cries the young man, opening his quick grey eyes. "Well, 'more know Tom Fool than Tom Fool knows.' I never knew any one in my life that had a 'companion'—of this sort, I mean. What may my unknown friend's name be?"

But at this juncture, before the name of his unknown friend can be confided to him, the old squire, waking up, urgently requests to be told what they are talking about, which information is communicated, in a succession of long dull roars, into his good ear. St. John takes advantage of the diversion to leave the room, and, running upstairs, knocks at Constance's door.

"Constance!"

"Who's there?" (Voice rather muffled—from under an avalanche of hair apparently).

"I. Can you come out and speak to me for a minute, if you are not in too great deshabille?"

"Certainly."

Ordinarily, Miss Blessington is a prude; but to appear for an instant before her betrothed in light-blue cashmere lined with blue satin, and her hair in golden rain about her shoulders, is, she thinks, for once permissible. Has he come to make some demonstration of affection?—to give her some warmer greeting than the nonchalant handshake with which they met? Or has he, has he—oh sweeter, warmer thought!—brought her a present from Ireland? Visions of Irish poplin, Irish lace, bog-oak and gold, cunningly fashioned together into bracelet or necklace, float before her mind's eye. In a moment, with a little affected coyness on her face, she stands before him; stands before him—and he does not even see her! He has opened one of the rusty casements in the passage, and thrust his head out, feeling the keen eastern blast blow against his throbbing brow with a sense of relief. He has evidently no gift in his hand, nor does he seem to be assailed by any very overpowering temptation to embrace her, blue and gold and white miracle though she be. Hearing her he turns, and the expression of his countenance is glum.

"I say, does this sort of thing happen every day?"

"What sort of thing?" (with a little pique at the errand on which she has been called away from among her cosmetics).

"This feeding, I cannot call it dining, like savages, at mid-day?"

"It is a fancy of my uncle," replies Constance, with the door-handle still in her hand; "he imagines that, if he dined later, he should not have time to digest his food before going to bed."

St. John utters an impatient exclamation. "In Heaven's name let him digest in bed, then; or, if not, let him dine by himself! I'm sure no one would object to that arrangement. Poor old boy! he can't help it; but it does take away one's appetite to see a very old man mumbling his food, like a toothless old dog over a bone."

"I suppose he may dine at what hour he chooses in his own house?" says Constance, coldly.

"Of course he may. He may go back to the manners and customs of the ancient British," rejoins Gerard, impatiently; "he may get up in the middle of the night and paint himself in blue-and-white stripes, instead of wearing coat and waistcoat, if he chooses—only he can hardly expect civilized beings to join him."

"I always think it right, on principle, to humour old people's whims," answers Constance, taking the high moral tone that she has adopted more than once since their engagement in any discussion with her lover, a tone symptomatic of what the postnuptial line of attack is likely to be.

"A very excellent sentiment, my dear," says St. John, a little mockingly, "worthy of being copied by little boys and girls after they have mastered straight strokes and pothooks; but to-night I must request the aged to humour my whim, and my whim is to absent myself from this symposium. I have got a splitting headache, and am altogether pretty nearly dead-beat. I have hardly a leg to stand upon: if you won't take it as a personal insult, I have a good mind to turn in at once. I have not been in bed, for any time worth speaking of, for the last ten days."

"Indeed!" replies Constance, freezing up, and looking as though tortures should not wring from her any question as to what had been the vicious pursuits that had detained her lover from balmy slumbers. "You will please yourself of course."

"If every one pleased themselves, and no one else, this would be a much more passable world to live in," retorts St. John, with a little misanthropy; "for then each person would get their fair share of attention neither more nor less, which is what they do not now."

But the last half of his sentence is addressed to himself, as his madonna has retired again within her shrine.

Meanwhile, for the first time since her brother's death, the "companion"—the nice, quiet, young ladylike person, whose only fault is being over-sensitive—is, like Constance, making a toilette. Since Jack's death she has daily put on her clothes, as a necessary preliminary to the day's work; but it has been a task full of weariness—devoid of pleasure. To-night, like Constance, she makes a toilette, and like Constance, it is for the benefit of the young man who does not know gingham from "gaze de Chambéry." It is not, however, with any faintest hope that her Sunday frock, any more than her work-a-day one, will bring back her lost lover to her side, that she puts the former on. The very strength of her faith in his honour hinders the possibility of his turning away from the woman he has promised to marry to any other woman from entering her head. Only, seeing, as plainly as if it were another's and not her own, the ruin of the face that meets her, daily and nightly, in the dim oval of the old glass in its tarnished frame, she wishes that that ruin might be revealed slowly, and by degrees (not *all at once*), to him that had once thought her so fair. For this one night, she would fain look like her old self—would fain be pretty plump Esther Craven, whose face, dimpled and *débonnaire*, men used to turn round in the street to look after—instead of the thin depressed "companion," whom if men looked at at all, it was only to pity her sunken white cheeks and sombre mourning weeds. Her Sunday frock is a lugubrious combination of cheap black silk and crape, against which her artistic eye has been revolting ever since she heard of St. John's coming. A little white tucker will not make her any the less mindful of Jack. And so she has been devoting most of the short winter daylight to the inserting of such a tucker, and to cutting the funereal body square. The alterations have been effected, now the Sunday frock is on: if it had been costliest velvet or satin, instead of papery silk at two-and-sixpence a yard, its black could not have contrasted better with the milkwhite of the long lily throat and swelling bust. Esther has lost flesh a good deal lately; but, being small-boned and thoroughly well-made, no unsightly hollows show as yet, like salt-cellars, beneath her collar-bones—not yet are elbows or shoulders sharp. Brilliancy of colouring is gone; but the head, arched like the Clytie's, is still left, and great plenty of night-dark hair to clothe it. Instead of the unnatural protuberance of a chignon, she has arranged this hair in the thick plain twists with which in the old time Miss Blessington's betrothed used—

.... "to   play
Not knowing——,"

and, so playing, spoke in loving commendation of them. In like twists Miss Blessington herself often disposes her locks—twists purchased by her for a considerable price from M. Isidore, golden hair being hard to match, and consequently expensive.

It is five minutes to six. The toilette is finished, and Esther stands before the glass considering it; but with none of the triumphant self-content with which a fine woman usually regards the victory that art and nature, fighting side by side, have achieved on the battle-field of her face. Colour had been Esther's strong point, and colour has gone from her; as it goes from a violet sent in a letter, or from a poppy dried between the leaves of a love-song. A raging desire for rouge, raddle, plate-powder—anything to bring back that flower-flush that used to need no persuasion to stay with her—enters her mind. But neither rouge nor raddle is near, and for plate-powder she would have to apply to the butler—an effort for which not even her great wish to appear once more red-cheeked before her ex-lover can nerve her. Suddenly, her eyes fall on a spray of scarlet geranium, that, plucked this morning in the conservatory, she has worn all day in the breast of her dress. A recollection comes to her of having, when a child, crushed one of those dazzling flowers against the face of another child, and of having laughed with pleasure at the scarlet stain. She snatches up eagerly some of the petals, and rubs them on her cheeks; the hue produced, though too scarlet for nature, is vivid and beautifying. She sets to work on the other cheek.

Esther is not a very cunning artiste; she has no idea of softening off edges with cotton-wool—of working deftly from cheekbone downwards. She is only possessed by a great longing to get back, for this one night, something of her old brilliancy. And in this she partially succeeds. The result of her labours is, indeed, a too hectic bloom; but the bright colour seems to fill up somewhat the hollowed cheeks—seems to bring back a little of the old childish *débonnaire* grace. Her labour ended, she runs downstairs quickly—not giving herself time for remorse at the meretricious nature of her charms, and listens, trembling all over, at the saloon-door before entering. There is no sound except the rolling grunts with which, unheard by himself, the old gentleman accompanies every respiration. A footman crosses the hall; the "companion" must not be caught eavesdropping; she turns the door-handle and goes in.

The old squire, with coat-tails under his arms, standing on tottery old legs before the fire; the old lady, in her evening-cap, sunk in armchair and Shetland shawls; Miss Blessington, with blue bands binding close her waved golden hair, and an expression of face less bland than usual, on the ottoman. No one else.

"How smart you are, my dear!" the old lady says, not unkindly, her faded eyes straying slowly over the square-cut bodice, white tucker, and cabled hair. "Is that in honour of Mr. Gerard?"

"It is rather thrown away if it is," says Mr. Gerard's future owner, with some temper: "St. John has chosen to make an invalid of himself to-night, and has gone to bed."

No need now for the geranium dye: a great hot blush burns through it—burns throat and brow and neck; she has *made herself up* in vain.

"Gone to bed!" repeats Mrs. Blessington, raising herself a little from among her pillows—"at *six* o'clock! Dear me, love, I hope he is not ill! I thought he seemed rather absent when he was talking to me before I went to dress; and he left the room so abruptly too! Are you sure, Constance, that he would not like something sent up to him?"

"He is quite able to take care of himself, I assure you—thanks, aunt," replies Constance, not without a vexed ring in her low flute voice. "If we served him right, we should accept him as the invalid he pretends himself, and allow him nothing but a little water-gruel or arrowroot."

"It seems so unnatural, a young man going to bed without his dinner; I'm sure, dear, I hope it is nothing serious," cries the old lady, with that righteous horror of death and sickness which, by some strange contrariety, one finds so often amongst the aged, so seldom amongst the young.

"Nothing more serious than the natural results of ten days' Irish hospitality," replies Constance, with a laugh, which, though low and highbred, is not mirthful; "men are so fond of one another's society when they get together, that they never can take it in moderation. I dislike bachelor parties particularly."

123

"He is making the most of his time, my dear—he knows it is short," suggests the old lady, smiling and nodding, and looking wise.

"Quite right, too!—quite right! Sensible fellow—knows when he is well off! So did I when I was his age—eh, Mrs. Blessington?" chimes in the squire, who, for a wonder, has caught the drift of the talk; chuckling to himself at the recollection—perfectly clear, though he forgets what happened yesterday—of the pleasant immoralities that have the weight of over half a century lying upon them.

"Dinner!" announces the butler, coming close up to his master, and bawling unnecessarily loud.

"You'll have to be content with the old squire again, Conny, my dear," says the old man, putting out his feeble arm; "you'll find the old fellows are best, after all."

"I quite agree with you, uncle—I think they are," replies Constance, gravely; and so, the old man supported on one young girl's arm, and the old woman on another's, the procession toddles solemnly, at a snail's pace, into the carefully-warmed and shaded dining-room.

"What a brilliant colour you have to-night, Miss Craven!" says Constance that evening; endeavouring vainly to get a strong light thrown upon Esther's countenance—the one small lamp, with its deep green shade, effectually baffling her.

"I went out in the wind, and it caught my face," answers Esther, hurriedly: involuntarily raising her hands to her cheeks and then snatching them away again, in the fear that the scarlet dye, staining them, may betray her secret.

"But there was no wind to-day, and I did not think that you had been outside the doors?"

"Yes, I was; I went for a run in the park just before dressing-time."

"It must have been quite dark."

"It is never *quite* dark out-of-doors; total darkness is a human invention, I think; there is always a sort of *owl* light."

Constance shrugs her shoulders: "*Chacun à son goût*, I prefer leaving it to the owls."

"It stifles me staying indoors all day; I have never been used to it."

Miss Blessington unbuttons her great eyes a little: "Really?"

"Yes, really."

"But there was no wind, surely?" persists Constance.

"Not a breath!" replies the other, absently, forgetting her former excuse for her brilliant face. "There never is any wind worth calling a wind in these low countries; the winds keep to the mountains, and very wise of them too."

"But you said it was the wind that had caught your face?" says Constance, raising herself from her lounging attitude with more animation than is customary to her.

Esther starts. "Oh! so I did—I forgot; I meant the air, of course."

Constance looks slightly sceptical, but is too well-bred to pursue her inquiries further; merely saying, languidly, as she rearranges the cushions upon which her stately shoulders rest posed, "Glycerine-cream is the best thing in the world for a chapped face."

"Is it?" answers Essie, guiltily conscious that a little cold water is the only glycerine-cream needed to effect the cure of *her* chapped face.

"Have you seen St. John since he came?" asks Constance, presently; the links that connect his name with her artificially-reddened countenance being painfully evident to Miss Craven.

"No—yes—no, not to speak to."

"You were out when he came, I suppose, weren't you?"

"No, I was upstairs."

"I have not told him you are here; it will be a surprise to him to meet an old acquaintance."

Esther gives an involuntary start of dismay. "Why did not you tell him?" she asks, hurriedly.

"*I!* Oh, I don't know; I have the worst memory in the world. I have intended to tell him in every letter, but I have always forgotten."

"Will he stay here long?" asks Miss Blessington's unsuccessful rival, in a low voice, bending down her head.

"I don't know, I'm sure; he is always so full of engagements, and I never allow him to refuse a good invitation on my account."

"Will your wedding be soon, Miss Blessington?" (spoken quietly and firmly).

"I really have not thought about it" (with a little yawn, as if the subject were rather a wearisome one than otherwise); "'sufficient unto the day is the evil thereof.' I don't suppose I shall be given more than two or three months longer; some time in the spring, I daresay."

124

"I always think it is a good omen when people are married in the spring," says the young companion, with a dreamy smile; "when the world is beginning all over again, it is right that people's new life should begin with it."

"Do you think so? I don't much believe in omens. May is certainly the best time for Paris. I have set my heart upon seeing the Grand Prix run for; unfortunately, St. John hates Paris."

"All men hate all towns, I think, except American men; 'good Americans when they die go to Paris,' somebody said, didn't they?"

"Did they? It was rather irreverent, don't you think? By-the-by, some one told me in the summer that you were engaged to be married; is it true? I hope you won't think me impertinent for asking."

"Not in the least; but it is not true."

"Really? How odd it is the way those sort of reports get about!"

"Very odd; people are singularly fond of pairing their neighbours, but they don't often hit upon the right pairs."

"Perhaps not," answers Constance, closing her eyes, and looking bored, whereupon Esther lapses into silence.

Every Jack has his Jill; but my Jill is probably in Siberia or Hong Kong, and yours is close at hand; so I marry yours, and you, being in Siberia or Hong Kong, marry mine, and we both rue it to our dying day.

CHAPTER XXXIII.

Next morning St. John wakes, recovered from his ill temper, his headache, and all the effects of his Irish saturnalia. Perhaps, had he known who it was that lay wakeful in a great ginger four-poster, two doors off, his slumbers would not have been so profound. The hounds meet twelve miles away, at Shepherds Hatch. By nine o'clock he is in the saddle, and riding quietly along the deep Essex lanes and wet fields, with a soft, south wind blowing in his face, and the grass, crisped by the slightest possible frost, beneath the horse's hoofs.

He is lucky enough to come in for the run of the season; has the satisfaction of seeing many better men than himself floundering, hatless and well-watered, in a brook, or getting croppers over stiff hawthorn hedges; over all which obstacles his grey, a new investment, of whose fencing powers he and his groom had been unjustly doubtful, carries him like a bird. As to whether his ladylove may relish this early preference of "bold Reynolds" to herself, any more than she relished his fatigue and headache last night, he troubles himself but little. He has no intention whatever of being a hen-pecked husband. When he proposed to her, he told her what he could give her, and what he could not—what she might expect, and what she might not: nor has this day's desertion been any departure from his half of the bargain. Somewhere about five o'clock he is back again at Blessington, splashed from head to heel; his tops, in which this morning you might have seen your face, all stained and discoloured; with a dab of mud on each cheek, and a third on the bridge of his nose. He runs upstairs lightly, whistling a tune, and has just reached the first landing, when, "Click-clack," he hears a woman's high-heeled shoes descending. It is Esther, who is walking listlessly down, with her eyes fixed on a great picture let into the wall—a large, white woman, with her clothes tumbling off, hurling her substantial person upon a spear; a young man, with arms like a blacksmith's, lying on the ground, making a profuse display of his charms, and, though with no very perceptible wound, evidently *in articulo mortis;* a fat Cupid blubbering hard by—the whole entitled "Pyramus and Thisbe."

St. John looks upward, to see who the author of the "click-clacking" may be. "Who the devil is this pretty girl?" is his first thought. His second—a thought that makes him stagger back with the colour hurrying from his healthy cheek—a thought full of anger, astonishment, desire, and pain—a thought that involuntarily he speaks aloud, is "Esther."

At almost the same moment she has caught sight of him. In her case, there is no surprise; but the pain is as great, if not greater.

"Yes, it is I," she answers, almost inaudibly, trembling all over.

His first impulse seems to be to rush away from her, to pass quickly upstairs; his second takes him to her side.

"In Heaven's name, what brings *you* here?" he asks, in a voice almost as low as her own, from intense repressed emotion.

No answer. His voice has carried her back, across the gulf of Jack's death, of her own servitude and failing health, to that night when, in the starry Felton fields, she had stood by his side, his beloved, promised wife. She is silent—struggling with a strong, vile, degrading temptation to fling down her tired head upon the shoulder of Miss Blessington's affianced husband, and weep out loud.

"Are you on a visit here?" he asks again, with stern brevity.

"Yes," she answers, bitterly, strengthened by his tone, in which there is small kindness, and much wrath; "I am paid fifty pounds a year to visit here."

"What *do* you mean?"

"I am Mr. and Mrs. Blessington's 'companion.'"

"Good God! You are here *always*, then?"

"Always."

A pause! Against his will his eyes dwell upon her, hungry and fierce, astonished at the alteration wrought in her whom he had once thought fairest among women. Faded, wasted, forlorn, to his cost he finds that he still thinks her so.

"Is this bondage to last all your life, then?" he inquires more collectedly, after a few seconds.

"Until they die, or until my voice fails."

"And what then?"

"I must look out for some other old people, to whom I can be ears, and voice, and feet."

"Good God! And what *can* be your motive?"

"One *must* live."

"I had thought the world wide enough for two people to walk apart," he says, with almost a groan. "I have entreated God that I might never look on your face again, and this is how my prayer is answered."

Another pause. "Tick-tack—tick-tack—tick-tack," goes a clock in the gallery overhead.

"You look extremely ill!"

"Do I?"

"You are wonderfully altered!"

"Yes, I know it!"

"What is it ails you?"

"Nothing."

"What does *this* mean?"—touching her black dress with a jealous pang of fear that his innocent rival, the "lout who gave her the sixpenny Prayer Book, and inscribed his name with a crooked pin on the fly-leaf," is numbered with the dead; and that the hollow cheeks, dejected droop of the head, and crape-covered garments are for him.

The tears crowd into her eyes; they know the way there so well now. She turns away, and leans against the banisters to hide them.

A light breaks in upon him. He remembers that she had a brother, her girlish rhapsodies about whom used to make him rather impatient.

"I see," he says, in a softer tone; "forgive me for asking."

Encouraged by his voice, she lifts her face towards him with a tearful smile.

"You may be satisfied, I think," she says, simply. "You have had your revenge; I have been punished almost enough."

Revenge is sweet, they say; but at this moment I do not think that St. John finds it so.

"You did not know that I was here?" she asks, presently.

"Know it!" he repeats, passionately. "Not I. Do you suppose I would have come within a hundred miles of this house if I had known it?"

"I will try to keep out of your way," she answers, meekly.

"For God's sake, do! It is the most merciful thing that you can do for both of us."

"I would leave this place to-day, if I could," she answers, humbly raising her wistful, deprecating eyes to his; "but I cannot. My daily bread is here—yours is not. Why cannot you go?"

He hesitates. "I ought, I suppose," he answers, doubtfully. "I will, if you wish it."

"It is as *you* wish," she replies.

Footmen are passing to and fro, through the hall, busy with preparations for dinner; any moment Mr. Gerard's blue-and-white angel may come sweeping downstairs and surprise them.

"I have not congratulated you yet, Mr. Gerard," Esther says, timidly.

"Congratulated me!—what upon?" he asks, absently, staring vacantly at her.

"Upon your engagement to Miss Blessington."

A shade crosses his face. "Oh yes, to be sure! I had forgotten. Thanks! you are very good, I'm sure."

"I hope you will be very happy—*quite* happy."

"Thanks. Wish that I may be Prime Minister, or Commander-in-Chief, or something equally probable, while you are about it," he says, sardonically.

"I wish you to be happy," she repeats, gently, "and I hope that is not improbable."

"Such a wish in your mouth is something like a butcher with his knife at its throat wishing a sheep a long life!"

126

A guilty sense of hypocrisy in wishing him happy whom, less than forty-eight hours ago, she had been congratulating herself on his certain misery, keeps her dumb.

"Why could not you have sent me word that you were here, and I would have kept away?" he asks, flashing angrily upon her.

"I asked Miss Blessington to tell you, but she forgot."

He turns away with a muttered exclamation, not benedictory towards his betrothed, between his teeth.

"I will try to be as little annoyance to you as I can," says the poor child, in bitter mortification. "You will be out hunting most of the day, I daresay, and, except when I am waiting upon either Mr. and Mrs. Blessington, I am not often downstairs."

He takes no notice of her submissive speech, but stands, with his eyes moodily downcast, upon the white stone of the cold carpetless stairs.

"Believe me, I would go away, if I could," she says, piteously. "I did not wish to be in your way; but I had nowhere to go to."

A shade of pity softens his stern face.

"Are they kind to you?" he asks abruptly.

"Yes—oh yes—quite kind."

"And what, in God's name," he says, slowly, as if the question were forced from him against his will, by the slender fragility of her figure, by the pallid delicacy of her face—"And what, in God's name, can have induced your friends to allow you to accept such a situation, for which you are about as well fitted as I for the archbishopric of Canterbury?"

"I have not many friends, and I did not ask the advice of the few I have."

"They ought to have given it unasked," he says, gruffly.

"So they did, but I did not take it."

"Well, it is no business of mine," he says, harshly, ashamed and angry at himself for his temporary lapse into friendliness. "God knows I have had as good reason to hate you, and wish you ill, as ever man had! I *have* hated you," he says, with fierce heartiness, "during the last three months, as I should not have thought it possible to hate anything so weak and tender. I *hope* I hate you still!"

Remembering how much deeplier she had sinned against that other, and with how godlike a fulness and freedom he had pardoned her, she feels her heart rise up against him.

"The worse case I see you in, the more I ought to rejoice—the more I *should* have rejoiced yesterday," he continues, with rapid passion; "and yet—and yet—"

He passes his hand across his forehead, pushing the hair away; and not even the dab of mud on his nose can hinder the expression of his countenance from having something of a tragical pathos in it.

"And yet what?" she asks, tremulously, moving a step nearer to him.

"And yet, for the life of me, while I am *with* you, I cannot. When I am away from you, I can remember what you *are;* when I am with you, I see only what you seem. Esther! Esther! why, in God's name, don't the two tally better?"

"Whether they tally or not can be of but little concern to you now, Mr. Gerard," she answers, with some exasperation.

His brown cheek flushes into shamed angry-red.

"You are right," he says, stiffly. "It *is* no concern of mine; I am sorry I needed reminding."

"Why must we waste time digging that poor old past out of its grave?" she says, with persuasive gentleness, as her hand lays itself lightly, as if half afraid of being shaken off, upon his scarlet sleeve. "Why cannot we let bygones, that" (with a sigh) "are so completely bygones, be bygones? I did you an injury once—not an irreparable one, you will allow, since it is already repaired" (smiling half-scornful, half-melancholy); "and my whole life since has been a punishment—O God!*what* a punishment!" (putting her hand for a second over her eyes). "I am tired of being punished now. We shall see very little of one another henceforth, but that little might as well be in civility as in incivility—mightn't it?"

"Civility!"—he repeats, without much of that quality in his tone—"civility between you and me! And what would that end in, pray? It would be oversweet at first, and bitterer than wormwood afterwards, as our former *civility* was. No—no! we will have no sophisms, no absurd Platonisms here! God forbid my thrusting myself into temptation again! We will say 'good morning' and 'good evening' to one another, as people would remark it if we did not. But for the rest, let us hold our tongues and keep apart; and as soon as I can do it, without exciting great question, you may rely upon my going; and then we shall have done with one another for good, I pray God!"

She bends her head submissively. "You are right, I think."

127

"Click-clack—click-clack," come other high-heeled shoes; "swish! swish!" a long dress trails along. From the heaven of the upper regions the blue-and-white angel is in the act of descent. Without another word, the two part—the woman going quickly down, the man as quickly up.

"Good morning, Conny! Rather late in the day to say 'good morning,' isn't it?"

This is his greeting, accompanied with a rather constrained laugh, to his future proprietor.

"So you and Miss Craven have been renewing your acquaintance upon the landing?" replies the divinity, smiling a little inquisitively. "I was looking down at you from the gallery; you looked so picturesque!"

"If being cased from top to toe in black mud is picturesque, I am eminently so," answers he, looking down at his legs to hide a transient expression of confusion. "Well, good-bye for the present; I suppose I must be going to adorn for this unearthly meal."

CHAPTER XXXIV.

No one ever accused the dinners *en famille* at Felton of being too lively; but, that evening, Gerard decides that they yield the palm, in point of perfect stagnation, to Blessington. There is, indeed, none of that lynx-eyed watching of the servants, none of that pouncing upon their minutest derelictions, which makes dining in Sir Thomas's company so thoroughly uncomfortable a process: no one calls the fat red-faced butler and the two blue-and-yellow footmen "hounds, louts, fools."

At Blessington, indeed, the servants have things pretty much their own way; and, accustomed to their master's total and mistress's partial deafness, have got into a habit of conversing with one another in a tone of voice considerably above that usually considered seemly in civilised *ménages*. With one member of the company (Miss Craven) St. John has entered into a pact to exchange no remarks, good or bad; a second member (Mr. Blessington) contributes nothing to the conversation but a series of inarticulate though loud mumblings over his food—with the exception of a question, addressed to the butler, as to what the viands upon the table under his sightless eyes consist of. "'Aricot—Volly Vong—Line of Mutton—Biled Turkey," enumerates that functionary, glibly, at the top of his voice. From a third member (Mrs. Blessington) St. John has already heard all that is to be said on the subject of draughts and sand-bags; and with the fourth member, conversation always drives as heavily as a loaded waggon dragged up a perpendicular hill.

The evening is but a prolongation of the dinner, with the additional disadvantage of there being no eating and drinking to employ the otherwise unoccupied jaws. "England expects every man to do his duty!" She expects every man who has the misfortune to be in the position of an affianced to sit, hours long, idle beside his betrothed—however ardently his soul may be sighing for a sheet of the *Times* or a whiff of Latakia: to hold converse with no other man, woman, or child, if she be in the room.

Since, at the entrance of the gentlemen, Constance looked up expectant, and since he has a vague idea that it is part of his share of their bargain to pay her all outward observance and attention, St. John seats himself on the sofa beside her. She sits rather forward, upright as a dart; he leans back, with his arms resting on the sofa behind her. It is not a caress; but, from a little distance, it has the air of one. The old gentleman, rendered surprisingly wakeful by the unwonted incident of the addition of a stranger to his little circle, insists upon hearing a pungent article on Gladstone and the Irish Church, over which he has fallen asleep in the morning, re-read to him by his little white slave.

"I am afraid I can hardly see, Mr. Blessington; there is so little light!" she has remonstrated, mildly.

"Light!—pooh!" repeats the old gentleman, gaily. "What do young eyes like yours want with light? They ought to be able to see in the dark, like cats. You'll be borrowing Mrs. Blessington's spectacles next—eh, Mrs. Blessington?"

"Mrs. Blessington is asleep, Mr. Blessington."

"Oh! Go on, then, my dear—go on. Let us hear what they have got to say for these rascally placehunters, who are trying to remove the landmarks of the Constitution for the sake of getting into office."

Her long damp evening rambles—rambles on which a mother would have put so decided a veto—have brought back Miss Craven's cold. She has been hoarse all day; and it is a well-known fact that hoarseness always becomes worse towards night: a tiresome little tickling cough interrupts her every moment. Add to which, her attention is completely distracted from the subject in hand by the involuntary and vain effort to catch what Mr. Gerard and his love are saying to one another. She would hardly have been repaid for her trouble had she succeeded.

128

"Had you a good run to-day?"

"Yes, rather a quick thing."

"Which horse did you ride?"

"The grey—one you have not seen. I bought her in Ireland of Brownrigg; *he* required more of a weight-carrier."

"Does she seem likely to prove satisfactory?"

"Very: she has a good turn of speed, jumps capitally, and is very temperate."

"Was it a large field?"

"Middling."

"Any one you knew?"

"Two or three" (with a yawn).

"You are going out to-morrow again, of course?" with a slight attempt at a pout, which is not even perceived by the person for whose benefit it is intended.

"No, I think not; it is five-and-twenty miles, and the trains do not fit: one gets lazy in one's old age. I suppose I shall agree soon with Brakespeare, of the —th, who sent seven horses down to Melton last year; and at the end of the season confessed that he hated hunting, and that he thought it a very dangerous amusement."

"Really?" answers Constance, who always takes everything *au sérieux*, opening her great eyes.

"No, not really—most assuredly!" he answers, laughing lazily. "On the contrary, I am nearer coinciding with the opinion of the Jewish gentleman, who said it would be a very pleasant world if there were no *shummers* and no *shabbaths*."

It is hardly worth Miss Craven's while, you will perceive, to lose her place twice, and get rated by her old employer, for the sake of hearing brilliant questions and answers of the above description. Though her jealous eyes are fixed upon the *Saturday's* columns, they see, none the less clearly, those two figures reclined upon the distant sofa. Once she sees St. John himself, and, stooping forward over his companion, speak with more animation than he has yet used. If she break the drum of her ear in the attempt, she *must* catch the drift of that remark—some delicious tender nothing, no doubt. She succeeds:

"By-the-bye, Conny, how was the lump on your pony's leg when you left home?"

As another and another article follow the first, Esther's cough becomes increasingly troublesome: her throat aches with the effort of reading: her voice at each paragraph waxes huskier and huskier. For several minutes past Gerard's answers to Miss Blessington's questions have been growing ever more wildly random; suddenly he leaves the sofa, and comes over to Mr. Blessington's armchair.

"Will you let *me* read to you a bit?" he asks, in that loud unmodulated roar that people unused to the deaf think the only method of making them hear.

"Eh! what does he say?" inquires the old gentleman, sharply, lifting his head, and peering blindly up in the direction whence the voice came.

"I asked whether you would let *me* read to you, for a change, instead of Miss Craven?"

"No—thanks, no," replies the old man, ungraciously. "Much obliged to you, but I cannot hear a word you say; you run all your words into one another."

"Do I? I daresay," rejoins Gerard, good-humouredly; "but have you ever heard me read? I think not."

"Begging your pardon, I have, though; I heard you read prayers here one Sunday evening."

"And I am afraid my mode of conducting divine worship has not left a pleasant impression," says the young man, laughing. "Well, but I promise to read as slow as ever you choose, and to count four at every full-stop."

"No—no," cries the old man, obstinately. "Get away with you, my dear boy! you are interrupting us. No offence, but we are very happy without you—aren't we, Miss Esther? You attend to your own business; we don't offer to help you in that—do we—eh, my dear?"

Baffled and vexed, St. John stands silent; and as he so stands, the young girl lifts her great meek eyes, dumbly grateful, to his. He has forbidden her to speak to him, but he cannot lay an embargo upon the gentle messages sent from those sorrowful shining orbs. His own meet them for an instant; then he turns away with a half-shudder.

"What a churchyard cough that girl has!" says Miss Blessington, fanning herself gently, as he reseats himself beside her; "it really quite fidgets one. Of course it is very unjust of one, but I always feel so *angry* with a person who goes 'cough, cough, cough' every minute."

"I feel angrier with the person who is the cause of it," answers Gerard, thoroughly chafed: "it is positive barbarity. You see what success *I* met with when I tried to relieve guard. Suppose you offer: you can always make him hear!"

"I should be delighted," answers Conny, blandly; "only, unfortunately, this damp weather makes my throat so relaxed" (touching the firm round pillar with two white slender fingers), "that I really should be afraid."

"Just try—there's a good girl," urges he, coaxingly; "you can stop in a minute if you find that it hurts you."

A mulish expression comes into her face; small good would persuasion, cajolery, threats, or promises do now!

"I am very sorry I cannot oblige you; but as I am to dine out on Thursday, and one is always expected to sing, I really must nurse my voice."

CHAPTER XXXV.

"When   the   days   begin   to   lengthen,
Then the cold begins to strengthen."

This ancient distich proves true in the year I am speaking of. Not later than Christmas does the moist mild weather last. With January the frost comes hurrying back; hanging great icicles on the house-eaves, throwing men out of work, and pressing with its iron finger the thin faint life out of half-a-dozen old almsmen and almswomen. The foxes have a little breathing-time—a little space in which to steal and eat three or four more fat capons and stubble-fed geese—before that evil day when their dappled foes shall tear their poor little red bodies limb from limb. Hunting is stopped, and men are hurrying up from the shires to London. St. James's Street and its hundred clubs are crowded. At Blessington everybody is pirouetting on the ice. St. John, passionately fond of all out-of-door sports, spends the whole day on the mere. One afternoon a large party comes over from Lord Linley's place, five miles away. Not in all Lord Linley's grounds is there such a stretch of smooth ice as the Blessington pool affords; and so they are all come to show their prowess on its hard flat face.

Esther keeps well out of their way. From her post of observation—the deep window-seat in the China gallery—she has watched their arrival, heard their gay voices in the hall, and then, unnoticed, unmissed, she has stolen out upon one of her long, dawdling, cold-giving strolls in the park: over the frost-crisped grass, under the branchy trees, whose staglike crowns cut the pale sky—up little knolls and down into dips where, in summer time, the fern stands neck high. At last she comes in sight of the mere; and, impelled by curiosity, trusting in her own insignificance to escape notice, sits down on a bank that slopes gently down towards the sheet of water, and looks upon the unwonted brilliance of the scene. Girls in velvet short costumes; bright petticoats, furs, hats with humming birds on them, curls, fair chignons, glancing in the cheerful winter sun. Fashion in all its folly and extravagance, but picturesque withal; it is as if a company of Dresden shepherdesses had stepped off the mantelshelf, and come tripping, dainty-footed, over the frozen water. Her eyes follow the shepherdess figures with eager interest—so seldom in her simple country-bred life has she been brought into contact with any of Fashion's bright daughters. The men have less attraction for her. Under no most prosperous conjunction of circumstances could she ever have been a man; but under happier auspices she might have been one of these fluttering butterflies—a prettier butterfly than any there, her heart tells her. Shylock's words recur to her: "Am not I 'fed with the same food, hurt with the same weapons, subject to the same diseases, healed by the same means, warmed and cooled by the same winter and summer?' Why, then, are they frisking about in purple and fine linen upon the ice, with half-a-dozen young patricians (in trousers of surprising tightness and coats of unequalled brevity) in their train, while I am perched here upon the all-alone stone, among these stiff cold sedges, with only the Canada geese, with their long necks craned out, screeching above my head?"

Meanwhile, Miss Craven is the subject of more remark than she is at all aware of.

"I say, Gerard," says Lord Linley's heir—a goodnatured ugly little prodigal, who is one of the shining lights of Her Majesty's Household, and goes among men by the *sobriquet* of "Gaolbird," for which he has to thank the unexampled brevity of his locks—"I say, Gerard, you ought to know all the remarkable objects about here: tell us, who is the *mourner* in the distance?"

St. John's eyes follow the direction indicated by his friend, and a shade of annoyance crosses his face. "Her name is Miss Craven, I believe," he answers, shortly.

"Uncommon good-looking girl, whoever she is!" says a second man, who has just stopped to adjust his skates; "I have been perilling my life among those d——d rushes by the edge, to get a good look at her!"

"Deuced good legs!" subjoins a third, remarkable for his laconism; taking his pipe out of his mouth to make room for his criticism, and fixing upon that part of a woman's charms which is always the first to enchain the masculine attention.

"She is vewy like a girl I used to know at the Cape," says a "Heavy," who has been vanquished in single combat by the letter R. "The *Fly* we used to call her, because when she settled on a f'la, it was mowally impossible to dwive her off."

St. John, who has been listening with ill-concealed anger and disgust to these comments—free as if they had been upon the points of a horse—on the charms of the woman for whom he has been trying to persuade himself that he feels inveterate aversion, turns to move away; but Linley's voice recalls him.

"I say, Gerard!—Gerard!"

"Well?"

"Do you know her?"

"Slightly."

"Introduce me, then—there's a good fellow!"

"And me!"

"And me!"

"My acquaintance with Miss Craven is not such as to justify my introducing any one to her," answers Gerard, stiffly, and so walks resolutely off.

"Sly dog!" cries Linley, laughing; "means to keep her all to himself—a nice quiet little game of his own."

"Means to drive a pair then—eh?" asks the laconic youth.

"Vewy seldom pays," says the "Heavy," sagely; "one or other invawiably jibs."

But Mr. Linley, being more in earnest than he usually is about most things, is not so easily balked. After many fruitless inquiries among the company, he at length appeals to Miss Blessington.

"Do you know, Miss Blessington," he says, peering up at her with his quick terrier-face (for her stately height exceeds his), "I have actually been putting the same question to twenty people running, and never yet succeeded in getting an answer? You are my last hope: who *is* that lady in black?"

"The lady in black!" repeats Constance, amiably—following, as her lover had done, the direction of his gaze. "Oh!" (with a little, slighting laugh), "nobody very particular; only poor Miss Craven, my aunt's companion!"

"Poor girl!" he says—his eyes still riveted upon the pensive oval face, and his interest in her not the least lessened by the information as to her social status, that Constance had thought so damning. He does not want to *marry* her; and for any other purpose a pretty woman is a pretty woman, be she duchess or fishwife. "It must be very slow for her, mustn't it? I always hate looking on—don't you? I always like to have a hand in everything, whatever it may be; it would really be a charity to go and speak to her, only I'm afraid she would take it as an insult if I went up and introduced myself."

"I assure you she is quite happy watching us," replies Constance, sweetly; being, for the most part, not fond of going shares with a sister fair one in any of the proper men and tall that are wont to gather about her.

But he is persevering. "Don't you think that a little improving conversation with me would tend to make her happier still?" he asks, banteringly, yet in earnest. "I tried to get Gerard to introduce me, but I could not make out exactly what was up; he seemed to take it as a personal insult. You won't mind doing me that good turn, I'm sure?"

"I shall be most happy, of course," she answers, hiding her displeasure under the calm smile which covers all her emotions, or approximations to emotion. And with apparent readiness she leads the way to the spot where, couched in her rushy lair, the subject of their talk sits unconscious, with her eyes riveted on the darting forms beneath her.

"Miss Craven, Mr. Linley wishes to be introduced to you."

"To *me!*" she says, starting; her eyes opening wide, and cheeks flushing with surprise.

Then two bows are executed, and the thing is done. Esther is not longer upon the all-alone stone; she has other occupation for her ears than to listen to the screeching of the Canada geese; she, too, like the other butterflies, has got a tight-trousered, short-coated patrician in tow.

"Linley has succeeded, do you see?" says the man to whom Esther's legs have had the happiness to appear "very good."

"Mostly does; it is a little way he has!"

"Who did they say she was?"

"Somebody's companion; old Blessington's, I think."

"Cunning old beggar! He knows what he is about, though he does pretend to be stone-blind."

"Old Blessington's companion, eh? I'm sure I wish she were mine."

"A sort of 'Abishag the Shunammite,' I suppose?"

These are some of the comments that the unknown beauty draws forth. Five minutes later, Miss Craven's scruples—such as never having skated before, having no skates, &c.—being overruled by her new acquaintance, she is sitting on the bank; and he, kneeling before her, is fastening some one else's unused skates on her little feet. A great desire for pleasure has come over her—a great longing for warmth and colour in her grey life, that looks all the greyer now in the contrast to the brilliant reds and purples of these strange lives with which it is brought into sudden contact. A great delight in the wintry brightness fills her—in the shifting, varying hues—in the bubbling laughter; a great impulse to laugh too, the spirit of youth rising up in arms against the tyranny of grief.

The low sun shoots down dazzling crimson rays on the mere's dirty white face. The swans and Solan geese are exiled to a little corner, where the ice has been broken for them, and where they have to keep swimming round and round to prevent the invasion of their little territory by the grasping frost. Girls that cannot skate being pushed about in chairs; "Whirr! whirr!" they rush along the smooth surface at a headlong pace. Men, with their arms stretched out like the sails of a windmill, advancing cautiously—first one foot, then the other—just managing to keep on their feet, and thinking themselves extremely clever for so managing. Other men and women flying hand-in-hand, from one end of the pool to the other, in long, smooth slides—as safe and secure as if running upon their own feet on the grass. Others, cutting eights, and all manner of figures, whirling round upon one leg, and making themselves altogether remarkable. One poor gentleman with his skates in the air, and head starring the ice; brother men laughing and jeering; pretty girls pitying—light laughter mixed with their condolences also. Eight people dancing a quadrille, *chaîne des dames:* in and out, in and out—right, left—go the moving figures, the cerise petticoats, the glancing feet. It is all so pretty and gay. When one has spent the best part of three months in weeping, when one has the quick blood of seventeen in one's veins, one longs to get up and run, and dance, and jump about too.

"There's no wind to-day," says Linley, turning his face to the north-east, whence a bitter breath comes most faintly; "when there is, it is the best fun in the world to get a very light cane chair and a big umbrella—to sit on the one and hold the other up; you can have no conception of the terrific rate that one gets along at."

"I should think it sometimes happened that the cane chair and the big umbrella went on by themselves and left you behind?" says Esther archly.

"Frequently, but that makes it all the more exciting."

"Does it?"

"Keep hold of the chair, push it gently before you, and try to balance yourself as well as you can," continues he, giving grave instructions to his new pupil.

"How *can* one balance oneself on things no bigger than knife-blades?" she asks, grasping desperately the chair-back.

"Rome was not built in a day," he answers, with a cheery laugh; "try!"

She obeys, and moves forward two or three timid inches; then stops again.

"I have that poor gentleman's fate before my mind's eye," she says, nervously. "I feel as if, by some natural attraction, one's feet must go up sky-wards, and one's head make acquaintance with the ice."

"No necessity at all," replies the young man, encouragingly. "That fellow is a duffer at everything; he is the very worst rider I ever set eyes on—holds his whip like a fishing-rod."

"Does he?"

"Look at that girl, now, with the purple feather! She skims along like a bird; she is as much at her ease as if she were in her arm-chair at home. By Jove! no, she ain't though!" For, as he speaks, "Thud!" comes the girl with the purple feather down in a sitting posture on the ice: men crowd round, inquire into casualties, pick her up again: off she goes!

"You must be more careful next time in your selection of examples," Esther says, smiling mischievously; "*that* one was not encouraging, you must allow."

Constitutionally timid, she stands hesitating, in half-shyness, half-fear, and whole dread of being ridiculous; laughing, reddening, dimpling in the happy sunlight—as pretty a picture as ever little terrier-faced member of the Household has seen.

"Perhaps you'd get on better if you tried walking between two people," he says, suggestively; "it is easier than with a chair. That is the way my sister began—I on one side, don't you know, and another fellow on the other. Here, Gerard, come and make yourself useful; give Miss Craven your arm!"

Gerard looks—has been looking all the while; sees the face, that had met him so pale and dejected three hours ago, transformed by the keen January air, and the excitement of the moment, into more than its old loveliness; sees the soft splendour of languishing almond eyes, the guileless baby-smile. It is the transient happiness of a moment that has wrought the change, and he, in his rough anger, attributes it to the insatiate rabid desire for admiration.

"She would flirt in her coffin," he says to himself, bitterly; and so answers, coldly, "I cannot—I have taken my skates off!"

"All right," says Mr. Linley, gaily, and then, in an aside to Esther, "On duty, evidently!"

"Evidently!" She assents with a faint smile, but her lips quiver with a dumb pain. "He need not have slighted me so openly," she thinks, in cruel mortification. "Perhaps if you gave me your hand I might manage to steady myself gradually," she says naïvely.

Mr. Linley has no objection whatever to having his hand convulsively clutched by a very pretty woman, even though it is so clutched, not in affection to himself, but in the spasmodic effort to maintain the perpendicular—in the desperate endeavour to hinder her feet from outrunning body and head. And so she totters along—amused, flattered, frightened; and far too much absorbed in considerations of her own safety, to be at all aware of the condescending notice that several of the more worthy gender are good enough to bestow upon her, though the conceit inborn in the male mind would have made them completely sceptical of that fact, had they been told it.

Meanwhile Miss Blessington, a little out of breath with her exertions, is resting on a chair, in bright blue velvet and a more delicate pink-and-white porcelain face than any of the other shepherdesses. Over her Gerard is leaning—frowning, sad, and heavy-hearted. Over and over again he has tried to turn his eyes to other groups, but again and again, contrary to his will, they return and fix themselves upon that slender staggering figure in black. Once he sees her on the point of falling—saved only by being caught with quick adroitness in her companion's arms. He draws his breath involuntarily hard. How dare any man but he touch her—lay a finger upon her fair person? One of the old simple instincts, stronger—oh, how far stronger!—than any of the restrictions with which our civilisation has sought to bind them—a great lust of raging jealousy—is upon him.

"I *hate* her!" he says to himself, fiercely; "she is a vile unprincipled coquette. Thank God, I found her out in time! Thank God, I washed my hands of her before it was too late! And yet—and yet—if I could but pick a quarrel with that fellow!"

What right has Gerard to object if every man upon the ground catch her in big arms, and hold her there under his very eyes? He has washed his hands of her, thank God! All his rights of proprietorship in womankind centre in the calm blue statue, smiling with even placidness on himself, on his poodle, on all the world—his Constance, whom no one is thinking of taking from him; his own—oh, blissful thought!—in life, in death, and in eternity!

In the meantime the remarks upon Esther vary from the wildly laudatory to the discriminatingly censuring.

"She is extwemely dark," says the *dwagoon*, as he would have called himself; "a thowough bwunette; must have a touch of the tar-bwush, I fancy!"

The stable-clock strikes four. Esther starts, as much as scullion Cinderella started at the chiming midnight. "I must go" she says, hastily; "I shall be wanted."

"Wanted?" he repeats, inquiringly. "And are not you wanted here? You cannot be in two places at once, like a bird."

"Mrs. Blessington will want me—I am her companion," she answers, colouring slightly. "I daresay you did not know it." ("He would not have been so civil to me if he had, I daresay," is her mental reflection.)

"Yes, I did."

"Who told you?—or have all 'companions' such a family likeness that you detected me at a glance?"

"Miss Blessington told me; and for the first time in my life I wished myself an old woman," he replies, sentimentally.

She laughs, a little embarrassed. She knows as well as he does that he does *not* wish to be an old woman, even for the pleasure of having her to carry his air-cushion and spectacle-case. But civil speeches are always more or less untrue, and none the less pleasant for that.

"If the frost holds," says the young man, suggestively—taking the small black hand which she has timidly proffered, not being by any means sure that it is etiquette for a "companion" to shake hands with lords' eldest sons—"If the frost holds, will you be inclined for another lesson or two? There is nothing like making hay when the sun shines—say *to-morrow?*"

Her face brightens for a moment; it is so pleasant to talk gaily, and be admired, and made much of, and reminded that there are other things besides death and poverty and servitude; then her countenance falls.

"To-day has been very pleasant," she says, naïvely, "but I cannot answer for to-morrow."

"Are you so changeable," he asks, with a laudable though unsuccessful endeavour to fashion his jolly little dog-face into an expression of reproachful sentiment, "as not to know to-day what you will like or not like to-morrow?"

"I know what *I* shall like," she answers, gently, "but I don't know what other people will. Would not you think it very odd if your valet were to make engagements without consulting you? *I* am Mrs. Blessington's valet."

She evidently thinks this argument so conclusive, and that it so decidedly closes the question, that he has no choice but to loose her hand; and she, having no other farewells to make, turns and passes homewards through the crisply rustling sedges.

"*Very* clean about the fetlock!" ejaculates the laconic youth, unable to raise his mind from her legs; following them with his eyes, as she climbs the grassy slope.

"Yes, but what howible boots! Whoever could have had the atwocity to fwame such beetle-cwushers?"

CHAPTER XXXVI.

The frost goes, but so does not St. John. He hunts all day, and all the long evenings lounges sedulously on the sofa beside Constance, trying to feel affectionate: trying to make her talk—trying, metaphorically, to pull the string at his fine wax-doll's side, to make her say "Pap-pa" and "Mam-ma" prettily. "Since I am to spend my life with this woman," he says to himself, heavily, "I must try and make the best of her."

And, alas! alas! the best is not very good. He is thirty now, and—the Gerards are a long-lived, tough race—he may live till ninety. He asks himself, now and then, in a sort of startled terror, is he to see opposite him at breakfast, every day for the next sixty years, this carven face, changeless as the stone saints on the walls of Felton Church? Of all the one-half of creation, is this unsuggestive, unresponsive, negative woman to be his sole portion? "It is her misfortune that she is not a woman of science," as Mr. Shandy mildly remarked of his wife, "but she *might* ask a question." Strive as he may against the conviction, the yoke that he has taken upon himself in careless apathy has already begun to gall his withers. And yet it was not (as you may imagine) *pique* that first made Gerard Miss Blessington's lover. It was partly that numb indifference as to anything that might happen to him, that always follows a great blow, partly sheer weariness of his father's importunities upon the subject of his marriage.

He is the last scion of a family that has come down in direct male line from a Norman robber: if it be tersely predicated of him on his tombstone that he died S. P., the Hall, and the lake, and the wide fat lands will go to some distant needy cousins, with whom Sir Thomas is at dagger's drawing, and for whom he cherishes a hatred livelier even than that which poachers, Irish beggars, and vulpecides inspire in his gentle breast. The fact of his responsibilities has been chimed into St. John's ears till he is rather weary of it: he has been hearing it for the last five-and-twenty years—ever since indeed, that solemn day when, petticoats being cast aside, he was invested with the virile dignity of round jacket and breeches.

"Why don't we cut off the entail?" he asks impatiently, one day, shortly after Esther's visit—a visit which has naturally given him a greater distaste for the subject than he had ever before experienced. "You and I together can do it, cannot we, Sir Thomas, and leave the property to the Foundling, or Hanwell, or to some hospital or penitentiary, where it would do a deal more good, I don't doubt, than it ever has in our hands?" But he does not mean it; his pride in the old house and the old name is as great, though not as offensively shown, as his father's.

"It's all your cursed selfishness," says his parent, strutting and fuming about, one morning, over the crimson and ash-coloured squares of the library carpet; puffing out his feathers, as it were, and beginning to gobble-obble. "You prefer your lazy, lounging club life, your French chef, and d——d sybarite habits, to everything else under heaven; you don't reflect that, when a man has been given such advantages as yours, he owes corresponding duties to his country and his estate, and—and—and his *father*——" concludes Sir Thomas, rather at a loss for a peroration.

St. John lifts his eyebrows almost imperceptibly at the last clause. "If you like to look out for a wife for me," he says, flinging himself indolently into an arm-chair, and speaking half-seriously, half-derisively, "and will engage to undertake all the bore of the preliminaries—love-making, dancing attendance, etc.—I have no objection to marrying, since the duty of continuing this illustrious race has been perverse enough to devolve on me, who, God knows, am not ambitious of perpetuating myself."

"Love-making!—pooh!" repeats Sir Thomas, contemptuously; "we need have none of that rubbish; respect and esteem are a deal the best basis to go upon; that's what your mother and I began life with——"

"And have continued undiminished up to the present day," says St. John, with a slight sneer. "Well" (yawning), "if you can find, amongst the wide range of your acquaintance, any young lady who is willing to respect and esteem me—which is not likely—or to respect and esteem Felton—which is more probable, and, after all, comes to much the same in the end—she may have the felicity of being your daughter-in-law, for all I shall do to hinder it: anything for a quiet life."

Sir Thomas turns his bright little fierce eyes sharply upon his offspring, prepared, at a moment's notice, to precipitate himself into one of his blustering, sputtering, God damning rages if he detect the slightest sign of mirth or derision on the young man's face. But none such is to be found; his downcast eyes are fixed with lazy interest upon his own substantial legs, stretched in black-and-crimson-ribbed stockings, straight before him. The ire of his parent's gaze is mitigated. "If you are in earnest," he says, surlily, "and not making a jest of this, as you mostly do of every serious subject, why—why—there's no use in going far afield for what one has ready to one's hand."

"Where?" asks St. John, thoroughly mystified by the Delphic obscurity of his papa's remark, looking vaguely round the room, out on the terrace, at the laughing, tumbling fountain, at the garden roller.

"Where?" repeats Sir Thomas, rather irritated at his son's obtuseness. "Why, here! not five yards off! in this very house!" Then, seeing him still look puzzled: "God bless my soul, sir! where are your wits to-day? How can you do better than Conny? That bit of land of hers down at Four Oaks dovetails into ours as neatly as possible; it seems as if it were intended by Providence," ends Sir Thomas, piously.

St. John gives a long, low whistle. "Conny!" he repeats, in unfeigned surprise. "I should as soon have thought of marrying my mother. Why, we have been like brother and sister all our lives."

"Fiddlesticks!" says Sir Thomas, gruffly. "She is no more your sister than I am. When I was young, if people were born brothers and sisters they called themselves so, and if they were not they did not. I hate your adopted brother and sister and father and motherhoods."

"Conny!" ejaculates St. John, again, reflectively.

The idea is thoroughly new, certainly, but it does not altogether displease him.

He is thinking of her approvingly, as the one woman whom, above all others, it would be impossible for him to love. After all, it is not a wife for him that is required; God knows, he has no desire for such an appendage; it is a mother for the heir to Felton that is wanted; and for that purpose she will do as well as another—better than most, indeed, being statelier, fairer, of better growth. If she can transmit to her progeny her own straight features, instead of Sir Thomas's bottle nose, or St. John's long nondescript one, so much the better for them.

"Well?" says Sir Thomas, impatiently, strutting up and down, with his hands under his green-coat tails.

"If she have no objection, neither have I; 'one woman is as good as another, if not better,' as the Irishman said," answers the young man, indifferently. "Well, Sir Thomas," rising and looking excessively bored, "I suppose I may go now, mayn't I? I promised Bellew to go down to the kennels with him, and as it is past twelve o'clock, I'm afraid my bliss cannot well be consummated to-day."

He wants an heir, and she wants diamonds, and so the bargain is struck.

"She is good to look at, and she does not pretend to care two straws about me—both causes for special thankfulness," he says to himself, with a sort of sardonic philosophy, after his decisive interview with his betrothed. "'On this day two years I married: Whom the Lord loveth He chasteneth.' Will Byron's summary of wedded felicity be mine also? Probably. I suppose one may think oneself tolerably lucky nowadays if one steer clear of Sir James Wilde, and if one's children do not bear a very striking resemblance to one's neighbour."

"And   I   know   he's   Mary's   cousin;
For   my   firstborn   son   and   heir
Much   resembles   that   young   guardsman,
With the selfsame curly hair."

Meanwhile Esther's little holiday is succeeded by no others; it remains one green oasis, with well and palm-trees, among long stretches of shifting, blinding, desert sand. Mr. Linley, indeed, has been to call, and has been rewarded for his attention by a three-quarters-of-an-hour *tête-à-tête* with Mrs. Blessington. Esther is aware of his presence; is visited, indeed, by a small and contemptible desire to go down and chat with the young fellow; feels a weak craving for the touch of a friendly hand, for the greeting of admiring eyes and courteous words. But, being dimly conscious that the small acquaintance she has already had with him has made Gerard conceive an even worse opinion of her than he had before nourished, she restrains herself, in her great desire to prove to him that she is not the insatiable greedy coquette he falsely thinks her; and stays upstairs in the cold, in her great bare barrack, curled up on the broad paintless window-seat, and vainly trying to read "Pamela"—the hairbreadth escapes from RUIN (in big letters), in the shape of a handsome and generous master, of that most austerely virtuous and priggish of waiting-maids being one of the newest works of fiction in the Blessington library.

And St. John hears of Linley's visit, and does not hear of Esther's little self-abnegation; and, too proud to ask any questions about the matter, pictures to himself soft *oeillades*, challenging smiles, hand-pressures, under the purblind eyes of the old lady, and, so picturing, eats his heart out with a dumb gnawing jealousy.

One evening, in one of her late lonely saunters (Miss Blessington never accompanies her on her walks), Esther has strayed outside the park paling into the road, lured by the splendour of a great holly-bush, all afire with thousand clustered berries, amid the dark glister of varnished leaves. Now, although having well understood (as

"Johnny   and   his   sister   Jane,
While walking down a shady lane,"

unfortunately for themselves, did not) that

"Fruit in lanes is seldom good,"

Esther has coveted those berries. Fond of bright colours as a child or a savage, she has been wrestling obstinately with the stout tough stems, and has come off ultimately victor, with only one very considerable scratch, and several lesser ones on each bare hand. This spoil, robbed from niggard winter, will make the old rat palace at home so bravely, warmly gay. As she strolls slowly along, considering her treasures, the sound of a trotting horse on the road behind her reaches her ears. She turns, and sees a glimmer of scarlet flashing through the misty light. Is it St. John coming back from hunting? If St. John have a figure light and spare as a jockey's, have a large red moustache, and a small questioning *retroussé* face, this is he; if he have not, this is not he.

"How de-do, Miss Craven?" says Linley, throwing himself off his horse, and coming towards her with ready right hand heartily outstretched. "Could not imagine who you were. I thought, perhaps, you were the spirit of a departed Blessington, and as I am rather nervous, and frightened out of my wits at ghosts, I had half a mind to turn and flee."

"Only curiosity got the better of fear," she says, smiling up at him, or rather down on him, through the steaming January evening; "you thought I might prove human, after all?"

"Why did not you come and see me the other day when I came to call upon you?" he asks, walking along beside her; "I believe you were at home all the time." In his heart he does not in the least believe it.

She does not answer; but, without thinking of what she is doing, picks off the berries, the procuring of which had cost her so many wounds, and strews them along the road.

"Were you *really* at home?" he repeats, a misgiving as to such having been the case crossing his mind, and giving his vanity a slight prick.

"Yes, I was."

"And knew I was there all the time?"

"Yes."

"A prey to Mrs. Blessington——?"

"Yes."

"And never came to my rescue?"

"Did you expect the butler and housekeeper to come and entertain you?" she asks, a little bitterly. "Have you forgotten what I told you the other day—that I am Mrs. Blessington's *valet?* I have as little concern with her visitors as the kitchen-maids have."

"But I was not *her* visitor," objects the young fellow, stoutly—"at least" (laughing) "I *was*, but Heaven knows I did not mean to be! However, 'God tempers the wind to the shorn lamb,' and I obtained a great deal of information gratis upon a subject on which I really never had reflected as seriously as, it appears, I ought to have done——"

"Draughts and sandbags! I know what you are going to say," interrupts Esther, breaking into a childish lighthearted laugh. "We do hear a great deal about them; but I don't mind now; I'm used to it. I fall into a sort of waking trance when the subject is first broached, and say 'Yes' and 'No,' and 'H'm' and 'Oh,' at stated intervals; it does just as well as listening all through."

Linley laughs too. He is always glad of an excuse for laughing. Life has been to him as yet only laughable or smileable.

"Not a bad plan," ha says, commendingly; "but, really now, I flattered myself I struck out one or two very original thoughts on the subject of sash-windows; I said several rather brilliant things, only she did not seem to see them. I hoped she would have found my conversation so improving that she would have asked me to come again; but she did not do anything of the kind."

"They never ask anybody to Blessington," says Esther, feeling the string of her tongue loosed, and experiencing, despite herself, great enjoyment in having some one to chatter to, at whom it is not necessary to bawl, and who does not answer her monosyllabically with *fade* chilly smiles. "They are too old to care for society; like Barzillai the Gileadite, they cannot hear any more 'the voice of singing men and singing women.' They have the clergyman and his wife to dine on Christmas Day, and there their gaiety for the year begins and ends."

"And yours too?"

"And mine too. But I don't wish for gaiety," she answers, gravely, with an involuntary glance at her crape, which has grown very brown, and rusty, and shabby genteel.

"It must be an awful fate being shut up with those two old mummies," says Linley, compassionately, his pity for Miss Craven made vivid by his personal recollections of Mrs. Blessington's conversational power. "I had rather live in a lighthouse, or sweep a crossing, by long odds."

"So would I," she answers, drily, "if any one would set on foot a subscription to buy me a broom."

"You have Miss Blessington now as a companion, at all events," rejoins he, glad to fix on any bright spot in his poor new acquaintance's mud-coloured life.

"Yes; she is pleasant to look at."

"And to talk to."

"She never talks."

"And Gerard? He is not particularly pleasant to look at, certainly——"

"Not particularly," she assents; feeling a hot glow steal all over her, as at an insult to herself.

"But when he is not in one of his sulks, as he was the other day—do you remember?—he is not a bad fellow, as fellows go."

"Isn't he?"

He looks at her with surprise. "Why, surely, living in the same house with him, you ought to know him, at least as well as I do?"

"I never speak to him, and he never speaks to me," she answers, shortly.

Linley bursts out laughing. "Good heavens! what a horrible picture you draw! You remind one of Mr. Watts's pretty little hymn—

"'Where'er   I   take   my   walks   abroad
How   many   poor   I   see!
And   as   I   never   speaks   to   them
They never speak to me.'"

Esther laughs; but anyone listening might have heard a melancholy ring in her merriment.

"Does *nobody* speak to *anybody* then at Blessington?" asks the young man, aghast at the state of things as revealed by his companion's answers.

"Mr. Blessington roars at Mrs. Blessington, and Mrs. Blessington roars at Mr. Blessington, and I roar at them both."

"And the other two—do not they speak?"

"We are, none of us, much addicted to conversation," she answers, grimly; "but, *en revanche*, what we do say we say very loud."

"Are you *all* deaf, then?"

"No; but when one lives with deaf people, one gets into the habit of thinking that the whole world is hard of hearing; one bawls at everyone."

"What an exhausting process!" he says, with a shrug; "takes a great deal out of you, doesn't it?"

"A good deal; lately, I have generally ended the day without any voice at all. I don't mind making short remarks at the top of my voice, but shouting out six columns of the *Times*, as is daily my pleasing task, is rather fatiguing."

"How inhuman of them to allow you!" he cries, indignantly, looking at the slender, fragile figure, at the childish face—so appealing, so touching in its utter paleness, now that he sees it without the temporary rose-flush of excitement.

"Not at all," she answers, simply; "they pay me for it."

"It would require very high pay to indemnify any one for the sacrifice of the best years of their lives to those two old fossils; I thought I was entitled to something considerable for standing the old woman for three-quarters of an hour the other day without uttering a groan," answers the young man, more seriously than he generally takes the trouble of saying anything.

"My pay is fifty pounds a year," she answers, frankly, "if you call that high."

Fifty pounds! It would not find him in cigars. He has thrown away five times that sum, before now, at lansquenet at one sitting.

Involuntarily his thoughts glance back over his own life—the luxurious sybarite life in which, hitherto, the heaviest misfortunes have been a too-prolonged frost, a disease among the grouse, the coming in second at a steeplechase, or the pressure of a heavy helmet on his forehead when on duty on a hot summer afternoon. Involuntarily, he compares this life of his with the existence of the slight frail child beside him: but the comparison is disagreeable, and so he stifles it, as he always stifles, on principle, every painful thought, as a sin against his religion of ease.

"Fifty pounds!—what a pittance!" he ejaculates.

"Do you think so?" she answers, surprised. "I think it is a good deal. Considering that they find me in food and lodging, and that I do for them only what any charity-school boy could do nearly as well, it is surely enough."

Her companion differs widely in opinion from her, but

"When ignorance is bliss 'Tis folly to be wise;"

and reflecting that it is fortunate that she is satisfied, on whatever insufficient grounds her satisfaction rests, he drops the subject, and continues his catechism on a different head.

"Have you no amusement of any kind—*none?*"

"Oh dear, yes! We drive into Shelford every day in a close carriage, with all the windows up."

"Terrific! And what do you do when you get there?"

"We come back again."

"And have you no visitors? Does no one ever come to call?"

"Yes; you came the other day."

"And am I a solitary instance of would-be sociability?"

"Not quite. Mr. Blessington gets into a panic about himself, sometimes, and thinks that he is drawing near his latter end; and he bids us all good-bye; and *he* cries, and *we* cry, and then Mr. Brand, the doctor, comes and reassures us."

"I had no idea that there was anything the matter with the old gentleman."

"No more there is. He has no more idea of dying *really* than you have; less, probably. You may break your neck out hunting, and he cannot well break his out of his armchair. When a person has got into such a confirmed habit of living as he has," she concludes, drily, "they find it extremely difficult to break themselves of it."

He smiles.

"After all," she continues, thoughtfully, "since it is wear-and-tear of mind, brain, and heart-work, that drives people to the churchyard, I don't see any reason why mere sleeping and eating machines should not go on for ever."

It would be impossible to imagine a more innocent dialogue than the foregoing, would not it? But the interlocutors have involuntarily fallen into a very gentle saunter, as two people that, finding each other's society agreeable, are in no haste to part. With his horse's bridle carelessly thrown over his arm, a small muddy scarlet gentleman strolls along with his face turned with interest towards his companion, who is chattering away to him freely and readily—not as having any particular partiality for him, but as being something young, friendly, compassionate.

This is the picture—invested by twilight with an air of mystery that it would not have worn in daylight—that salutes the eyes of a second and larger scarlet gentleman, splashing home through the puddles on a tired horse. As he passes them, Gerard (for it is he) pulls up his horse into a walk, for he would not have the incivility to cover any woman with dirt, even though the woman in question be a vile greedy coquette, to whose insatiable vanity all men are meat. Then, raising his hat stiffly, he rides on without speaking. As he trots homeward through the dusk, the thought flashes into his writhing heart: "It was an assignation! She arranged it with him on the day he came to call. Damnable flirt! Is not she satisfied with *two* ruined lives? Is she fool enough to think that Linley will marry her? A nice time of night for a respectable young woman to be out walking with a man she has only seen twice in her life! And I heard her tell Mrs. Blessington the other day that she never went outside the park-gates! Liar! What man was ever deep enough to be up to a woman's tricks? She'll go to the dogs, as sure as fate, if she is left to herself! Pshaw! I daresay she knows the way there already. She is *so* young; shall I warn her? Shall I speak to her? Not I. Thank God, it is no business of mine!"

"Gerard!" says Linley, as, having passed them, he strikes into a brisk trot—looking as if he were going to his own funeral, and just about to join the *cortège*. "Certainly being in love don't improve him; he is not half the fellow he was last season."

But Esther, in the moment of his passing them, had caught a glimpse of the eager white anger of his face, and she hardly hears. "I'm afraid Mr. Gerard thought it odd my being out so late," she says, trembling with recollected fear of those altered, wrathful eyes.

"Well, and if he did?" cries Linley, impatiently.

"It *is* very late," she says, looking round into the dusk; "it must be, by the light. I never noticed how dark it has grown since you overtook me."

"It is no darker than it was before Gerard passed us," he answers, rather nettled.

"No, but—"

"Why, how scared you look!" he interrupts her. "You don't mean to say you are *afraid* of him?" (incredulously.) "If I were you, I don't think I should pay much deference to the opinion of a person who, as you say, never has the civility even to speak to you."

She is silent.

"It is the authority of his eye that awes you, I suppose?" says the young man, vexed and sneering:—

"'An eye like Mars', to threaten and command.'

"*Threaten!* Yes—I can testify to that!"

Hearing his words, Esther recovers her self-possession, and speaks with some dignity: "You are quite wrong. Mr. Gerard's opinion has no influence whatever on my sayings or doings; it would be very ridiculous if it had. It was merely that his look of surprise reminded me of what I ought to have recollected without reminding, that I *should* have been home an hour ago."

"Wanted again, I suppose?" says the young man, with the air of an aggrieved person. "I wish you were not in quite such request; you are always being wanted."

"There is a stile close here," says Esther, evidently in a hurry to be off; "if I cross it, and make a short-cut across the park, I shall be home twenty minutes sooner than if I went by the road. Good-bye."

"Good-bye," he says, reluctantly. "I'm not a bloodthirsty fellow generally, but I wish that Gerard had broken his neck over that bullfinch that he came to grief over to-day, before he had come poking his ugly nose here, where nobody wanted him; at least I did not, and, to judge by your face, neither did you. Well! when are we to meet again, I wonder?"

"Never!—some time or other—soon!" answers Esther, hastily and contradictorily, running up the gamut of adverbs in search of the one most likely to obtain her release. Having gained that object, she jumps over the stile, and disappears into a sea of mist.

Meanwhile St. John, having arrived at Blessington, and given up his horse to a groom, enters the house; but the confinement of roof and walls is insupportable to him. So he goes out again, and, walking up the avenue, stations himself at the gate. There, resting his arms on the topmost bar, he stands, straining his eyes down the road by which he expects to see Esther and her companion make their appearance.

"They will defer their parting to the last moment—that is of course," he says to himself, in his lonely pain. "Well," taking out his watch and minuting them, in order to drink the cup of his jealous misery to the dregs, "it is not more than a mile and a half from here to the place where I passed them; let us see how long a time they will manage to be in doing the distance."

He has not long to wait. Before five minutes are over he hears the sound of a horse's feet. "Linley must not see him watching them," he thinks, with a sort of shame at himself, and so steps back into the shade of a great tree.

Linley rides by *alone*. His face is turned towards the house, in whose great black façade the lighted windows make oblong-shaped red glories; his eyes are trying to fix upon Esther's casement. Of course he hits upon the wrong one, and directs his sentimental gaze towards the apartment where, with wig off and teeth out, Mrs. Blessington, aided by her maid, is slowly moving through the stages of her dinner toilette.

"She must have taken the short-cut across the park," thinks Gerard, with a sense of unwilling relief. "Afraid of my telling tales of her escapade, I suppose."

He retraces his steps down the avenue, and, following a back road that skirts the kitchen-garden, reaches another gate that leads into the park, and there stands and waits again.

The short-cut has proved rather a long one. Part of the park has been fenced off, to keep the deer and the Scotch cattle separate; a gate which she had reckoned upon finding open, she discovers to be padlocked, and has to make a long circuit round to another gate.

As she toils weary-footed through the wet grass, vague alarms assail him that watches for her. Can any evil have come to her in the darkness? Most improbably in that still, safe park. After a while, and when his reasonless fears are beginning to gather more strongly about his heart, he hears the sound as of some one running pantingly. Esther is not so good at running as she was in the old Glan-yr-Afon days. She has been flying along in hot haste, with a mixed fear of Scotch bulls and goblins in pursuit. As she approaches the gate, Gerard opens it for her. Seeing it swing open without any apparent cause, she gives a great nervous start; then, discovering the motive cause of the phenomenon, drops into a walk.

"It is rather late, Mr. Gerard, I'm afraid, isn't it so?" she asks, with some hesitation at this disobedience to his command of silence. And yet, surely, if he had meant not to speak to her, he would not have come thither.

Two speech-gifted human beings could hardly be expected to meet with less civility than two pigs, who would at least exchange a grunt.

He looks at his watch again. "It is ten minutes to six," he replies with punctilious politeness.

"Is it *really?* I had no idea how the time went," she says, apologetically, "until your look of—of—*surprise* reminded me."

The line of defence she has hit upon is unlucky.

"Really!" he answers, stiffly.

"I had not noticed how the light had gone, nor anything about the matter," she continues, innocently, floundering at every word into deeper disgrace.

"I daresay not," he replies, freezingly.

She had addressed him, penitent and humble, willing to take a scolding in all submissiveness, but the chill brevity of his answers turns her meekness to gall.

"When one is in pleasant company," she remarks, with a rather hysterical laugh, "one forgets the flight of time."

"Undoubtedly," replies Gerard, endeavouring to conceal his anger under an appearance of calmness, and unable to manage more than one word at a time.

"If one has not taken a vow of perpetual silence, it is a great relief to have a little conversation with a person who is neither *deaf* nor *dumb,*" she says, emboldened by exasperation.

"An immense relief, no doubt," he answers, in deep displeasure. "And yet, if you will allow me," he continues, unable to resist the temptation to lecture her—"who am so much older than you, and can have no interest in the matter but your own advantage—to give an opinion, I should recommend your choosing a fitter time of day for your meetings, even with so desirable and congenial a companion as Mr. Linley."

"Beggars must not be choosers," she answers, sulkily. "You seem to forget how very small a portion of the day I have at my own disposal."

He draws himself up to his full height, and a stern expression makes his lip thin. "I was right," he says internally; "it was no accident!" Then aloud: "I apologise, Miss Craven, for interfering in your affairs, in which, God knows, I have small concern. I only thought that, as you are so young, you might not be aware that *nocturnal* walks with a man of Linley's character are not advantageous to any woman's reputation."

"I know nothing about his character," retorts she, defiantly; "I daresay it is as good as other people's. All I know is, that he is very kind and civil to me, which is what nobody else is nowadays."

Then, to avoid the disgrace of seeming to court his compassion by tears, she darts from his side, and rushes to that harbour of refuge—her great, bare sleeping-chamber.

CHAPTER XXXVII.

Time goes by. Since Joshua, God-bidden, commanded sun and moon to stand still, who has been able to stop it?

Gerard still remains at Blessington—remains, despite the six-o'clock dinners; despite the inarticulate and inharmonious mumblings with which old Blessington takes away the appetites of such as feast with him; despite the utter failure of his endeavours to draw from the mind of his betrothed any ideas but such as *Le Follet* and *Le Journal des Demoiselles* had just put into it. Latterly he has abandoned the attempt, has taken to reading the *Times, Field,* anything in the evening, instead; has even, in his despair—modern works of fiction being, as I have before observed, unknown at Blessington—waded through two chapters and a half of "Pamela," which Esther had inadvertently left on the table. Sometimes, to his own surprise, he catches himself wishing that his wedding-day were over. "When we are married, we need never speak to one another," he reflects. "Thank God, we shall not be so poor as to be obliged to keep together from economy; a dinner of herbs and hatred, or, worse still, indifference therewith, *would* be hard to digest; she may go her way, and I mine. I will get up a great stock of beads, and looking-glasses, and red calico, and make an expedition to Central Africa; learn some euphonious African tongue, all made up of Ms and Ns; and carefully abstain from engaging in arguments upon the immortality of the soul with intelligent natives."

Now and again conscience's voice thunders at him in the recesses of his soul: "You are paltering with temptation. Arise!—flee!—begone!" But he, strong in the innocence of his acts and words, replies doughtily: "Temptation is there none for me here. The occupations of my life are such as they would be at home; I am struggling to know and like better her with whom my life is to be passed. As to that other woman, I see her rarely, speak to her never, look at her as seldom as it is possible to me."

And, in the meantime, that other woman droops like an unwatered flower, day by day. When the mainspring of a watch is broken, must it not stop? If hope, the mainspring of life, be broken, must not life stop—not all at once, as the watch does, but by gentle yet sure degrees? A slow fire burns in the child's veins; before this man had come, she had peace—a sad stagnant peace, indeed, but still peace. *Now* she lives in a state of perpetual concealed excitement. True, they meet but rarely, speak to each other never; but the same roof covers them both. From her outlook in the China Gallery, she can watch his going forth in the morning, his coming back at evening. At breakfast and dinner he sits opposite to her; she can study his face, with stealthy care, lest she may be observed, while he drives heavily through slow trite talk with her that fills the place in his life that, for a golden day, from one sundown to another, was Esther's. Sometimes they meet upon the stairs; her black dress lightly touches him, as they pass one another dumbly. At night she lies awake, waiting to catch the sound of his footfall in the gallery past her door; has to wait long hours often; for he, unknowing that any one takes note of his vigils, sits in the smoking-room far into the small hours, puffing out of his well-coloured meerschaum great volumes of smoke—wishing, not seldom, I think, that he could puff away Constance, his beloved, into smoke volumes and thin air.

Fed by no kindly words, nourished only upon neglect and cold looks, Esther's love for Gerard yet strikes out great roots downwards—shoots forth strong branches upwards. A tree of far statelier growth it stands than in the days when the soft gales and gentle streams of answering love fanned and watered it. Who cares for what they can have? Who cries for the moon? It is the intermediate something—the something that lies just a handbreadth beyond the utmost stretch of our most painfully-strained arms, that we eat out our hearts in longing for.

Esther never goes beyond the park palings now, deterred by the fear of being waylaid by Linley. She need not have been alarmed. As long as she came naturally in his way, he was delighted to see her: as we stoop and pick gladly the fruit that drops off the tree at our feet. He had even, on a day when the frost forbade hunting, and when he had got tired of skating, taken the unwonted trouble of riding over to Blessington, to warm himself at the fire of those great black eyes, that have still for him the charm of novelty upon them; but women, many and fair, came too readily to his hand to make him very keen in the chase of any one individual woman. In former generations men used to be the pursuers, women the pursued. In this generation we, who have set right most things, have set right this also. *Now*, the hares pursue the harriers, the foxes the hounds, and the doves swoop upon the falcons.

During these latter evenings Mr Blessington has been very alert and wakeful—has insisted on being read to from tea to bed-time—a liberal hour. But, however hoarse and voiceless the young reader may be, Gerard never now comes to the rescue, never interferes, though the frequent teasing cough of the "damnable flirt" goes through his heart like a sword. With steady certainty, through frost and thaw, rain and shine, through all the alternations of an English winter, the young girl's health declines. To all but herself is this fact evident, and she, unaccustomed to illness—never having seen the signs of premature decay in others—thinks it is but a little weariness, a little languor, a nothing. It will pass when the swooned world revives into spring and the buttercups come.

Sunday is here again, the initial letter in the week's alphabet:

"The   Sundays   of   man's   life,
Threaded   together   on   Time's   string,
Make   bracelets   to   adorn   the   wife
Of the eternal glorious King."

Ah me! the languid, yawning Sundays of most of us will make but sorry bracelets for any one, methinks. Sunday—the day on which the Shelford shopboys and shopgirls walk about gloriously apparelled, arm-in-arm, man and maid, filling their lungs with country air,—day on which the gentlefolks, such as are men of them, debarred from horse and hound and cue, smoke a cigar or two more than usual over the instructive pages of Messieurs De Kock, Sue, Balzac, &c.; while such as are women, being for the most part piously disposed, hold Goulburn's "Thoughts on Personal Religion," or Hannay's "Last Day of Our Lord's Passion," open on their velvet laps, and kill a reputation between each paragraph.

On this especial Sunday Esther has risen, feeling feebler, more nerveless than usual. Something in the influence of the weather—soft, sodden, sunless—weighs upon her with untold oppression. She would fain not go to church, remain at home, and lie on her bed; but this cannot be. Foremost in importance, in indispensability, among her duties are these Sunday ones. If the weather be tolerable, Mr. Blessington is always scrupulously punctual in attending Divine worship. Leaning on his valet's arm, he totters up the church, in his old tail-coat, tightly buttoned over his sunken chest, and, arrived at the Blessington pew, is deposited in a little nook thereof, partitioned (in some quirk of his, while he could yet see) from the rest. In this nook there is room for two people—to wit, for Mr. Blessington, and for the happy person who is to guide his devotions. And to conduct Mr. Blessington's prayers and praises is, I assure you, no sinecure. Almost entirely deaf, almost entirely blind, he is yet resolute to take a part in the services by no means less prominent than the clerk's. It is, therefore, his attendant's duty to shout the responses in his ear, in order to give him some clue to the portion of the ritual which has been arrived at and to check him with elbowings and nudgings, when his aberrations from the right path become so flagrantly noticeable as to distract the attention of the other worshippers. But too often, however, the attempts at repression on the part of the acolyte are so much labour lost. In the region of darkness and silence in which his infirmities have placed him, the old man frequently becomes impatient of the slow progress of the service as notified to him by the roars of his companion. Not seldom he proclaims, in a voice distinctly audible throughout the building, the point at which, according to his reckoning, priest and people should have arrived. "And with thy spirit," cries the squire, with unction in his deep, tremulous bass, while the sleek young rector's gentle "The Lord be with you" does not follow till five minutes later. In the Creed there is but one course to pursue: to start him, if possible, fair—happy, indeed, if he does not insist on turning to the altar somewhere towards the close of the second lesson or beginning of the Jubilate,—to start him fair, I say, and then in despair, give him his head. Fervently, loudly, rapidly, he announces his belief in the articles of the Christian faith, while parson, clerk, and congregation toil after him in vain. Occasionally—especially at such portions of the service as refer to our need of forgiveness, our sinfulness, our mortality,—he breaks out into senile tears; too deaf to hear his own penitent sobs, he has no idea of the loudness with which they reverberate through the church. Strangers, hearing, perk their heads up above their pews, and then fling them down again on their pocket-handkerchiefs convulsed with inextinguishable laughter; but the greater part of the assemblage are used to these spasms of grotesque devotion—it is only "t'oud squoire."

Esther always draws a long breath of relief when

"Lord,   have   mercy   upon   us!
Christ,   have   mercy   upon   us!
Lord, have mercy upon us!"

has been safely tided over without any unusually noisy burst of lamentation.

On the Sunday I speak of "t'oud squoire's" prayers were more unruly than usual. Whether it was that Esther's weakened voice was unable to guide them into the right channel, or to whatever other cause assignable, certain it is that his vagaries were more painfully evident— ludicrously to the congregation, distressingly to his family—than on any former Sunday within the memory of man. Many heads turn towards the Blessington pew; even the rector—meekest among M.A.s—looks now and again with gentle reproach at the old man, who is, with such aggressive loudness, usurping his office of leading the devotions of his flock. A proud woman is Esther Craven when the Liturgy comes to a close. In the sermon there are, thank God, no responses for the congregation to make; it is not even customary to cry, "Hear, hear!" "Hallelujah!" "More power to you!" at intervals. In the sermon, therefore, the old gentleman composes himself to sleep, and there is peace.

The Blessington pulpit is to-day occupied by a stranger—a Boanerges, or Son of Thunder, in the shape of a muscular, half-educated, fluent Irishman—a divine who would fain *flog* his hearers to heaven, show them the way upwards by the light of hell's flambeaux—one of that too numerous class who revel in disgusting descriptions, and similes drawn from our mortality. It is impossible to help listening to him, and difficult to help being sick. Esther listens, trembling, while he descants with minute relish on "the worm that never dies." The worm that never dies! Surely, a terrible picture enough, in its simple bareness, without enlargement thereupon! With imagination rendered more vivid, and reason weakened by sickness, the unhappy girl pictures that worm gnawing at her brother's heart—gnawing, crawling, torturing eternally. She covers her face with her hands; it is too horrible! A sort of sick feeling comes over her—a giddy faintness. If she can but reach the open air! She rises unsteadily, opens the pew-door, and walks as in a mist down the aisle, between the two rows of questioning faces, and so out. As she passes through the church-door she staggers slightly, and catches at the wall for support. Gerard, watching her anxiously, sees her unsteady gait, and the involuntary gesture of reaching out for some stay for her tottering figure. Instantly, without giving thought to the light in which his beloved may regard his proceeding, he, rising, quickly follows the young girl. She has just managed to reach a flat tombstone, and there sits, with her face turned thirstily westwards, whence a small soft wind blows fitfully.

"You are ill," he says, bending solicitously over her, and laying aside in that compassionate moment the armour of his coldness.

She does not answer for awhile; then, drawing a long breath, and trying to smile: "The church was so close," she says, sighingly; "and that smell of escaped gas always makes me feel faint, and—and" (with a shudder)—"that dreadful man—with his metaphors all taken from the charnelhouse!"

"I wish he were there himself, with all my heart," answers Gerard, devoutly; "he might there frame metaphors to his taste at his leisure."

"And it is so terrible to think that it is all *true*, isn't it?" she says, fixing her great awestruck eyes upon, his face, as if trying to find comfort and reassurance there; "that the reality exceeds even his revolting word-painting; that we *shall* be *loathsome*, all of us!—you and I and everybody—young and old, beautiful and ugly! How *could* God be so cruel as to let us know it beforehand?"

"Knowing it beforehand is better than knowing it at the time, which, at least, we are spared," replies St. John, composedly.

"But are we?" she cries, eagerly: "that is the question! Latterly I have been beset by a fearful idea that death is but a long catalepsy. In a catalepsy, you know, a person seems utterly without consciousness or volition; breath is suspended, and all the vital functions; and yet he feels and sees and hears more acutely than when in strong health. Why may not death, too, be a catalepsy?"

"Absurd!" he says. "My poor child, it is thoughts like these, gone wild, that fill madhouses. According to your theory, at what point of time does your catalepsy end? When we are dissolved into minutest particles of dust does each atom still feel and suffer?"

"My theory, as you call it, will not hold water, I know," she answers gravely, "but it does not haunt me any the less. There are times when one cannot reason—one can only *fear*."

"You should not give way to these morbid fancies," he says, chidingly; "they are making you ill."

"Am I ill, do you think? Do I look ill?" she asks, with startled eagerness.

The havoc worked in face and figure by the last few months is too directly under his eyes for him to answer anything but truthfully. "Very ill."

"You don't think I'm going to *die*?" she says, lowering her voice, and laying her hand on his arm, while her great feverish eyes burn into his very soul. "People are not any the more likely to die for being thin and weak, are they? Creaky doors hang the longest."

"Die!—God forbid!" he replies, trying to speak lightly. "Let us banish death from our talk. I suppose it is this place of tombs that has made him take such a leading part in it. Come, you are not at all fit to go back into church, and I am not anxious to hear the tail-end of that wormy discourse. The smell of brimstone is quite strong enough in my nostrils already. Let us go home!"

So they return to the house, and he still shows no inclination to leave her. He draws a chair for her near an open window, and stands with his hand resting on the back. It is almost like the old times—the old times that he thinks of,

"As   dead   men   of   good   days,
Ere   the   wrong   side   of   death   was   theirs,   when   God
Was friends with them."

Something in the recollection of those days makes soft his voice, which is not wont to be soft. "You are not fit for this life," he says, stooping down his face towards her small wan one. "It requires a tough seasoned woman, in middle life. Tell me why you have undertaken it? Why are you not—not married?"

She turns away, crimsoning painfully. "Because no one has asked me, I suppose," she answers, trying to speak banteringly.

"But you were engaged when—when we parted?"

"Yes."

"And you are not now?"

With ungovernable, unaccountable impatience, he awaits the slow brief answer.

"No."

"Had he then—h'm! h'm!—*discovered* anything?" Gerard asks, finding some difficulty in framing the question politely.

She fires up quickly. "*Discovered* anything!" she repeats, indignantly. "Do you think it is impossible for me to be honest even *once* in my life? I told him myself."

"*You* broke it off, then?"

"No, I didn't."

"*He* did?"

"Yes."

"Poor fellow! he had good cause to be angry," says St. John; the old bitterness surging back upon him, as he reflects on the cowardly duplicity that had made waste two honest lives.

"But he was *not* angry," she cries, eagerly: "he was grieved—oh, *so* grieved! Shall I ever forgive myself when I think of how he looked when I told him?" (her eyes gazing out abstractedly at the "Rape of the Sabines," as her thoughts fly back to that quarried nook on the bleak autumnal hillside, where she had broken a brave man's heart). "But he was not angry. Oh, no! he never thought of himself! he thought only about me! Ah! *that was* love!"

"He would not marry you, however?" says St. John, exasperated at these laudations, which he imagines levelled as reproaches against himself.

"No," she answered quietly, "you are right; he would not marry me, though I begged him. But that was for my sake, too—not his own; he told me that he could not make me happy, for that I did not love him. He was wrong, though. I did love him—I love him now. If I did not love the one friend I have in all this great empty world, what should I be made of?" she concludes, while the tears come into her eyes.

"You have a great capacity for loving," says St. John, who, though not usually an ungenerous fellow, is maddened by the expressions of affection, the tears and regretful looks bestowed upon his rival. "I envy, though I despair of emulating you."

"Men have but *one* way of loving," she answers, gently; "women have several. I love him as the one completely unselfish being I ever met. I agree with you, that the way of loving you mean comes but once in a lifetime."

At her words, and the fidelity to himself which they so innocently imply, a fierce bright joy upleaps in his heart—a joy that clamours for utterance in violent fond words, in the wild closeness of forbidden embraces; but honour, that strong gaoler that keeps so many under lock and key, keeps him too.

"For Love himself took part against himself
To warn us off; and Duty, loved of love—
Oh! this world's curse, beloved but hated—came,
Like death, betwixt thy dear embrace and mine,
And crying, 'Who is this? Behold thy bride!'
She push'd me from thee."

He only holds out his hand to her. "Esther, let us be friends. I am tired of this silence and estrangement; let there be peace between us!"

"I have always wished for it," she answers meekly, laying her little trembling hand in his—"you know I have; but let us be at peace *apart*, and not *together*; that will be better. How long," she asks, impulsively, lifting quivering red lips and dew-soft eyes to his—"how long—how much longer—do you mean to stay here?"

"Why do you ask?" he says, in a troubled voice, hurt pride and hot passion struggling together. "Surely in this great wide house there is room for you and me; I am not much in your way, surely?"

"You are," she answers, feverishly—"you are in my way; you would be, in the widest house that ever was built. Every day I long more and more to be a great way off from you. I think I could breathe better if I were."

He does not answer: leaning still over her in a dumb agonised yearning, that—with the chains of another still dragging about him—may not be outspoken.

"That day we met upon the stairs," she continues, eyes and cheeks aflame and lustrous with the consuming fire within her, "you promised me you would avail yourself of the first opportunity to leave this place; a month or more is gone since then. Surely the most exacting mistress could spare you for awhile now? Why have you broken your word, then? Why are you here?"

He is silent for a few moments, questioning his own soul—questioning that conscience whose monitions he has hitherto so stoutly resisted. Then he speaks, a flush of shame making red his bronzed cheek: "Because I have been dishonest to myself and to you. This place has had an attraction for me which I see now it would not have had had *she* only been here. I linger about it as a man lingers about the churchyard where his one hope lies buried."

"Don't linger any longer, then," she cries, passionately, taking his hand between both hers; "don't be dishonest any more! Tell *yourself* the truth, if you tell no one else, and go *at once*, before it is too late; for if you won't, *I* must!"

She is weeping freely as she speaks; her tears drop hot and slow, one after another, upon his hand.

He flings himself on his knees beside her, his mastery over himself reeling in the strong rush of long-pent passion.

"You tell me to go," he says, in a voice choked and altered with emotion, "and in the very act of telling me you cry. Which am I to believe, your words or your tears?"

"My words," she answers, trying to speak collectedly, and by gaining calmness herself to bring it back to him. "I have been dishonourable once—you know it; don't let me have the remorse of thinking that I made an honourable man palter with temptation—made him sully his honour for me. If *I* am the inducement that keeps you here, *go; for my sake, go!* I say it a hundred times; promise me you will go—*soon, this week.* Let me hear you swear it; you will not break your oath, I know!"

He is silent; hesitating to take that step of irrevocable banishment—banishment from the woman that he cast away in righteous wrath, and in whose frail life his own now seems to be bound up.

"Swear!" she says again, earnestly, with a resolute look in her soft face. "I beg it of you as a favour; for if you won't, though my only chance of daily bread lies here, I must go to-night."

The determination in her voice recalls him to his senses. "I will not drive you to such extremities," he says, coldly. "Give me only till to-morrow morning—twenty-four hours cannot make much difference to you, and a man going to be hanged likes to have a little respite—give me till to-morrow, and I will swear whatever you wish."

"That is right," she answers, trying to smile through her tears. "Some day you will thank me; you will say, 'She was a bad girl, but she did me one good turn!'"

The people are flocking out of church; the squire, in a low pony-chaise, driven by a groom as old and toothless as himself, and drawn by a pony (considering the comparative ages of horses and men) also nearly as old, is bowling gently up the drive.

"I must go," Esther says, rising hastily; "Mrs. Blessington hates red eyes as she hates a black dress, and for the same reason!"

CHAPTER XXXVIII.

At Blessington no one goes to church twice. It is the bounden duty of every Christian man, woman, and child to go to church in the morning; it is the duty of only the clergyman, the school-children, and the organist to go to church in the afternoon. The old people sleep side by side in the blaze of the saloon-fire; being, both of them, happily deaf, they are undisturbed by each other's grunts and snores.

Since the beginning of St. John's visit, the north drawing-room has been made over to him and his betrothed to be affectionate in, so that they may enjoy, uninterrupted, those fits of affection to which all engaged people are supposed, and sometimes unjustly supposed, to be liable. Whether they have reached the requisite pitch of warmth on the afternoon I speak of is, to say the least, doubtful; but, all the same, in the north drawing-room they are. Constance leans back in an armchair, rather listless. She is fond of work, and it is not right to work on Sunday: her feet repose on a foot-stool before her—her eyes are fixed upon them: she is thinking profoundly whether steel buckles a size smaller than the ones she is at present wearing would not be more becoming to the feet. St. John sits by the table; his left hand supports his head; his right scribbles idly, on a bit of paper, horses taking impossible fences, prize pigs, ballet-girls, little skeleton men squaring up at one another. He, too, is thinking—but not of shoe-buckles. He has got something to say to Miss Blessington—something unpleasant, unpolite; and he cannot, for the life of him, imagine how to begin to say it. Chance favours him. Miss Blessington, happening to look up, catches her lover's eyes fixed, with an expression she had never before seen in them—not on herself, as she, for the first second imagines, but (as a second glance informs her) on some object outside the window. Her gaze follows his, and lights upon "nobody very particular—only poor Miss Craven!" who, with head rather bent, is trudging by towards the garden. "How ill that girl looks!" she says, pettishly. "I really believe those sort of people take a pleasure in looking as sickly and woebegone as possible, in order to put one out of spirits,"

The opening he has been looking for has come. "Constance," ho says, bending his head, and speaking in a low voice, "what fatuity induced you not to send me word when you found that that girl was here?"

"You forbad me ever to mention her name to you," she answers, coldly; "and, to tell you the truth, I thought it was a good thing that you should see her. If you had not met again, you might have carried a sentimental recollection of her throughout life, which you can hardly do now that you have seen with your own eyes how completely she has lost her beauty."

St. John lifts his head, and stares at her in blank astonishment. "Lost its beauty!"—that

"Face   that   one   would   see,
And   then   fall   blind,   and   die,   with   sight   of   it,
Held fast between the eyelids."

145

"Lost her beauty!" he repeats, in a sort of stupefaction.

"Well," she replies, languidly, "why do you repeat my words? You know I never admired her much. I never can admire those black women, but that is a matter of taste, of course. It is not matter of taste, however—it is matter of fact, that whatever good looks she once had are gone—*gone*."

Gerard smiles contemptuously. "I do believe that you women lose the sight of your eyes when you look at one another."

"What do you mean?" she asks, with some animation. "Is it possible that you don't agree with me as to her being quite *passée?*"

"I think her, as I always thought her," he answers, steadily, "the loveliest woman I ever beheld; a little additional thinness or paleness does not affect her much. Hers is not mere skin beauty: as you say, tastes differ, and I like *those black women*."

"That is a civil speech to make to me!" she answers, reddening—an insult to her appearance or her clothes being the one weapon that has power to pierce the scales of her armour of proof.

St. John smiles again. "When we engaged to marry one another, did we also engage to think each other the handsomest specimens of the human animal Providence ever framed?"

"It is, at least, not usual for a man to express an open preference for another woman to the girl to whom he is engaged."

"It is no question of *preference*," he answers, quietly. "I had no thought of drawing any comparison between you and Miss Craven at the moment; I was not thinking of you."

"You said she was *the* loveliest girl you had ever seen!" objects Constance, pouting.

"So I did—I do think her so," he rejoins, calmly. "If there is some defect in my eyes, hindering me from seeing things as they are, it is my misfortune, not my fault. Cannot you be content," he asks, banteringly, "with being the *next loveliest?*"

She turns away her head, too indignant to answer.

He changes his tone. "Constance," he says, gravely, "when I proposed to you, did not I tell you, honestly, what I could give you and what I could not? Love (odd as it may sound between engaged people), and the blind admiration that accompanies love, I had not got to offer you; this is true, is not it?"

"Perfectly true," she answers, resentfully; "and as I am not, nor ever was, one of those inflammable young ladies, who think that *burning*, and *consuming*, and *melting* are essential to married happiness, I did not much regret its absence. I have always been brought up to think," she continues, having recourse to the high moral tone which is her last sure refuge, "that respect and esteem are the best basis for two people to go upon, and I think so still."

"But do you and I respect and esteem one another?" he asks, half-cynically, half-mournfully. "Is it possible that I can respect you, who, though you did not care, or affect to care, two straws about me personally—though you knew, at the time I asked you to marry me, that I was madly in love with another woman—were yet willing to give yourself to me, soul and body—to be bone of my bone, and flesh of my flesh, because I was a good *parti*, as the vile phrase goes? And as for me," he ends, in bitter self-contempt, "what is there in all my idle wasted life, from beginning to end, that any one can respect or esteem?"

"Has this struck you now for the first time?" she asks, drily. "I am not aware of any change in our relative circumstances since our marriage was arranged; I suppose our feelings towards each other are much what they were then, when you were troubled with none of these scruples."

"And what *were* our feelings then?" he asks, bitterly; "what brought us together? Was not it that our properties dovetailed conveniently into one another, as Sir Thomas says—that it was advisable for both of us to marry some one—that we were of suitable age, and had no positive distaste for one another: was not this so?"

"I suppose so," she answers, sulkily.

"And yet," he continues, sternly, "although I had laid bare to you all my wretched story—although you were well aware that I was utterly without the safeguard of any love to yourself—you yet let me fall into this temptation—the cruelest I could have been exposed to—without a word of warning. Was this fair? Was this right?"

"Since you put me on my defence," she answers, with anger, "I must repeat to you what I said before, that it seemed to me the best method of curing you of your ill-placed fancy for Esther Craven—a fancy which she repaid with such disgraceful deceit and duplicity—was to let you see for yourself what a wreck she had become!"

"You meant well, perhaps," he rejoins, with a sigh that is more than half a groan; "but it was terribly mistaken—terribly ill-judged; it has done us both an irreparable injury."

"I am not aware that it has done me any injury whatever," she answers, coldly, mistaking his meaning

"I was not alluding to you," he replies, curtly.

She makes no rejoinder, and he, rising, begins to walk up and down the room with his hands in his pockets. He has made his meaning clear enough, surely, and yet she does not appear to see it. As she continues resolutely silent, he stops opposite to her, and speaks earnestly, and yet with some embarrassment, as one who knows that what he says will be unpleasing to his listener.

"Constance, I must tell you the truth, though I suppose it is hardly of the complexion of the pretty flattering truths or untruths that you have been used to all your life. But, at least, it is better that you should hear it now, than that we should tell it one another a year hence, with mutual, useless recriminations; there is no use in disguising the fact that you and I do not feel towards each other as husband and wife should feel."

"Pshaw!" she says, pettishly, turning her head aside; "we feel much the same as other people do, I daresay."

"If," he continues, very gravely, "marriage were a temporary connection, that lasted a year—five years say—or that could be dissolved at pleasure, there might be no great harm in entering upon it with the sort of negative liking, the absence of repugnance for one another, which is all that we can boast; but since it is a bargain for all time, and that there is no getting out of it except by the gate of death or disgrace, I think we ought both to reflect on it more seriously than we have yet done before undertaking it."

"It is rather late in the day to say all this," retorts she, indignantly. "You have known me all my life; you must have been well aware that I never could enter into those highflown, romantic notions, which I have heard you yourself ridicule a hundred times. These objections should have occurred to you before you proposed to me, and not now, when we have been engaged two months, and when our marriage has been discussed as a settled thing by all our acquaintance."

"You are right," he answers, quietly. "They should have occurred to me before; but, in justice to myself, I must say that they would never have occurred to me: I should have remained in the same state of supine indifference to everything in which I came here, had not you yourself thrown me in the way of Esther Craven."

She sits upright in her chair; her pale, handsome face paler, harder than usual, in her great anger. "The drift of this long tirade, when translated into plain English, is, I suppose, that you wish to marry Esther Craven instead of me?"

He is silent.

"Is it so?" she repeats, her voice raised several notes above its wonted low key.

"When I am engaged to one woman," he answers, slowly, reluctantly, yet steadily, "I hope I am not dishonourable enough willingly to harbour the thought of marriage with any other."

The Gerard diamonds flash before her mind's eye: they are so big, and numerous—necklace, aigrette, stomacher. The idea of seeing them gleam restless in Esther's hair, on Esther's fair neck, is insupportable to her. She will not release him, ardently as he wishes it; she will hold him by a strong chain that will not snap—his honour.

"I am glad to hear it," she answers, coldly. "In common fairness to me, you could hardly have entertained such an idea. It is a great disadvantage to a girl to be engaged, to have her engagement as widely known as mine has been, and then to have it broken off; people never think the same of her again."

He turns to the window, to hide his bitter disappointment. "Very well," he answers, calmly; "things will remain as they are, I suppose, then? I only thought it right to warn you how small a chance of happiness there is in a marriage so loveless as ours: for the rest you must blame yourself."

CHAPTER XXXIX.

Night's black sheet drawn off the other half of the world is thrown over us; the dark side of the lantern is turned towards us. Esther has fallen asleep, with almost a happy smile upon her soft, parted lips. She is forgiven; and is there any sweetness like the sweetness of being pardoned, having sinned? He no longer hates her! That was not hate that looked out of his quick, keen eyes to-day, as he leant over her while she sat, dizzy and faint, on that churchyard slab, or as he knelt in strong emotion at her knees. And now, though at her own telling, he is going away from her to-morrow—though, when next they meet, either they will have put off mortality's tatters, God will have laid

"Death, like a kiss, across their lips;"

or else, to look and lean as he looked and leant to-day will be deadly sin—yet creeps there a sorrowful joy about her heart. He has given her back the past—the short, happy Felton past; no one can take it from her again; not even Miss Blessington, who has taken all else—present and future and all. She is dreaming of him now—dreaming that she is sitting in the library at Felton, in the fragrant gloom made by the lowered Venetian blinds, by dark oak bookshelves, by plentiful sweet flowers, and so sitting hears the sound of his quick feet coming along the passage. He is at the door—he is opening it. But, ah! what is this?—it will not open; it is stiff on its hinges. He is pushing it—pushing gently, pushing hard—but it will not move. What a stealthy noise it is he makes, as if he were afraid of some one hearing him! She starts up, broad awake; it is not all dream; there is some one pushing stealthily, yet audibly, against a door. For the first bewildered moment of sick fear she imagines that it is her own door on which this attempt is being made; but a moment's listening undeceives her. The sound comes from underneath her window, apparently. It is not rats this time; a rat, with all its ingenuity, would be puzzled to make a noise so distinctly human. Upon her mind there flashes suddenly the recollection of a door leading into the garden beneath her casement, but not so immediately beneath but that she can see it; a door that stands wide open all the summer through, when people step from house to garden, from garden to house, a hundred times a day, but which in winter is rarely used. She sits up motionless, while round her utter darkness surges. The noise is repeated: push—push! creak—creak! it is as if some one, with hand and knee, were attempting to obtain entrance. When light is withdrawn hearing becomes preternaturally sharpened; in an instant she has jumped out of bed, and run barefoot over the cold boards to the window. There, pulling aside the blind, she, trembling all over, peeps out. Moon is there none, but the joint light of countless star-squadrons, faint though it be, is yet strong enough to enable her distinctly to make out the figure of a man pressing itself against the door in question. With bodily eyes she at length looks upon that burglar, whom, with the terrified eyes of imagination, she had so often beheld. Whether he wear a crape mask or not it is too dark to discern. What *is* she to do?—she, in all probability, the only wakeful, conscious being in all that great house. For a minute she stands irresolute, while a rushing sound fills her ears, and her teeth chatter dismally in the cold. Shall she alarm the servants? But how to reach them? She does not even know the way to their sleeping-places. They are miles away, in the other wing of the house, where she has never been. Shall she go to Miss Blessington? At least she knows the way thither, though it is some distance off. But of what avail would that be? Of what use would two girls be, any more than one, against the onslaught of daring unscrupulous robbers? Shall she betake herself to St. John, whose room is but two doors off? No sooner does this idea suggest itself to her, than she puts it into practice. Hastily striking a light, and wrapping her dressing-gown round her, she opens her door, and, flying down the passage, knocks loudly at Mr. Gerard's. But Gerard, having a not particularly bad conscience, and a particularly good digestion, is a sound sleeper. She knocks again, more violently, almost to the flaying of her knuckles: "Mr. Gerard!—Mr. Gerard!"

"Hullo! who's there?" responds a sleepy voice.

"It's I! Esther!" she cries pantingly. "Open the door, please—this minute—quick!"

"*Esther!—you!*" says the voice, perfectly awake this time. "What on earth is the matter?—wait one second!"

He hurries on his clothes, and then hastens to accede to her request of opening the door.

"Are you ill?" he asks, anxiously, seeing her lean against the door-post, with death-white cheeks and terror-struck eyes.

"No—no!" she answers, hoarse and breathless, while St. John, candle, and door, all seem to be dancing a jig round her. "It is not I, but there's a man—getting into the house—by the garden-door. I saw him!"

"The devil there is!" replies the young man, with animation. "Here, give me your candle, and I'll go and see what he wants."

"No—no!" she cries, with all a woman's unreason. "Don't go; you must not!" (though for what other purpose she had sought his assistance she would have been puzzled to say). "I won't let you; you'll be killed!" and so, gasping, stretches out her white arms towards him, and, letting drop her candle, falls insensible, in the total darkness, into his embrace.

For a month past or more, the dream that has pursued Gerard night and day—unchecked in sleep, in waking faintly repressed by considerations of honour—is to hold that fair woman's form in his arms; and now he so holds her in reality. And yet, as the fulfilment of our wishes seldom affords us the gratification we had anticipated, so it is with him. Now that he has got her, he does not quite know what to do with her. Shall he, encumbered by his beautiful burden, grope his way back into his room, and lay her down there, while he goes and investigates into the cause of her terror and swoon? But the household, being alarmed, may find her there; and, so finding, would not the reputation of her, most innocent, be endangered? Her head droops heavy in its perfect lifelessness on his shoulder; her soft warm hair caresses his cheek in the blackness of the night. He looks down the passage. From Esther's open door a flood of light streams; at all events there is a candle left burning there. In a moment he has borne her into her own chamber, and has laid her most gently down upon the ginger-moreen bed. He has no time to try and revive her now. "Perhaps it was only her own imagination, poor child!—her own imagination, and those infernal rats!" is the hasty thought that has crossed his mind; but looking through the window, as she had done, he sees, as she had seen, a man's dim figure in the starlight. Without a moment's delay, without casting another thought even to the fair swooned woman he leaves behind him, Gerard runs down the corridor, his blood pleasantly astir with the thought of a possible adventure—through interminable dark galleries, down the gleaming cold of white stone stairs, through hall, saloon, north drawing-room, and justicing-room—till he reaches a narrow short passage that leads to the garden door. As he and his light draw near, the noise suddenly ceases. He stands still for a moment, expecting to hear it repeated, but it is not. Setting down his candle, therefore, he advances towards the door and unfastens it—it is secured by an old-fashioned catch inside—opens it, and looks out into the night. At first he can discern nothing but the chill wintry garden, and the million stars scattered broadcast over God's one great unenclosed field of the sky; but a second glance reveals to him a dim figure crouching indistinct in the shadow of a projecting buttress.

"Who's there?" he cries, in a loud clear voice.

No answer.

"Who's there?" he repeats. "If you don't answer, I'll fire."

Firing, in this instance, must mean using the flat candlestick as a projectile, for other weapon has Mr. Gerard none. Hardly have the words left his mouth, however, before the figure springs forth from its hiding-place, and stands erect before him.

"Don't fire, sir, please; it's I."

Livery-buttons flash in the starlight: behold the culprit revealed!—a young and lighthearted footman, who has on one or two previous occasions been suspected of a too great proclivity towards the nocturnal festivities of the "Chequers." A sense of infuriation at the bald tame end of the adventure gets possession of St. John.

"What the devil do you mean, sir, skulking here, alarming the whole household, and frightening the young ladies out of their senses?" he asks, with a gruff asperity not unworthy of his papa.

"If you please, sir, I was only—only—taking a bit of a walk in the park, sir."

"A likely tale!" cries St. John, angrily. "A walk in the park at this time of night! Come, don't let us have any lies, my good fellow; that is covering a small fault with a much greater one. You were at the 'Chequers,' I suppose? Come, out with it!"

"If you please, sir," replies the man, hanging his head, and looking very sheepish, "there was a young woman, as come all the way from Shelford, and as she was a bit timid, I promised to send her home."

"A young woman!" repeats St. John, repressing an inclination to smile. "Well, next time, you must be good enough to choose more seasonable hours for your meetings with young women."

"And when I come back, sir, I found all the house made up for the night, and I could not get no one to hear me; and I thought as how, very like, I might find this 'ere door open, if so be as Betsy had forgot to bolt it, as she mostly does, only it is so plaguy stiff on its 'inges——"

"And, for a wonder, Betsy had not forgotten to bolt it," interrupts Gerard, drily. "Well, don't let us have anything of this kind again, or, I warn you, you'll be packed off without a character."

Relieved at being let off so easily, the young fellow slinks away, and Gerard retraces his steps upstairs again. He cannot help laughing as he thinks of poor Esther's tragic fears, of her agonised pleadings: "You *must* not go! I won't let you go! you'll be killed!"

"If I'm never in nearer peril of death than I was to-night," he thinks, "I have every chance of outliving Methuselah. Was ever mountain delivered of so contemptible a mouse?" He laughs again. "'I won't let you! you'll be killed!' Poor little thing! I wonder has she come to herself yet! I must let her know that this bloodthirsty villain has not slain me outright this time." Having reached her door, he pauses and listens. There is no sound within. He knocks gently—no answer: knocks again—still no reply. Half-hesitating, as one that stands doubtful on the threshold of a church, he opens the door and enters. The light burns on the dressing-table, and she lies still prone, where he had laid her, on the bed, still completely insensible. This swoon is horribly deathlike:

".................But   she   lies
Not   in   the   embrace   of   loyal   death,   who   keeps

149

His   bride   for   ever,   but   in   treacherous   arms
Of   sleep,   that   sated,   will   restore   to   grief
Her snatch'd a sweet space from his cruel clutch."

Her head is thrown back, and her round chin slightly raised. Over the tossed pillow wander the tangled riches of her swart hair; nerveless on the counterpane lie the white, carven hands and blue-veined wrists, on which the faint fine lines make a tender network. Half-shadowed by her dressing-gown, half-emerging from it gleam bare feet,

"That make the blown foam neither swift nor white."

He leans over her, gazing with passionate admiration at the heavy shut lids and upward curling lashes—with passionate admiration mixed with sharp pain; for he can see, plainlier now in this long quiet look than in the hasty, stolen glances he has hitherto given her, the purple stains under closed eyes, the little depressions in the rounded cheek, the droop of the sweet sorrowful mouth. Iachimo's words recur to him—Iachimo's, as he gazed in his treachery upon the sleeping beauty of Imogen:

"................   Cytherea!
How   bravely   thou   becom'st   thy   bed!   fresh   lily!
And   whiter   than   the   sheets!   That   I   might   touch!
But   kiss—one   kiss!   Bubies   unparagon'd,
How   dearly   they   do't!—'Tis   her   breathing   that
Perfumes   the   chamber   thus.   The   flame   o'   the   taper
Bows   towards   her,   and   would   underpeep   her   lids
To   see   the   enclosed   lights   now   canopied
Under those windows...................."

But looking at a person with ever such warm approbation will not recover them from a swoon. What is he to do? He is horribly puzzled, so seldom before has he seen a fainted fellow-Christian. Vague ideas of having heard of burnt feathers held under nostrils recur to his mind. But whence to obtain feathers, unless he takes a pair of scissors and snips a hole in the feather-bed? There is nothing in all the great room more feathery than the stumpy end of an old quill pen, with which Miss Craven is wont to indite her small accounts. Another specific flashes before his mental eye. Smelling-salts! He walks to the dressing-table, and carefully overlooks its slender load: brushes and combs, a Bible, and a fat pincushion—neither essence, unguent, nor scent of any kind. Esther's toilette apparatus is but meagre. Shall he throw cold water over her? What! and deluge all the ginger moreen bed, thereby making it an even more undesirable resting-place than it is at present? Quite at a loss what to do, he returns to the bedside, and begins to chafe her cold hands between his two warm ones. Then he stoops over her, trying to discover any smallest sign of returning consciousness. When his lips are so close to hers, how can he help laying them yet closer? Men seldom do resist any temptation, unless it is very weak, and the objections to it very overwhelming. This temptation is not weak, and there are absolutely no objections to it. No one will ever know of this theft—not even the person upon whom it is committed: it will do her no harm, and to kiss her even thus unknowing, unreturning, gives him a bitter joy. But, having once kissed her, he refrains himself, nor lays his lips a second time upon hers. Something of shame comes over him, as one that has taken advantage of another's helplessness—one that, for an instant, has let the brute within him get the upper hand of the man. Only he caresses gently her two cold hands, and his eyes dwell on her face, watching longingly for the first small symptom of back-coming life. His patience is rewarded, after a time; after a time there comes a quivering about the eyelids, a tremor about the mouth—then a deep-drawn sighing respiration. Always with a sigh does the soul come back to its dark cottage, having journeyed away from it for awhile. The curtain-lids sweep back from the spirit's windows; and, pale and clear, her eyes' dark glories shine upon him, conscious yet bewildered. Then a little stealing red, like the tint that dwelt in a sea-shell's lips, flows into each pure cheek; then comes full consciousness, and with it recollected terrors. "Where is he?" she asks, in a low frightened voice. "Is he gone?—did he get in?—did he hurt you?"

"He was not a very formidable burglar, after all," Gerard answers, with a reassuring smile: "it was only Thomas, who had been seeing his sweetheart home, and was trying to get into the house without being heard."

"Oh, I'm so glad! But" (her eyes straying confusedly round the room) "how did I get here? When last I remember any thing I was in the passage."

"I carried you here."

"And then went and found out about this man?"

"Yes."

"And then came back here?"

150

"Yes. I hope you don't think me very impertinent," he says, apologetically; "but I could not bear the idea of your lying here, insensible, without any one making an attempt to bring you round."

Recollecting what his own method of bringing her round had been, his conscience gives him a compunctious stab. She blushes furiously, and, raising herself into a sitting posture, begins to twist up her hair with both hands.

"You are better now," he says, tenderly, but with perfect respect; "I will go."

He moves towards the door, but, before he can reach it, it flies open hastily, and Constance, dishevelled, dressing-gowned, flurried out of all likeness to herself, bursts in. "Oh, Miss Craven! I'm so frightened! I heard people talking outside——*St. John!!*"

Mrs. Siddons might have been defied to crowd more solemnly tragic emphasis into one word than does Miss Blessington into the innocent dissyllable, "St. John!"

"Well!" replies St. John, tartly, vexed past speaking at being discovered in such an utterly false position.

"I suppose I may be allowed to ask what brings *you* here?" she says, drawing herself up to her stately height.

"You certainly may," he answers, endeavouring to recover his self-possession; "and I have not the slightest objection to telling you. What brought me here was the endeavour to recover Miss Craven from a faint into which she fell on coming to tell me—as the only person within her reach—that a man was, as she imagined, endeavouring to break into the house."

Even to his own ears this tale, as he tells it, sounds wofully improbable.

"And you took no steps to prevent him?" cries Constance, quickly; her fears for her personal safety, for the moment, outweighing the claims of outraged virtue.

"Pardon me! I did; but having discovered that it was only one of the footmen, who had been accidentally locked out, I came back to tell Miss Craven so, if she were recovered! and, if not, to give her that assistance which anyone human being may render to another without being called to account for it."

Having spoken, he folds his arms, and confronts her, calm and stately as herself.

"I should hardly have imagined it was *your* business," she replies, with scarce-concealed incredulity. "May I ask why you could not ring for the servants?"

"Because, as you are well aware," he answers, trying to quell his rising anger, "if I were to ring from now till doomsday, not a soul would hear me; all the bells ring downstairs, and the servants' bedrooms are at least a quarter of a mile distant up-stairs."

"Why could not you have come to me, then?"

"The impropriety would, in that case, have been at least equal," he answers, sarcastically; "and, to tell you the truth, such a course never occurred to me."

Something in his tone irritates her. "It is, of course, no concern of mine," she says, with icy coldness. "If Miss Craven chooses to receive the visits of gentlemen, HERE, at two o'clock in the morning, it does *me* no harm!"

She moves towards the door, but he places himself between her and it; and, grasping her wrist with unconscious roughness, speaks in a voice low and hoarse with anger, while his roused wrath glances upon her from out of his grey eyes—the eyes that hitherto have looked upon her only with indifference.

"Constance! what do you mean by these insults? How dare you give utterance to them? Is your own mind so impure that you cannot believe in the purity of others?"

"You must allow that it is at least an equivocal position," she answers, half-frightened by his stern looks, but keeping resolutely to her text.

"It is," he answers, remorsefully; "I allow it—I bitterly feel it. And yet, if it were only myself that were concerned, I should scorn to descend to any more explanation than that I have already given you; but for the sake of this most innocent girl, whom by my folly I have compromised, I swear to you, Constance—I solemnly take God to witness!—that it is exactly and simply as I have told you. Miss Craven had not recovered from her insensibility more than two minutes before you came into the room; I was in the act of leaving it as you entered. This is the whole plain truth: do you believe it?"

She does not answer.

"Do you believe it?" he repeats, earnestly.

The mulish look comes into her face—the look he has begun to know so well.

"It cannot be of much consequence to you whether I believe it or not," she answers, still with that freezing calm of voice and face. "You have, at all events, adopted the best method of obtaining your release from that engagement, which you so broadly hinted, only yesterday afternoon, that you wished to be free from. You have your wish—you are free!"

151

"As you will," he answers, gloomily. "God knows there never was much love in our connection; an iller-mated pair never came together; it was a mere matter of business on both sides. But, as to saying that the pure accident which has brought Miss Craven and me into slight and transient collision to-night can have any influence upon the conclusion or continuance of our engagement—it is tantamount to telling me that what I have sworn to you, upon my honour as a gentleman, to be true, is false!" he says, his face growing white and fierce.

"Is it?" she says, with a quietly enraging smile; having that confidence in the shield of womanhood, which makes so many a woman gall a man to the uttermost, and expect him to stand by, serene, polite, and smiling. "Unfortunately," she continues, "I am behind the spirit of the age; I am shackled with obsolete old notions of propriety and decency; and therefore—as you have no longer any smallest control over my actions—will you be so good as to allow me to go?"

He drops her hand instantly, and, opening the door for her, bows his head haughtily, saying, "Go! I have neither the wish nor the power to detain you;" and as he so speaks she passes out.

Meanwhile Esther, having slidden from her bed, stands with trembling limbs, grasping the back of a chair, and gazing from speaker to speaker with a world of surprise and horror in her great innocent eyes. As Miss Blessington leaves the room, St. John turns to her:

"My darling!" he says, with an accent of passionate remorse, "how will you ever forgive me for having exposed you to this!"

She turns away from him, and covers her burning face with her hands. "Go!" she says, faintly—"go, this minute! Don't say another word! Don't give her any more reason for her wicked slanders! Go!"

And he goes.

CHAPTER XL.

Of the three persons whose repose has been disturbed by the amours of Thomas the footman, only one is able to take up again the thread of interrupted slumber. Miss Blessington, having returned to her chamber, and having meditated calmly for a quarter of an hour on the knot in her destiny she has just untied, and having given one great sigh to the memory of the Gerard diamonds, lays down her golden scented head on her pillow again, and sleeps the sleep of the just. Miss Blessington has well nigh mastered the secret of eternal youth and perennial beauty—incapacity for feeling any emotion. It is hardly likely that the god Sleep, who loves a quiet house, will visit two such unquiet temples as the brains of St. John and Esther: he goes away from them utterly, taking his gentle poppyheads with him.

St. John walks miles and miles up and down his bedroom carpet, pondering, deeply and vexedly, not on what his own course of conduct shall be—*that* he is already determined upon—but on what effect Miss Blessington's coldly sceptical reception of his wildly improbable yet true tale is likely to have upon Esther.

And Esther herself, having conceived a mortal aversion for the shelter of the ginger-canopied pavilion, wraps a great shawl round her, and, sitting down on the deep window-seat, watches for the first streaks of dawn, which, on these winter mornings, are long, long coming. Though it is a winter night, her hands burn hot and dry; for the last few days she has had a sharp pain in her side—to-night it is getting yet sharper; it begins to hurt her to draw her breath. Two thoughts keep buzzing about her brain: "I am going to be ill," and "I am going to be turned away." She throws aside her shawl, but the dry burning still continues. She has sat here for hours now, and the dawn's feet are beginning slowly to climb the steps from the eastern gate. The battle between day and night is yet undecided; almost equally they divide the sky between them. Perhaps it is the night's excitement that has given her this fever; perhaps the cold morning air would refresh her. She waits until day's victory is complete, and then—being already dressed—puts on her hat and jacket, and steals noiselessly downstairs, to the garden door that has been the cause of so much mischief, out into the garden between the brown earthed beds, where the winter aconite's small yellow heads and green tippets are beginning to push themselves into sight, and thence into the park.

There is no wind abroad, only heavy rain-clouds outwalling the infant sun, and the unarmed air has a piercing chillness in it. Esther has not proceeded far, and is standing thoughtful on the brow of a little knoll, from whence one looks down on the dark flag-fringed pool, when she is aware of a footstep behind her; and the next instant St. John Gerard stands by her side.

"What have you come here for? Why have you followed me?" she asks, turning upon him in hasty dismay. "Miss Blessington's windows look this way—she will see us together."

"Let her see us," he answers, doggedly.

"She will never believe that it was by accident we have met," cries poor Esther, in great agitation.

"She will be right, then; it is not accident."

"She will think that it was an appointment!" she says, clasping her hands in unfeigned distress.

"Let her think so!"

"It is very well for you to talk in this way," she says, with passionate reproach. "You are a man—you may defy the opinion of the world; but is it so easy for me?"

"Why should her opinion concern either you or me?" he inquires, gravely. "What is she to either of us? Did not you last night, with your own ears, hear my dismissal pronounced?"

She stoops her head until her hat almost conceals her face from him.

"She was angry," she says, in a low voice; "she will be sorry for the things she said; she will forgive you."

"Will she?" he answers, quietly smiling. "I think not; to tell you the truth, I don't mean to ask her."

She lifts her face, suddenly earnest, to him.

"You *must!*" she says, eagerly. "You must explain to her, as you tried to do last night, that what happened then" (a painful blush) "is no possible reason why her engagement to you should be broken off. You must convince her of this—you must, indeed; for my sake *you must!*"

He looks down, frowning heavily.

"When a galley-slave's chains have been knocked off, must he handcuff himself again?"

"Why did you handcuff yourself at first?" she asks, with impulsive vehemence. "Whose doing was it but your own? What madness first impelled you to ask her to marry you?"

"Because," he answers, with emotion, fixing his upbraiding eyes upon her—"because I was smarting miserably under the blow you had just given me—you, who had made me mistrust everything attractive, and womanly, and innocent-seeming. I was obliged to marry some one; that is one of the many curses attached to being an eldest son, and the last male heir of an inconveniently old family. I said to myself, 'She is too dull to deceive me, too passionless to disgrace me.' I chose her because she was, of all the women I knew, the one least capable of calling forth emotion of any kind whatever in me—consequently, the one most powerless to make me suffer."

The words of his defence came quick and hurried. She is silent for a moment; then, uplifting imploring eyes to his: "Mr. Gerard," she says, tremblingly, "the twenty-four hours you asked me to allow you yesterday are nearly expired: have you come to say 'good-bye' to me? If so, it is well; you remember your promise?"

"I remember it," he answers, slowly, "and I am prepared to—*break* it. Don't look so reproachful, Esther! I am ready to make you as good a one instead. I am ready to swear," he says, his face all kindling in the grey cold morning with eager passion—"I am ready to swear to you that I will never leave you again, unless you send me away, until death do us part. Will that promise do as well as the other?"

She gives a little cry of astonishment. "What do you mean?" she asks, faintly, moving a step farther away from him.

"I mean," he says, solemnly, his countenance all shining with the light of a great new joy, "that I am sick of my life without you, Esther; and you—you are sick of yours without me, aren't you?"

She cannot deny it, and is unwilling to allow it; so keeps a troubled silence.

"There must be some reason," he continues, passionately, "for your failing health, for your thin white cheeks, for your total loss of beauty" (with a smile), "as Constance tersely worded it yesterday. Am I right; or is it my conceit that makes me think that I have some concern in the change?"

"You are mistaken," she cries, hastily—the idea that pity for her miserable appearance has brought him back to her flashing gallingly across her mind. "I was very fond of you—*very;* it was a great grief to me when you threw me away from you; but I could have done without you, if—if—I had not lost my boy."

She turns away, to hide her quivering lips and swelling tears: it is so seldom that she speaks of her dead, that the mere naming of him seems to make his loss the clearer.

Gerard's face falls a little. "Could you?" he says, simply and sadly. "No doubt! I was unreasonable to suppose that *I* could be indispensable to any one."

They walk on in silence side by side. It is beginning to rain, heavy drops ushering in a winter storm. The deer-barn is near—the deer-barn, with steep red roof, lichen-painted, standing on a little rise, among a company of ancient hornbeams, whose twisted trunks lean this way and that. For the last twenty years, every young lady that has come to stay at the hall has sketched the deer-barn.

"This is not fit weather for you to be out in," Gerard says, solicitously glancing at his companion's slight figure and fever-bright eyes. "Let us shelter here till the storm is over!"

Having reached it, Esther stands watching Heaven's quick large tears falling heavy on Earth's chill breast; St. John walks up and down on the rough earth-floor, buried in thought. At length, rousing himself, he approaches Esther, and speaks, calmly at first, but with increasing vehemence as he proceeds:

"Esther, I have been thinking what a short section of my life, counting by days and weeks, the time that I have known you forms; that month at Felton, when we had scarcely eyes or ears for any one but each other, and this month here, when we have hardly exchanged two words. I suppose I know very little about you, *really;* you may be a very bad worthless girl, for all I know to the contrary. God knows I have not had much reason to think you a very good one; and yet, good or bad—well, as you say, and as I have no reason to doubt, that you can get on without me—I cannot, for the life of me, bear any longer the dragging of the endless empty days without you. Esther!" he says, with passionate hunger in his eyes, "I *want* you! I *must* have you for my own! Is there now any reason why I should not?"

"Have you forgotten," she asks, with a melancholy smile, "the night when you told me that you would never forgive me, either in this world or the next? What have I done since to make you change your mind? I am no different to what I was then—unless, perhaps, I may be a little wickeder; I have been most unhappy, and adversity makes one wicked."

"I suppose I have lost my senses," he answers, with excitement; "but it seems to me now that, even were you to deceive me again, as you did at Felton—if you were to cheat me, and tell me falsehoods with the same baby-innocent face that you did there—that even then I should not repent of my bargain. Of two evils it would be the least; it would be better than never to have possessed you at all. Only, child, one thing I beg of you," he continues, with reproachful entreaty: "if you mean to trick me a second time, don't let me find it out for a little while! Let me be happy for a year—a month—a week!"

Her eyes rest on the ground, and a painful red spreads on either cheek. Despite the honest yearning love that vibrates along his voice, she cannot cast out from her heart that galling suspicion that has stolen there.

"You are very good," she makes answer, in a constrained voice; "and it is very generous of you trying to hide your real motive; but I can see it: it is *pity!* You look at me, and think, 'She was a pretty girl once, and now she has grown old and thin and plain, and it is all for love of me!' Yes, it is pity!"

"You are right," he answers, earnestly; "it is pity, profound pity, for the most miserable, discontented fellow upon God's earth—to wit, myself."

She raises her eyes slowly, and fixes them searchingly on his eager flushing face; and, looking, can doubt no longer.

"If I was over-harsh to you that night at Felton," he continues, rapidly, "and I am willing now to own that I was—for, after all, it was not against me that you had most greatly sinned—I have, at all events, paid heavily enough for it. What do you suppose I have suffered during the last month, watching you day by day wearing out your young life in a cold servile drudgery—hearing you strain your poor little tired voice in the interminable readings to that insatiable old man! Essie, I'm not a particularly pleasant fellow to live with—sometimes I believe I am particularly unpleasant—but, at *my worst,* I'm not so bad as old Blessington."

At that she laughs a little, but shakes her head.

"Why do you shake your head?" he asks, manlike, pursuing the hotlier the more she seems to hold back. "Is it," he says (a heavy fear quickening his pulses, and making his voice come thick and harsh), "that you want to tell me by signs, what you dare not tell me in words to my face, that the old love is *dead,* killed by my hard words that miserable night at Felton? Oh, love! it must have been but a weakly thing, if a few rough words could kill it."

She does not answer.

"You *did* love me once, Esther," he continues, vehemently; "I know you did! I knew it then, only, in my blind rage, I affected to disbelieve it. You *must* have loved me, when you, who had always been so shy, so reserved, so maidenly to me, of your own accord—do you recollect, sweet?—held out your arms to me, and flung yourself upon my breast. God only knows how hard it was for me to put you away!"

At the recollection his speech calls up, her face is stirred with a convulsive emotion; but still she holds her peace.

"Esther, speak!—and yet, perhaps, when you have spoken, I shall wish that you had kept silence. Say anything you will, do anything you will, only don't kill me by telling me that so sweet a thing can be *dead!*"

She lifts her heavy eyes to him, and in them is the look of a hunted animal. "Why do you torment me with these questions?" she asks, passionately. "If my love for you is dead, you ought to be thankful; for, while it was alive, it brought nothing but misery to either of us."

"If you think so, it must indeed be dead," he answers, deeply wounded.

"Why will you insist on driving me into a corner?" she asks, with the accent of a person rendered irritable by pain. "Why will you force me to make admissions that I don't want to make? What is the good of my owning that I love you still, when I am determined never to marry you?"

"*Never to marry me!*" he repeats; unable, in his immense surprise, to do more than say her own words after her. A man is always overwhelmed with astonishment at the idea of any woman not being overjoyed to espouse him.

"Never to marry you!" she reiterates, steadily. "I was a bad-enough match for you before—without fortune, position, or connexion; people would have pitied you then for being drawn into such a marriage; but now——"

"But now, what?"

"But now that I am a *companion*," she continues, with a bitter pride—"an anomalous animal, just two shades higher than the lady's-maid in my own estimation, and probably not that in any one else's—a companion, too, of whom people can say the things that Miss Blessington will say of me now——"

"What do you mean? What sort of things *can* she say?"

But Esther maintains a shamed red silence.

"That you are completely *passée?*"

"No, not that!—that would not concern me much."

"That the way you cough in the evening fidgets her to death?"

"No, not that."

"That you are over-sensitive, as these sort of people always are?" (with a faint mimicking of Miss Blessington's slow languor of articulation).

"No, not that."

"What then?"

"You *must* remember the things she said; you were there, and it is not more than five hours ago," she answers, with some impatience.

"I forget every word she uttered except three."

"And what were they?"

"You are free."

"She did not mean them," says Esther, trying to speak with dispassionate calmness; "she was under an erroneous impression when she said them; she will take you back again."

"Take me back again!" he repeats, angrily. "Good heavens, Esther! are you bent on driving me mad? Not satisfied with refusing me point-blank yourself, are you determined to insult me, by forcing upon me a woman for whom, as you know—as you must have known from the first moment you saw us together—I have never felt anything but the profoundest, coldest indifference?"

"I meant no insult," she replies, apologetically: "I only meant to say what is true—that *she* is a suitable match for you—that *she* is your equal."

"Is she?" he retorts ironically. "You are very good, I'm sure; I ask for bread, and you give me a stone. For God's sake, Essie, if you will have nothing to say to me yourself, at least spare me the degradation of listening to your kind and disinterested plans for my welfare!"

Under this severe snub, Miss Craven remains silent.

"Is it," he continues, presently, his indignation being a little cooled, "the mere fact of my being well-off that damns me in your eyes? If so, I think I may plead 'not guilty,' seeing that this oppressive wealth of mine lies on the other side of Sir Thomas's death—an event probably, at least, as distant as the millennium."

She gazes out (not seeing it the while) at the driving rain, while a troubled look flits over her small grave face; but she says neither "Yea" nor "Nay."

"When I am asking you to give me your whole sweet life," he cries, impulsively, snatching one of her little cold hands, "are you so ungenerous as to wish me to have absolutely nothing to offer you in return?"

Still silence.

"Essie!" he says, drawing her nearer to him, and looking resolutely down into her timid reluctant eyes, "I don't ask you to have pity upon me—that is a puling, cowardly way of making love, I always think; if the only road to a woman's heart lies through her compassion, I had rather never get there at all—but I ask you to pity *yourself*. To be my wife, ill-tempered and jealous as I, no doubt, should often be, would be distinctly a better fate than to be old Blessington's drudge. Child! have you no pity for yourself?"

"None whatever," she answers, with emotion. "I am not in the least sorry for myself; I richly deserve everything that is come to me. As long as I am unhappy myself, I can better bear the recollection of my vile conduct to the best and loyalest lover ever any woman had; if I began to be happy, I think my remorse would kill me."

He drops her hand suddenly, with a gesture of anger.

"I have been sacrificed to him once already," he says, fiercely; "am I to be sacrificed a second time to a sentimental recollection of him—to the mere memory of his perfections?"

She raises her rejected hand and its fellow deprecatingly towards him. "Don't be angry with me," she cries, pleadingly; "this has nothing to say to him; the reason why I will not marry you is that I am a *mésalliance* for you."

"That is my concern, I imagine," he answers, stiffly.

"I think not," she rejoins, gently. "You have lost your senses, as you told me just now; you are mad, and I am sane; therefore I can judge better than you yourself what is for your good: some day you will agree with me."

"Never!" he replies, emphatically; and with that, she standing nigh, and the temptation being mighty, he flings his arms *sans cérémonie* about her supple body, and strains her to his breast.

Outside, the rain streams down with a continuous quiet noise; the dappled deer are herding their branchy heads together under the old leafless hornbeams for shelter. For one moment Esther lies passive in her lover's arms, yielding to the bliss of that rough embrace; and, after all, among the blisses that we wot of, what is there so great as,

"After long grief and pain, To feel the arms of your true love Round you once again?"

Then her recollected resolution comes back. "Let me go," she says, faintly; "this is not right!"

"Right or wrong," he answers, doggedly, "it is the one moment worth being called 'life' that I have spent since I was fool enough to cut my own throat by parting from you."

"Let me go!" she says, again; and he, holding her still prisoner, but putting her a little farther from him, that he may the more distinctly see the workings of her countenance, says steadily:

"Essie, I am not unjust; I will let you go this instant, to any quarter of the world that you wish, without a word of remonstrance, if you will only look up in my face and say, 'St. John, I don't love you.'"

She lifts, with infinite difficulty, eyes in which pride and shy passion are fighting a duel to the death, and falters: "St. John, I don't——" but, in the mid-utterance of that falsehood, her voice fails suddenly, and she buries her burning shamed face on his breast.

"I knew it," he cries, triumphantly, dropping a light kiss—for has not her hesitation confessed him her owner?—upon her bent head. "I risked my everything upon that test, and it has not failed me. Even your miserable pride, Esther, could not constrain you to such a lie! With your heart beating against mine, as if we had but one between us, your lips did not dare frame those ugly words."

She gives no verbal answer; but, with head shame-drooped, tries, with trembling hands, to push away the arms that so closely, warmly bind her.

"Oh love!" he cries, with an accent of impatient but tender upbraiding, "are you struggling to get away from me still? Am I never to persuade any good thing to stay with me? Will you never forgive me the sin of being an eldest son? God knows it is not my fault—that it was not my choice to be born amongst the drones! Oh, Essie, is it just of you to punish me for what I cannot help?"

"I don't wish to punish you," she answers, trembling (seeing that she wished to be away from him, he has released her from his arms). "The real way to punish you would be to let you have your will—to say, 'I will marry you, St. John!'"

"In God's name punish me, then! No one ever took chastisement meeklier than I will this."

"And what would the end be?" she asks, sadly. "You would be insanely happy for a little while—a month—two months, perhaps—and then you would get tired of me. There is nothing in me, I think," she says, simply, "to keep a man's love after the first madness is over: I never had anything but a pretty face, and now even that is gone in the eyes of every one but you."

"What! in Linley's?" he asks, with a half-jealous smile.

She blushes, but goes on, without heeding the enquiry. "Some day you would wake up and say, 'I have thrown myself away;' and I—I prefer to say it for you now, while it is yet time."

He makes a movement to interrupt her, but she continues. "When a person has once lost confidence in another, they can never get it *quite* back again; you would never *quite* trust me. Only the other day you thought hard things of me, because I seemed grateful to Mr. Linley for talking friendly to me: I saw it in your eyes as you rode past us that night: and—which is the last and greatest reason of all—you would not like people to say of your wife the things that Miss Blessington will enable them to say of me."

"Even granting," breaks in Gerard, with indignant violence—"and God forbid my ever granting anything of the kind!—that it is in her or any one else's power to blast your reputation, what pleasure could it possibly give one girl to sully the good name of another, whom she must know in her heart of hearts to be as innocent as herself?"

"None whatever, perhaps, if I remain as I am," she answers, collectedly, though a little bitterly. "As Esther Craven, I am too insignificant to clash with her; but if I were to be your wife—if I were to be her successor in that position for which she is, in her own and her friends' opinion, so well suited—would not she be likely to give her own explanation of the change? She would describe things as they seemed to her, and people would believe her."

"Let them!" he answers scornfully. "If you loved me perfectly, the only people that existed in the world for you would be yourself and me."

"I do not love you perfectly, then, I suppose," she answers, calmly; "for not even the enormous happiness of being with you always, of being half your life, could compensate me for the degradation of bringing you a sullied name."

He turns away, with hands clenched and lips bitten, in the endeavour to be master of his useless surging rage.

"St. John," she says resolutely, laying her hand upon one of his, "you have made me two promises—one that you will go away and leave me to-day, and one that you will leave me never until I send you away. I keep you to the first: I send you away."

"But I will not be sent," he cries fiercely, giving the reins to his passion. "The conditions under which that promise was made are utterly changed; the obstacle that parted us *then* no longer exists: there is none between us now but what is of your own raising. I am, therefore, no longer bound by that oath; I will not go!"

"Very well," she answers, sighing: "then I must; and when one is to have a foot or a hand cut off, it is best to do it at once. St. John, I will not sleep another night under the same roof with you! Goodbye!"

But he turns away sullenly. "You may say 'goodbye' to me, but I will never say 'goodbye' to you: death is the only 'goodbye' I will accept as valid between us."

She makes no rejoinder, but, slipping from his side out into the wild wintry rain, flies across the park away from him.

"Esther!—Esther!" he calls after her: but the "drip, drip" of the great swollen rain-drops from the eaves of the deer-barn is his only answer.

CHAPTER XLI.

The rain ceases, and St. John endeavours to work off his disappointment and rage in a very long walk. When he at length re-enters the house, the two old people are hobbling into luncheon, and Miss Blessington sweeping, slowly and alone, after them. Her face is serene, and, to his surprise, wears no bellicose expression towards himself. To tell the truth, during three hours of point-lace work, the Gerard diamonds have kept flashing and gleaming, restless-bright, before her mind's eye. She has been telling herself that she was over-hasty in the relinquishment of them—has been resolving to make one effort, if consistent with dignity, for their recapture.

"Does Miss Craven know that luncheon is ready?" asks St. John of the butler, when they have all been seated for some minutes.

"If you please, sir, I don't think that Miss Craven is coming to lunch."

"Why not?—is she ill?" he inquires, anxiously, perfectly indifferent as to whether his anxiety is remarked or no.

"I believe she is rather poorly, sir."

Luncheon over, the old people are convoyed back to their arm-chairs. Gerard stands with his back to the hall-fire, with the *Times* in his hand. Constance, under some pretext of looking over the day's papers, lingers near him.

"I have been telling my aunt about our alarm last night, St. John," she says, as sweetly as usual.

"Indeed!"

"And its tame prosaic *dénouement.*"

"Indeed!"

"I am afraid I was unreasonably angry with you for what was evidently a mere accident; but when one is nervous and frightened, one really does not know what one says. I'm sure I have the vaguest recollection of what I said."

"I remember distinctly what you said, Constance."

"Indeed!" (with a smooth low laugh). "You don't bear malice, I hope? Things are much as they were before, I suppose?"

He lays down his paper, and looks at her steadily with his clear grey eyes. "Things are between us as they have been all our lives up to last October; as they have been since then, they will never be again."

She turns away quickly, to hide the mortification which even the cold pure mask of her face cannot wholly conceal.

"That is what I meant," she answers, quietly—with great presence of mind endeavouring to prevent her defeat from being converted into a rout; and though she deceives neither herself nor him, the effort to do both is at least laudable.

And Esther, interrupted midway in the packing of her few and paltry goods by the sharper recurrence of that pain in her side, lies on her bed, shut out by the strength of that bodily agony from all power of mental suffering. The excitement of the night—the exposure to the chill morning air—the thorough wetting undergone in her wild run through the park, amid the driving rain, have hastened the coming of that great sickness with which for weeks past she has been threatened.

Darkness falls: dinner-time comes. Presently the housemaid, who had formerly given her the laudanum, knocks at her door.

"Dinner, please, miss."

"I cannot go down," answers the poor child, rather piteously, sitting up, and pushing away the tumbled hair from her flushed cheeks, while her eyes blink in the candle-light. "I don't want any dinner; I'm ill!"

"Dear me, 'm! you *do* look bad!" exclaims the woman, drawing nearer to the bed, and speaking with an accent half-shocked, half-pleased; for, in a servant's eyes, the next best thing to a death in the house is a serious illness. "Would not you like to have Mr. Brand sent for?"

"Oh, no—thanks!" replies the girl, sinking wearily back on her pillow. "I daresay it will go of itself."—"If I did send for him, I have no money to pay for him," is her mental reflection.

The evening drags away about as heavily as usual in the saloon. Gerard, having ascertained that Miss Craven is still in the house, and has consequently broken her resolution of not sleeping another night under the same roof with him, tries to content himself with the idea that to-morrow—her temporary indisposition probably past—he will have another opportunity of reasoning and pleading with her. About nine o'clock Miss Blessington's maid appears at the door.

"Please 'm, might I speak to you for a moment?"

"Certainly," answers Constance, graciously, rising and walking off to the demanded conference.

Constance is always polite to her servants; it is a bad style, middle-class to be rude to one's inferiors.

"If you please, 'm, I really think as something oughter to be done for Miss Craven; she is uncommon bad, poor young lady!"

"What is the matter with her?" inquires the other, placidly; "nothing but influenza, I daresay; it always goes through a house."

"Indeed, 'm, I don't know; but she has a hawful pain in her side, and she can scarce draw her breath, and she is hot—as hot as fire!"

"Good heavens!" cries Constance, thoroughly roused by this gay picture; "I hope it is not anything *catching!*"

Reassured on this point, and having ordered the attendance of Mr. Brand, she returns unruffled to the fireside.

"What was that mysterious communication, Constance?" asks St. John, lazily, quite willing to be amicable now that their relative positions are made clearly evident.

"She only came to tell me that Miss Craven was very unwell," she answers, carelessly. "Servants exaggerate so; I daresay it is nothing!"

"What is the matter with her?" he asks, hurriedly.

"I really don't know," she replies, drily; "you had better wait till Mr. Brand comes, and ask him."

Ten o'clock! The old couple are trundled off to their separate apartments: and Miss Blessington, having bidden St. John a cold "good-night," sails, candle in hand, up the grand staircase, to that sleep that never fails to come at her calm bidding. Gerard foregoes his evening pipe, because the smoking-room does not look to the front. In painful unrest, he unfastens the shutters of one of the saloon-windows, and, raising the stiff and seldom-opened sash, leans out, looking and listening—looking at the maiden moon that rides, pale and proud, while black ruffian clouds chase each other to overtake her. Mr. Brand is out, apparently; for half-past ten has been struck, in different tones—bass and treble, deep and squeaky—by half-a-dozen different clocks, and still he has not arrived. At length, to the watcher's strained ear, comes the sound of wheels descending the steep pitch, from Blessington village; then a brougham's lamps gleam, issuing from between the rhododendron banks, and roll, like two angry eyes, to the door. In his feverish anxiety, and impatience at the long tarrying of the sleepy footman, St. John himself admits the doctor; and, following him at a little distance, as he is ushered upstairs, sits down in his own bedroom, with the door wide open, ready to pounce out upon the small Æsculapius, as he passes along the gallery at his departure, and learn his verdict.

The visit is rather a long one; to St. John, sitting still in his idle impatient misery, it seems as though the sound of Esther's opening door would never come; but never is a long day. At length the welcome sound is heard; and the young man, precipitating himself into the passage, comes face to face with a small elderly gentleman, shiveringly taking his way down the unwarmed ghostly old corridors.

"Is it a serious case?" he asks, abruptly, framing the simple words as they rise from his full heart.

Mr. Brand stares, surprised, at his questioner's blanched face. He had imagined that his patient was a little friendless orphan companion, whose life or death—save as a mere matter of compassion—were subjects of almost equal indifference to the people under whose roof she lies, panting out her young life.

"*Serious?* Well—oh! I assure you there is no cause for alarm, my dear sir," he says, imagining that he has got the key to the mystery; "it is nothing infectious, I assure you—nothing whatever!"

"That is not what I asked," rejoins Gerard, bluntly. "I don't care whether it is infectious or not; is it *dangerous?*"

"Are you any relation of the young lady, may I ask?—brother, perhaps?" inquires the little doctor, peering inquisitively, though under difficulties—for the abundant wind is playing rude tricks with the flame of his candle—into St. John's sad brown face.

"No—none."

"Well, then, to be candid with you, it *does* look rather serious," he answers, with the careless deliberate calmness which those whose half-life is spent in pronouncing death-warrants seem insensibly to acquire: "a sharp attack of inflammation of the lungs, brought on by neglect and exposure. By-the-by, can you inform me whether there is any predisposition to lung-disease in Miss—Miss Craven's family?"

"I know nothing about her family," replies the other, gloomily. He has no reason, beyond the probability of the thing, for supposing that she had ever had a father or mother, much less a grandfather or grandmother. Mr. Brand retires, completely mystified; and St. John, re-entering his room, throws himself into an arm-chair, and, covering his face with his hands, sends up violent voiceless prayers for the young life that is exchanging the first passes with that skilfulest of fencers, whom the nations have christened "Death!" In all his rough godless life he has had small faith in the efficacy of prayer: but, on the bare chance of there being some good in it, he prays wordlessly in his stricken heart for her.

Before they have done with him, the inmates of Blessington Hall have grown very familiar with Dr. Brand's face; night and morning, night and morning, coming and going, coming and going, through many days; for the adversary with whom the child is wrestling has thrown many a better and stouter than she—and the battle is bitter. It is of little use now that she hate the shadowing ginger curtains of the vast old wooden four-poster; there must she lie, through all the weary twenty-four hours, in paroxysms of acutest pain, in fits of utter breathlessness, in agonies of thirst. Grief for Jack, love for St. John, shamed concern at Miss Blessington's damaging story and insulting words, are all swallowed up in the consuming craving for something to wet her parched lips, to cool her dry throat—something to drink! something to drink! By-and-by, with the pain, she becomes light-headed—wanders a little—"babbles of green fields;" babbles to the uninterested ears of the sleepy tired nurse, of the twisted seat under the old cherry-tree, of the tea-roses up the kitchen-garden walk, of the yellow chickens in the rickyard. Then her delirium grows wilder: the green flabby Cupids on the walls come down out of the tapestry, and make at her. One, that is riding on a lion and blowing a horn, with fat cheeks puffed out, comes riding at her—riding up the bed-quilt, riding over her. Then the black and gold cocks on the old japan-chest, that, with neck-feathers ruffled, and heads lowered, stand ever, in act to fight, change their attitude: come pecking, pecking at her—pecking at her eyes; and she, with terrified hands stretched out, fights at them—thrusts them away.

"And thrice the double twilights rose and fell,
About a land where nothing seemed the same,
At morn or eve, as in the days gone by."

And it comes to pass, that there falls a day when these sick fancies pass—when the pain and breathlessness pass—and when Esther lies in utter exhaustion, weak as a day-old babe, whiter than any Annunciation lily, between her sheets. Eyes and ears and power of touch are still hers: but it seems as though all objects of sensation, of sight and sound and touch, reach her only through a thick blanket. She can see, as if at an immense distance off, shrouded in mist, the faces of doctor and nurse as they lean over her, and then, turning away, whisper together. She cannot hear what they say; she has no wish to hear—she has no wish for anything; only she lies, staring, with great eyes, straight before her at the bed-hangings, at the ceiling, at the little countless pigeon-holes in her toilet-table. One of the windows is open; and heaven's sweet breath circulates fresh and slow through the quiet room.

It is Sunday; the village people are clustering about the church-door; the violets, like blue eyes that have slept through winter's night, are opening under the churchyard wall. The bells are ringing; now, loud and clear—"ding-dong bell! ding-dong bell!" almost as if they were being rung in the still chamber itself—they come; now, faint and far; the wind has caught the sound in his rough hand, and carried it otherwhither. Whether they ring loud or faint, whether they ring or ring not at all, she has no care; she has no care for anything. She is very weary: it seems as if there were but a faint life-spark left in her; she can scarce lift her hand to her head. Now and then they raise her up, and, without asking her consent, pour brandy and beef-tea down her reluctant throat. She is *so* tired! Oh! why cannot they leave her alone! The slow hours roll themselves round; the people have gone into church, and have come out again.

Mr. Brand is here still; he is entering at the door; he is leaning over her. What can he have to say that he must needs look so solemn over? "My dear Miss Craven," he begins, with slow distinctness, as if he imagined that her illness had carried away her powers of hearing, "Mr. Winter is here; would not you like to see him?"

Mr. Winter is the meek M.A., whose voice the old squire drowns.

She fixes her great eyes,

"Yet larger through her leanness,"

upon his face—wondering as a child's just opened upon this strange green world. "I—why should I?" she asks, in a faint astonished whisper. She cannot speak above a whisper.

The good man looks embarrassed. "You are very ill," he says, indirectly.

"Am I?"

"And people in your situation generally wish for the holy offices of a minister of the Church."

"Do they?" She is too feeble to join one link to another in the simplest chain of reasoning. She has failed to grasp his meaning. He looks baffled, uneasy.

"My dear young lady," he says, very gravely, "it is very painful for me to have such a sad task to perform; but I cannot reconcile it with my conscience not to tell you that, in all human probability, you have not many more days to live."

Through the thick veil of her weakness and its attendant apathy pierces the sting of that awful news: her eyes dilate in their horror and fear, and she falls to weeping, feebly and helplessly.

"Don't say that—it is not true. How unkind you are! I don't want to die; I'm so young; I have had so little pleasure!"

"We must submit to God's will," says the doctor, a little tritely. It is so easy to submit to God's will towards one's friends and acquaintance.

She does not answer, but raises her hands with difficulty to her wasted face, while the tears trickle hot and frequent through that poor white shield.

"Have you any relations that you would like to have sent for?" inquires Mr. Brand, not unkindly; stooping over her, rather moved, but not very much so. Often before has it been his portion to say, to youth and maid and stalwart man, "Thou must die!"

"I have no relations," she answers, almost inaudibly.

"Any friends?"

"I have no friends."

"You have, then, no wish to see any one?"

"No. Stay," she says, as he turns to leave her, reaching out her hand to detain him; "are you *quite* sure that I shall die?" (Her lips quiver, and a slight shudder passes over her form, as she utters the words, "Is it *quite* certain?")

"It is impossible to be *quite* certain in any case," he answers, slowly; "while there is life, there is hope, you know; but—but—I cannot buoy you up with a false confidence."

She lies quiet a moment or two, regathering her spent strength. "How long do you think I shall live?"

"It is impossible to say exactly," he replies, gravely. "A few days—a few hours; one cannot be certain which."

Again she is silent, exhausted with the slight effort of framing a sentence. "Ask Mr. Gerard to come and see me—*now*—*at once*—*before I die!*"

He looks at her in astonishment, with a half-suspicion that she is light-headed; but her eyes look back at him with such perfect sanity in their clear depths, that he must needs abandon that idea. He cannot choose but undertake her commission at her bidding.

And St. John comes. They are singing the "Nunc Dimittis," which, saith Bacon, "is ever the sweetest canticle" in the Church, as he crosses the threshold of that room, and draws near that bed on which, but a few short nights ago, he had seen her, with his covetous lover's eyes, lying in all her round dimpled beauty. There comes no greeting blush *now* into her cheeks—the cheeks, that the sound of his far-off footfall had been wont to redden. How can she, that is the affianced of great Death, blush for any *mortal* lover? Her eyes lift themselves languidly to his face; and, even in the "valley of the shadow," dwell there comfortably; though in that countenance—never beautiful, and now made haggard by watching, with reddened eyelids and quivering muscles—a stranger would have seen small comeliness.

"So I am going to die, they tell me!" she says, whisperingly—says it simply and mournfully.

Gerard cannot answer; only he flings himself forward upon the bed, and devours her thin hand with miserable kisses.

"Perhaps it is not true! Oh, I hope it is not, St. John!" she says, falling to weeping; in her feebleness and great dread of that goal to which all our highways and byways and field-paths lead:
"Death, and great darkness after death!"

Still no answer.

"Cannot they do anything for me?" she asks piteously.

He lifts his head; and in his eyes—the eyes that have not wept more than twice since he was a little white-frocked child—stand heavy burning tears.

"Nothing, darling, I'm afraid," he answers, in a rough choked voice.

"There is *no* hope, then?"

"Oh, poor little one! why do you torture me with such questions? I *dare* not tell you a lie!"

"You mean that I am *sure* to die!" she says, faintly, with a slight shudder, while a look of utter hopeless fear comes into her wan face.

He throws his arms about her in his great despair. "Why do you make me tell you such news *twice?* Is not *once* enough?"

"It is *quite* sure! Oh, I wish I was not so frightened!"

His features contract in the agony of that moment; an overpowering temptation assails him, to tell her some pleasant falsehood about her state; but he resists it.

"As far as anything human *can* be sure, it is so," he says, turning away his head.

"Are you sure there is no mistake?—is it *quite* certain?"

"Quite."

"Then"—essaying to raise herself in the bed, and reaching out her slight, weary arms to him—"then kiss me, St. John!"

Without a word he gathers her to his breast; fully understanding, in his riven heart, that this embrace, which she herself can ask for, must indeed be a final one; his lips cling to hers in the wild silence of a solemn last farewell.

"I'm glad you are not angry with me now," she whispers, almost inaudibly; and then her arms slacken their clasp about his bronzed neck, and her head droops heavy and inert on his shoulder.

And so they find them half an hour later: he, like one crazed, with a face as ashen-white as her own, clasping a lifeless woman to his breast.

CHAPTER XLII.

Lifeless! Yes! But there are two kinds of lifelessness: one from which there is no back-coming—one from which there is. Esther's is the latter. Although a member of that fraternity whose province it is to kill and to make alive has sapiently said of her, "She will die!—she has not week to live!" Mother Nature has made answer, "She shall *not* die; I will save her alive! She has yet many years." And Esther lives. For many days, it is hard to predicate of her whether she be dead or alive; so faintly does the wave of life heave to and fro in her breast—so lowly does life's candle burn. But though the candle burn low, it is not blown out. By-and-bye strength gathers itself again, and comes back to pulse and vein and limb.

At seventeen life holds us so fast in his embrace that he will hardly let us go. To the sick child there come sweet sleeps; there comes a desire for food—a pleasure in the dusty sunbeam streaming through the window—in the mote playing up and down on ceiling and wall. I marvel will the bliss of spirits at the Resurrection dawn, feeling the clothing of pure new bodies, surpass the delight that attends the renewal of the old body at the uprising from a great sickness? The blanket that hung between Esther and all objects of sensation is withdrawn: full consciousness returns, and remembrance; and in their company, untold shame—shame at not having died! The celandine's greenish buds are unclosing into little brazen wide-awake flowers in the hedge-banks: the crocuses in the garden-borders hold up their gold chalices to catch the gentle February rain and the mild February sunbeams; in the wood-hollows the mercury—spring's earliest herald—flourishes, thick and frequent, its stout green shoots. About the meadows, small gawky lambs make a feeble "ba-a-a-ing." It is drawing towards sundown. The window is open; and near it, on a beech bough, a thrush sits, singing a loud sweet even-song.

Esther has been fully dressed for the first time, and has been moved into an adjoining dressing-room. In the small change of scene, there is, to her, intense delight—delight even in the changed pattern on the walls, in the different shape of the chairs—even in the brass handles of the old oak chest of drawers. Every power seems new and fresh—every sensation exquisitely keen; in every exercise of sight and sound and touch there is conscious joy. She has been amusing herself making little tests of her strength. She lifts a book that lies on the table beside her; it is small and light, but to her it seems over-heavy; she has to take two hands to it. She makes a pilgrimage from her arm-chair to the window—she has to catch at the wall, at the furniture, for support; but she gets there at last, and, sitting down on the window-seat, looks out at the quiet sky, blackened with home-coming rooks—at the pool made flame-red by the westering sun—at the peeping roof of the distant deer-barn. That little bit of roof brings a flood of recollections to her, and first and foremost amongst them stands St. John and her last interview with him. Although she is quite alone, a torrent of red invades cheeks and throat and brow, even to the roots of her hair. "*I sent for him*," she says to herself, with a sort of gasp; "*I asked him to kiss me*, and *I did not die!* How horrible! I must never see him again." Then she falls to thinking about him: whether he is still in the house? whether he has made up his differences with Miss Blessington? whether he is very joyful at her own recovery? whether he is not penetrated with the ridiculousness of her impressive leave-taking, which, after all—oh bathos!—was no leave-taking at all? "He must never hear me mentioned again," she says, twisting her hands nervously together. "Perhaps he will forget it in time; perhaps he will not tell any one about it. How soon shall I be well enough to go?—in a week? five days? four? three?—and whither am I to go?"

Aye, whither, Miss Craven? There are but two alternatives for her—the Union and Plas Berwyn. She must swallow her pride, and return to the Brandons: to the long prayers; to the half-past six tea and bread and scrape; to the three bits of bacon at breakfast; and to the perusal of the *Record* and the *Rock*: she must induce Mrs. Brandon again to advertise for a situation in a pious family. This morning's post has brought her four pages of doctrine, reproof, and instruction from Miss Bessy, and, lurking within them, has come a short, sweet, metrical prayer, adapted to every Christian's daily use:

"My heart is like a rusty lock,
Lord, oil it with Thy grace;
And rub, and rub, and rub it, Lord,
Till I can see Thy face."

There is no time like the present; she will write now. She has drawn paper and pens towards her, when the door opens, and her friend the housemaid enters. Doctor and nurse have fled,

"Like bats and owls,
And such melancholy fowls,
At the rising of the day."

"If you please, Miss Craven, do you feel well enough to see visitors?"

She looks up astonished. "I'm well enough for anything; but I'm sure I don't know who is likely to visit me."

"Mr. Gerard was asking whether he might speak to you 'm?"

"Certainly not—I mean yes—No.—Yes, I suppose—if he wishes," replies the girl, stammering hopelessly.

Miss Craven looks rather small, and excessively childish, sunk in her huge elbow-chair; a white wrapper envelopes her figure; her hair, which she has not taken the trouble to dress properly, is twisted up in the loosest, unfashionablest, sweetest great knot at the back of her neck; while a cherry-coloured ribbon coquettishly snoods her noble small head: the innocentest, freshest, shyest rosebud-face, and the liquidest southern eyes, complete the picture. St. John apparently treads hard upon the heels of the messenger, for, before permission is well accorded him, he is in his mistress's presence. Upon his brown face is untold gladness—in his eyes enormous love; and in them lurks also a look of half-malicious, half-tender mirth. She rises, and then sits down again, in unutterable confusion; and at length holds out her hand with distant diffidence to him, while as intense a blush as ever made mortal woman call upon the hills to cover her, bathes every inch of her that is visible. Her cheeks feel like gigantic red globes, over which her eyes have difficulty in looking. *His* eyes, laughing, pitiless, yet impassioned, refuse to leave her.

"You did not give me so cold a greeting when I last saw you, Essie?" he says, with an enraging smile of passionate triumph.

She turns away her head, and covers her face with both hands; but, in the interstices between her fingers, the lovely carnation blazes manifestly vivid.

"Oh, don't—don't be so cruel!" she murmurs, in a stifled voice.

"The truth can never be cruel!" he says quietly, smiling still; and so kneels down on the floor beside her.

But she only murmurs, "Go away; *please* go away! please let me alone!"—the words coming half-broken, half-lost, from behind the covering of her hands.

He puts up his, and tries to draw away the screen from her shamed discomfited face, saying, "Look at me, Essie!" But she, with all her feeble strength, resists.

"I cannot!—I cannot!" she cries, vehemently; "don't ask me! Why didn't I die? When they saw I was getting well, they ought to have killed me. Oh, I wish they had!"

"I'm rather glad, on the whole, they did not," he answers, gravely; and so, with one final effort, he being strong, and she being weak, he obtains possession of her two hands, and her face lies bare, unshaded—dyed with an agony of shame—clothed with great beauty—under the hungry tenderness of his happy eyes.

"To think of making one's last dying speech and confession, and then not dying after all," she says, in torments of confusion, yet unable to restrain an uneasy laugh. "It is *too* disgraceful! I shall never get over it! *Never!*—NEVER!—*NEVER!!*"

"Time, which mitigates all afflictions, *may* mitigate yours," he replies, gaily, unable to resist the exquisite pleasure of teasing her.

She turns from him with a petulant movement of head and shoulder. "Why don't you go?" she cries, the angry tears flashing into her eyes; "I hate the sight of you!"

At that he grows grave. "Essie," he says, slipping his arms round her as she sits, shrinking away from him in the deep chintz chair, "in that awful moment, when you thought—and God knows I thought so too—that we were saying 'goodbye' to one another for *always*, the barriers that your wretched false pride had built up between us were knocked down; try as you may, you can never build them up again."

"I knocked down plenty of barriers, I'm aware," she answers, ruefully. "You need not remind me of that!"

"Never to be built up again any more—never any more!" he says, his mirth swallowed up in great solemn joy.

She has fallen forwards into his embrace; he holds her little trembling form against his heart—a posture to which she submits, chiefly because it affords her an opportunity of hiding her face upon his shoulder.

"Never any more!" she repeats, mechanically, and then there is silence, save for the thrush, that trills ever his high tender lay. Presently Essie stirs, and whispers, with uneasiness, "St. John!"

"Well?"

"You won't tell any one, will you?"

"Tell them what?—that you and I are going to be married? By this time to-morrow I hope to have told every one I meet: I am not so selfish as to wish to keep such good news to myself."

"No—I don't mean that; but you won't tell any one about—about—about *that?*" This is the nearest approach she can bear to make to the abhorred theme.

"Esther!"

"And you'll promise never to joke about it?"

"*Never*, by the holy poker!"

"And you won't twit me with it when we quarrel?"

"What! you contemplate our having little differences of opinion?"

"Of course," she answers, laughing; "when two such ill-tempered people come together, how can it be otherwise?"

"Quarrel or no quarrel," he cries, passionately kissing her sweet shy lips, as one that can never be satiated with their tender warmth, "we are together now, for bad and good, for fair weather and foul, till death us do part! Say it after me, Essie; don't let ours be a one-sided compact."

And Essie, obedient, murmurs after him, "Till death us do part!"

And so it comes to pass that in the sweet spring weather, when the ground is a carpet of strewn cherry-blooms, when the cows stand knee-deep in buttercups, and the brake-fern is uncrumpling its tender fronds, the church-bells ring out, and they two are wed.

And the sun, that shines down on the bravery of the wedding pomp, as bride and groom pace by, shines also hotlier, with a more brazen sickly glare, on a soldier's grave, over which, three days ago, his comrades fired the parting volley on Bermuda's sultry shore.

The name of the soldier to whom Heaven has granted his discharge is Robert Brandon. Esther Gerard may spare her remorse now; treachery of hers can wound that loyal heart, on which the worm feeds sweetly, never more! Not unknowing of the good fortune of the woman he had so madly, miserably, nobly loved, has he passed away. In his poor schoolboy scrawl he had written her a little simple, badly-worded note, bidding, "God bless and speed her on her way!" The tears had fallen hot and thick upon the paper; but he had wiped them off, and she had never guessed them. He has hoarded his scant pay, has denied himself many of the small comforts that to his brother-officers are bare necessaries of life, that he may send her a wedding-gift befitting Gerard's bride. And he had gone about his wonted ways with no moping martyr's airs, unshaken in his simple creed that, since God wills it, all must be for the best. His honest laugh, if it come seldomer than it used, yet is none the less hearty and genial when it does come. And then, that pestilence which, at stated seasons, never forgetting its appointed periods, visits that tropic clime, comes and lays its heavy hand on the shoulder of many a fair-haired youth; and, among the first, upon the stalwart shoulder of Robert Brandon. And he, with no life-hating madness, with no quarrel against fate, yet not all unwilling, having stoutly fought life's hard battle:

"Surrenders   his   fair   soul
Unto his Captain—Christ!"

THE END.

Printed in Great Britain
by Amazon